The Undoing Dance

Praise for the Book

'An ace storyteller, Srividya Natarajan is a vastly gifted dancer who learnt from the legendary bharatanatyam guru Kittappa Pillai and trained under the musician T. Brinda. *The Undoing Dance* is an unputdownable saga of devadasis, written in a language that has the fragrance of jasmine garlands and incense, and the light of oil lamps in temples. And the reader will marvel at Natarajan's razor-sharp critique of the world of bharatanatyam dance, its politics and its social milieu' **Sunil Kothari**

'This is one of those rare books which hides a broken musical anklet between the pages, the tinkle of which will entertain and unsettle the reader thus leaving her soul disturbed and serene all at once' **K.R. Meera**

'A slice of cultural history that has remained shrouded in innuendo has been skilfully woven into an unputdownable novel. That the author has first-hand knowledge of the dance style and its nuances is apparent on every page' **Mallika Sarabhai**

Praise for *No Onions Nor Garlic*

'Luminous wit' *Tehelka*

'A delight' *India Today*

'Indian humour at its best' **Khushwant Singh,** *Telegraph*

'One of the finest fictional critiques of caste society' *Outlook*

'Wickedly funny' *Journal of Commonwealth Literature*

The Undoing Dance

Srividya Natarajan

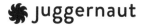

JUGGERNAUT BOOKS

KS House, 118 Shahpur Jat, New Delhi 110049, India

First published by Juggernaut Books 2018

ISBN 9789386228895

Typeset in Adobe Caslon Pro by R. Ajith Kumar, Noida

Printed at Manipal Technologies Limited, Manipal

To Nigel and Richard

The Wedding Ring Dance

I dance in circles holding
the moth of the marriage,
thin, sticky, fluttering
its skirts, its webs.
. . .
Underneath the soil lies the violence,
the shift, the crack of continents,
the anger,
and above only a cut,
a half-inch space to stick a pencil in.
. . .
And I keep dancing . . .
and the same radio plays its songs
and I make a small path through them
with my bare finger and my funny feet,
doing the undoing dance,
. . .
letting my history rip itself off me
and stepping into
something unknown
and transparent,
but all ten fingers stretched outward,
flesh extended as metal
waiting for a magnet.

Anne Sexton

LINEAGE

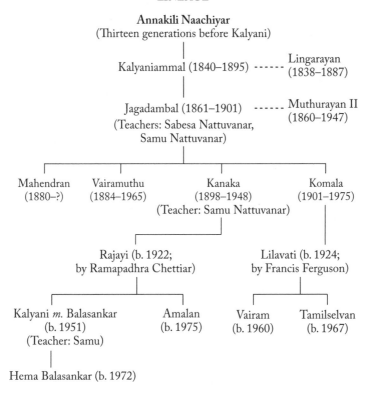

Annakili Naachiyar
(Thirteen generations before Kalyani)

|

Kalyaniammal (1840–1895) ------ Lingarayan
(1838–1887)

|

Jagadambal (1861–1901) ------ Muthurayan II
(Teachers: Sabesa Nattuvanar,   (1860–1947)
Samu Nattuvanar)

| | | |
--- | --- | --- | ---
Mahendran (1880–?) | Vairamuthu (1884–1965) | Kanaka (1898–1948) (Teacher: Samu Nattuvanar) | Komala (1901–1975)

Rajayi (b. 1922; by Ramapadhra Chettiar)   Lilavati (b. 1924; by Francis Ferguson)

Kalyani *m.* Balasankar (b. 1951) (Teacher: Samu)   Amalan (b. 1975)   Vairam (b. 1960)   Tamilselvan (b. 1967)

|

Hema Balasankar (b. 1972)

1

Hema
Madras, May 1992

Before Kalyani, who moved like light on the river, there was Rajayi, who could improvise like a poet full of drink. Before Rajayi there was Kanaka, who played male roles better than any man, who danced like thatch on fire, leaping across the temple's flagstones and landing with luminous accuracy on the last beat of a seven-beat cycle.

Before Kanaka was her mother Jagadambal, the king's mistress, who rode with the Raja to the boarhunt, straddling her Kathiawari mare in her dancing woman's flared trousers. Before Jagadambal was Kalyaniammal, whose way with the veenai's strings made war-hardened soldiers cry, for which skill her lover Lingarayan III honoured her by placing her in one pan of a scale and heaping the other pan with gold for her.

Thirteen generations of singers and dancers, dasi women, all the way back to Annakili Naachiyar at the beginning of the eighteenth century. All that skill, all that craft, wrapped in Kalyani's skin, and I never thinking of her as anything but 'mother' until her fortieth year.

In the Madras Literary Society's dusty stacks I found 'Callianicarah: A Brief Historical Account', by Colonel Dufferin. 'In 1864,' Colonel Dufferin writes:

> In 1864, Lingaroyan III, the twelfth Rajah of Callianicarah, decided that it was impossible to hold out against the British army. His neighbour to the North, Tanjore, had been absorbed into the Empire for want of a natural heir; his neighbour to the west, Poodoocottah, had acknowledged the suzerainty of the government of Madras, and of HM the Queen.
>
> Lingaroyan disbanded his standing army the following year. That included the two hundred militiamen who lived in the vast compound of his mistress Callianiammal, the chief dancing girl of the temple. After these retainers were dispersed, her family was housed in a smaller building on Musicians' Street, and the lands she owned returned, in large part, to the Rajah.

Lingarayan's treasury was gradually drained by tax and tribute to the British Raj. When he admitted that he could not keep his promise to gild the finials over the southern gateway of the Kalyanikkarai temple, Kalyaniammal gave back the gold he had packed on the scale against her weight.

'Lingaroyan educated his son Mootooroyan in British ways,' wrote Colonel Dufferin, who styled himself 'An Examiner of Antiquities'. 'Mootoorayan ascended the Callianicarah throne in 1887, after twelve years under the tutelage of a wonderfully expensive Cambridge man. The thirteenth Rajah wrote poetry in Tamil, Telegoo and English, travelled all over Europe, and has collected the most extensive archaeological library in all of South India.'

In Muthurayan's time, the cantonment at Kalyanikkarai grew big enough to have a church, a mission house, a police station, and a press. And a Lock Hospital, for the 11th Madras Infantry was bringing syphilis and vexation to the bazaar prostitutes on the edge of the cantonment.

'Round up the clapped-out whores,' Colonel Dufferin growled, one day in the summer of 1897, tired of having his men in the sick bay. The doctors in the Lock Hospital poked and prodded the privates of the bazaar women; they quarantined the infected ones. But Colonel Dufferin – a man of the world, a man who dined with Augustus Harris at his club, and hoped to hear Nellie Melba during his next furlough – would not have dreamt of arresting the dasi courtesans who were under the protection of king and temple. In fact, he found the self-righteousness of the anti-dance campaigners repugnant. He freely admitted that the nautch parties were fascinating.

When the new District Collector made his first visit to the Kalyanikkarai court, in 1900, Colonel Dufferin sat beside him at the nautch party given in his honour.

'I say, there's a fiddler,' the Collector said. 'The fiddle isn't native to these parts, surely?'

'An import. A court musician in Tuticorin adapted the instrument to native music. This Rajah's father borrowed the 11th Madras's bandmaster – a Belfast man, a civilian – about thirty years ago. Beastly uncomfortable chairs, what?'

The young violinist, grandson of the musician who had been apprenticed to the Irishman, was a master now. His bow slid over the strings like a foot over oil. Listen, the musical cognoscenti at Muthurayan's court exclaimed, the *ni*-note in this scale is altogether novel. It is a new mode, they said, created by the Raja himself.

'Never have quite learned to like these melodies, Dufferin,' the Collector mused. 'The tunes the native bands play during the processions sound more pleasing.'

'At the procession yesterday, they were playing "The Galway Piper". Part of the bandmaster's legacy, my dear fellow.'

'"The Galway–"! Why, of course. To think I didn't recognize it!'

'Well, the rendering does transform it. The Rajah's dance master set steps to the song, so that Collectors could be entertained with it. Ah, here's the delectable Jagadambal. The most celebrated of the nautch dancers in these parts. The Rajah's mistress.'

Jagadambal stepped out from behind one of the gilded rococo pillars into the sudden hush that had fallen over the assembly. She touched her dance master's feet and took her position on the floor while the musicians set the mood: neutral, relaxed, waiting, right hand on hip. If the audience had been challenged to break her aura down into its elements, they might have mentioned the shimmering Banaras silk she wore, or the impudent angle of her shoulders, or the poise of her neck, or her level gaze, or her detached focus on the music rather than on the effect of her beauty. No matter; her presence vibrated in their nerve endings.

When Jagadambal began to dance, the court's dignitaries and the visiting princelings watched her interpretation of the poetry with scholarly attentiveness. The white men, riveted despite their suspicion that they were somehow being implicated in some heathen ritual, understood nothing of the shapes her bejewelled hands hung in space. Through the intricate lattice-work of the screens on the balcony, the Raja's wives and their women friends kept the beat, and studied the cut of her blouse, and wondered which goldsmith had made the unusual mango-pattern girdle she was wearing.

In the middle of the recital, the doorkeeper scuttled into the durbar hall and sank to his knees before the Raja, his head hanging in helpless mortification. Keen though his ceremonial spear was, he couldn't very well have run three British ladies through their middles with it.

The women swept into the assembly. They held up placards: *Stop the Traffic in Temple Children! Save the Innocent Babes!*

Muthurayan had heard of these women. Arriving in his town in the wake of the white officers, these prune-faced daughters of pastors stood up in the bazaar on stages made of tables tied together, and fulminated about the sinfulness of Hindu customs. They had bought a printing press. They published the *Callianicarah Herald*, full of articles about how the voluptuous sighs and languishing glances of the dancing women were corrupting the morals of young men.

'Mr Collector, do you know that this dancer is a lewd woman, a woman without a husband?' one of the women cried.

The court dignitaries stared at the intruders as they might have stared at some strange growth or affliction that disfigured a beggar. Should they explain that the dasi women had divine husbands better than any mortal ones? Were not they themselves, the men in the assembly that had been so rudely disrupted, the men chosen by dasis here on earth: zamindars who owned great swaths of paddy field, and merchants, and lawyers, and princes like Muthurayan? What could these women who looked like shrivelled saltfish know of the unimaginable exchanges of pleasure between a dasi dancer and her patron?

Since neither the Raja nor her dance master had signalled for her to stop, Jagadambal went on dancing. The mirrored walls splintered and amplified her reflection. Her master sang louder, and the women singers, Jagadambal's dasi sisters, took their cue from him. Suddenly the durbar was ringing, booming, reverberating with music and dance.

'We are here to save our fallen sisters, imprisoned from childhood in the darkness of the jungle temples!' the boldest of the interlopers shouted, struggling to be heard. The Collector raised an eyebrow; Colonel Dufferin muttered something about 'the hysterical crusade'.

'Go back to the door,' Muthurayan said to the despondent guard. He rose courteously. 'Welcome to our durbar,' he said, shaking hands, in the European manner, with the bold one. 'The ladies of the court will make you comfortable.'

The women hadn't expected an antagonist as tall or as imposing as this. He walked them towards the curving stairs, and they went up meekly enough, a little intimidated by the large turban he wore on special occasions, and by the fierce moustache that hid his smile.

Behind the lattice, the boldest one began again, in halting Telugu. 'Surely you ladies must understand that we must at least save the innocent babes!'

'Shush!' said the Raja's oldest wife. 'Be quiet, watch. In this part of the song, the singers will repeat a single line thirty, forty times. Each time they sing the line, it must sound a little different from the last time. And Jagadambal must go on improvising until they change the line. They have to be infinitely resourceful, you know; they are turning different facets of that line to the light.'

On the polished oxide floor of the Raja's durbar, Jagadambal's footwork inscribed a stylized map of the Raja's authority. Here, in the east, in the west, in the north, in the south, and everywhere in-between (her gestures proclaimed, with bitter formality) were the Raja's fifty-four kingdoms; and here was the Raja himself, whose sexual potency filled the granaries with rice and brought beautiful women to his bed.

A woman came up the stairs to talk to the white women. She tripped over one of the placards, sat down on the other.

7

'Listen,' she hissed. 'You people are making great nuisances of yourselves. We dasi women are married to the god of the big temple in this town that was built before your ancestors knew how to cook meat. We are fertility walking on two legs; we can never be widowed. The brides bring us their wedding beads to string. We bring good luck to each naming ceremony in this town. We broker bargains with the ferocious goddesses who send epidemics. Ask the Raja's wives. If we stopped dancing, disease would consume the town, the harvest would wither on the stalk!'

'It is true, what she says,' the oldest Rani said.

'Can you not reason with your husbands, you poor, wronged wives?' the white woman said. 'Do you feel no anger at all? '

'My husband,' the royal goldsmith's wife retorted, 'keeps a small house with the most talented singer in all of Kalyanikkarai.'

'Anger?' said the youngest Rani's cousin. 'You mean because he lies down with her? Goodness me. It's a mercy he gets *that* from his dasi mistress. Better her than me. With the eight children and the paddy fields and the house and the elders to look after, I don't have time for *that*.'

In the durbar below, Muthurayan slumped down in his chair. 'Jagadambal,' he was thinking, 'is no longer a hummingbird of affirmation, sipping from the cup of royal favour. She is a nightingale, singing with her breast against a thorn. This is a dying culture; these white buzzards will strip it clean.' He rubbed his tired eyes as Jagadambal concluded her recital with 'God Save the Queen' – that Irish bandmaster's legacy, now a part of her repertoire – and meditated on the vicissitudes of patronage in English because he knew no other language so adapted to the expression of irony.

By the 1920s, most of Kalyanikkarai's dasi dancers had lost or had squandered away their protection. Some of them ended up in the bazaar, and into their houses too, as into the houses of the bazaar prostitutes, the police burst, covering up embarrassment (for they knew these women, after all, they used their services too) with innuendo and harsh laughter.

'Serves them right,' the respectable wives said. They were beginning to see it all differently. 'Serves the whores right for thinking they could take our husbands from us.'

Then the policemen began to raid the houses of the courtesans on Musicians' Street. They came at last to the house that was Lingarayan's gift to Kalyaniammal.

'It is a fact,' a missionary called Rachel Carstairs wrote, 'that numbers even of moral and religious people have permitted themselves to accept and condone in Man what is fiercely condemned in Woman. This double standard punishes our fallen sisters for their sins, but turns a blind eye to the wrongdoing of the men who are surely equally to be blamed, men who are public figures, generals, officials, district collectors, even kings.'

'It's not the men's fault,' said the good wives, the brahmin ladies who, by that point, had started their own Save the Dasi Child organizations. 'How can they resist the seductions of these loose women? How silly and accepting we were, once, even feeling proud that our men had mistresses. Well, we're glad someone is doing something about it.'

By the 1950s, there was nothing but shame and disgrace in the name of dasi. After Kalyani exchanged the dancer's life for the life of a brahmin wife, she never spoke of the family she had been part of before she married my father, not even to me. And my father never once mentioned that my mother had an extraordinary gift.

When I was a child, I once cycled along a lake, with the sun low in the sky, and a runner of light came straight towards me on the water, no matter how much my path on the bund twisted. The first time I saw Kalyani dance reminded me of that sight. I waited for the symmetry to be lost, for the pattern to dissolve, for the ordinary chaos of human flesh, but Kalyani seemed to move, always, with the bright flawless geometry of light. It took my breath away.

2

Kalyani
Madras, 8 April 1990

'Have the papers come?' Balan said.

'I'll have a look.'

I put his tumbler of coffee down on the bedside table and went to the window with mine. Beyond the balcony, the gravelled drive curved towards the wrought-iron gates. The sun cleared the rooftops beyond the gates as I scanned the road.

The paper-man sailed up on his Atlas every morning. Through the window I would watch the arabesque of right leg over the saddle, the stand kicked smoothly under the rear wheel, the papers thrust between the bars of the gate, the leg as it drew the arc in the air again. But there was no paper-man today. Only Vijaya was there, her shadow pointing towards me on the drive, a grim iron spike. She was nipping the thick, pink blooms from the arali shrubs and dropping them in her basket. The flowers were for her gods. They had to be picked before the milk-man, the spinach-woman, the knife-sharpener, and the paper-man, plying their several trades, brushed against them and contaminated them with their flesh.

To the right of the arali trees, the vivid bougainvillea, unfit for the gods, curled over the whitewashed compound wall. The magpies darted through the thin haze, waiting for Vijaya to go. In the middle of March they had come, the black-and-white magpies, to the mailbox that hung from one of the gateposts. They flew in and out of the mail slot carrying oddments of twig and leaf and hair and cotton wool. The nest began on a Saturday. Hema had sat with her back to the wall, following its progress. She had taken a book because she was preparing for her final examinations, but it lay in her lap, face down. The shadows of bare branches fell across her face. The summer-flowering trees had shed their leaves; the afternoon was saturated with the scent of leaf meal; the gravel was sending up plumes of heat. Everything was still, somnolent, suspended. Only the magpies laboured.

'Amma,' Hema called to me, holding the mailbox door open. Another Saturday, a week after the birds had begun the nest. The gul mohar tree had burst into red flame. 'Amma, come down and look!'

Hema at six years, playing with the children next door, had called up to the balcony in the same imperious voice – Amma, come down, look, look at us! – the youngest of the group, the unchallenged leader, running like an acrobat on the mossy compound wall, arms flung out for balance. I was always there to be summoned: a woman who had nothing to do. I might have been leaning with my elbows on the balustrade (always, in the bathroom mirror, my elbows were white from the whitewash of the balcony), listening to the children hiding among the shrubs, watching them vault over the wall and scamper away to the back of the neighbour's house. I might have been daydreaming, floating away from the hum of the traffic and the shrill protest of the neighbour's toddler, who had been left out of the game; hearing, threaded into the laughter and quarrels of these children, the voice of a child far away, calling: Look, look at me!

'Amma, come down and look!' Hema had called. I went down into the garden. Four verdigris eggs lay among the feathers and hair in the bowl of the magpies' nest. I wrapped an arm around Hema's shoulders – she was as tall as me now – grateful that she still shared her pleasures with me, wanting to mark the moment with some bodily gesture.

Three of the four eggs hatched some days later, and the fourth lay in the nest, a speckled blue failure. When the magpies were away foraging, Hema and I opened the mailbox door and watched the chicks. They were scraps of muddy-pink flesh, their eyes unseeing. Dowdy feathers sprouted along their backs. When they sensed movement, their beaks opened like cavernous clutch purses. They were delicate, touching, comical; I had to resist the urge to let them nestle in the palm of my hand, to stroke them.

'It's a myth that birds will reject their chicks if they smell of humans,' Hema said. But I didn't believe her.

The house to which Balan had brought me after we were married was on a quiet side street near College Road. It was full of patterns for the eye to rest on. When I looked down, the black and ivory tile squares were comforting and reposeful. Outside the bedroom window was a balcony that ran the length of the house's facade. Tall fluted white pillars rose at intervals at the end of the balcony and held up the roof. When I leaned back in the wicker chair that had been set on the balcony for my use, I could see the roof beams, mahogany against white plaster, geometrical.

An Irish bishop had lived in this house once, and had suffered from tropical fatigue, and had had improvements made. Blinds of woven vetiver hung between each pair of pillars on the balcony. In the evenings, when they were rolled up, the fragrance of arali and magnolia drifted up to the balcony, and the brainfever bird's slow, melancholy ascent through the chromatic scale. In the afternoons I let the blinds down and watered them, cooling the house.

Balan used to sit with me on the balcony once. Sometimes, when we sat together, I would slip my hand into his and exclaim: 'This house is so beautiful, Balan.' Later, his matching wicker chair was put away because he had no time. I had too much. It ballooned out around me, empty, full of meaningless tasks. While Balan travelled, I sat on the balcony, waiting for him or for Hema to come back, from the airport or from college. When Hema was a child I had more to do. Now she was finishing her third year of college; she was independent – far more independent than I ever remember having been – clever, secretive, lost in her books. I missed the feel of her hair drifting through my fingers as I combed it, of her chin cutting into my breast as we read a book together.

'Kalyani,' Balan said. He pushed the sheet off his legs and sipped from his tumbler. 'The papers?'

When we were younger and more egotistical, he took offence if I ignored a question he had put to me, and I was hurt if his mind wandered away from me in mid-conversation. But after sixteen years of marriage, there was room for parallel streams of thought that never intersected.

'Not yet,' I said. 'It's too early. Your mother's still down there, picking flowers.'

I had asked the paper-man not to push the papers into the mailbox because of the nest. He had shrugged. 'Easier for me. But you watch for the papers and take them in, or some porukki boy will swipe them and sell them back to you.'

'Kalyani.' Now there was a faint edge to Balan's voice. 'Your coffee's getting cold.'

I half turned away from the window.

'Balan,' I said, 'did you call Padmasini?'

'About what?'

'The recital – that New Jersey student. She insisted particularly that you call today. If you can't be chief guest, she said, she needs to find someone else.'

'Well, she's already got my name on the invitation card. Seems a bit redundant asking me after the fact, hmm?'

'Oh, Balan. I remember telling you that Padmasini had asked, and I remember you calling her to say you were available. Two months ago.' He probably remembered too; this was his way of rebelling against duty.

'I suppose I must go.' Balan yawned, blew out his breath, flexed his neck this way and that. On the wall behind him, the Graces danced, their torsos twisting elegantly. The Botticelli print had grown dingy over the years. A film of dust was trapped inside the frame, and the flowers and fruit and figures no longer stood out from the dark leafy landscape. 'But I'm dreading it. I'm going to have to tell Padmasini I'm bumping her from the festival in the US.'

'*Again?*' A knot of fear formed in my chest. I touched my coffee to my lips. Too sweet. Balan's mother Vijaya made the coffee the way Balan liked it, sweet, bitter, thick as marsh-mud. I asked her once if I could make my own coffee; she said I could, after she was dead. I didn't bring the subject up again. I suppose I could buy one of these new electric kettles and plug it into a socket in this room.

'She'll probably make a worse stink than she made last year,' Balan said.

'Has NATAC Delhi cleared it? Dropping her, I mean?' Perhaps they would stop Balan, perhaps that man he was always talking to, Akhil, would overrule Balan.

'Akhil is pretty sick of Padmasini. I've simply *got* to ease her out. I don't suppose you have any ideas about how I might do this tactfully.'

NATAC was the National Academy of Traditional Arts and Culture. It was part of the Indian government's effort, the brochure said, to preserve cultural heritage and to promote new artistic work. Dancers and artists and singers thought of NATAC as their passport to foreign lands. They forgot the expansion and remembered only the acronym.

In south India, my husband *was* NATAC. A man so powerful it was unsettling. Casually, carelessly, he picked up a promising singer and elevated him to fame; without a thought, smiling pleasantly all the while, he dropped a dancer who had outlived her attractiveness. He sent government cheques to this one, cut off food and drink to that one. The honours and awards the government had instituted, the money that went with them, the chance to be seen, the applause of critics, the tours abroad: all these were his to hand out or snatch away. In his palms were flashing currency signs from every corner of the world. All the strings were looped around his fingers; the puppets danced when he chose, and flopped on their sides when he was done.

It was not an easy job, Balan said. Dancers and musicians were such tiresome, such fragile people.

Balan rubbed his face, making his day-old beard rasp. 'Janaki should go to the US this year. Her presentation values are much better than Padmasini's.'

They were arch-rivals, Padmasini and Janaki. Padmasini was about Balan's age – fifty-one – and ageing rapidly. Janaki was younger, better-preserved, slick and opportunistic.

'It's about time Padmasini retired from the stage,' Balan said.

Even as recently as two years ago, Balan would not have used this dismissive tone. He would have said, in the wry voice of a man acknowledging a woman's success, 'What a woman. You should watch her.' That was what he

17

said to me the day he suggested that I send a book I had written to a publisher. 'If you want to learn how to make contacts, watch Padmasini,' he said. 'She knows how to work the system, the government, the public, the press.'

To make his point, he bought me a large shiny book called *Bharata Natyam: The Soul of India*. Padmasini had written it. It was full of pictures of Padmasini.

'Look at her book,' Balan said, 'how she calls it a history of dance in India, and uses it for personal publicity. Brilliant.' Balan was mentioned on the Acknowledgements page.

Now Balan was saying, 'She is past her expiry date. NATAC Delhi – Akhil, at any rate – says she runs a bharatanatyam factory, and it manufactures substandard goods.'

'She still has the older audiences eating out of her hands,' I said. 'And she has this new following among young Hindutva hotheads.'

'But her students, Kalyani! All of them undifferentiated *clones*!'

What did he expect, now that dance was no longer craft but pure vanity? The older dancers battened on the desires of the young ones. The young ones wanted to be seen, to be ornamental. There were no stars among them. The older ones, having tasted stardom and wanting to keep its benefits for as long as possible, taught the young ones their steps, and as they taught them, they stamped out all signs of succession. When death harvests the older ones, there will be nothing left but burnt stubble.

'She should make room for the next generation,' Balan said. 'For her own students at least.'

'I don't think she's ready to make room for anyone,' I said. 'Maybe – Balan, maybe you should let her go on the US tour. Just one more year.'

Last year, when Balan had dropped Padmasini from the Festival of India in Paris, he had pretended that NATAC had made the decision behind his back. Padmasini had known better. She had gone to the press; she had pestered Balan until he said, 'Padma, I can't back down now. I'd look a fool. I never cave in to public pressure. But next year, it will be your turn to go to the US I promise.'

But here was Balan saying, 'Padmasini's approach has gone stale. Janaki, now *she's* really got an eye for what will sell.'

'Yes, she has.'

Janaki's work appealed to America-born-and-bred Indian-Americans who had grown up on those glossy posters of India where the sea is an improbable ultramarine, where the beach is clean, where the women are tribal beauties. It appealed to white people who wanted to celebrate the emancipation of Third World women.

'Her female power angle will go down well with the next generation.' Balan laced his hands behind his head. 'You could learn from the way she works that line.'

I wondered sometimes if Balan remembered how, when he and I were newly married, we lay tangled in damp sheets, thighs still locked together, and talked of Art and Nation.

'What kind of society is this?' he burst out one night. 'It seems to recognize almost no deep compulsions except procreation and the making of money.'

Balan's own compulsion was to open the world's eyes to the unsuspected riches of traditional art. He was going to rescue folk arts from neglect. He was going to search the small towns and villages for the unsung, the unassuming, the forgotten masters. When he found them, he would bring them to the cities, and help them earn a living. When Hema was older, if she showed a talent for singing or dancing, he said, we would take her to a teacher from one of the old towns.

By the time Hema was ten years old, Balan was saying, 'Dancers need an *angle*, you know. Dance, these days, is like politics. You can't get anywhere without a platform. You can go the social work route – work with slum children or cripples or the blind and get into the papers that way. You can go the innovative route – you know, do bharatanatyam to Tchaikovsky or stir some aikido or Martha Graham into the usual stew. Or you can take the spiritual line – do mythological dance dramas, like Padmasini, get a godman or two to bless your work in public. Well, Padmasini's angle works.'

How had the Balan I married become this purveyor of cynical practicalities? From the way he cheerfully deflected any suggestion that he had changed, I understood that, of all the questions in the world, this was the one question I must not ask.

When Hema was eleven, she began lessons in Padmasini's dance school. 'At least she'll get somewhere,' Balan said.

But she got nowhere. Eight years later, she was still Padmasini's student, not learning much, fretting, hating her classes. She was the ugly duckling that had grown into an ugly duck, or at any rate a plain one; why would she want to keep learning, when she knew Padmasini would never put her on stage? But Balan would not hear of letting her stop her lessons.

'Balan,' I said, 'if Padmasini doesn't get a Festival slot this year, do you think she'll let Hema stay on in her school?'

Balan struck his forehead. 'I hadn't thought of that–'

'It will be awkward. Maybe this year Padmasini could be on your US list. Maybe next year you could move Hema to another teacher, and it won't be so embarrassing.'

'Yes.' Balan frowned. 'Or maybe it's time to arrange a new teacher for Hema.'

A sudden pincer of heat stabbed my forehead. What had Padmasini said? 'So you never got around to telling Balan about your mother?' I felt sweat pooling under my breasts. The ceiling fan over the bed, whining monstrously, slashed the light from the window into long spathes of bright and dark.

'Now, Balan? Just like that?'

'If necessary. I'm sure I can come up with some little sop to keep Padma happy. There's that lifetime achievement award–'

'NATAC's new award? I thought that was for someone from a hereditary dance-teaching family. Padmasini is hardly that.'

'We could ask Padma to – wait, I've got it – to film or

interview the person. Maybe make a documentary, for national TV.'

'She'd never want to do that. It would mean sharing the limelight.' I looked out of the window again. The paper-man was late. Dust rose in eddies on the road.

'She'll do it if the money is good enough,' Balan said. The bed creaked as he swung his legs off it. 'The show – the one Padma wants me to be chief guest at – is next Saturday. I'd like you to come along, Kalyani. It will be terribly boring without you. One of those spavined NRI girls who don't know the meaning of the songs they're dancing to – Kalyani, you're miles away. What are you thinking about?'

'Oh, the magpies.'

The magpies, wonderfully busy, flying away from the mailbox urgently, and returning with beakfuls of food.

'What?'

'The birds, Balan – they've made a nest in the mailbox. I showed you last week.'

'Yes, of course, the birds. By the way, how's the new book coming along? Madhu and um–'

'Mohan and Mala.' I groped for a lie, then thought of Enid Blyton, and went on fluently. 'They've fallen into a cave with an underground stream. I'm going to have to get them out somehow. I'm so tired of them both. Mohan is so bossy and so – so unpleasantly knowledgeable, Mala is just so permanently panic-stricken.'

Balan laughed. 'You've been listening to Hema too much.' He reached for his shirt. 'You sound like her when she is in one of her feminist rages.'

There was no Mohan and Mala book this year. But

22

Balan wouldn't know that; he never read anything I wrote, though he often expressed polite curiosity. I was writing something new. My notebook was full of fragments of my family's history. It was not yet a coherent story. What would I do if it took shape, how would I publish it? I put off thinking about that for the moment. I kept my notebook hidden.

Joseph the driver had been with our family for twelve years, but Balan's mother held that you could not trust any man with a nineteen-year-old virgin. Perhaps she was right – what do I know? When Hema was driven to dance school twice a week, or when she was driven to the shops, I sat in the back of the van with her. She resented it.

'Oh, *hell*!' she said, 'Do I look like I need a chaperone? Amma, can't you tell Vijaya Paati to mind her own business?'

Hema wondered why I couldn't change the world. Why, she said, reading my last book, why couldn't poor incompetent Mala find a way out of the ruined temple? Why did Mohan have all the bright ideas? Why was Mala afraid of heights and spiders when Mohan was afraid of nothing? Why didn't I just go out and get a job? Why didn't I simply defy Vijaya's edict that I never cook in her house and – well, make dinner one evening?

'Amma,' she said, rolling her eyes. 'So *what* if you're not brahmin? Who believes in all that pollution shit? Why should stuff like that matter in this day and age? Amma, *how* can you be so passive?'

When I went shopping, I lingered outside bookstores, drawn by the pseudo-optimism of the self-help shelves: *Cycling Your Way to a New You*, *How to Think Better of Yourself*. I wondered if I should buy a bicycle. What could I do to give my life some shape or meaning? If I Learned Estonian in Thirty Days, would I be a different woman? I saw Hema, striding to college in her jeans, saying casually, 'My generation, liberated.' I saw Vijaya, a tear in the canthus of each flinty eye, saying, 'You've killed him, you bitch. When you stole our son from us, you broke our hearts. You killed my husband. I hope you are happy now.' And my mother, Rajayi, saying, 'You don't worry your head about me. I will survive.' How was I to explain to Hema that I was trapped in the amber of transition, and had neither my mother's strength nor my daughter's? Oh, what was the use of appealing to habit, to helpless femininity, I thought, each Thursday evening and Saturday morning, as I sat in the back of the van on the way to Padmasini's dance school, and noticed the grey hairs multiplying on Joseph's head.

Padmasini performed archetypal femininity on the stage, but refused to admit its burdens into her life. I met Padmasini's mother and her aunt – twin sisters – soon after Hema began her lessons. Padmasini was in her early forties then, looking at the end of her childbearing years. Misreading the degree of our intimacy, the twins recruited me to persuade Padmasini to marry.

'Ask her why she won't marry, Kalyani. Talk some sense into her head. You are her friend, her little sister.'

When the twins spoke to me, I could not tell which was which. They wore identical saris; their hair grew silvery at the same rate; their faces blurred into each other. One was a widow, but they both wore a small black pottu, as if to say they took half shares in widowhood, turning the red pottu of fecundity into the black one of renunciation, and half shares in wifehood, in that they wore pottus at all.

'Yes, ask her. Why won't she get married?' They sat with their arms touching at the shoulders.

Embarrassed, I asked Padmasini in front of them.

'Because I live for my dancing,' Padmasini said. Deadpan; as if she knew it was a cliché, and had ceased to believe it herself, but found it a handy phrase.

'Ask her, doesn't she want children,' one of the twins prodded.

The twins had only this one child between them. They had been mothers to Padmasini together. 'My mothers,' she said, when she spoke of them. They treated her single state as a lifelong burden that they had somehow brought on themselves, first by engaging a dance teacher's services when she was ten years old, and then by bringing her to Madras to begin a career on the stage.

'Ask her, who will look after her in her old age,' the other one said.

'Money will look after me,' Padmasini said, not waiting for me to ask. 'I will make enough money from my dancing to pay to be looked after in my old age.'

Padmasini did not need to make money. She had inherited her home and her wealth from her childless uncle. He had been a successful lawyer in Kalyanikkarai, and a member of the Madras Legislative Assembly. Padmasini's aunt had been married to this lawyer, and her mother to his brother, so the lawyer was Padmasini's uncle twice over.

'But what about loneliness?' the twins wailed. 'Who will keep you company?'

To me, Padmasini said, 'There was a time when I could have crooked my little finger and men would have come crawling. It seemed great fun then, being half-woman, half-goddess, desirable and entirely out of reach.'

So Padmasini had remained defiantly single. Had she imagined the queue of suitors growing longer or holding steady, had she gloried in the heartbreak of the rejected? Was it because it was impossible in those days for a woman to be a dancer and also to have what people called a *normal* life? To live a normal life: to bear children, one after the other, to put the husband's needs first, to massage the inflated egos of in-laws. Or was it that she had watched her own father settling too many arguments with his fists?

The twins lived with Padmasini most of the time, for propriety's sake ('Only one kind of woman lives on her own, and you know what kind *that* is!'). But Padmasini said her mother had her own reasons for living in Madras. Her father was a brute; her mother had moved her possessions and her affections from Kalyanikkarai to Madras by degrees, until she lived here with her sister and daughter more than she lived at home with her husband. He was left to the care of servants. Nobody blamed her.

Two months before the magpies had begun their nest, I was keeping Padmasini company in her bedroom while Hema went through the motions of a dance lesson in the fashionably thatched rooftop school.

Padmasini sat at her dressing table in her blouse and petticoat, and I sat on the edge of her bed.

'I'll be frank with you, Kalyani,' she said. 'If Balan turns me down again for both the big festivals, I shall blame you.'

'Padma, he won't listen to me. Especially not about things to do with his work.'

She put her left forefinger to the corner of her eye and stretched the skin of its lid. The brush in her right hand began its viscous journey at the inner corner of her eyelid. The stroke began with a flourish, ended on a note of tremulous anxiety. She waited a moment, blowing upwards to aid the drying, then let her eyelid go. The skin stayed in place, inelastic, reticulate as the underside of a leaf. The eyeliner gleefully flooded all the rucks and crinkles of her two score and ten years.

'How did those eyeliner queens do it, my God,' she said, studying the mess, 'Brigitte Bardot, Audrey Hepburn, Meena Kumari? You have more influence over him than you think. You just need to *use* it. People who are besotted with their wives generally listen to them – if pushed.'

On the bedside table was a 1961 Deepavali issue of the *Ananda Vikatan*. I had seen it before; it carried a two-page profile of Padmasini. When I picked it up, the magazine fell open at that profile. She must have been about twenty years old when the profile was done. In one picture she wore a silk sari and full make-up; her hip was thrust out and she was swinging a tennis racquet. In another picture she was dressed as the poet Andal. In the third, she leaned negligently against a Studebaker. In those photographs, she was indeed feminine in an old-fashioned voluptuous way, big-bosomed and wide-hipped. Her dance might even have meant something then. Now she was obscene and lazy onstage, cynically adapting the grammar of the dance to accommodate her own body's exhaustion. Offstage, she was lonely and brittle. Dance was the tiger she had caught by its tail. There was nothing to do but profit from the discomfort.

'Did you ever tell Balan you were from Kalyanikkarai?' she said. I looked up, startled, but she was swabbing her eyelid with cotton wool. I could not read her expression.

'No, I never told him.'

'I thought not. You're a sly one. I've always wondered why. He seemed to think you were born and brought up here in Madras. So you never got around to telling him about Rajayi – about your mother?'

'No. No, I never did.'

'Yes, I thought you were hiding something. You asked me not to mention her, and I never have. I've never asked you why. I just did as you asked.'

'Yes.'

Between Padmasini and me was the artificial, transient intimacy of women undertaking the origami of each other's sari pleats, women slapping at their wrinkles and peering at their blemishes in front of each other. I am not sure why. Perhaps because Balan and Padmasini's

28

mothers had taken it for granted that we would be friends. Perhaps because we had both grown up in the town of Kalyanikkarai, where my mother still lived, though we had not known each other as children. Perhaps because we were related in a roundabout way: my mother had been the mistress of the uncle who had offered Padmasini shelter in Madras.

'So Balan has no idea your mother was my uncle's keep? Or that you could be my uncle's child?'

'Padmasini, I don't know who my father is,' I said. 'My mother never told me.'

Her uncle's picture had always hung on my mother's wall. I had drawn my conclusions, but I had no way of knowing if they were the right ones.

'It's dangerous to keep secrets, isn't it? Your mother hid things from you, and you're hiding things from your husband.'

I listened to my heart, its tattoo of fear. 'Yes.'

'Balan knows you are from a dasi family – why would you not tell him this little detail? Then you can see your mother once in a while.'

'I can't. It's complicated, stupid, but I can't.'

'I wonder what would happen if he found out about your mother.'

Her voice was cool, but she was threatening me – blackmailing me. She had never done that before. What exactly did she know about me? Gossip from my part of the town did not usually reach the wealthy part where her father lived. Besides, she had never, as far as I could tell, visited her father since she had come, at the age of sixteen, to live with her uncle in Madras. She was as cut

29

off from her home town and from her roots as I was from mine. What did she know?

'I hate this mirror,' she said suddenly. 'It makes me look fat.'

She stood up and pulled the string on her petticoat tighter. It made the flesh bulge above it. She lifted her breasts one by one and pushed them higher in her blouse. She tucked the end of the sari into the petticoat.

'My father's ill,' she said. 'The doctor says it's an aneurism. Do the pleats?'

'That's a – a thin place in an artery, isn't it?'

I knelt before her while she made the pleats. Her smell came off her in layers. A glaze of perfume, and behind it, fruity lipstick, pressed powder, foundation, dry-cleaned silk, sweat.

'Mm-hm. My mothers have just found out. He's doing all right now, but they say I must go home soon to see him. I've never understood this urge to forgive and be forgiven by the sick. I hate him as much as I ever did.' She watched in the mirror as I lined up the pleats and swept my hand down flat along the edges, the pressure of my palm overwhelming older folds made when the silk was starched and pressed, leaving blade-sharp pleats clean as a Chinese fan. 'Oh, by the way, there's a girl from New Jersey who's doing a show two months from now. I want Balan to be chief guest. Tell him to call me, okay?'

'I'll tell him. Will you go see your father?' Padmasini's father still lived in that town, among the family's rice-fields. He had tolerated her dancing for a few years, but when she was fifteen or sixteen, had disowned her because she had chosen dancing as a career. With curses, she said, with a bruise or two on her face; but she had her uncle in Madras, and he had taken her in.

As she tucked the pleats in, I saw the flesh of her belly, smocked with deep indentations left by the petticoat string. I thought of the tree in Kalyanikkarai where the villagers hung the organs of dead cattle.

'My mothers don't think he'll last through the summer,' she said. 'If they are not dramatizing things and he really is dying, then I'll go. There's the house and the land. That doesn't change anything about the US Festival – talk to Balan. Don't forget. Maybe I can take Hema along this year.'

What did I feel for Padmasini? I felt the pity of the married sister for the barren spinster. I felt the mild amusement of the slender sister for the woman who was always on a diet that didn't work. I felt the envy of the hobbled animal for the free one. And beneath those other feelings there had always been fear. The fear flashed up, like light on the point of a knife lying casually on a table, like a shark's fin breaking surface among swimmers, after that conversation two months ago.

My life was a layered confection of lies. Lies that had been told to Balan's extended family about who I was, and the slightly different lies that had been told to his colleagues. Only Vijaya and Hema (and all the domestic help, heaven help us) had been let into the truth of my – what a ghastly word – *origins*. It was Balan's word. 'Kalyani,' he said, before we were married, 'I don't care about your origins. Not a bit. But you will be asked about your origins, and we must all have a clear story.' Some of the lies began there; others were added later.

On good days Balan was sure he knew everything there was to know about me. On bad days he feared that there were things I had kept hidden even from him. The bad days outnumbered the good. Balan's love for me was a constant fatiguing struggle to render me more transparent to him. Balan wanted to be included. Included in what? What did he see in my life – stripped bare, bones without flesh, calendar without events – that he wanted a part of?

Balan and I forgot, sometimes, which lies had been told to which people, and there was the odd social error. More frighteningly, I forgot what lies I had told him. Who, I thought, panicking, were the characters in the story I had told him? Whom did I suppress, whom did I modify? I did most of the original lying years ago. The lies I told later were maintenance lies. Sometimes I thought it was pointless to keep them up. It seemed silly, like acting out a parody of a Victorian novel.

In a doctor's waiting room, once, I flipped idly through a magazine: the agony aunt suggested that happy marriages were founded on honesty. I will be honest, I thought on the way home. Through some tiny three-cornered rip in the fabric of untruths I let Balan glimpse the truth. A song was all it took. He recoiled. His eyes pleaded with me: restore the illusion. I found that Balan was a Victorian after all. To have Revealed All or to have Shared My Past would have been fatal to everything that anchored me – my marriage, our home, Hema, my continued contact, however tenuous, with dance. I felt like a sleepwalker waking with one foot stretched beyond the lip of a precipice, about to tread down into nothingness.

None of the things I concealed actually made me ashamed. That was part of the reason why I almost gave them away. But I was filled with shame that I had so little courage. I was ashamed that I had been untrue to my craft and to my people. I was ashamed of the wrong things. I tried to remember to be ashamed of being born into a dasi family. I tried to remember that I had married a brahmin man.

Some days I felt acutely that the flimsy structure I had built would come tumbling down. I was afraid of the faces that swam up out of the past, of talking in my sleep, of the letters that Balan received, of the wind in the corn. Standing by the window, looking down at Vijaya as she denuded the arali tree, I searched among the morning sounds for signs of my danger, for assurances of my safety. The raucous call of the crows, the high sweet chatter of the bee-eaters and sparrows, the gurgle of the pipes in the bathroom as Balan brushed his teeth.

Everything was in order. Beneath me the household stirred.

It would be all right. Padmasini would not betray me. I would not betray myself. I would remember which things I had told Balan and which things I had blacked out. Balan would not leave me, Hema would not abandon me. Balan had loved me passionately once, and I had loved him. Perhaps we still loved each other, though I didn't know, I didn't *know*. A brahmin way of life was slow creeping death by customary practices and taboos and timidity. Was being a wife just a habit, then, that one could not give up?

The paper-man's bicycle wobbled up to the gate. Even before it stopped, his leg swung over the back of it. He balanced the frame against his hip. I ran down the stairs.

I had not noticed that it was a different paper-man, but it must have been. When I reached the gate he was already cycling away. The newspapers were not tucked into the bars of the gate, but had been forced down the mail slot.

I opened the door of the mailbox. If it had been the weekday paper, perhaps those soft half-fledged bodies would have withstood the weight. The heavy Sunday papers had fallen on them like bricks. Not one of the three had been spared. Their down looked ragged (how did the fur of dead animals clot into points, the feathers of dead birds stiffen so quickly?). The last blue egg had broken. I could not bear the reek of its putrefaction, I could not take out the papers with the spatter of pink and red crushed flesh upon them.

The magpies were on the electric wire above the road. Could they smell their dead? Would they feel grief, bereavement, a sense of the horrible futility of the food in their beaks? Would they peck at the dead chicks, trying to make them eat? Let their parenthood be nothing more than a matter of instinct, I prayed. Let them build another nest in a safer place and raise another brood.

But I could not stop the grief in myself. I wept for the birds, ashamed of myself, because Balan would have said I was a silly idiot (surely Kalyani, in the broad scheme of things – you are overreacting – come now, admit that your grief is a little disproportionate, he said, when I confessed that I had left the papers in the mailbox because of the dead chicks.) When I turned back to look, the magpies were fluttering above the mailbox, attacking the part of the papers that stuck out of the slot.

3

Kalyani

Kalyanikkarai, 1957–1961

My forty years have been divided into distinct parts: the parts when I was allowed to dance and the parts when I was not. In my mother's house I danced; in Aunt Rachel's house and in Balan's house, I could not. In Balan's house, especially, the pressure of immobility grew so great that I thought I might go mad. For years I lay under the creaking ceiling fan that hung over Balan's bed and mine, hoping it would fall and crush one of my legs. The sight of other people dancing awoke in me the sort of ache I imagined amputees felt. If my leg were crushed, and I were cut off from dancing by forces beyond my control, it would – I thought, in the early years of my marriage – be easier than knowing I might have had the use of my limbs if they had not been pinned down, irrecoverably, by propriety.

When I stopped singing the old padhams my mother

had taught me, I noticed that the ache of my phantom limb grew duller.

The big pillared hall in my mother's house, in Kalyanikkarai, was dark and cool until I was five years old. And then one summer, the year I turned six, it was bright and hot. All morning the hot ribs of light from the window shrank as the sun rose higher; they crawled backwards across the red oxide floor, over the worn teak of the swing that hung off to one side of the hall. The house was smaller that summer, and there was a new front door. There were voices on the other side of the wall.

One day that summer, I sat on the swing while my mother bent over her trunk. When she straightened up, a crimson cotton sari was in her hands. She flapped it out of its folds. She ripped the borders out, rolled them up, and stuffed them back in the trunk.

Amma tied one end of the red strip to a window bar. The window was a dazzle far away across the room and the red streamed towards me like a long tongue. Amma wore a splash of the same crimson on her forehead. Her shoulders were dark clay from the Kalyani's banks, smoothed, polished with water.

'Eley, Kalyani,' she said, holding the soft middle part of the sari. 'Come here.' Amma's veins ran along her forearms like blue branching rivers over dark loam.

'Stand still, child. Hold this end of the sari. Pull hard, like this.' Amma put the loose end of the cloth into my fists, and made me grip it tight and flat against my belly. I was wiry like Amma, and beginning to be tall. I looked at my hands beside hers, and they were soft and white. I liked the feel of the stretched cloth. It was like the tug-o-war rope at school, it made me feel my strength. But I also liked to fret, and keep Amma's attention, because when she became absorbed in work, I felt she did not care for me.

'Aaah,' I said, wincing. 'It hurts.'

'If you think this hurts,' she said placidly, 'you wait till Samu Vathyar has finished with your *thayya thai*. Your thighs will be on fire.'

'I don't want to dance,' I said, wriggling in her arms.

'Keep the cloth stretched, like a good girl,' Amma said, 'and listen to the story of your name.' Amma's palms were rough against my knuckles. 'Lean away from the window. There. Long long ago, Gangai poured down from the heavens, to wash the world clean of sin.'

I leaned away from the window; my mother took me by the shoulders and turned me around and around, keeping the tension in the cloth.

'Her power was too great for the frail earth.' She half spoke, half sang the story. 'To soften it, Siva-Peruman caught her in a knot of his hair first, before sending a trickle to the mountains below. People bathed in her waters, washing their sins away.'

I walked into the taut red. Every time I turned, it licked me up some more. It wrapped itself tighter and tighter around my stomach until I fetched up on the barred square of light under the window. I looked up and saw the parakeets wheeling green and dizzy above the neem tree. 'Kee! Keeya! Keeya!' they cried.

'One day, Gangai went to a rocky hill in the south and

offered sacrifices to Sivan. "I am tired of sin, Lord," said Gangai to Siva-Peruman when he appeared before her. "Give me a sister to share my burdens." So Siva-Peruman made Kalyani and set her flowing from the very spot where Gangai prayed.'

I writhed inside the red that made me stiff as a plank from chest to hips.

'Hush. Then a king conquered that hill and built a town near it and called the town Kalyanikkarai. He saw Siva-Peruman in a vision, in the mist rising from the river.'

'It's too tight.'

'"Here, in this very place," Siva-Peruman told the king, "you will build a temple for me and celebrate my festivals." And so the Kalyanikkarai temple was built.'

'And so I am called Kalyani.'

(Later, in the Madras Literary Society library, I would find an English version of the story in a book called *Myths and Legends of South India*, by an American folklorist. She had written that a twelfth-century ruler of Kalyanikkarai had commissioned this legend to establish his right to build the temple and rule the fiefdom.)

'It is a beautiful name,' Amma said.

'I can't *breathe*,' I moaned.

'If Samu Vathyar hears you fussing, he'll break your legs. It's an honour, a teacher as great as him teaching a little titch like you.'

The summer before, the roof had made a low wavy fringe over the window, like an eyelid almost shut. Standing at the window, I could see the lowest section of the neem's trunk, but I couldn't see where it forked into branches. At the end of the year, a storm whipped the tiles away and smashed them against the wall. When it rained, we took our mats to the other end of the room.

'Can't we stop the rain, Amma?' I asked.

'No one makes pipe tiles any more in Kalyanikkarai. They are Madras tiles, and to repair the roof we have to go to Madras.'

I waited, imagining a trip on the train, and a return with a basketful of red tiles. (Now I know there had been no money to repair the roof.)

So that summer, which was the beginning of my dancing life, I could see up into the neem's branches. The parakeets were cracking the neem pods inside their red beaks, making the bitter milk splash on their neck feathers. The sun poured into the house. I shut my eyes tight, and the insides of my lids glowed like live coals. I opened them and watched the parakeets. Amma's body hid them when she untied the end of the cloth from the window bar, and they came back again when she stooped to tuck it into the red band around my belly. The end of the cloth was crumpled with being knotted, powdery with rust.

(One window bar in Amma's house was bent like a bow, disturbing the pattern of hard black verticals in the bright patch on the floor. It had been pressed into service as corseting technology for over a century.)

'You must–' Amma said, on the day of my first dance lesson, folding my wrist as far back as it would go, not stopping until I winced, and placing it on my hip over the red band, '–keep a straight back in Samu Vathyar's class.'

She braided a heavy kunjalam into the end of my plait.

She took my face in her palms and looked at it critically. 'Hmm, you'll do.' She kissed me. 'Put on your slippers,' she said. 'It's hot outside.'

On the street, with my slippered feet, I rubbed out the hopscotch squares that the neighbours' girls had made by dragging their heels in the fine dust. They played in a group, and I could hear them every day, arguing: you stepped right on the line, I saw you, you just made up that rule, you dropped your tile, didn't she drop her tile? Once, I said, 'Yes, she stepped on the line, I saw her.' They rounded on me: 'Who asked *you*, you stupid thing?' I never questioned much the fact that they would not let me play with them. For as long as I could remember it had been like this. I was not unhappy. I found ways of occupying my solitude at home and in school.

Three houses away, Samu Vathyar sat on a wooden chair in a pillared hall larger than my mother's, one leg crossed over the other at the knee, his hand holding his foot, his body charged with nervous energy.

'I've told you all a hundred times, there will be no more dance teaching in this family.'

'Let the child learn,' Vadivel said. He was Samu Vathyar's third son and the only one of his sons who still lived in Kalyanikkarai. 'She is our Rajayi's daughter, she's bound to be good.'

My black-and-gold kunjalam swinging at the end of my plait, my red sash tight around my waist, I was a supplicant in the temple of dance.

'They're calling the tevadiyas whores,' Samu Vathyar

said. My mother's lips tightened. 'What does that make us, then, Velu? Do you want to be famous as a pimp? The other castes are mocking us. I cannot hold my head up without shame. When something has come to the end of its time, and is ready to die, it must be allowed to die. This dance is finished. Better to sweep the floor in some rich man's house than keep it alive.'

'The child is eager to learn,' my mother said. It was a lie; I didn't care. 'So many high-caste girls, brahmin girls, are learning to dance, and you are teaching them. Why would you turn Kalyani away?'

Samu Vathyar was quiet for a long time. Then he sighed. 'All right, Rajayi. For your sake. But this dance business is a vampire. It climbs on people's backs. It will have your blood and the child's blood and Velu's blood.'

They spread a cloth on the floor and poured rice grains on it for the ritual of beginning to be a dancer. My mother took me by the hand and planted my feet on the rice.

'Turn your feet out,' Samu Vathyar said. 'More. More. *More.* Don't tip forward like that.'

He took up his stick and began calling the first step, in the slowest speed: *thayya thai.*

Amma held my ankles and made my feet stamp in time to the stick. *Thayya thai*, *thayya thai.* The rice grains jumped up brown around her glass bangles. By the time I finished my *thayya thai*, my thighs were on fire. Samu Vathyar proved every bit the curmudgeon she had warned me about.

'Down!' he shouted. 'Bend your knees! Open them wider! Go further down! What are you sticking your behind out for? Tuck it in!'

42

And by the time I finished learning the next step, the *thayyum thatha*, my arms were on fire too.

'Hold your elbows higher,' Samu Vathyar growled. 'Even if a pack of monkeys jumps on your arm, it must not drop below the level of your shoulder!' I imagined balancing monkeys on arms I held stretched like a bow. He was free with his tapping stick. He threw it at my feet when they were not turned out enough and he threw it at my wrists when they drooped. Luckily for me, he was in his sixties and his aim wasn't very good.

Every day, for three years, I ran down the street from Amma's house to Samu Vathyar's house, smelling dust laid with water, smelling neem, straw and woodsmoke. I remember in his yard the flamboyant flowers whose stamens I wore like a moustache. I remember playing knock-the-cock's-head-off with the stamens, and popping yellow buds against my forehead.

When I woke in the morning in Amma's house, I smelt dew on leaf meal, and coral jasmine by the back door. Summer came through the window in a fat prong of light, full of drifting motes. Amma lived on Musicians' Street. It was just the two of us. None of the other women on the street talked to her, and none of the other children on the street played with me. Women turned their faces away and spat on the pavement when Amma went to the market, but I did not understand why, and after a while it did not matter.

'Your mother is a tevadiya,' they said in my school.

'What is a tevadiya?' I asked Amma. The question had

festered for a long time because she had never answered it properly. Now I was afraid of the answer.

She sighed. 'A tevadiya is a woman who sings and dances and . . .'

'And what?'

'And helps with temple worship.'

Sometimes the town boys climbed on the high wall behind the house and threw rubbish into the backyard. Amma watched and said nothing. If I shouted at them, they shouted back: 'Tevadiya mundai!'

'Their parents teach them those words,' Amma said.

'Tell me what they really mean.'

'You leave those boys alone.'

We left them alone; but they came into the yard and tore down Amma's jasmine creeper. They threw broken glass into the yard, and we had to tread carefully when we went to the privy in the night. Once, in the morning, I saw Amma's footsteps all the way back to her sleeping place, marked in blood. She had forgotten about the glass.

As I grew older I did not hear this word as often. Perhaps the people intimate enough with the old town to know my mother had moved away, or had lost interest; perhaps I had stopped caring.

In spite of the boys, until I went to stay with Aunt Rachel, I felt safe in Amma's house. The walls were so thick that when a layer of bricks caved in on the inside, as they had done here and there, there was no damage visible from the outside. Above us the ancient ribs of the roof lined up, black against tiles that were discoloured like old people's gums. I could tell by the sound where the squirrels were streaking over the tiles. There was a wooden sign with English letters above the door, and I amused myself by throwing a ball against the sign and catching it again.

Three photographs hung on the wall and were honoured and garlanded on special days. One was of my grandmother, Kanaka. I had never seen her. She was light-skinned and straight-backed; her right hand rested on the back of a chair, her other arm hung easily at her side, slightly away from her hip. A chain of gold coins hung around her neck. The second picture was of Amma's dance master and mine, Samu Vathyar. His head was thrown back; a waxed black moustache hid his mouth. And the third picture was of the man my mother always called 'the Vakil', as if there was only one lawyer in the whole world.

'She is ready,' Samu Vathyar said after class one day.

'For what?' I asked Amma when we walked home. 'What am I ready for?'

'Your arangetram,' she said. She looked happy and proud. 'Your first time dancing on the stage before people. It's to be at the temple.'

Samu Vathyar came with us to the market to choose my ankle bells. The brass bells lay in a huge basket and he shook each one, listening to its sound. He picked some and set others aside. 'Keep those for the cows,' he said to the shopkeeper, who looked annoyed. We took the bells to be stitched in rows on cloth. We chose a red sari for me to wear when I danced. Amma held it against me and tipped her head, studying the effect.

She smiled a lot; she was happier than I remembered in a long while.

Every evening for a week, the mridangam player came, and the clarinet player. The rehearsals went on for hours.

'Again?' I said. 'From the beginning?'

'Again,' Samu Vathyar said implacably. This time he put away the tapping stick and the little plank; he tapped out the beat with cymbals. If I made a mistake we began over. The varnam seemed to have no end. Amma sang it over and over, and Vathyar watched my feet with a frown.

'Enough,' Amma whispered to him at last. 'She'll be too tired for tomorrow.'

On the morning of the day I had waited for and dreaded, Amma oiled my body under the overhang of tiles over the back veranda of the house. On three sides of me, sheltering me from the eyes of the boys who climbed the back wall, she had stretched an old sari around poles. With my nails I scraped designs on my hard ovoid belly; in the middle I wrote: *tha-dingina-thom*. The oil came up into my fingernail and left a pale skin-coloured design against the darker, saturated skin that smelt of ginger root and cumin and pepper. I bunched my flesh in my hands and felt the pleasant soreness of the muscles underneath. Amma took the tongs, pulled pieces of wood from the fire in front of me and put them in the brazier. She fanned them with the palmyra leaf. Blue wispy flames jumped up. She brought water from the well in a bucket, and poured it into the ancient black brass tub on the fire. Inside the house, the swing creaked.

'Someone's in the house,' I said.

'What?'

Amma pushed her hair away from her face with the back of her arm, and stared at the back door. Her sari was soaked from my splashing water on to it. She went in.

'Shut the door, don't let whoever it is come here before I get my clothes on,' I called out, but she didn't hear.

'I cannot believe this foolishness,' the voice in the house said. I did not remember having heard it before. 'Haven't you had enough trouble from this dance?'

Amma didn't stop to express amazement, or to ask what she was talking about. She replied exactly as if they – she and the voice – had had the same quarrel a hundred times before.

'What else can I give the child?' Amma said. 'What else am I good for?'

'Rajayi, girls are doing everything under the sun today. I hear she is a clever child – she can become a teacher or a nurse. Listen, I understand that you took up dancing to make your mother happy. You did it to keep her promise to the god.'

'If I did not give up dance altogether, it was only partly for my mother's sake. The other part, Komala Chithi, is my *love* of it. Surely you can understand that.'

'Yes, I can understand that kind of love. In you. Does your daughter love dance the way you do? What right do you have to make a dancer of her? Don't you want her to have a future? What future is there when the Act has banned the dance in temples?'

'The Act makes me angry. It was wrong of the government to take away our way of life. If it banned women from dancing, Komala Chithi, how do we account for all the women who are dancing today? Samu Vathyar has more students today than he ever had. Even Velu, his son, is teaching young girls.'

'*Brahmin* girls. No one will point a finger at them. When *they* do it, it is art; when *we* do it, it has only one name.'

'It is *our* art. It has been *ours* for generations. We are its guardians. This is why we must keep dancing, Chithi, this is why Kalyani must dance.'

'Rubbish. You live in the past, you are quoting from that petition – that desperate, hopeless petition that was supposed to turn the tide in our favour. Look at the world today, Rajayi. I am an old woman, and I can do it – why can't you? Why are you stuck in this – this mentality of the village?'

'In Samu Vathyar's class, I see every day how badly the brahmin girls dance. They understand nothing, have no knowledge of the music, the poetry, the kind of thinking that gives this dance life. I cannot bear to think of them dancing in public, ruining this form, while Kalyani, who is so good, is hidden out of sight–'

'If a local landlord, one of these hard-drinking minors, asks tomorrow to become her patron, what will you say?'

'I'll say no. We don't have to do *that* any more. She can teach a class.'

'Does anyone want to learn from a dasi woman?'

'Chithi, stay and watch her. I don't say this in front of her, but her movements are so fine, her steps so clean. You watch tonight.'

The neem leaves rustled, and I sneezed.

'I had better go wash the oil off her,' Amma said,

'or she will be ill by this evening. Sit, I'll make coffee afterwards.'

Amma came to the back of the house again and washed my hair with herbs and crushed hibiscus leaves. She called the rivers as she poured hot water over me: 'Ganga, Yamuna, Saraswati, Narmada, Sindhu, Kaveri, Kalyani!' She rubbed my spindly limbs with a towel, tied a petticoat around my body, and we went inside.

'This is my Komala Chithi, your great-aunt,' Amma said. 'My sister Lila's mother.' The lady rocked slowly back and forth on the swing. She was tall and white-haired, but she looked a lot like Amma. Amma brought in the brazier and sprinkled frankincense over the red coals. I threw my hair over my head and over the brazier, the incense drifted through the strands, and I sneezed again.

'Krishna!' Amma said automatically, to keep off bad luck.

The temple's floor felt hard and cool under my feet. The audience sat anywhere it liked. My great-aunt sat with my mother on a step, holding a pot of water for me to drink from. Samu Vathyar sat on a platform with the other musicians. I barely noticed the audience; my whole intent that evening was to please Samu Vathyar, to make him say *'Balle!* Well done!' Amma warned me that he would never say it. Light shone on me from the great brass lamps on either side of me, but I felt it came *from* me, from inside my body. I remembered all the steps and all the abhinayam, in the right order. I made no mistakes.

When it was over, Amma and Samu Vathyar and I went to make an offering to the god. Amma took the ash on her thumb and stroked it across my forehead. Samu Vathyar put his gigantic hands on my head to bless me. I was sure he was going to say 'Balle', perhaps whisper to save me from getting a swollen head. But a man stepped out from behind a pillar and said something to Amma, and her hand shook, and ash fell on my face and all down my lovely red sari. I looked up and waited, but her face was like stone, and she was looking at the man the way children look at a teacher who is going to hit them.

When I woke up the next morning, my great-aunt was saying, 'I told you there would be trouble.' The swing moaned as she rocked: *cree-cree, cree-cree.* 'I warned you.'

'I didn't think – I didn't expect – that threat was made so long ago, I almost forgot.' Amma was crying, a rare and frightening sight. She was sitting up against the wall. I turned away, pretending to be asleep.

'Get her away from here. I'll arrange it, Rachel Carstairs will take her.'

'Ray-chel?'

'Kokku Missy. The one I worked with when I first went away from here. She now has a full-fledged orphanage.'

'An orphanage, for children whose mothers are alive?'

'She looks after children of families like ours, educates them. See what they are saying about mothers in our community, Rajayi. Here, read this.'

A rustle of paper. Amma's voice, saying sadly, 'And you, you believe this about me? That I am not fit to raise a child? When you left Lila with my mother, did you think that dasi women were terrible mothers? What do these people know?'

'If the whole town starts to see her as prey – you saw what the Inspector said last night. You've seen what they can do to people like you. I will go to Rachel right away. If you are lucky, she will have a place for the child.'

Which child? No one told me anything. I was never asked if I would like to do this or that. Swiftly, Amma or someone else would decide, and I won no arguments by crying, and I learned that there was no going back. That weekend, Amma cut up two of her best saris, and began to make skirts for me. She sewed for three days, quickly, with fierce concentration. Then for three days after the skirts were ready, when I was wondering if she would let me try them on, she sat in a corner by herself, not speaking to me. I knew better than to ask questions.

I loved the moment when the calendar spun around in Kalyanikkarai, from dry heat to rain. I loved the sky when it turned grey and gravid, the lazy spirals of wind that whipped the dust and leaves into eddies.

Three weeks after my arangetram at the temple, the sky over the hills cracked open like a giant bronze basin. The cracks flared white, forked and slithered into the curve of horizon. A spitting rain made tiny craters in the dust of the schoolyard. The clouds towered up, storey upon storey, and cannoned into each other.

When the school bell rang, I jammed my books into my satchel. Clattering my knees against the benches,

I ran into the rain that sloped down on the land now, heavy as a ploughshare. The schoolchildren dashed, wet-shanked, shouting with gladness, through the brush which the town women gathered for brooms. I followed them. They ran through the cattle paths and tunnels of weed on the Raja's property. They stopped in the shelter of the big archway to tear notebook pages into squares. The ditches were filling up, canals for paper boats. They shook water on themselves out of the Raja's cashew trees; I stood near them and the tree rain fell on me, making my tumbled hair starry.

When I got home, soaked and sneezing, a cart stood outside the door. Not a bullock cart, but a jutka. I shivered. The man driving the jutka had already put my things into the back. Amma kissed me, cold hands cupping my face, her face like stone.

'This lady will take care of you now,' she said. 'You will go with her and be like her child.'

The lady who had come to take me was white as a ghost. She lived in Nallur, five miles away. I had first seen her when I was three or four years old, at the temple, drawing in her book. I had heard people laughing at her as she strode through the town with that drawing book under her arm, a long ugly woman with no lips. Later, after I read the English fairytales in her library, I would think of her long swinging stride as the stride of the seven-league boots. She had many pockets, full of pencils and pens, in her practical skirt. When she passed by, the boys in my class had balanced on one leg and jerked their arms up and down like wings.

She hadn't been seen so much in recent years. She

must have been getting too old for Kalyanikkarai's uneven, boulder-filled hills. She must have been nearly seventy when she came to collect me. To me she looked a hundred years old.

'For this you made me skirts?' I asked Amma. 'To send me away?'

Amma put her arms, so cold, around my body, and rocked me gently. I locked my arms around her neck.

'Why must I be sent away? Why?' I buried my face in the smell of her neck. She stroked my back, while Kokku Missy pried my hands loose.

'Is it because I didn't dance well? Did Vathyar say I didn't dance well? I'll dance better next time, Amma. Amma, tell her to go away.'

'You have a great many burrs in your skirt,' the white lady said. Somehow, between the cart driver and my mother, they had hoisted me into the jutka. I set my heart against my mother then, but I watched her for a long time, because she came out into the road, her feet splashing in the puddles, her arms hugging her belly as if it hurt, and walked after the jutka until it swung right around the bend of the hill, and suddenly I couldn't see Kalyanikkarai any more.

4

Kalyani
Nallur, 1961–1970

Kokku Missy. I examined her neck through my tears. Yes, it was long, but wattled with age, more like a turkey's neck than a stork's. In the jutka, she told me I would have to be *sen-sible.* 'Me – Aunt Rachel,' she said, pointing to her chest. 'My name. I call you–' She poked me in the ribs. I barely understood her Tamil. 'I call you *Callie.*' Later she told me 'Callie' meant 'beautiful' in Greek, and had been her grandmother's name.

I sneezed and wiped my nose with the end of my wet skirt.

'No *hand-kerchief,* I think?' Kokku Missy said. She mixed Tamil and English words, but she clicked her tongue to show disgust the way my schoolteachers did. 'You have much to learn.'

At the mission house, Aunt Rachel said, 'You go bath.' I looked in my bag for the clothes Amma had made for me.

'I took those things away, Callie,' Aunt Rachel said. 'They were *un-suitable.*'

I was given a bed to sleep on for the first time in my life. I lay on white linen and pressed down on the mattress around me, marvelling at the way it yielded.

'Handkerchief' and 'unsuitable' were among the first English words I learned; 'unsuitable' was Aunt Rachel's favourite word.

My strongest memory of her was of her long skirt sweeping by me, the edges whisking away my toy of the moment – a paper boat, a heap of flowers – and me crawling after to snatch my playthings back as soon as her skirts deposited them somewhere. All the while her voice would be calling out sharply to someone in the kitchen or the garden. Through the ruffled lace curtains of her study I would see her haranguing visitors into raising money for the Cradle-Babies' Cause, or writing in her journals.

On the wall of Aunt Rachel's office there was a large picture of a man with rippling brown hair – when I was better informed I knew it was Jesus – gathering four fair, golden-haired children into his arms. 'Suffer the little Children to come unto Me', the caption below it said in a flowing script. Until Aunt Rachel explained it to me, I thought it meant that children should suffer, and be ripped from their homes to be brought to Jesus. I thought it meant that some girl five or six years old should howl like a sad puppy because she missed her mother ('Let her cry, Callie, it is good for the soul! We must never give in to a child's tantrums – you will spoil that little girl so!'), that she should cry with hunger because she was not allowed to eat a thing under Aunt Rachel's roof

55

without first learning to pick it up with a fork and knife, sitting with a white starched napkin on her lap, that she should give up the soft cotton flowered skirts her mother sewed for her and wear a stiff blue dress down to mid-calf when she was young, and a white sari with a blue border, like a widow from a Seth's house, when she was older. That the Lord's Prayer should be her introduction to the English language – Aafatha-inyeaven, halobeethynay, thykingdomcome, thyvillbeedone, onathaastisnewan, and so on, until buddeliwerr us promeewilamen would let her begin the task at hand, eating, or reading, or sewing.

'Suffer the little Children to come unto Me,' Aunt Rachel spelt out to me, when, bathed and clean and dressed in a blue pinafore, and equipped with a handkerchief into which I was instructed to blow my nose, I was taken to her office on my first day in the mission house. 'If you are a good girl, Callie, I will teach you how to read. We'll begin this very week.'

Under Aunt Rachel's erratic tutorship, I learnt English so fast I astonished myself. I was given free access to the mission house library. First I devoured the fairy tales, then the heavy crimson tomes with gold lettering and 'Mudie's' printed on the spine. *Jane Eyre*, *Wuthering Heights*, *Vanity Fair*, *Mary Barton*, *Nicholas Nickleby*.

As I learned to wash and sew and help with the cooking, my heart asked the question: why? Why did my mother send me here? Was it because of my great-aunt? Because instead of saying '*Balle!*' Samu Vathyar said I was a hopeless dancer? (I imagined this; I never had time to learn what he thought of my dance.) Because of the man who had stepped out from behind the pillar the night of my recital at the temple?

When I was not washing and sewing and cooking, I was reading. Aunt Rachel was delighted with my progress. 'Wonderful,' she said. 'Unbelievable. The Lord works in mysterious ways. Now you can teach the young ones.'

Most of the children who came to the mission house missed their homes in the first few weeks, and then settled down. But I had let anger at my mother cloud my grief during my own first months at Aunt Rachel's house. I had spent a year at the mission house before the suppressed misery and longing washed over me like the tide. Suddenly I began to dream of Amma – her hands, her voice, her smell – all the time.

'I would like to go home,' I said to Aunt Rachel.

'This is your home, Callie.'

'To see my mother.'

'I'm afraid it cannot be thought of, dear.'

'For just one day,' I said. 'Please, Aunt Rachel.'

'Callie, I'm afraid, from what I hear, your mother's home has become completely unsuitable for a young girl.'

'Why?'

'Your mother is – she–'

'Entertains men?' I said.

'Now who – now where in the world did you hear that?'

One of Aunt Rachel's friends had used that phrase only the week before; I heard through the curtains and it stuck in my head. With contempt in her voice: 'Rachel, this work you do with the children of these temple prostitutes is admirable, but ask yourself this – well, take Callie, for instance. Don't you think all you did when you brought her over all those months ago was make it easier for her mother to entertain men?'

I want to ask Rajayi now; to go back to Kalyanikkarai and ask her, without anger, did you send me away when I was nine, so that you could entertain men? But in Aunt Rachel's house, I lived so completely outside my mother's world that the question lost its urgency. In fact, I lived outside the world of Hinduism altogether: according to Aunt Rachel, all Hindus were damned anyway, men or no men, and had fire and brimstone coming to them.

At the mission house, I began to understand the talk about my mother. I began to understand why people despised us, why the boys had thrown rocks at the house, and why they had called us tevadiya women, dasi mundais, whores, bitches.

Almost two years after I was brought to the mission house, a man came to see Aunt Rachel. I recognized his face: he was 'the Vakil', the man whose picture hung on my mother's wall. He entertained the orphanage children by taking off his turban to show how bald he was. I wondered if he was my father. He spoke to me briefly and disappeared into Aunt Rachel's office. I retained a blurred impression of patrician features, shining skin, a strong smell of soap, a gentle mouth.

Soon after this visit, when I had almost stopped wanting to see Amma, Aunt Rachel changed her tune about my going home. Once every few months I climbed into the jutka; it would take me to Kalyanikkarai and deposit me in front of Amma's house, and three days later it would collect me again.

'You must not forget the Lord when you go to see your mother, Callie,' Aunt Rachel would say, before I left for Kalyanikkarai. She'd say, 'You must try to imagine what the Lord would have you do with your time there.'

I was not likely to forget the Lord. In Nallur, we went to church often, at least two or three times a week. At first, the new style of worship seemed drab. The worshippers were subdued. My eyes searched for colour (where was the pink of the sandstone, where the saffron of chrysanthemum garlands, the splashes of scarlet kungumam like blood on the stone, the flickering lustre of a hundred brass lamps?); my ears for sound (where were the brass bells, the drums, the pipes, the people intoning, singing, groaning out their demands?); my nose for smells (where were the perfumes of jasmine, smoke, camphor, oil? the slightly rotting smell of coconut water over the stone drains around the sanctum? the feral reek of bats, the odour of ancient stone?).

When my eyes became the eyes of a different person, I finally saw colour in the church. The sun came around to the other side of the stained-glass window, and Jesus glowed, walking on water. The rosewood pews were polished. We put lilies and roses in the vases above the altar, we lit the candles, and I admitted that the church was a holy place. As its hushed walls became sacred in my eyes, the festive brightness of the temple became garish. The faith I had known melted away from my horizon like an island in the mist. My mother became a blurred wraith.

When I came home from the mission house, I saw the sign against which I had thrown my ball for years. I read it for the first time, because it was in English, struggling a little with the longer words, but recognizing their import: 'It is hereby noted that the occupant has been warned against transforming minor girls for immoral purposes.' When Amma opened the door, her hands shaking and clumsy, and swept me into her arms, I flinched from her.

Amma knew at once that I was judging her.

'Who was that who came to see me at Aunt Rachel's?' I asked Amma that night, when she rolled out the sleeping mat for me. 'The man in the photo?'

'The Vakil?' she said casually. 'He is a great man. Kalyanikkarai's best lawyer. And an MLA now, in Madras.'

'He's bald,' I said. I tried to ask if she was entertaining men, but my tongue would not push the words out. She sat beside me on the mat, gently waving a palm leaf fan over my body. I looked around the house for whatever I thought was evidence that men had been there, but there was nothing. Everything looked as it had when I left, only older and more decayed.

The newspapers said Rachel Carstairs single-handedly did the work of the Lord in Kalyanikkarai. 'Single-handedly' only meant that she had no Europeans around her, I suppose. It wasn't as if she got down on her knees and scrubbed the floors. There was an army of dark-skinned local women – Mariam and Vasanta, Kutty Rachel and

Assumpta, Chandra and Malli and Kumudha – women with white teeth and coarse hands and blue-green tattoos of Hindu prayers still vivid on their forearms, to help with actually bathing and feeding the children. My band of women who have taken Christ into their hearts, Aunt Rachel called them. When I was older, I became one of their number, beating the white linen against a stone slab to get the dirt out, and teaching the English alphabet to the 'orphans', children of two and three who had been taken from their mothers as I had been.

When I was sure Aunt Rachel was asleep, I crept into the beds of the youngest newcomers and held them while they sobbed for home. I heard Aunt Rachel say, of the mother of a small child who had been brought by the police to the mission house: 'Good lord, how she bucked and screamed, as if she were giving up her life, not her child.'

It was understood that the children were brought to the mission house for their own good. Aunt Rachel's most urgent desire was to rescue *infant* girls from dasi women. 'The younger they are, the purer they are,' she explained. She knew all this for sure, without a moment's doubt.

'The presumption of these women!' Aunt Rachel exclaimed. 'They behave like queens when they don't have two rupees to rub together!'

Three or four years after I began visiting my mother, I realized that Kalyanikkarai had grown very strange to me. Every time I went back, I would think: what am I going to do here? There was nothing to do. It was so quiet it frightened me, especially in the evenings.

One evening, when Amma was teaching me a padham, the town boys, now grown to manhood and full of drink, began to throw stones at our windows for old times' sake. Amma and I sat on the mat while the stones hit the wooden shutters and the bars. I had forgotten how it was; how upset I had always been that Amma wouldn't move, wouldn't stop them or shout at them.

When their witless laughter died away, we resumed the song:

Why have you come here?
That woman's house is not on this street. Go away.

At Aunt Rachel's house I had companions. The other girls and I were always sewing something for the mission, or painting, or going to church. We sang:

We don't want to march in the infantry, march in the infantry,
We don't want to march in the infantry,
We are in the armless drill.

It seemed too fatiguing to go up and down between the mission house and my mother's house, between Nallur and Kalyanikkarai, between Jesus and Sivan, between padhams and marching songs; to change my way of eating and sleeping and dressing, to adapt to a different world every four months. There was another thing: I felt uncomfortable going to the temple after going to church all those years. I was determined to stay aloof from Amma's religion. I believed what Aunt Rachel told me, that it was superstitious. I feared that I would be struck down. Especially because of the house.

Amma's house was beginning to crumble more and more quickly, or perhaps, because of the gaps between my visits, the process was more visible to me. I couldn't sleep thinking about it. When I went back to the mission house after one of these visits, Aunt Rachel read a passage from the Bible which I never forgot. 'Behold,' she read, 'there came a great wind from the wilderness and it smote the four corners of the house and it fell upon the young men, and they are dead.' I would lie on my mat in Amma's house and worry myself sick, imagining that this would happen to Amma and me because we were heathens. The four corners of the house would buckle suddenly; the roof would collapse; we would lie dead and unregarded under a mountain of rubble.

I found it convenient to revive my anger with my mother, and brood once again on the fact that she had given me away. I began to believe that she did not deserve to have me back. So after four years of going back and forth, when I was about fifteen, I said, 'Aunt Rachel, do I *have* to go to my mother's house?' and Aunt Rachel said, 'Not if you don't want to, dear,' and I stopped going back to Kalyanikkarai. Just like that.

I never asked my mother how she felt about it.

By the time I was nineteen, Aunt Rachel began to slide towards senility. She was in her seventy-eighth year, physically still strong and active, still striding down the dusty road to the church. But once there she left her own prayer book behind, or took the church's hymn book home. She left her umbrella leaning up against the stained glass door and forgot to call in at the bakery on her way home. All of which made the parish priest write to her devoted Australian nephew. That nephew, already worried because his letters had gone unanswered for several months, arrived in Nallur one Christmas Eve, paid off the domestic help, relocated the few orphans still living there, and left me enough money to close up the place. He said I could stay as long as I liked before closing up. There was an excellent local lawyer I could contact for any legal help. I did not recognize the lawyer's name, but when I met him, he told me he was working for Sundaram Iyer, the Kalyanikkarai Vakil. That was the man I thought of as my father, the man who had come to the mission house once and made jokes about his bald head. I felt some pride at the thought that he had trained this 'excellent' lawyer.

As her nephew strong-armed a loudly protesting Aunt Rachel on to the Madras train, on the way to Victoria, Australia, she turned and gave me a stricken look. It was the look she gave the forsaken umbrella when it was returned to her by one of the children, or the hymn book when the padre courteously asked for it back. Parched, upright Aunt Rachel, headed for Australia after so many years of the Lord's armless drill.

Aunt Rachel asked me to put her books and papers in order after she left, and gift them to the Raja's library. The diaries and letters among them gave me a clearer impression of the person she was, and explained the vagaries of her attitude to dance. Answering the call put out by the Church of England's Zenana Mission, for 'a lady of culture and some missionary experience, preferably to be secured from England', the young Rachel Carstairs had come to Nallur in 1920.

Almost as soon as she settled down in Nallur, Aunt Rachel had begun to write angry letters to Muthurayan, demanding that he ban the dedication of dasi girls to temples. 'The Raja has no shame,' Aunt Rachel wrote in her journal that year. 'He declines, he says, to be swept into the new morality as easily as some of his compatriots.'

There were several letters to Aunt Rachel from my great-aunt Komala, going back forty-five or fifty years. They were always about the same thing – the slow pace of the anti-dasi campaign. It must have been quite something, the poor Raja dealing with the two of them. Aunt Rachel and Komala had written terrible pamphlets about the Raja. Aunt Rachel wrote to my great-aunt about coming back to the mission house aching with frustration, carrying baskets full of coffee and fruit and gifts that the Raja had given her.

The white authorities to whom Aunt Rachel had appealed – all the way up to George Willingdon and George Stanley – ignored her. 'How different are your nautch parties from Drury Lane?' they asked her. The townspeople brushed her off.

Compensating for these setbacks, Aunt Rachel appears to have sprayed a sort of maddened altruism in all directions. When her mission superiors suggested that she exercise some restraint, she asked to be given independent control over her own territory. They hemmed and hawed. They wrote several letters, which I found among her papers, expressing doubts about the wisdom of the move, to which Aunt Rachel no doubt responded with all the force of her implacable will. They gave in. Rachel Carstairs was becoming used to having her way.

In 1925, she decided to start a proper day school for the children of her fallen sisters.

'Education will be their salvation,' she wrote in her journal. 'They will learn to read and do sums. They will be exposed to the best and noblest books ever written since the Bible. Note: apply to mission for library funds.'

She received her funds, and she sent to England for second-hand books. They arrived at the mission in trunks: Bible storybooks, hymn books, picture books with fairy tales, the classics of English fiction, volumes of poetry, improving literature, and bound sets of the *Girl's Own Paper* and the *Boy's Own Paper*. This was the mission house library. After Aunt Rachel's departure, it became one of the best-stocked District Central Libraries in south India.

Rachel Carstairs explored the countryside in her spare time, and wrote about it. A cutting from the *Madras Antiquities Gazetteer* credited her with this description:

Rising sharply behind the Callianicarah temple is a series of granite and sandstone rocks that are embedded in the sides of majestic hills. The Calliani river makes a sort of cuff around these hills. There are iron oxide deposits in their higher reaches, and the river gushes a russety red.

A legend explains the river's colour. A dancing girl who was the mistress of the reigning Rajah was taken to the riverbank and beheaded by his soldiers for being unfaithful to him. But the dancer had raised the standard of dancing in the temple to such a degree that it was the talk of the kingdom, and the God Siva had been pleased. He restored the dancer to life, gave her back to the king, and asked him to build a shrine on the easterly hills. Siva is supposed to have said, 'In the shrine, set an image of me dancing and make sacrifices to me and celebrate my festivals here. But to make me different from the Lord of the Dance in Chidambaram, have the right leg of my image raised, not the left.' But the dancer's blood turned the river red forever.

That is the legend as it was told me, without a blush, by a priest at the temple. Later, when I enquired about the authenticity of the story, some people said the story was certainly not the original legend. The priest himself was notorious for having taken a dancing girl as his mistress, though his wife was still alive. But it is a picturesque enough tale.

Now a small shrine perches high up on the crest of that hill, and very few people if any will brave the steps that have been cut into its almost sheer granite face.

I see in the disposition of these great piles of granite the hand of a higher Authority than the heathen god the Hindoos have enshrined in that temple. A great mushroom-shaped rock is so exquisitely balanced on two small rocks that it has rocked in the wind these many centuries without ever tumbling off its perch. Who could fail in this hallowed place to see the hand of the Highest?

Aunt Rachel became a ruin-enthusiast, and when she was not on cookhouse fatigue in the army of Christ, she began painting with a box of water colours. She wandered over the landscape, producing 'Hindoo Lady', 'Indian Cuckoo', and so on, but also 'Temple Rocks' and 'Strange Gods', in which Kalyanikkarai's heathen architecture was faithfully if unsympathetically captured. This eccentricity of hers became the ground of a reluctant friendship with the Raja. There were several sketchbooks among her papers, and the palace library gladly took them from me, framed the vignettes, and hung them in the gaps between the shelves in the reference room.

Between 1927 and 1947, the Raja and Aunt Rachel had dinner together every other week, and arguments during the fish course. They discussed architectural styles over dessert. The Raja favoured the Nayaka style; Aunt Rachel thought it too florid. When Muthurayan died in 1947, she was heartbroken. His son, she wrote in her journal the next year, was a spineless man, of no account whatsoever. Anyway, by then, in 1948, the Devadasi Act had been passed, and India was independent of British rule. Even the young Raja's nominal power was about to be taken from him.

Aunt Rachel gradually lost touch with my great-aunt after Komala became a Self-Respecter. That must have been in the late 1930s. My great-aunt was making speeches all over south India about the evils of caste and the devadasi system, but she had also renounced Christianity and proclaimed herself an atheist. This conversion was the occasion for Aunt Rachel to make several furious remarks in her journal.

I read Aunt Rachel's journals and thought: what an odd mind; what a full-blown eccentric this woman was. She had started off very puritanical. She joined an organization called AILOWS, the All India League Opposed to Woman Suffrage. She was President of the local chapter of the Society for the Prevention of Vice, and of the Temperance League. Then her journals were full of a writer called Quimby. Then she began to read Madame Blavatsky and Annie Besant. So Aunt Rachel's mystical education went on, in a sort of parallel groove to her Christianity, and it ended up complicating her religion. She must have struggled mightily with her conscience. She was very sincere; really she was. I realized that when I was eleven – the time she began to let me visit Kalyanikkarai – she had begun to half change her mind about dasis. By my nineteenth birthday she was telling me, in strict confidence, that all roads – not Christianity only – led to God, and that Christ was only one of the great prophets. She even made me write a letter to my great-aunt Komala on her behalf, telling her that dasis were not sinners, but vestal virgins. Her last letter to the editor of the *Callianicarah Herald*, before she left for Victoria, was about the double standard of morality. 'Even moral and religious people,' she had written, 'condemn women who are not chaste, and accept men who wallow in the fleshpots.'

'Callie: shd. she go to her mother?' she had written in her journal, about ten years earlier, '*What* a dilemma. Needs her mother's touch, perhaps, I don't know much about that side of things. But those dens of *vice*, those dance classes! Give me direction, Lord.' And later, 'Callie goes to her mother once in three months. Gentlemanly lawyer from Madras – reassurances – extracted promise from Callie's mother through him. The visits seem to have done the child some good.' And still later, 'Callie not going to mother any more. Is this moral transformation? Is it *right*? Guide me, Lord.'

When I finally went home to Kalyanikkarai, at the age of twenty-one, my mother was alarmed to see me back. Especially on a Sunday. Aunt Rachel had worried that I would dance when I went back home, and she had only sent me back on weekdays, so that I wouldn't compound the sin by dancing on the Sabbath.

The coral jasmine tree had shed its flowers all around itself in my mother's backyard. It was one of the things that had survived the years; it still perfumed the mornings. A hoopoe touched down among the bruised petals, strutting, flexing its crest. A fan in Aunt Rachel's hands on a nervous Sunday opened and shut like that, I thought.

How strange that there would be no more fans and no more churches and no more Aunt Rachel.

'Tell me about our ancestors,' I said to my mother one evening, sitting cross-legged on the grass mat. 'I am old enough now to hear the truth about who I am, who *we* are. Tevadiya women.'

Give me a way to come back, I was saying; help me kick myself loose from the shame that is dragging me down like pondweed.

My mother understood. She lit a lamp and stuck an

incense stick into its stand, to keep the mosquitoes away.

'This home we live in,' she said. 'It was built by the Raja of that time – Lingarayan – for our ancestor – my great-grandmother – Kalyaniammal. And was improved by that Raja's son for my grandmother Jagadambal. Your great-grandmother.'

'What was she like, Jagadambal?'

Jagadambal, my mother said, walked with the low-hipped, swimming gait of long-haired women. With a gold weight at its end, with rubies flashing all down its length, her braid was like a glossy black serpent, striking one well-rounded buttock and then the other.

'Walks like a queen,' the dazzled townsfolk said, every last man burning with unspoken lust, the temple's priests included. 'Like a goddess,' they sighed, giving up all claim to her.

For she belonged to the king.

'They called her "Rani",' my mother said. The Queen. She walked up Musicians' Street and East Main Street to the palace, strutting (as woman was never meant to strut, said the jealous ones) like a peacock, like a proud horse coming home from battle, like a buck showing off his horns. 'They say she swanned along as if the sunshine was for her alone, as if the street, the crossroads, the town, the whole country was just a carpet under her feet. "Arrogant bitch!" the townsfolk cursed her. And then they admired her: "Look at the Queen go, look, eley! Have you ever seen anything as fine as that, people?"'

Jagadambal danced in the court for the Raja, Muthurayan, but it was her dance in the temple that entitled her to lands, and temple food, and honours during the big festivals. While the common people stood among the oil-darkened pillars, she and her fellow-dancers mimed, outside the door of the sanctum, a stylized version of the priest's worship inside. In the flickering illumination of a hundred and eight brass lamps they entertained gods and worshippers, their dance an amalgam of sex and craft and ritual. Their ankle bells drew crowds to join the gay flambeau-lit processions through the four streets around the temple's tank.

Amma trimmed the wicks to make the lamp burn brighter.

'Muthurayan paved the whole length of Musicians' Street so that the sharp stones would not hurt Jagadambal's feet when she walked to his palace in the evenings. He planted trees to keep the sun off her lovely face. The paving remained intact for decades.'

(Then the elected government of Kalyanikkarai ripped it up to put down a modern tar road. Since then, every monsoon, the road grew pocked with ruts and potholes; the trees, all but one, had been cut down.)

'Muthurayan gave her bangles and rings, necklaces and ear studs. In those days, there was still money in the treasury. Look,' my mother said, stretching out her arm with one gold bangle on it. 'All that is left of the jewellery that belonged to Jagadambal. My mother made me promise to wear it always, for her sake.'

In 1901, when Jagadambal fell ill with a stomach disease that would not go away, Muthurayan ordered that straw be put down on the road outside her house so the carts might pass softly and not disturb her. When she became worse, he sent his own carriage down to her house, and had her brought to the women's quarters in the palace. But even the Raja's personal doctors could do nothing to save Jagadambal.

When they brought him the news, Muthurayan was in the temple. 'Let her have the full honours,' he said.

'So the widowed god of the temple mourned your great-grandmother Jagadambal for ten days,' my mother said. 'The god mourned, because she had no successors, and he was as much a widower as the Raja, for in all Kalyanikkarai no one would dance like that, or walk like that, or be called 'the Queen' in quite the same way again. The people who know about these things – old-timers like your aunt Lilavati, like Samu Vathyar – say that real dancing died with the dasis. What came afterwards was decline, self-indulgence, the cult of mediocrity. As for patronage, Kalyani, patronage died with the old Rajas.'

The room was full of the smell of sandalwood.

'If Jagadambal had lived some years longer,' Rajayi said, 'she would have prevented the failure of our family's fortunes, and the quarrels and betrayals that doomed her grandchildren to poverty. That was the kind of woman she was. '

The next day, we sat under the neem tree, with the cannonball creeper winding around its trunk, and my mother began again to teach me the padhams that my ancestors had sung and danced, in the perfumed durbar hall of the palace, where the walls – she said – were made of mirrors and the pillars were gilded.

The padhams I could no longer sing. They had been

swept away – by what? By history, perhaps; by change; it had begun like a draught under the door in my great-grandmother's time, and by my mother's time had become a bitter howling wind strong enough to blow the house down.

Perhaps writing about the change would let me go back and undo some of the damage. And writing would at any rate be a substitute for the songs I could no longer sing, and for the movements that were forbidden to me.

5

Vijaya
Madras, 8 April 1990

Balan inherited this sprawling house from his father, and every day I thank god for it. There are rooms enough for all of us, and there is space between me and the woman. The servants don't steal. Well, Kuppu the cook does, but only sometimes. She has a sweet tooth. Everyone I know from Kumbakonam does. She hides away pieces of jaggery when she is cooking and sucks on them later. I tell her off, but she takes no notice. Still, all in all, being from Kumbakonam, she is a solace to me, even though she grumbles all the time.

In the shrine which I had Balan's father build for me, I have the picture of Rama-Sita-Lakshmana in the middle and all the other gods around it. Tirupati Balaji is on blue velvet, framed in silver, on the side wall. I can shut the door of the prayer room and make garlands for the gods. Kuppu showed me how to fluff out and stretch a ball of cotton between my palms until it got long enough for a garland. The cotton comes from the silk cotton tree in our own garden – I open the pod and strip the seeds from the fluff with my own hands. Kuppu showed me how to dip my thumb and forefinger in turmeric paste and pinch the cotton at two-finger intervals. Roll, stretch, fluff, stretch, pinch, pinch, pinch. The garlands come out nice. Fluffy white cotton flowers and pinched yellow cotton stems. When I pinch, I think of the woman's skin. May the gods mark that flesh with scars. Today I am making a garland for Balaji.

I woke up with a headache again today, the *worst* one in months, and Kuppu brought me the Vicks, though I said quite clearly I wanted the Amrutanjan. I've tried them all, Vicks, Zandu Balm, Tiger Balm, Amrutanjan. They don't help much, but then I don't expect them to. The doctor rolled his eyes when I saw him last week. You again, he was implying. But he didn't say it aloud, because he makes money off me.

'Nothing wrong with you,' he said, after looking at my tongue for a minute. 'Nothing wrong with you. You worry too much. That will be fifty rupees.'

'You shouldn't charge me a paisa,' I said, 'seeing as you don't seem to know how to cure a headache.'

Perhaps there is a tumour in my brain. If I die of it, Balan will realize at last how he has wounded me, how ill he has made me. It will be too late for Balan to cry over me. I hope my spirit gets to watch him shrivel up with remorse.

What have I not tried for my headaches. Look, I said to Kuppu this morning, I wear black strings on my wrist and around my neck, each one blessed by a priest. I swallow bottles of pills, take cold baths and hot baths, burn coconuts out on the street to take away the evil eye that is over me and this house. I collect money in a silk knot and take it every month to a different temple's collection box. I fast every second day. I make the priests in different temples say different prayers for me, hoping one temple or one particular archanai will have the power to break the evil. And still my head aches.

Kuppu only said, 'What do you want me to do?'

'Bring me the Amrutanjan,' I said to her, and she brought me the Vicks. Miserable old hag.

When I told Balan how my headaches wouldn't go away, he said, 'Amma, if you were only a little happier, you would get fewer headaches.' What kind of answer is that? Happiness, happiness. How can a woman in my position be happy, Balan, I wanted to shout. Happy, in a household that is a constant affront to the gods, where I don't know what is clean and what has been polluted? Happy, with my daughter-in-law enjoying luxury and leisure, scheming behind my back, poisoning my own son's mind against *me*, the only protector of his interests? I don't miss a thing. I am watchful as an eagle. I must be *happy*, when that sly bitch keeps sneaking off to the post office on foot so she needn't leave her letters on the hall table for Joseph to post? What is she afraid of? That I'll see a man's name on the envelope? I've seen how she smiles at strange men who come to the house looking for Balan. I've seen how she creeps up to her bedroom with her letters and her notebook and locks things up in her cupboard.

I wanted to tell Balan about the letters, but I swallowed what was on my tongue, because he has made it clear that the woman is not to be blamed. It is bitter to be silent.

She was late – again – coming down yesterday.

'It's not as if your wife needs to come downstairs early enough to make your coffee from scratch,' I said to Balan. 'Who makes the decoction, who puts the coffee powder in the filter, who boils the water and the milk? The woman could at least come down in time to take it up *hot*.'

'Amma, you could let Kuppu bring up the coffee,' he said. 'And her name is Kalyani.' That was it? My damn-fool son, still defending his wife, *still* not over whatever blind bewitchment made him pick a woman of her caste in the first place. The gods should have poked her eyes out when she was born.

This new way of being married is an outrage. Why should this slut have the affection of her husband? *I* never had that, god knows. What is this new thing they call *love*? Duty and children were enough for respectable women of my generation. All my life I devoted myself to duty, all my life I bore the slights my husband heaped on me. If I was angry, I locked the anger up in my heart. I demanded nothing for myself. And my rewards are these – a son who has married a dasi tart, whose father was of god knows what caste, and a daughter in America writing to say she has divorced her husband.

Muruga, Balaji, save us all. The divorce I pray for every day does not happen. Instead, my own daughter leaves the man who was chosen for her by her father. She tells me about it after it is all over. Already there is a new man. I don't even know if he is a brahmin. My daughter, changing husbands as easily as changing saris. Now she writes that she's coming here, leaving her new husband in Chicago, to spend the summer with me. Every other year she comes, bringing some useless stupid gadget from America, waiting to leave almost as soon as she arrives, to go and waste her time with her friends in Bombay and Delhi. I have seen my grandsons twice in all these years. She never brings them down. And maybe that is a good thing, because what I saw of them I didn't like.

It was bad enough with Balan's father. He was all right when my parents married me to him, but later, in his middle age, he was the talk of the town. He said I didn't understand. He said his interest in the dasi women was pure. As if my nose could not smell another woman on him, as if I had gone blind and couldn't see where he had brought back a streak of jigina on his cheek. Glitter from the pottu on a whore's forehead. Glitter doesn't wash off well, it sticks to the skin. Why would a man smell of soap and toothpaste when he came back home at night, on top of whisky? Why would he suddenly bring home a jasmine string for me when he had never done that before, not even when we were young? So you bought them for *her*, I thought, and she wasn't at home today. I *tore* the flowers petal by petal and threw them in the trash. It took me an hour to shred that string of fat, double-layered flowers.

'You don't have to sleep with those women to have your good name spoiled,' I said to Balan's father. I kept up the story about his pure interest. It was easier that way. I was afraid of driving him right out of my life. 'People see your car parked in front of their houses. That Lilavati's house. What were you doing there last Friday? Kuppu says the whole of George Town was talking about it.'

'You know very well what I was doing,' he said. 'I arranged a chamber concert for Lila, and I was attending it. I asked you to come with me. Vijaya, there are so few people who can sing in that old style. Come with me, just once. If you hear her music, you will know what I mean.'

'I will not know. I *never* want to know. They say you are learning dance from her.'

'No—'

'No? Kuppu says you are.' I gave Kuppu bus fare and she went to George Town and brought back the news.

'All right, I am. Just one or two old traditional pieces – no one else around remembers them.'

'*Why?*' I burst out. '*Why* do you have to make a fool of me by running after these cheap women, by doing unmanly things?'

'I am trying to preserve our heritage, that's all.'

'Heritage!' It was a fine word for sensuality and self-indulgence. It was one thing to make marginal annotations on copies of the *Abhinaya Sara Samputam*, in the name of heritage; it was quite another thing to be running after flesh-and-blood dancers full-time.

'I won't have any *heritage* in my house,' I told him the day I found the album. It was full of pictures of those dasi scum. All the dance reviews and articles he wrote had been cut out of newspapers and stuck in it. I found it in the drawer of his desk. He never knew I could open that drawer. I had a key made. When I opened the book, a stink like sewage came up out of it. In one picture he stood smirking, with his hand on Lilavati's shoulder.

I burnt that scrapbook, I burnt it before his eyes, even though he wept at the loss of his precious pictures. I had to *clean* the house.

'No good will come of mixing with that lot,' I told him, over and over. 'It will be the ruin of us.' What was he thinking, bringing dasi dancers to Madras, when we'd have been better off if they'd died of famine and pestilence in their villages? Spending his Saturdays with Krishna Iyer, that crackpot who used to wear women's clothes and make an ass of himself dancing like a dasi whore? They called themselves Pro-art Progressives, those heritage-preservers. That was what the articles in the album said. I watched the fire curl them up black, my husband and Krishna Iyer and the other idiots and all their flashy protégés. The wind blew away the ashes of all those letters to *The Hindu* about the need to bring dasis from the small towns to teach our girls dance.

I was never one of the socialites – those Tamil women who dressed like Punjabi women or like white women. Lipstick, chiffon saris, drinking with their husbands. What would I do with make-up? I knew my husband slept with me from duty rather than from appetite; as soon as his dutiful seed started a child in me, he would stop. And I wasn't one of the small-town gossiping wives who gave each other company and comfort when their husbands went straying. I was too proud for that. I had nowhere to turn. It was all inside me, the suffering. It still is.

So, doctor, so, Balan, where was the secret of happiness in this life I led?

Lilavati! Oh, she was cheap. All dasis were cheap and common. Jamabandhi inkwells. Anyone could dip their pen in them. That's why dasis became film actresses and danced half-naked and didn't care a jot if men pawed them all over their bodies, for all eyes to see. You never saw girls from good families going into the movies in those days. The directors were looking for any loose woman in her early twenties – if she could sing, if she had good features, if she didn't know the meaning of modesty and morals, they'd make her Sita or Savitri in a film. I never went to see those films. It was an *abomination*, casting these prostitutes as goddesses. That Lilavati didn't even get goddess parts. She was just good enough to be an extra until some director found her appetizing and rented a house for her. He paid her for space in her bed by making her Ahalya in his film. Who would have thought the chaste Ahalya of legend would wear a tight sequined bodice and tight pants and dance like a bazaar whore for Gautama Muni.

Everyone knew Lilavati had a child by that director – what was his name? Then he dumped her. She drifted from man to man, acted in one or two rotten films that flopped.

What was there in a woman like that that Balan's father should take up with her?

'The dasi style of singing and dancing is dying,' he said, and I retorted, 'Let it die, then, and good riddance.'

Lilavati made so much money off the people Balan's father introduced her to that she rented a bigger house in George Town, put petrol in the tank of her broken-down Herald car and showed up smelling of the wine shop at music concerts, even the ones by respectable folk. It got so bad, I stopped going to concerts.

I appealed to the father in that man. 'What sort of example are you setting for Balan? Do you want him to think it's all right, seeking the company of loose women?' I said.

I must have a black spot on my tongue, seeing how prophetic I was.

I'm trying to remember how old Balan was when he said he was going to join that NATAC organization. They had just started the south India branch then – it must have been twenty-four or twenty-five years ago.

'For this we spent money?' I cried. 'For *this* your father put you through college?'

His father and I had both wanted Balan to be a lawyer. It was a family tradition. He had agreed, but said he would do an MA in Philosophy first. His father had indulged him.

'My father thinks promoting the arts is a good idea.'

'At least your father's interest in the dasis is *pure*,' I said. I kept up the facade with Balan, because I was so afraid of where his father's example would lead him.

I told Balan's father what his son was saying. '*Now* see what your foolishness has led to,' I said to him. 'Talk him out of it.'

'Promoting the arts?' Balan's father said. 'Eh, Balan, surely you are not going to take up that pimp's calling?'

But Balan was determined. He was stubborn even as a boy, and Hema, now, she's just like him. Balan was interviewed for the job. His father promised me he would stop the NATAC people, but in the end, he told me that he couldn't. As if I didn't know how half-hearted his efforts were. He pretended to try only to shut me up. They gave Balan the job. A couple of years later they gave him a promotion, and he started meeting singers and dancers.

'Let's get him married quickly,' I said to his father. 'It may stop him from ruining his life in the arms of some dasi slut.' It took a while, but we found a good brahmin girl from near Kumbakonam. She was musically talented too, and Balan likes music. I thought everything was settled. Then when she became pregnant, she bloated up and got high BP. The doctors stood upside-down to save her when she was birthing Hema, but she had convulsions and died about three hours later.

'You see what happens when there is so much evil in the house,' I said to Balan's father. 'You see what the gods do to punish us.'

After that, Balan's father gave up his dasis. I heaved a sigh of relief.

How was I to know that the gods were going to test me again?

How quiet it was, how peaceful, for those three years after Balan's wife died. How subdued he was. He went to concerts because he had to, it was part of his job, and I went with him when the singers came from respectable families. It was a good time for me, though I was worn out from looking after the baby – I was not a young woman any more – and from worrying that Balan's job would lead him back to the dasis. That Lilavati was still around, but she had grown fat and repulsive, so I thought Balan was safe. We took Hema with us to the concerts, because Balan wanted her to listen to music. Such a cheerful, accommodating baby she was, no sign of the wicked stubbornness that is coming out in her now.

A year after his wife died, I started to ask Balan if we could find a second wife for him, but he said no. So I waited, knowing he was a man with a man's bottled-up needs, and feeling sure he would come around to my way of thinking.

Then Balan started running off to concerts, night after night, and he did not want me along. Sometimes he took Hema, sometimes he did not. I knew something was happening. I knew he was caught in some woman's snare. He started talking his father's talk about reviving the forgotten arts. Who cared? By then the dasi women were wiped out, and no one wasted time regretting that fact.

He kept her hidden from us for months. His own parents.

'There is someone,' I said to his father. 'Balan is keeping some loose woman hidden from us.'

Balan's father did not believe me.

'I was an idealist too, Vijaya,' he said to me. So very foolish, so trusting of his son. 'In any case, if Balan is interested in a woman, how do you know she is not a woman of good family? When he is ready, he will tell us, and we will make it formal. The lad has been through a lot, after all.'

'*Ask* him. There is someone, and I have a bad feeling about it. If you ask him outright, he won't lie to you.'

'Why don't *you* ask him?' he said.

'He won't talk to *me*!' It was true. When I asked him questions, Balan would smile and shake his head. Then he would walk out of the room, closing the door gently to show he was not fighting with me. I would go to the door afterwards and open it and slam it shut, hard, enjoying the noise, slam, slam, hating my life.

Every day, for two months, I said to Balan's father, 'Find out. Find out, or before you know it, a dasi's whelps will be eating your salt and taking shares in your property. I am not a lawyer like you, but I can sense it in my gut.'

So finally he asked. And hearing the truth from Balan was the very worst thing that ever happened to me.

There was indeed a woman.

'Art and life need not collide like this, Balan,' his father said. Balan just smiled.

'I am a broken woman, Balan,' I said. 'You have killed me. You have shattered my heart.'

'Nonsense, Amma,' Balan said. 'You look perfectly healthy.' He was happy, in such a glow that he scarcely noticed how depressed I was. Yes, I was a broken woman. I told Balan's father I would die if I had to welcome a casteless interloper under my roof. My headaches became unbearable.

'Do something,' I said. 'Or I will die.'

Balan's father asked the woman to come and see him.

'Come here, paapa,' Balan's father said to her, speaking to her more kindly than she deserved. 'All these years I've worked to help your community, and this is how you repay me?'

She could have said something. She could have cleared out, the bitch. She didn't. Stood there silent and sullen in front of us, her fingers locked together, staring down at Balan's father's gouty toes. I'd bandaged them myself that morning.

'Offer her money,' I said in Balan's father's ear.

'Is it money you want, paapa?' Balan's father said.

Now she will take the cash and run, I thought. Balan will know her true colours.

She shook her head. She stood very straight and brazen and shameless.

'I don't mean a little money. Ten thousand?'

'No,' she said.

'Twenty thousand.'

'No, I don't want money.'

'Offer more,' I said, because I thought – I was sure – I saw her hesitating.

'Fifty thousand, then. Put it in a bank, or buy shares – I'll even tell you what to buy – and it will be enough to keep you comfortable all your life.'

'No,' she said.

'You won't be happy, you know,' Balan's father said.

'It won't last,' I said. 'He'll kick you out. He'll kick you into the gutter.'

She began to cry. Balan came running in to protect her.

'What are you saying to her?' he asked his father. Taking a whore's side against his own flesh and blood.

'Who is her mother?' his father asked him. 'Who is her father? What do you know about her? Where is she from? Is she clean or diseased?'

'Her mother is dead–'

'I know these dasis and their families.' Yes, there was no denying that he did. 'Is there a child in all that community that can name its father? A gaggle of prostitutes–'

'Appa.' Balan's voice had a dangerous edge to it. Once, when he had disagreed violently with his father, he had left the house and it had taken us three months to find him. He was our only son.

'An alliance with a respectable family,' his father said, 'a decent wedding. Forget about the dowry, even. Could a man ask his son for less? What about your younger sister? Who will marry her if this scandal gets about?'

Nothing we said made any difference. I wept day and night, I prayed to all the gods, I even went on a pilgrimage to Tirupati. That was when I bought the silver Balaji for whom I am making the garland today.

'Will you mock the Arundathi by showing it to a tevadiya hussy?' I cried. Arundathi, the star of constancy and chastity, which a man shows his bride on their wedding night, saying, will you be as faithful as that star? 'Will you touch her feet to place them on the stone?'

In the end, we had to let the wedding take place. Concealing her origins was the best we could do. She told us she was from here, from Madras, so we told our relatives she was an orphan brahmin girl from Pudukottai.

Who knows what the slut had done, whom she had slept with. At the wedding I said I would drape her sari. It was the right of the bridegroom's mother. I didn't want to see the flesh that my son would possess that night – it was more painful than anything I have done, it was polluting. But I knew women who had made sure of the virginity of their daughters-in-law before tying the sari. I stripped her naked. Our bodies were more alike than I would have believed, though hers was young. When I was her age, I had the same body, and my sisters mocked me, called me a stick of wood. My husband felt obvious revulsion at the hardness of my bones. No doubt he liked to lay his head on Lila's fat thighs. Now, it appears, skinny women are fashionable.

The woman had large breasts for her size. I looked for stretch marks, but her skin was like cream, and if she had any they did not show up. I wanted to scratch her, leave ugly stripes on her flesh with my fingernails. I looked at her nipples. I wanted to tear them off.

She stood shivering in front of me with her underskirt clutched to her privates, looking as if she would clamp her ugly dancing thighs around my hand if I so much as touched her there. She was scared all right. What did she have to hide?

'What should I call you?' she said.

At the last minute I didn't have the courage to look at her privates. I had not stripped Balan's first wife, so I was not sure what else to look for. If I had let my older sisters into the secret, they would have found out what I wanted to know, but I was too proud.

I made her drop the underskirt and tied the crimson silk of the wedding sari around her waist. I pushed her this way and that with deliberately insulting hands, always keeping the silk between her flesh and my hand.

Silk destroys pollution, I remembered – when the Muslim hakim in my village took a brahmin woman's pulse, we would ask him to put silk over her wrist and touch her veins through the cloth.

'Should I call you – Amma?'

What a question to ask me, what a moment. I didn't know what to say. She even reached out a hand to me. I did not touch it. I have not ever touched her, then or since, not once. If I had touched her, I would have left burns on her skin, I hated her so much. I gathered spit in my mouth and could have spat in her face, but I swallowed it again. She would go crying to Balan in front of the guests. So I just made pleats and made her tuck them in at her waist, almost not breathing at all; I took the sari between her legs and wound it around her shoulder. Suddenly I was so angry that I blurted out: 'Is it honey you secrete, or what, that my son wants to suck your cunt?'

I didn't care if it was language I had never used before. I wanted to skewer her eyes, break her limbs. No brat of hers would be allowed to come into my part of the house.

'May your marriage be blighted, shani,' I said. 'If you ever start a child, may it wither in your belly.'

'I'm a broken woman,' I told Balan and his father after the wedding. I was exhausted. Three days of fending off all the nosy relations, passing the girl off as a brahmin orphan, when every movement of her body, every step she took made it clear she was of a shameless caste. Having to lie to my own sisters, feeling relief when they went away. How many questions they asked, my god.

'I have nothing left to live for,' I said. 'Let my gods come and take my life away.' I was laid up with chest pain. Of course my sisters came back to take care of me – they said – but they snooped and asked me what was wrong, and I couldn't tell them.

How could I tell them? Our parents had been cursed with four girls, and had spent their lives laying up dowry to marry us off. When my two oldest sisters were ready for marriage, the dowry was only enough to attract grooms who were government clerks, grubbing their lives away. My third sister was given to an officer in the Railways. I was the youngest. When it was my turn, my father had a promotion, and more money, and so he looked more confidently for a groom from a rich family. Balan's father was a lawyer. Before my wedding, my sisters said of Balan's father, if only he were a little younger! A little better-looking! As if my marrying him hadn't lifted them all out of privation. He helped them build houses, helped their husbands to better jobs.

Only I, of all the sisters, had a husband who had power, who had influence, who had money to pamper me. Ah, I was so proud, coming home to my parents for the first Deepavali, stepping off the Tanjavur Mail with two new heavy gold necklaces around my neck. My trunk was full of silk saris for my mother and sisters. I had a new bedroll, with a satin cover. It paid me back amply for their sneering.

Then my husband had to start that lunacy of helping the dasis, and my sisters sniggered behind my back.

So when everyone was poking and prying to find out what was upsetting me, I couldn't very well weep and be weak in front of them. They smelt scandal, but I made sure they couldn't locate the source.

Then Balan's father complained of chest pain too.

'I haven't got much time,' he said, a couple of weeks after the wedding.

'Oh, stop complaining,' I said. I was ill and unhappy, but he wanted all the sympathy. 'You'll be up on your feet in two days.'

'My feet will be up all right,' he said. 'They'll be taking me out of here on a litter.'

I fully expected Balan's father to go on complaining about the stringiness of Kuppu's beans, the corruption of the government, and the small size of newspaper type. I fully expected him to go on binding exotic rose grafts to the stems of his spotted yellow ones and grumbling that they would not take. To go on sending out to Bhavan's Publications for commentaries on Sanskrit verses.

But a month later he was gone. Poor man. I invented some reason why that woman had to stay out of the death ceremonies. I didn't want her to pollute the rites, and stop his soul from going to his ancestors. The relatives peered at her and at me and speculated more frantically than at the wedding. The dasi women Balan's father had helped sent garlands, but they had the grace not to show their faces. I threw the garlands in the gutter behind the house.

After they had all gone, leaving me alone in the house with the woman, I found the notes Balan's father had scribbled in a tiny hand on the margins of the *Abhinaya Sara Samputam*, and I cried like a child. I went to the woman and showed them to her, and said, 'Look. This was the great man you have killed. May you be cursed forever. He is watching you now, from above, he can see everything, he knows everything.'

I hoped for years that Balan's father would come to me in a dream and tell me how to end Balan's marriage, but he never did.

It is true I suffered unspeakable miseries when I was a wife. But a widow is an inauspicious person, and I felt all the good fortune draining from this house when they took Balan's father's body away. Now I had to live under Balan's rule. One thing I said to Balan: if he had a child by this woman, I would never touch the child or let it pollute our kitchen.

'If you have a child, Balan,' I said, 'you will bring it under this roof over my dead body. I will drink rat poison and die and lie across the threshold.'

'Amma, for heaven's sake–'

'That is not empty talk,' I said. 'I owe that much to the memory of your poor father,' I said.

Balan promised there would be no children. I don't know what they did – perhaps she was barren, from having had too many abortions. But there have been no children, these sixteen years, and I do not expect there to be any now. This is my only consolation.

I watch the woman all the time. This morning I saw her come through the door and run up the stairs as if a demon was at her heels. I ran to the window to see who she had been speaking to at the gate. The man had gone.

Next time, she won't be so lucky. My eyes miss nothing. I have seen her hiding things in her cupboard.

I told Balan, 'What is wrong with a man having the key to his wife's cupboard?' but he laughed and said, 'Amma, you have the strangest notions.'

Such a blind, besotted fool. I am having a key made. When I show Balan the letters she hides in that cupboard, when I show him the gifts and tokens from the man she writes to, Balan will see the truth of her whoring soul.

6

Kalyani
Madras, 1973

In 1973, my mother and I came to Madras from Kalyanikkarai, and stayed with my aunt Lilavati for nearly six months. Rajayi – my mother – and Lila were first cousins. A cycle rickshaw brought us from the railway station, through narrow winding streets, to George Town. It stopped before a modest house with a tiled roof. The door opened, Lila waddled down the steps, and the two women clung to each other. The rickshaw driver, waiting to be paid, dropped his hand and stepped back, watching them with a whimsical grin. They were an odd couple – my mother dark and spare and showing her age, Lila still startlingly beautiful and startlingly fleshy.

I studied their faces, standing in the dusty street with my belongings at my feet. Their gladness in each other's presence was unmistakable. It made me wish I had a sibling.

Lila paid the rickshaw driver and took the bag with the broken handle from Rajayi.

'Just look at you,' Rajayi said, laughing, letting go of the bag and trailing her hands down Lila's plump butter-coloured arms, which tapered to fragile porcelain hands. 'You still have no elbows, Lila.' She splayed out her fingers, pointing. Then one noticed her sinewy bronzed arms, her palms large and flat like lotus leaves, the strongly defined fingers, bones jutting out at each joint. Dark shining branches after the rain. But Lila had no elbows, no joints; she seemed to be flesh all the way to her core. That anatomical detail fascinated me, because I took after my mother in being all assertive elbows and big bony feet. Lila's movements were economical, unselfconscious. Her sari covered heavy legs and revealed feet fine as frangipani petals.

When my aunt Lila began to tell me about her own childhood, I realized that her mother had given her up too. Lila didn't seem to hold it against her mother; she barely remembered her. When I asked her about her father, she said, a note of pride in her voice, 'My father had the distinction of being the first man in Kalyanikkarai to die of electricity.'

Lila's mouth was dainty, vividly scarlet from chewing betel. She talked through the betel juice, her lower lip jutting slightly to cup it in her mouth, her words slurring. I was mesmerized by the scarlet juice that showed between her lips.

When Jagadambal died in 1901 (my Lila Chithi said one day), her motherless children were brought up by their aunts, and the Raja, half acknowledging the children were his, gave them all the help they needed. There were two brothers, and two sisters, Kanaka and Komala. There were no grown men in the house.

The girls began dance lessons with Sabesa Nattuvanar's son Samu when they were eight and six years old. Samu was not yet famous then. He was only about ten or twelve years older than the sisters, but shrewd and demanding. The girls had their stage debut when they were twelve, and were married to the god. They danced together.

When Kanaka and Komala were engaged to dance at a wedding, their master, Samu Vathyar, acted as their manager. He collected the fee (and it was a tidy sum, since paired dancers were a novelty in Kalyanikkarai) and split it seven ways. He pocketed two shares. The dancers only got a seventh, after the four musicians had been paid. This was the custom; they did not question it. Samu was a great master, and they respected him above anyone else in their lives.

When the sisters came of age, rich men made offers to take them as mistresses. The man Kanaka chose was an ebony-skinned zamindar. He treated her with respect, and lavished money on her. Her second and only surviving child was born in 1922. The child was named Rajalatchmi, but everyone called her Rajayi.

Komala's first lover was a good catch, but he had an epiphany about the evil of his ways one evening, when he was watching his children playing in the yard, and he took a vow to be monogamous. He renounced Komala. Komala was only twenty-one years old then. A dasi woman had to live: a celestial husband was good for many things, but an earthly patron was still vital. The town waited to see whom Komala would give herself to.

The town said Komala was too outspoken for her own good. She had no modesty. She said what she liked, and once she even cheeked Samu Vathyar. She would sometimes rile people just for the fun of it. For instance (Lila said), there was the time Komala was bathing by the river, and a group of boys went by on the path meant for women. Komala was holding a sari loosely around her breasts, not draped, and had thrown her hair over her head to dry in the warm wind.

'Hey,' one of the boys shouted, because he was thirteen or fourteen and showing off to the younger boys, 'look, the wind will blow the tevadiya woman's hair right off and she'll be bald!'

'It's all right!' Komala shouted back. 'The hair on my head grows all the way up from its roots down here!' And she whipped the sari open to give the boys an unimpeded view of her mons. Their jaws dropped, and they fled. It was an old dasi joke.

And there was the time during a performance of the 'Kalyanikkarai Kuravanji' in the temple, when the actor singing the opening song had added insulting wordplay to his lyrics. He was drunk.

Komala had walked off the stage.

'It's unheard of,' the elders said. 'Who would have thought it, a chit of a girl showing disrespect to the whole audience, to all of us, walking off like that!'

So they had watched, beady-eyed, for further signs of

temper and rebellion. Even so, they were shocked when they were told that Komala had been seen with that engineer Ferguson.

That happened after the first time the police came to the house on Musicians' Street.

'We've come about the new pipes,' the police said.

'Pipes?' said Kanaka, eyeing the men suspiciously. 'What for?'

'The Raja is sending engineers to put in these pipes in all the dasi houses. It seems the Dorais are insisting that he do this, because they are doing it in the bazaar-women's houses. Seems some people want their women clean.' The men behind him snickered. Someone made a dirty joke.

'I don't know what the white people think we use our wells for,' Komala said. 'We've always had a perfectly good well in the backyard. And we are not like those dasis who have relationships with those poxy white soldiers.'

'Still, it's an order, and you'd better move aside so our engineer can rig up the pipes.'

'I'm Ferguson, ladies,' the engineer said, bowing. 'Pleased to meet you.' The workmen carried his tools in as Komala watched. One thing led to another, and when the pipes were all set up, Ferguson had asked Komala to be his mistress and Komala had agreed.

The elders of the temple were outraged. It was not because the engineer was a married man. It was not because he was in the employ of white people. It was because he was a casteless mongrel.

The perfidy of it! Komala, beautiful plump Komala with the round breasts and the tiny, provocative dimples, holding the hand, and god knows what else, of a half-caste nothing! A Eurasian! They threatened her with excommunication.

At the forefront of the campaign against Komala were her own two older brothers, who had fattened themselves and their families on her money for half a decade now. Even as boys they had shown signs of becoming no-account hangers on, neglecting their lessons with their tavil-drum teachers. Even Jagadambal, even the Raja, determined to make them self-sufficient, had not been able to make them work at anything for two days together. Their stance was not unusual for the men in the dasi community. Kooja-thookis, people called the men of the dasi families: waterboys. Bootlickers who in their youth scurried with unsure steps after their mothers and sisters, and in their middle age gambled away the wealth that the women brought into their homes. Grumbling, always, about inheriting nothing. The men-about-town who smoked and played cards with them despised them: men ought to be men, they said, they ought to have control over their families, not be emasculated pimps. But they drank whisky with the emasculated pimps, fingering their gold chains and fantasizing about getting a free night with one of the girls.

Komala ran away and set up house in Nallur. Her lover built the house for her, and she had electric lights in it.

'Always the fighter-cock,' her brothers said.

In 1924, Komala had a child by Ferguson, a daughter, who turned out exceedingly fair. Komala called the baby Lilavati, after the woman mathematician of the sixteenth century.

'But she has this reddish hair, poor thing,' the gossips said. 'Imagine that, a child with red hair.'

'See?' Komala's brothers crowed three years later. 'Our Komala got what was coming to her, all right.'

Someone turned on the pumphouse mains when Komala's Eurasian lover was repairing an irrigation pump on the Raja's land. Some people said it was murder. Some people blamed Ferguson's wife, but nothing could be proved.

The workmen brought the news to Komala's brothers. 'The Colonel in the military is devastated. He was a good engineer, that man, even if he was one of those halfbreeds.'

'He's left our Komala high and dry, hasn't he, now, the half-caste loverboy?' one brother said. 'Not a paisa to her name, not a scrap of land. His wife got everything.'

'Now she'll come crawling back to everything she left behind,' the other brother said. 'We'd better make a move.'

Before Komala came back to Kalyanikkarai, they found a lawyer, seized almost everything she owned – some rice fields, even her jewellery – and had it transferred to themselves.

They justified themselves to the community. 'She's forfeited her rights. She has lost her caste.'

They tried to claim the house on Musicians' Street, but their sister Kanaka still lived there with her daughter, Rajayi, and her aunts, who were still alive, and the grandchildren of the oldest aunt, who were still too young to be married. Kanaka went to court and won the battle to keep the house.

But Komala did not come home after all. She gave up her property without a whimper. It turned out that she had been listening to the words of that Christian woman they called Kokku Missy: Rachel Carstairs. By 1925, Kokku Missy had begun to convert a few educated people to her way of thinking. Komala was one of her first full-fledged converts. She not only saw the logic of Kokku Missy's argument about the dedication of girls to temples, but she also embraced the Christian faith.

'Stands to reason,' her brothers said. 'First she sleeps with a half-breed, now she becomes a Christian. Her own gods are not good enough for her. Ever ready to be disloyal to her own.'

Kokku Missy recruited Komala to be her chief assistant. At that time, there was no room for a small child in the mission house, and Komala left her daughter Lilavati, only two years old, with her sister Kanaka.

'Unnatural woman, leaving her child behind,' her brothers said, feeling a cloudy and uneasy satisfaction in these developments.

'This was how Rajayi and I,' Lila Chithi concluded, putting one frangipani-soft hand on my mother's thigh, 'though we had different mothers, grew up under the same roof and learned to love each other as only sisters can love.'

Lila's hair, bearing traces of her Celtic ancestry, was coppery-red and silky. She leaned back in her chair on to her plait, found its bulk uncomfortable, and twisted it around over her shoulder, letting it snake down over her breasts. Her plait was a living, sexual thing; it flew over her shoulder; it coiled and uncoiled as she played with it; it lashed a startled man in Pondy Bazaar when she whipped around to greet an acquaintance. A picture came back: my mother's thick black plait lying over the long ridge of spine that showed through her thin blouse, as she sat with her back to me, her sari trailing on the floor, one hand rolling the pestle round and round, the other pushing the lentils closer to the well of the grindstone. By the time we came to stay with Lila, the grey unobtrusive knot at Rajayi's neck had no vitality in it.

In the mornings Lila lay in bed with a puffy face and deep purple shadows like bruises under her eyes. An empty bottle often lay on its side under the bed, and the familiar smell of stale gin was everywhere. Slowly, in the afternoon, she knit herself back together. In the evenings she wrapped herself in silk, took her silver betel leaf box and her beaded handbag, wound flowers into her hair, and stepped gaily outside her George Town house. In the morning she walked as if her knees hurt; by the evening, there was something jaunty about her gait. She rode her sputtering Herald to music concerts as if it was a gilded chariot. She had an enormous appetite for people and for pleasure. She studied the people of the evening – the singers and dancers, the drummers and clarinetists, the violinists and the flautists and the patrons of the arts – with frank curiosity. She chuckled at the violinist's presumption and clucked over the singer's ineptitude. She tried to draw me in. But I stood aloof, not wanting to know anyone, not really wanting to hear

Lila's gossip about this one's wife and that one's lover, this man's tragedy and that woman's triumph.

'Let's go to the Rasika Ranjani today,' she said, about three months into our visit. 'Brinda and Mukta are singing.'

The singers were from a dasi family, like Rajayi, like me. Their music was slow and accretive, secret and passionate. It was like a woman tidying her cupboard, finding there old love notes, and empty perfume bottles kept for the beauty of their glass; finding beads that had never been made up into a necklace, and the toys and tokens of beloved children. The padhams pierced the barriers of anger and indifference and grief that I had raised over months. I felt myself alone, as if the roof had blown quietly away and I was adrift in some emptiness between bright planets, my whole being contracted into quivering, humbled response. I felt the universe humming around me, and suffered guilt, because in the midst of strife and poverty I had let myself be exalted by music. The singers' voices reminded me of my mother's voice years earlier, strong but subtle, exquisitely sensuous. I looked at my hands because I did not want to look at the ordinary sweating faces around me; in my fists I tried to hold their music as if it was beads, or stars.

When we joined the file of people leaving, a man was standing across the room, and his eyes were fixed on me.

Lila nodded towards him and whispered, 'That one. He can't stop looking at you.' She had her betel leaf box open; she was rubbing lime paste on the back of a leaf.

She folded the leaf and said softly, 'Balasankar, his name is. Not a musician, but a government man. A fixer. Plenty of money. I knew his father.'

I looked at him. Not with Lila's candid gaze, but obliquely. He was good-looking in a brahmin way, fair-skinned, and refined in his features. He was talking to a woman. Lila told me her name: Padmasini Mahadevan. I had seen her pictures in a magazine years earlier; they had called her a rising dancer in the article, and presumably by now she was risen and shining.

The man was holding a sleeping child over his shoulder, her arms curled loosely around his neck, her long silk skirt rucked into folds under his arm. The child shifted and turned, smacking her lips sleepily, and the light caught a delicate thread of spit at the corner of her mouth. The sight woke some memory in me, of being carried in a man's arms. I could not recollect having been carried like this; there had been no man in my mother's circle, as far as I could remember, who might have carried me with such absent-minded protectiveness. I felt powerfully that I had mislaid something, and it bothered me that I could not remember what it was. The music had left me thin-skinned and vulnerable.

'His wife died two-and-a-half, maybe three years ago,' Lila was saying. 'In childbirth. The little girl never knew her mother, poor mite.'

The man glanced sideways at me again. I turned away and then turned back, drawn by that tableau across the room. The man leaned forward and asked his companion a question. Her eyes flicked over me carelessly. She answered him, shrugged, led him away. He looked back once before he passed through the door, and the image was haunting in the afterglow of the music: a man and his sleeping child, his face refined, her hair tumbling over his shoulder.

'It's a good time to leave,' Lila said, taking me under my bony elbow. 'We've piqued his curiosity.'

I did not answer when she asked me what I thought of him. I was unhappy that my mother and Lila between them had decided that my future lay in marriage.

Vijaya said later that I had seduced Balan in a spirit of calculation. It was not true. If I had a besetting vice, it was passivity. All my life I have been confused, and have longed for clarity. Each of the women who had brought me up, my mother and Aunt Rachel, had appeared for a while to believe strongly in some truth, and each one had failed to act on her belief. I had wavered between their worlds and their truths, and had found that just as I declared my loyalty, the truth had shifted, and the world had changed. I have always been uncomfortable in my own skin, as if I was wearing a hair shirt made to somebody else's measurements. I stopped at every moral crossroads, paralysed, unable to choose. How would I seduce a man like Balan?

But always, after succumbing passively to someone else's plans, I blamed them when things went wrong for me, and allowed myself the luxury of bitterness. Not the hard clear-edged bitterness that in other people leads to action; a soft bitterness, a cursed wallow. I blamed everyone: Rajayi, Lila, Aunt Rachel, and Velu, my dance master. I wanted to get away from them all. I did not know how to do this except by putting another human being in their place.

Balan; I toyed with the idea: Balasankar.

'This isn't one of your pond-tiddlers,' Lila said to Rajayi, a dozen concerts later.

Lila's feet peered out of her sari, tiny, softly fleshed. Silver anklets bit into their skin, leaving a series of shallow dinges. My mother sat beside her, Lila's veenai over her lap. The day we arrived at Lila's house, she had fallen on the instrument the way a hungry child falls upon a favourite dish. She had dipped her fingers, spatulate from years of playing, in the salve. Her hands had rested on the ivory frets as if she did not know where to begin. She had stroked the strings, testing them, testing her fingers, her eyes closed, and then had played as if she had never stopped practising.

'Who isn't a what?' Rajayi said, looking up from the veenai.

'This Balasankar. He is the big catch,' Lila said.

At each concert we attended, somehow, the 'fixer' had been present. We had talked, a few times, about the high points of the music that evening, about composers we both liked. At the most recent concerts, he had looked for me and come straight over to sit by me.

'After everything we've been through, you and I, Lila,' Rajayi said, 'surely you're not saying she should become his keep?' The fingers of her right hand plucked the strings at the gourd end; the fingers of the left hand rocked and caressed them where they passed over the frets, nudging the notes of the Mukhari padham a haunting quarter-tone away from true.

'Not his *keep*, Rajayi, his *wife*. You wait and see. This fish will want marriage.'

'Why would he? Men like that don't marry women like us. You're not planning to hide her caste, are you?'

'Our Kalyani's so fair she could be passed off as a brahmin girl. But those brahmin customs, heavens – she'll give herself away. No, Rajayi, that will never work.'

'So then?'

'You should see his face when he looks at her. If she says she will be at a concert, he shows up. He makes excuses to spend time with her. He asks me if I want coffee and takes her with him to buy it. He's smitten all right. We'll hold out for marriage or nothing.'

'We'll get nothing,' Rajayi said, her eyes half-closed. Her voice was dry, her face expressionless. But the strings were twanging and moaning softly in the background all the time. 'Who'll want to marry a woman from our caste? And a brahmin, of all people!'

'Didn't a brahmin man marry M.S. Subbulakshmi?'

'Oh, that MS is a beauty, and talented enough for ten women.'

'Was I not nearly married myself once?'

'But you weren't in the end, were you?'

'I only missed marriage by a whisker, I tell you. And our Kalyani is every bit as beautiful as MS.'

'Lila, what if he beats her? You know how it comes over the men, that they've married a woman with our way of life–'

'Look at me. Not married, but I got beaten anyway. Rajayi, you know as well as I do that we're damned if we do and damned if we don't. Think about it! At least this way she'll live in comfort.'

Lila's life was a shambles, everything she built fell apart again. Somehow she kept up her spirits and her dignity; somehow she felt contentment. She asked for very little. She was cheerful about her second-rate career as a comedian's sidekick and screen wife, she was cheerful about having been mistreated by the director to whom she had almost, if not quite, been married.

'And Kalyani's dancing—'

'Oh, she'll have to give up dancing,' Lila said.

Amma looked at me with troubled eyes. 'Kalyani, child. What do you think?'

I was unhappy, befuddled. I treasured my stigmata, examined them. I was insufferable, I realized later. I wished the wind would trepan me, blow away a segment of my skull, release the past like a flood, so that I could start afresh, with only a present and a future. I wanted to sink into something that would stay steady under the weight of my trust. I felt a dull desire for respectability, comfort, cessation of conflict.

Very well; I would give up dance. Dance had given me up, after all. In return for this gesture I would have, perhaps, the steady affection of a man.

I sat in the room with them, refusing the part I was being offered in the drama of planning. They remembered me, my predicament; they forgot me and spoke of the past. They had been parched for each other's company. During the day, their voices rang sharp with irony, scorn, mockery. So-and-so's singing, a travesty; parading up and down the octave with his chest thrust out like a pigeon, Lila said. Another one's veenai-playing, Rajayi said, all scholarship and no feeling. A third one's padhams, they said, unbearable; driving the notes with a bull-whip.

In the evenings, their voices – Lila's moistened by gin – waxed rich with remembered fragments of music and family history, waxed tender with love. The veenai went on in my dreams, throbbing and fading, accompanying the hum of their voices, now bubbling with hilarity, now sad.

'When I first saw you, your face was pale,' Balan said later. It was the pallor of depression, but he romanticized it. 'You looked remote, immune from loving. A Botticelli woman.'

But I was ready to love. I had let hope edge out regret, and had become intrigued by Balan. I had been slow coming to this feeling, but I wanted my arms to be full, my heart to be engaged, I wanted to hear my laughter mingling with a man's comfortable laughter. I had to make a choice. It must have been my choice, though I felt that my hand had been forced.

At the December concerts that year, we learned more about each other, Balan and I. Not very much. We still met under the gaze of others.

Then Balan asked Lila if he could speak to me in her house.

'With Kalyani's elders present, of course,' he said. That

was how Lila grew certain that he wanted something more than a quick affair.

Lila said, 'Rajayi, you leave this to me. You forget your daughter for the moment, go back to Kalyanikkarai and let her have a life. You must go back home. If they know about you they'll find out too much about her.'

'I hope you will be happy,' Amma said again and again, her hands on my shoulders, just before she went back to Kalyanikkarai. 'This is hard to do.' Softly, when Lila was away buying a sari for me, she said, 'That man – he knows no more of you than the hunter knows of the bird in the mist; he just snatches at it.' I looked away, refusing to meet her anxious eyes. 'If he treats you badly, remember you can always come back home.'

So I had given up my mother again. Rajayi went back to Kalyanikkarai. Lila, exulting in her success as manager of my affairs, told everyone I was an orphan. There was the first lie, as heavy as a flail. It may not even have been necessary, but it had been uttered and could not be taken back. It was too late to change anything. Kalyanikkarai was suppressed too. What if Balan knew people there, what if he traced my family? All would have been known, as Lila dramatically put it.

Lila was terribly damaged, but full of hope and efficiency. Her knowingness about men, her certainty that she could handle them, may have led her to commit blunders that a woman less confident and less bruised would not have committed. Perhaps she was entirely wrong about Balan. He was outside her range of experience.

After Rajayi left, Lila's driver and I cleaned the George Town house from end to end. The furniture was ugly, irreducibly shabby – rexine sofa, Formica-top tables – but it made a difference that the bottles were gone, along with all the litter of our own stay. The house smelt of Mansion Polish. Brass gleamed; dolls dressed in regional costumes stood in a glass-fronted cabinet. On a grass mat, the veenai glowed, and an engraved brass table was laden with fruit.

'I haven't cleaned the house properly since Balan's father stopped coming,' Lila said. She chuckled. 'Did I tell you that he was my patron once? He was as hungry for me as this man is for you. The difference was that he was married.' She was ebullient, humming to herself, scrubbing vessels and wiping down the window bars where the dust had been allowed to collect for years. She burned incense sticks, and the fragrance of sandalwood ousted the reek of gin. She hung a fresh string of mango leaves over the door. She dusted the pictures of her younger son on the wall. He was an assistant director in one of the big studios in Kodambakkam now. It wasn't much of a job – he was the one who held the two pigeons that billed each other or the flowers that touched to signal that the hero was kissing the heroine offscreen, but he said he was watching and learning from the cameramen every second he could, and was going to move up soon. Once in a while he sent Lila some money and a film poster. Lila had faith in him.

Lila sat me down with her tambura in my lap. 'Sing,' she said. 'He should catch you in the middle of a song. They are a musical family. His father used to learn music from me and write down the notation for the old padhams. It's a pity your mother had to sell the veenai before you were old enough to learn. It would have made a marvellous shot.'

'Don't, I don't want to pose.'

'Do as I say, child. You are young and silly. Too bad that Kokku Missy made a Christian out of you – she took all the woman out of you. You haven't been taught anything about attracting men. It's our caste's dharma, seduction, do you know that?'

I sang a half-hearted padham or two, my eye on the door. After all the preparation, Balan didn't come.

I said, 'I'm tired of this game. I am going back to Kalyanikkarai.'

'Already she is tired. We've barely begun. If not Balasankar, then some other man. We've been over this before, Kalyani. What will you do back in the old town?'

'I will teach in the school. I can teach English, and not many people can do that in Kalyanikkarai.'

'Did you not try in the school? Your mother said they wouldn't take you. Think. If you keep this man's love, if you learn how to ask for gifts, you can squirrel something away and help your mother out instead of being a burden and a worry to her.'

'I will try again at the school. There is a new principal.'

Lila nagged me for the rest of the evening. But I felt I had made up my mind. In a desultory way, with some relief (I had given up too much, I was thinking already; now I could have back what I had given up), I began to pack.

7

Kalyani
Madras, 1974–1989

The day after I had made the decision to go back to Kalyanikkarai, just as the driver came in with a fresh supply of gin, Lila's doorbell rang. Lila drank up and whipped her glass under the bed.

Balan was saying, 'Forgive me, I couldn't come yesterday. Is Kalyani home? May I talk to her?'

Lila waved the driver away, and waddled to the kitchen to make coffee. Balan came over and sat beside me. He put out two fingers hesitantly and ran them down my forearm. Then he looked at his fingers.

'Have you ever caught a butterfly?' he said.

'Yes, when I was a child.' My voice shook; I felt gauche. 'I wouldn't now.'

'The iridescence from its wings stays on your hands. I feel that I might touch you and be left with particles of glamour on my fingers.'

Desire running down his fingertips along my skin to the hair on the nape of my neck, the glow of all the things happening to my flesh. My mind went blank.

'Now I've embarrassed you,' Balan said.

'No. It's just that I don't know what you mean,' I said.

'I don't think I could live without you,' Balan said. 'I have come to ask if you will marry me.'

Lila came in with the coffee then. I got up and ran past her into the bedroom, my face burning. The windows shook to Lila's tipsy laughter at my awkwardness. She accepted the proposal on my behalf.

In my head I heard my mother's voice singing:

The bird wheeled above the hunter,
He caught only the bird's shadow on the rock.

Balan defied his parents to marry me. Their unhappiness settled like an acrid fog over the house.

His mother's face: it was as if an indifferent sculptor had carved it by slashing downwards at a block of wood. After the wedding, she declared herself broken, and without further interest in life. At breakfast every morning, she relived her sufferings of the night before: the chest pain, the consciousness of the dread presence of the god of death, the dream that his noose was about her throat. Balan listened patiently, if inattentively. He took her to the hospital and they began a series of tests.

To me it appeared that Vijaya was flourishing mightily, and that she looked set to live out her fourscore years despite the constant irritation of my presence under her roof. Her very malevolence was a charm against extinction.

One evening, Balan's father said something about a pain in his chest too. Vijaya said it must be heartburn. He went to bed and did not wake up again. Vijaya blamed me for his death. In the midst of grief she found the energy to inflict new kinds of humiliation on me.

Vijaya's gods were caste-conscious. She had not a moment's doubt that they were all brahmin. She observed ritual as literally as she could. She bemoaned the fact that she had to drop some of the more obscure elaborations. She pursed her lips; she feared contamination. Only brahmins were allowed to cook in Vijaya's kitchen. The cook was a brahmin; I was not. What Kuppu the cook prepared I carried to the dining room, if Vijaya was fasting, or upstairs to Balan. The storeroom was always kept locked. All the keys for the household, to every cupboard and door, dangled in a bunch at Vijaya's hip.

'Would it be such a bad thing,' Kuppu said to me one day, 'to let you help an old woman who is made to grind the batter in a grinding stone when other people have machines to do this work? That one chills my old bones. She and her show of loving the gods. All eye-poking, punishing, happiness-blighting tyrants.' Kuppu wiped her hands on her sari. 'Here's coffee for your husband,' she said. Suddenly she poked me in the chest, and her watery eyes swam up before my eyes. 'I too was young and had a husband once. Let it be; what is gone is gone, for you and for me.'

As a wedding gift, Balan bought me a large print of Botticelli's *Primavera*, so that I would understand what he meant when he called me his Botticelli woman.

'Look,' he said, making a face. 'White people's idea of dancing. Elongated, asexual blondes playing Ring-around-the-Rosy while Zephyrus blows raspberries at them. No wonder the Dorais lusted after flesh-and-blood dasis in the old princedoms!' But he didn't really mean the mockery; it was his way of distancing himself from the enthusiasms of his boyhood. He said he used to copy Botticelli's pictures in his sketchbook over and over again when he was a boy, until he realized that it was part of the colonial upbringing of all wealthy Indians, this fascination with white people's women and white people's art.

'Your skin,' he said on our wedding night. The picture had been framed and was propped on a shelf against our bedroom wall. We were trying to decide where to mount it. He stood behind me and slid his hands under my sari and undid the buttons on my blouse. 'Your skin.'

He rolled the silk of the blouse away from my shoulders so that it came down and trapped my arms. I watched my own skin emerge in the soft light of the bedroom and shine back at me from the glass on the picture.

'Like a watered rose. Like a river. At midday.' He trailed his fingers over the flesh of my shoulders, and now I was like the women in the picture, half-clad, the drapery of sari sliding away from my breasts. 'A million flecks of light. Caught by Botticelli's brush tips.'

'I'm not so tall,' I said doubtfully, trying to slow my breathing, to match his mood, exactly halfway between impersonal aesthetic pleasure and sexual excitement. 'Not so pretty.'

He felt the heft of my breasts. His cupped hands grew moist with the sweat that collected in the fold between my breasts and ribcage. 'No,' he said. 'More beautiful. The same fair skin, the same fragility, but so sensuous. So warm.' He picked out the hairpins that held my knot in place and my hair sprang free. He watched it come down over my shoulders, down my back, over my hips. He pulled my body back against his. I felt my nipples tightening. It was his desire, not mine, not yet.

His arms were around my waist, untying my underskirt. 'You're not as tall,' he said, 'but beauty lies in the proportions. You have the same proportion of torso to leg.' The cloth fell away. My skin was stretched over bones that were strong rather than fine. I carried no flesh except on my breasts. He touched my jutting pelvic bones. 'These bones – they make you look naked.' His voice was suddenly thick, he sounded drunk.

'Kiss me,' he said.

My lips drifted past his.

'That's not a kiss.'

'I don't know how.'

'And you're supposed be a dasi dancer?' Was this some kind of test?

'They didn't give me kissing lessons in dance class.'

He was delighted, he laughed with relief.

'You are designed for the stage,' he said. For a second I felt wild hope. Then he said, 'What a pity no one else will see you.'

From the time I was a child I had imagined myself bound by love to someone who was both lover and father, someone principled and uncompromising. I would be all soft tendrils, he would be the hard trunk. Balan's masculinity lay in his principles and his intellect, not in his physique. He was older than me. He was the privileged son who had chosen to read philosophy at university, deliberately rendering himself unfit for most practical and worldly occupations. He loved books. He took me to the Madras Literary Society library, and while the assistant made up my membership card, we climbed the ladder to stand on the slotted aluminium racks. I was ravished, as I had been at Kalyanikkarai, by the rows of old editions shedding book dust, by faded gold lettering, by names: the Brontës, Dickens, Eliot, Hardy, Longinus, Plato, Sainte-Beuve. And at last by Balan, who refuted Bishop Berkeley in the margins of his copy of *Three Dialogues,* who talked with fervour of Art and Nation, who was an idealist, a passionate man.

The *Primavera* print was hung above the bed. Botticelli's Graces danced hand-in-hand two inches off the verdure while Zephyrus's wind-face blew at them, past the figure of Flora. Flora unclothed, Flora verdant, covered in blooms. Later, many years later, I thought, why, Botticelli painted the first supermodels in the fifteenth century – blank virginal faces, languid sashay, diaphanous drapery. Am I like that? I thought. A graceful mannequin, empty and ornamental?

On my twenty-fifth birthday, Balan bought an antique Miraj tambura and placed it beside the bed, so that I saw it when I woke in the morning.

'My birthday gift,' he said. 'To you.'

I took the tambura on the bed, laughing with incredulous delight, and tested the strings. They were out of tune. With my left hand I turned each peg at the end of the tambura's long shaft. The wood was rich, the colour of chocolate. My right hand plucked each string at its midpoint. I set the pitch of the strings, and the tambura's gourd produced a rich resonance.

Balan said. 'Is there something wrong with it?'

I looked up. He was studying me.

'What?' For a few minutes I had forgotten he existed.

'You were frowning.'

'Was I? I frown horribly when I'm concentrating. Balan, thank you,' I babbled, 'thank you.'

I tugged gently at the ends of the silk thread that ran under each string at the bridge. When the silk was in the right place the note thickened, trembled, flowed into the other notes. Balan, sitting on the bed beside me now, bent down and put his ear against the ivory inlay on the gourd of the tambura and I brushed the mantharam string with my forefinger, the man-string my mother called it, thick, made of copper, not steel like the high Sa and Pa strings. The other strings hummed in sympathy.

'It is in perfect tune,' Balan said. 'I can hear all eight notes from low Sa to high Sa. Sing that song for me. That one you were singing in the bath last night.'

When the wind blew, bearing rain
I didn't water my garden.

When my garden turned to dust, I wept, beloved.

My voice was tremulous from lack of practice. I would have liked to start with the scales and geethams and varnams, build it up, sing properly as my mother had taught me, but I sang to please him:

In the moonlit time, on the riverbank
he took me in his arms
and no one was there.
When I saw his flawless golden body,
oh, how easily, like a fool,
I became his plaything
my friend.

'You must never stop singing,' Balan said.

I looked up again, taken aback. 'Why would I want to stop?' The tambura went on humming under my fingers. I wanted to sing more.

'You must always sing for me here, in the house. Only never in public.'

'Yes, of course.'

'No one but Amma and I know about–' he broke off, embarrassed, '–about your uh – talent. Amma would be devastated if people knew. I can't do that to her.'

'No, you can't.'

He smiled and kissed my forehead, leaning over the shaft of the tambura.

Balan was tender and gallant, and we had patches of great happiness. Every evening, at first, he waited for Vijaya's announcement that she was ready for bed. It was our cue for going upstairs, for sitting together on the balcony. He would hold my face in his palms, and gaze into my eyes, and let me gaze into his and drown in the passion there. If Vijaya held him back with conversation, as she often did, his hand would creep up and clasp my hand on the sofa, under the fabric of my sari. We behaved like a pair of children stealing forbidden sweets under the nose of a stern headmistress.

I was content when Balan was with me. I was happy, too, when I was with Hema, walking her to nursery school or weighing down one side of the seesaw in the park. But I missed my earlier life, I missed Kalyanikkarai and everything it contained; in sharp, painful flashes, I missed dancing acutely. If somebody had said to me: leave all this behind and you can be a dancer, I might have flown away.

'Your first wife,' I said once, hesitantly. I was thinking of the first time I saw Balan and felt the hollowness in me echoing the hollowness in him. 'Do you miss her?'

He shook his head. 'I married her out of duty. She was a sweet-natured woman, not sophisticated. You are the woman I chose for myself, out of my heart's desire.'

Later, when I became dependent on Balan, when my separate self had dissolved irrevocably, he seemed to barely notice me. It was broken – the enchanted weathervane that had always swung him towards me. I could not read him any more. His life bubbled with event; he was beginning to make his trips around the world, trips he took without me. I was becalmed in an old house full of patterns.

When I asked him for outward signs of love, he was

amused and indulgent at first, then a little impatient. 'Haven't you gotten used to it yet? Do I have to keep reassuring you? Haven't I told you I care for you?'

Yes, last month, last year. It is not enough. Tell me again. Tell me again, keep me going for another week, two weeks.

'What an appetite you have for this. Men – we are different, I suppose, we tire of this.'

'Why won't you tell me what you know I want to hear? Tell me something, talk to me tonight, Balan. Sweet nothings will do,' I said, laughing, and he deliberately took up my laughter but ignored the begging beneath it.

I looked up at the Graces. They needed no men; they made a perfect circle of femininity. I held myself tight and thought: with whom shall I make that circle of sisterhood? Padmasini? I dared not speak of Balan to Padmasini; once or twice I began a complaint, and then bit it back, knowing that if I threw the small disloyalty out, it could not be reeled in again. Marriage, I learned, is a lonely place when one's husband must also be one's sister and one's mother and one's friend.

I struggled to make my pride overcome my need. I withdrew from Balan, and searched for other pleasures and certainties. I read books. I took up the tambura, shut the bedroom door against him. I cast about for a song without associations, but everything was painfully connected to the people and the place I had left behind.

My mother's legacy of songs and dances was now lodged against my ribs like a thorn. The old padhams my dance masters had taught me went through me like knives. Some phrase would jump out of the song containing within it all that I was cut off from: the sound of water gushing from irrigation pipes into paddy fields, the smell of oil and camphor from the temple walls, or the feel under my feet of a red-oxide floor.

You keep saying the wrong thing, my daughter.
It doesn't seem to matter how I wear myself out saying it:
You keep saying the wrong thing to your man.
Why do you do it?
His father is a big man, Siva himself.
You let every little thing annoy you,
It is the woman in you.

I pushed the songs back down when they surfaced in my memory, my nerves taut and shuddering with the effort; but sometimes, when I wasn't thinking, I would pluck the strings of the tambura and the words would come back to me.

Is there anger mixed with his love for you?
That is natural enough.
What is the use of my saying these things?
You're like the man who listened
To the Ramayanam all night, and in the morning asked:
And what was Raman to Sitai again?

Samu Vathyar, my mother's dance master, had taught my mother that song and my mother had taught it to me. My mother had sat under the cannonball orchid in the backyard and I had sat on the step across from her.

Souls may sing when all heart strings are broken, I read somewhere.

I switched on the radio, learned new songs.

I drifted away from Balan when I was singing.

If I was sufficient unto myself, if I was singing with my eyes closed, if I was remote from him, in a world he could not understand, he clattered over to me, accidentally kicking my music book into a corner, apologizing wryly. He sat down and took me by the chin so that I had to open my eyes like a sleeper jerked awake. He searched in my eyes for my soul. He was troubled when I was opaque to him.

'What are you thinking now?'

'I'm trying to remember the words of this padham. I've forgotten the second verse.'

'What do you think of when you sing those padhams? I imagine such things going on in your head.'

Sometimes, before the song was finished, he wanted to make love. He wanted to pack, he wanted to sleep, there was a plane to catch. He rustled the pages of a book he was reading. He opened the door, looked in, mimed an apology, shut it again; two minutes later he opened the door again. He would not let the air settle around me. There never was enough time to finish a song, to build it up slowly, to draw out its meaning.

'I would never come between you and your music,' he said. There were accidents, though. He broke his arm when I started working on some manuscripts that Padmasini had bought, that she had given me to transcribe. He was touchingly dependent on me for reassurance; he seemed afraid I would fly away while his arm was in a sling.

'They asked me at Hema's school, if I'd teach the

children music,' I said one day. 'One of the teachers heard me humming something in the waiting area.'

'An interesting idea. You need to do something with your talent. It's not as if you will be on the stage.'

'And I would be doing something for people, like you.' I began to write a syllabus in a notebook.

'What's the matter?' I put the notebook down and touched Balan's shoulder.

'Shoulder acting up again.' He had chronic frozen shoulder. He had developed it when he was a young man. He kept it at bay by exercising his neck, but when he was tired it bothered him. I stayed home and nursed him. When I went back to the school, they had found another teacher.

I began to sing only when Balan was away, but even that was hard; I felt his hand on my throat, stroking me, stopping me. The tambura stood in a corner, against the wall, coated with a fine layer of dust. He saw me wiping it with a rag.

'Poor love. The tambura needs a case, doesn't it?'

He had a master carpenter come in and measure the instrument, and build a wooden case for it. I put the instrument away in its new case with the glass top, grateful and confused. The case looked like the coffin in which Snow White lay, in the picture book in Aunt Rachel's library.

Especially when she heard my padhams, Balan's mother was reminded that I came from a family whose women sang and danced, shamelessly, in public.

I imagined faceless people, their eyes hidden, speaking out of typewriters and store shelves, like the wheat in the story of Midas. 'You can never be entirely sure, can you, Balan. Once a dasi, always a dasi.' The voices grew more urgent and spoke out of jewellery boxes when I was dressing to go out, hanging in my ears the earrings he bought me. Above all, when I was singing, they spoke out of the strings and the dark polished gourd of the Miraj tambura he had given me. Whose voices? We had told no one. Whose voices, then? You always hurt your foot in the same place, the family that is ruined will be ruined again, the voices reminded Vijaya.

Balan snubbed her gently when she said things about me in front of him, but her shadow fell across everything we did in the early years of our marriage.

'Why is there no child yet? Who knows? Who knows what infections have passed through her womb?'

'Amma, be quiet!'

'Very well, I won't open my mouth again in this house. Where is she today?'

'She has just gone to the library, Amma—'

'Do you know for sure? Who knows whom she is meeting, a woman like that? Who knows what lies she is telling you? Once a dasi, always—'

'Amma! I won't listen to you talking about my wife like that!'

'Very well. When trouble comes, remember I warned you. Remember you brought it on yourself.'

When I came back, from the library, from Hema's school, Balan would be in a rage.

Balan controlled his rage. He knew how to break in on me when I was singing. He would walk into the kitchen, for instance. He would wash an apple, weigh the knife, and set its edge to the red skin. He would look up for a moment; if he heard nothing but my humming, or even my radio, if he heard no cheerful babble of love and welcome–

'Oh! Damn! Damn!' Loud, louder than the music. I would come around the door at once, though his mother did not like me in the kitchen.

'What is it?'

'I cut myself. It's nothing.'

I would think, he has broken in on me again. 'Oh, it's a big cut. Let me wash that; let me put a bandage on.'

Yes, I would think, as he held out his hand, letting the blood bubble out thin and startling in the sink, yes, he has broken in on me again.

He began to have arguments with me about disturbing his mother, about – only once, this – having rescued me from a life of shame, only to have me turn against him and seek that life again. He could not say to himself: I want to control her. He was a generous rescuer, he wanted me to forget that I had been saved. And being grateful for this, and loving him in my own way, I accepted his demands.

'He keeps breaking in on me,' I would say to myself, angrily; and then I would say, 'But I have so much to be grateful for.'

I gradually stopped singing. I understood the role my gift would play in our life: something sweet, a matter of history, a part of my self that was nevertheless not to

128

be expressed. After I had stopped singing for a while it became increasingly difficult to start again.

I cut myself in desperation.

'What is this?' Balan said, touching the scars as we lay in bed. He switched on the lights, examined the criss-cross weals. 'Have you been cutting yourself? What is happening to you? What are you using to–'

'Balan, it's nothing, it's – all right, a razor blade.'

'Give me the razor blade, Kalyani. This cannot go on.'

'I threw it away.'

'Listen to me, Kalyani my love. I want order and regularity. I've had my fill of family disputes and female jealousy. There was too much misery in this house when I was a young man, and things haven't changed much. Has anyone been nasty to you?'

Your mother is never anything but nasty to me, I could have said. Her hatred follows me like tar smoke around the house. It gets in my throat.

'No,' I said. 'No one.'

'If you are upset about something, you can tell me, can't you?'

'Yes, of course I can. There's nothing.' Nothing I can tell you about.

'Then what did you do this for?'

'I don't know.'

'Aren't you happy?'

I hedged, prevaricated, and with a sigh decided that this small form of self-expression would have to go. What would I do then? Where was I going to put frustration if

I could not even put it in on the skin of my inner thigh?

'What you need,' Balan said, 'is a creative outlet. Why don't you write for children?'

Hence Mohan and Mala. It took me six months to write the first painful draft of the first story. The brother and sister: the girl I had called Hema, the boy I had called Amalan. Amalan was strong and clever; he protected Hema from catastrophes carefully constructed so as never to cause nightmares (for I remembered the books I read in a strange library far from my mother; I remembered the sweat-damp sheets and the terror in the dark when I dreamt of the animals spanking the elephant's child with their trunks and hooves and paws; when Mr Brocklehurst punished Jane; when a boy jumped suddenly off a dream chair and began to hang squealing puppies from the back of it).

I read the first book to Hema, who was six years old then. She could read fluently, but not longhand. She liked the story. 'But I don't want the girl to have my name,' she said. 'It's *my* name.'

So I called the girl Raji. Amalan and Raji. Balan recommended a publisher, an old school friend.

'Good plot, good style,' the publisher said. 'But Amalan and Raji? Odd names – too Tamil, and Amalan is too – uh – non-brahmin. It's mainly brahmin kids who read, you know. Especially English books. I'd use good simple pan-Indian names.'

So I changed the names: Mohan and Mala.

The editor at Longman Press liked the names: 'Mala and Mohan, perfect. You know, casteless, regionless, but Hindu.'

Mohan and Mala calmed me down, gave me something to do. The first book sold for a thousand rupees. But in two years, *The Adventures of Mala and Mohan* was a series, and I was making enough money to, at last, send about five thousand rupees every year to Kalyanikkarai, to my mother. This annual tribute kept my guilt at bay.

Every year Balan bought me a notebook so that I could work up my latest story. This year, I took the notebook from its package and looked at the cloth cover, thinking: there is nothing in these stories I write, after all. Nothing to make me drop my hands into my lap with the consciousness of a work finished, to make me say: I have done this. My writing was drab, derivative. I felt tremendous irritation, suddenly. I felt boredom. My hands were restless, and almost before my mind was aware of what I was doing, I began to stroke words on to the creamy paper.

Six months into our marriage, Balan was asked to oversee an art restorer working on a temple mural that had just been discovered. He took me with him every day. Balan took photographs, documented the process, and brought in scholars to identify the style of the mural; I simply watched. Slowly, with infinite patience, the restorer uncovered the glowing earth colours of the sixteenth-century mural under the acrylic crust of the modern painting. Kalyanikkarai my past, Madras my present. My body was a palimpsest, I thought, watching him, the dull square lettering of middle-class morality, of brahmin rules, covering the old curlicues of the love-poem of years ago.

I began to ask Lila questions about her ancestors; her ancestors and mine. Vijaya had told me I must never meet her, but I did, on the quiet, if only to collect the letters my mother sent me at her address. I also spoke to Lila on the telephone. I began to write down what she told me; I wrote from memory of things my mother had said; I remembered Samu Vathyar's anecdotes about his ancestors who had been linked with mine in a long chain of teachers and pupils; and I found pieces of information in the old gazetteers at the Madras Literary Society.

I dreamt that an art restorer worked on me, dissolved the shallow false city away from my skin, let the old town appear. I dreamt of unpinning the present and finding the past intact. I dreamt of making everything continuous, of making myself clear.

The dreams and stories filled up the notebook that Balan had given me for my 1990 Mohan and Mala book. I hid the notebook in a shawl in my cupboard. Balan never snooped, but nothing was safe from Vijaya.

I was a traveller, turning around now, on that lovely, lonely road, walking back towards the place where I began. Exercising limbs stiff from years of inaction, doing the undoing dance.

8

Hema
Madras, 14 April 1990

The Madras dance world is a Malebolge of backbiting and malice, of rehearsals broken up by tantrums, of poaching of musicians, of choreographers spitting at each other like alley cats after stealing each other's ideas. By the end of the last December season, I decided that I was going to stop dancing. Amma and Appa dragged me along to too many performances. All this *culture* was choking me.

'I don't want to go to dance class any more,' I said to Appa one Saturday morning.

Appa was working at his rosewood desk. Files marked 'NATAC 1990' in bold letters lay open before him. He looked at me over his glasses. 'Do you have an exam or something?'

'No.' I've never taken days off from dance class for exams – he should have known that. 'No, I mean I want to stop for good,' I said.

133

'Has something happened?'

'No,' I said. 'I hate it, that's all.'

'*Hate* it? After all these years? Why?'

'Because of all that stupid artificial sexiness camouflaged by talk about the human soul and the divine soul,' I said.

He blinked. 'What?'

'Padmasini's dance dramas make me gag. I hate the pining, languishing nayikas. I hate the phoney spirituality.'

Padmasini's dance dramas upheld the virtues of traditional Hindu womanhood in every cranny of the world. Eyelashes fluttering, rubbery lips wobbling, she played all the young heroines herself. Radha, Sita, Draupadi. Always the same harrowing cliché of come-hitherish but coy maidenhood. God knows why, but her audiences still bought tickets. In some mofussil backwater, I could understand; but in Madras, where all the old fogies prided themselves on their taste? There was no accounting for it.

Since Padmasini was too busy jet-setting to teach in her own school, her senior students did the job. She had turned them into astonishingly exact replicas of herself, and now they groomed the next generation of copycat dancers under the fake ethnic thatch. Clones teaching clones once removed – even Appa admitted that. Daughters of millionaires, granddaughters of MPs, sisters of film stars, all learning from the senior clones to imitate Padmasini's every twitch and mannerism, down to that tic of the muscle on the side of the nose – I looked it up, it's called the nasalis muscle – that made her look as if she was holding back a sneeze. The clones married men earning dollars in happier parts of the world. Then they got their chance to set up copycat dance factories. In Maine or Maryland or some place.

Appa put down his pen slowly and stared at me. So I said, 'I hate never making any progress. I hate being taught by those second-rate senior students.'

'My god, Hema.' He looked as if he was going to explode. He made an effort, managed to contain himself. 'Respect your teacher – that was the first thing they taught us. Mata, pita, guru, daivam!' I wondered sometimes if he ever had any actual thoughts any more, as opposed to pious stock-phrases. 'Is someone feeding my little girl these ideas?'

'No!' Feeble, awful, rotten cliché. His 'little girl'. 'Appa, no one has to feed me anything. Your little girl can think for herself,' I blurted out. It sounded stupid as soon as I said it. I just hate clichés, even my own.

He was studying my face as if he had never seen me before. He was pitying me. I knew what he was thinking: she wants to stop dancing because she is plump and dowdy, because she wears glasses, because she will never look graceful in a costume.

'You are right,' he said, quietly. 'I suppose I have been too busy. I've missed–' Oh, spare us the Hollywood moment.

He hesitated and went on. 'I've felt guilty about being such an intermittent parent. I suppose I've covered up my guilt, even to myself, by treating you like a little girl. You know,' he laughed awkwardly. 'I'm not around to see the changes, so I pretend there have been no changes. Well. I'll try to stop.' He rubbed his neck. I felt sorry for him suddenly. Something or the other in his body was always bothering him.

I became embarrassed and began to babble. 'I just – I think I'll finish my BA in English and do an MA, maybe a PhD I want to be a journalist. I could write about dance, if you're keen that I do something artsy-fartsy.'

He winced. 'Your Amma and I have actually been talking about moving you to a new teacher. Why don't we discuss this after Padmasini's show tonight?'

'Okay,' I said, a bit disconcerted at how easily he'd given in. I happily resigned myself to one more show. After that, I said to myself, no more.

Joseph dropped us off at the show. Amma checked her hair in the rear-view mirror, gathered the pleats of her crimson Kanchipuram into the tips of her fingers and stepped out of the van. I didn't bother fixing my hair. People who look like me can't afford vanity. I was wearing a really dowdy brown sari, the kind these dancers wouldn't be seen dead in: my small gesture of defiance in the middle of the general dazzle.

I hung back a bit because I hated being seen with Amma. At forty, she was still gorgeous in a thirtyish kind of way, and when people saw us together, they couldn't help speculating about whether we were related or not. Men's eyes, I noticed, were irresistibly drawn to her. The women looked at her a lot too, but with a good deal less pleasure.

The show was in a wedding hall, not a proper theatre. Someone had tried to make the place look festive. Tinsel streamers had come loose from the pillars and were trailing in the petrol blotches on the ground. It all looked tawdry and depressing. The portico stank; the cement trash bin had been built too close to it, and it was overflowing. Joseph, leaning on the horn, took the Maruti away through the yapping, snarling pye-dogs that fought each other for the stale remains of a wedding feast. I braced myself for agonizing boredom. With the interminable English translations of the Telugu and Tamil songs, with the speechifying and garlanding and the socializing during the interval, it would be close to three hours before I could go home.

Appa was due to arrive soon; he was coming straight from the office. In the dingy lobby, Amma and I wavered, assailed by doubt.

'Are we in the wrong place, do you think?' Amma said. All around the perimeter of the wedding hall we saw the stalls of a fundraising fair. We stepped back to read the banner slung across the entrance. Painted clumsily on yellow cloth was the legend *Brahmin Ladies Club Annual Sale Sale Sale*.

'Surely even Padmasini hasn't sunk to sharing space with—' Amma stopped, searching for a phrase.

'—incense stick cooperatives and home-made halva,' I said. She hid a grin with her fingers. Padmasini had grown careless about what Appa called 'production values'.

'She has really begun to take her constituency for granted, hasn't she?' Amma said softly.

'Uh-huh.' And why shouldn't she, when she had been a fixture for the last thirty years on the Madras dance scene? When her students' relatives were conveniently distributed across the world? The Miami Mami, the

Amsterdam Auntie, the Singapore Sis, all ready to arrange performances for the revered teacher. In Canada, where some clone's brother owned a television channel, in the US, where another clone's aunt three times removed was a diplomatic wife, tickets to her performances sold out almost before they were advertised. So Padmasini went around pissing against posts everywhere from Sydney Harbour to Jacob's Pillow, with her troupe of exotic bharatanatyam dancers. There were lots of worshipful, ignorant diasporic Indians out there, yearning pathetically to suck up little dribbles of culture from the motherland.

Last year, when Appa cut her from the festivals abroad, she sent up such a howl of outrage that they covered her story on the front pages of the national papers.

'Why does Padmasini need you?' I had asked Appa then. I was rather naive in those days. 'Why does she need NATAC?'

'It works out cheaper,' he said absently. 'The plane fares get taken care of by NATAC; then everything else is pure profit.' Then he realized that he was insulting my guru, and clammed up.

She had never taken me on any of her foreign tours, and I knew she never would. The dancers who got to go with her were three inches taller than me, skinny-waisted, and very, very pretty. There was a side effect she didn't seem to notice – they made *her* look like a root vegetable.

Amma and I stopped in front of a shelf of video cassettes that said 'Learn Classical Dance in 30 Days!' and 'NRIs! Learn Dance by Correspondence!' What blind urge towards self-expression made people invest in a thing so palpably absurd?

I liked libraries. I felt at home in them, I loved the smell of books. I had three on the go; I was itching for the show to be over so I could get back to Virginia Woolf, Iris Murdoch, Isaac Bashevis Singer. I detested social gatherings. They were full of posturing phonies. Every movement I made felt gauche. Standing there in front of a display of Taj Mahal replicas built out of improbable materials (white plastic beads, pith, papier maché, icing sugar), I felt like a sun-dried chilli becalmed in syrup.

Amma unclasped her handbag and took out the invitation card. The gold lettering said that the danseuse – I don't know why, but they always referred to the dancer as 'the *danseuse*' – had come all the way from Newark, New Jersey, to perform Bharat Natya in Madras, in this wedding hall, on that very evening. Bharat Natya: where did they get a spelling like that? We looked around for someone with official powers of clarification. Standing beside a pistachio-coloured pillar was Padmasini's representative, one of my fellow-students who got to tour with Padmasini. There was no mistaking it. Her sari, her hyperbolical earrings and her smile – switched on and off with jolting, high-voltage fakery – proclaimed her another dancer – or *danseuse*, even – who, had fate but decreed it, might have been on stage herself, in that wedding hall, on that very evening.

'Excuse me,' Amma said to her. 'Is there a bharatanatyam performance here tonight?'

'Yes, madam!' Coruscating flash of teeth. 'Over there, madam! Shall I take you?'

We peered in the direction of her outflung arm,

distracted by the clatter of two-dozen bangles, and made out the stage between Jams and Pickles and Granny's Herbal Skin Remedies.

'No, we'll find our way.'

'Please – can I give you a brochure?' The girl held out a tray.

Amma took a brochure, I took another. No fear that the brochures would run out at shows like this.

I examined the New Jersey dancer's picture on the brochure, checked her position on a looker scale of one to ten. I guess even ugly women play that masochistic female game: Is She Prettier Than Me? Yes, she was a nine, disgustingly ornamental, she'd get taken on tour. Late teens, hair dressed high on her head, garnets framing her forehead and hanging from her ears, her neck, her wrists. Her feet at a badly judged angle, her palms together. Her face split by the vapid, overripe, meaningless, self-satisfied smirk of ethnic glamour. She could have been a hostess from an Air India in-flight magazine. Already, said the brochure, the *danseuse* has been hailed by *connoisseurs* – those ubiquitous, disembodied arbiters of taste, so prodigal of praise – as the next great sensation.

Then the girl with the brochures caught sight of the name on the invitation card Amma was holding.

Spellbound. 'Not *the* Mr Balasankar! You are Mrs Kalyani Balasankar! Why didn't you say so earlier, madam?'

The girl slalomed, tripping on the hem of her sari, throwing awestruck glances over her shoulder at Amma, past the little knots of guests who were looking distractedly for the best seats. Not the seats with the best

140

view of the stage, but the seats best placed for a quick exit. I could tell from their hunted looks and dragging feet that they were the dancer's sisters and her cousins and her aunts, captives of that old beast Family Obligation.

Moments later, the *danseuse*'s mother materialized, and fastened herself to Amma's wrist, as if she was afraid of losing her in the crowd. If she'd had handcuffs handy, she'd have used them.

'I'm so *thrilled* you could come, Mrs Balasankar,' she breathed tenderly. 'Padmasini-teacher has told us so much about you.' She was anxious to let us know that Appa's importance had not escaped her. She led Amma and me past the stalls with little irritating caresses – 'Look at those cute handmade teddy bears, madam!' – and attentions – 'Can I get you something to drink, er–? Coke?'

'No,' I said shortly. 'Thank you.'

'It's becoming so terribly expensive for us non-residents to perform in Madras these days.' The woman hovered, her breath fanning Amma's cheek conspiratorially. 'The manager of this hall – *hall!* – it's not even a proper concert theatre, see how dirty the curtains are – I couldn't believe it – he demanded thirty thousand rupees upfront as soon as he heard that we had come from New Jersey. Just to use the stage, madam.'

Amma clicked her tongue in perfunctory commiseration, her eyes searching for Appa. I had no sympathy to spare; to me the girl in the brochure was one of the ten thousand spoilt daughters of rich parents who patronized the silkworm and the gold mine. I hated these America-based, 'non-resident' Indians. They were turning classical dance into a reserve for the aesthetic games of the superfatted rich. They were driving talent out of circulation. Let them pay through their cosmetically altered noses. I saved my sympathy for the talented and hopeless, like the girls in my dance class who came from middle-class families. (There were no really *poor* ones, of course – Padmasini screened everyone). They knew they'd never, *ever* be able to afford a stage debut. It was vile and unfair, this glorification of moneyed mediocrity. When I thought about it, I wanted fire, I wanted tornadoes, I wanted swords, bloody from tang to tip. I wanted to perform some supreme act of violence to mark the death of intelligent patronage of the arts.

The woman wittered on: 'You can imagine our other expenses, madam – paying Padmasini-teacher and the orchestra, buying saris and jewellery, printing invitations and brochures. Just because we are living abroad people think our dollars grow on trees. My husband wanted to give up the whole thing. He said, "If that's the attitude here, then Madras doesn't deserve to see our Srikala perform." But I said, "Madras is the Mecca of bharatanatyam; some appreciative people are sure to be there." Would you like a snack?'

'No, no thanks.'

There was the usual chatter around me.

'Nice pendant.' A soft insecure voice. 'Remind me to buy one like it.'

'Oof, isn't it hot?' A strident voice. 'Where shall we pick up some dinner?'

'I hope they wind up by nine. Orient Dragon's takeout closes at ten.'

'Think there'll be speeches during the interval?'

'Ayyo, I hope not. The chief guest is that man from NATAC. Oh my god, don't look now, but the tall fair fellow in the sherwani, by the Taj Mahals. Okay, look now – that's him. Balasankar.'

'The one with the briefcase?'

'Uhh, no, that's the dancer's uncle. The other one. Now he's turning around, towards us. He's the secretary of NATAC. He can really promote a dancer or finish her career. You'd better meet him, he's a really *really* big cheese.'

At these dance recitals, professional dancers (or their mothers and their fathers and their sisters and their cousins and their aunts) heard the alarm of an internal clock going off. The 'schmooze alarm', I called it once. Appa found the word very funny. 'Time to suck up to *this* cultural kingmaker,' the clock reminded the dancers, 'if you want to make *that* Festival of India in blank blank.' In those blanks my father could fill in the name of any destination in the fascinating world that lay butterflied before him, exquisitely interconnected. Paris, New York, London, or even Mattawamkeag, Maine, where they were, Appa said, building a brand-new lotus-shaped Hindu Cultural Centre.

I watched as Appa's distinctive head, with its steel-grey hair, bobbed past soapstone goddesses and beaded lunchbags towards us, already anointed with the Brylcreem of flattery, bouncing the fluorescent light. Immediately the idolatrous sea of mothers and fathers and aunts engulfed him. He approached, a large crumb of Gorgonzola held aloft by a swarm of scurrying ants. A girl dove down and touched his feet; the mother of another, elbowing the dancer's father out of the way, offered him an album of photographs. Appa must have cut a ribbon. They'd forgotten to take the scissors from him. The open blades swung in his hand, endangering Hand-Embroidered Pillowcases.

Appa was still a handsome man, I suppose, and a slim one. When I was eleven or twelve, I wondered how, with two parents as wirily built as Amma and Appa, I had ended up plump. I asked Amma why I didn't look like her at all. She explained that I was her stepchild. I had known this dimly, from things the relatives said when they gathered at weddings and funerals, but I had never ingested the fact or owned it. Amma made Appa unlock the drawer in his cabinet where he had stashed pictures of my biological mother. I couldn't feel anything for the woman in the photographs. In the wedding albums she looked touchingly awkward, a chubby woman with a lugubrious expression and a gaudy sari that looked all bundled up around her. In the pictures when she was pregnant with me, she sat plumply and more cheerfully among plump women – her sisters, Appa said, sitting down with me at last to help me figure out who was who – and they were packing bangles on her wrists. Her hands looked swollen. She was a plain-looking woman. I suppressed the thought because her face was my face, and besides, she was dead.

The dancers and their mothers surrounded Appa,

wanting, wanting, wanting. The danseuse's mother prised the scissors carefully from his fingers, and pressed a glass of lemonade into them. The jaded eyes of the older women assessed the worth of their rivals' saris. The young dancers grew cross-eyed with watching others watching them. Their jaws were paralysed with smiling. They were all thinking of the power of Appa's hand, of what it could do with a flick of the wrist and a trail of ink on a chequebook or a contract. Against the cooing, treacly, sycophantic medley of networking voices, Appa's own tones were gruff and staccato.

The gushing voices grew quiet for a moment and heads turned to look at someone behind me. I turned too, and saw Janaki Kotiswaran trimming her silken sails and swishing up to Appa. She grimaced at the sight of the other dancers. But when she spoke to Appa, she had a smile on her face, the rictus of one who had firmly grasped the nettle of public relations. You could hear her thinking: how gracefully I handle the necessary inanities! With how much more finesse than all the others I wear the mask of impersonal seduction!

Janaki's eyes were intelligent, restless, dishonest. They flickered from face to face, testing the effect of her presence on the world. She was the daughter of a long line of entrepreneurs who could turn a profit from anything under the sun: from the distress of housewives whose husbands would not save (Madras Chit Funds), from the new craze for Tanjore paintings (Chitrakala Arts).

She despised people who didn't have initiative. She was a beauty in a tall slinky way, and rumoured to be the blonde woman calling herself Angelique or Veronique or something, on the centrespread of a 1977 *Playboy* issue, but no one knew for sure, because who in India had access to back issues of *Playboy*?

Janaki was married to a man called Kotiswaran. The press called him the Biscuit King. His biscuit company produced a special Hi-Energy Helthi Glucose Bikki that the Indian Test Eleven depended on for nutrition during international tours, or so his advertisements claimed. The Indian Test Eleven were doing badly, but Mr Kotiswaran was enormously and serenely rich, a patron of the arts. He funded Janaki's dance shows, which had two themes *in toto* – Indian women are powerful goddesses, or Indian women are oppressed victims. Sometimes she managed to convey that Indian women were oppressed victims *and* powerful goddesses. Apparently these shows went down well abroad. The shows were visually elegant. Janaki spent lavishly on sets and worked with a designer who engineered the 'look' of each production.

Amma wedged herself into the crowd around Appa, and he leaned towards her to hear what she was saying. He clutched at his hair, shook his head. Seeing me unprotected for the moment, the Biscuit King lunged forward and without warning took my cheek between thumb and forefinger. I stumbled and bit my tongue. Amma noticed and hurried over. Her face was rigid with worry. She was not herself at all. She disentangled me from the Biscuit King, but not before he had slapped me heartily on the back a couple of times. I coughed. I wanted worms, I wanted vultures. I wanted to make a drinking cup of my enemy's bald skull. I wanted to put my hand into the hornet's nest and churn it about.

'Don't hang back!' old Biscuit roared at me, struggling against the adenoidal volume of the two sisters, dressed in parrot-green saris, who had begun to sing devotional songs on the stage. Why did religious fervour always have to be expressed through the nose? To Appa, 'So this is your daughter er – Hema, hey, Balan?' He reached out to pinch my cheek again, but somehow Amma was there between us. 'So, Balan, is NATAC making you work hard?'

'Yes, well, the usual,' Appa said. 'Last month I was supervising the Festival of India in Paris,' Mothers and daughters plucked at his sleeve, cut him off from us, hung on him like an encrustation of barnacles. Many of them would leave as soon as their purpose – meeting Appa – was achieved; they wouldn't stay for the show.

'I'm sorry, Madam, but I can't make any appointments right now. I have urgent personal matters to attend to.' There were tired pouches under Appa's eyes. He hadn't noticed the lemonade stain on his sherwani. Someone must have jostled his arm.

'No, I'm afraid I can't meet your daughter this week. I'm leaving the country soon to attend the International Innovative Dance Conference in Chicago. No, sir, I don't know when I will be back. Thank you for sending the press-cuttings.'

'Such a busy man!' the mothers and fathers marvelled resentfully.

'My granddaughter, Ranjani,' a pot-bellied man said,

holding out a picture. 'The day Ranjani started dancing it was clear that she was another Kamala Laxman. By god's grace, *if she gets a chance*, she will show the whole world how an Indian child can dance. The whole world.' He looked significantly at Appa.

Appa smiled noncommittally. 'We must encourage creativity,' he said. He lowered his lemonade glass and studied its contents with a vacuous eye. The danseuse's mother took him urgently by the arm, muttering something about the Press, and swept him away again.

'Such a busy man!' Biscuit exclaimed. Conversation flagged suddenly, as if everyone could only be bright and alert when Mr Balasankar of NATAC was around.

'How was the trip to France, Mr Kotiswaran?' Amma asked.

The Biscuit King nodded as if she had made a statement. 'Good. But when I was returning, unfortunately, all my luggage was misplaced. Some fellows at the airport booked it on another flight.'

Janaki sighed languidly, a siren's sigh. 'To Brazil.'

I rejoiced at this loss. I hoped the luggage had disappeared into an equatorial rain forest, never to be found again. I hoped some species of ape was rifling the burst suitcase – gigantic underpants tumbling out into the mud, blending with animal smegma. Maybe the Biscuit King hadn't had time to buy a replacement toothbrush; when he leaned towards me, he reeked.

The front row was made up of special red velvet-covered wingchairs, marked 'Reserved'. The danseuse's mother dusted cushions with an officious tissue. She massaged the Biscuit King into one chair, Appa into another. Amma and I made shift with whatever chairs we could find. Amma was definitely worried about something. She was picking at the tassels at the end of her sari. Her eyes were on Appa, not the stage.

The danseuse's father scuttled up. 'So glad you have come to be the chief guest, Mr Balasankar. So honoured.'

'What's wrong?' I whispered to Amma.

'I'm worried.'

'I know. Why?'

'Appa is going to scratch Padmasini from the US Festival.'

'Oh. I can't wait to see the fireworks.'

'Appa has some kind of filming project in mind that he is going to throw out – a crumb for Padmasini.'

'I bet the crumb will just make her madder than ever. And Janaki's here – is she going to the US?'

'Yes. Oh god, it's going to be ugly.'

'Oh god, it's going to be fun.' I might almost enjoy the evening.

We waited for the performance to begin. It was gaspingly hot. The fans were too high up to be much help. The nasal sisters had stopped singing. A microphone was being temperamental. A baby began crying and was taken out, its receding wail broken into hiccups by rough joggling. Behind the backdrop the dancer walked up and down busily, her ankle bells proclaiming her location. On a rug at stage right, the musicians tuned their instruments. The mridangam player tested the pitch of his drum – *dhim* – *dhim* – *dhim* – raising the note infinitesimally with a *tap*! of his wedge and stone, over the thongs that bound the stretched skin to the wooden barrel. *Dhim – dhim – tap – tap*. It was a pleasant sound.

The Biscuit King splayed his fingers comfortably on his thighs and leaned forward.

The microphone was dragged downstage and the girl of the brochures and the earrings shuffled a sheaf of papers. We had to endure English translations before each piece on the programme. I couldn't bear their agonizing godwottery, the unintended comedy of their 'Sakhi, bring my Lord without delays' and their 'O Preserver of the Universe, we offer Thee obeisance'. Who the hell says 'obeisance', anyway?

Beside me, a gold watch flashed on a wrist raised to point. 'Look, there's Padmasini. You'd think she'd get someone decent to do her hair. Isn't it ghastly?'

'She charges her students seventy-five for a debut performance.'

'Seventy-five *thousand*?'

'That's what they say. And a silk sari and a gold necklace on top of that.'

'Hmm. I wouldn't be at all surprised. My daughter's teacher charges almost as much and she's not even famous.'

'Why don't you switch to . . .' –mumble mumble, while I slapped ineffectually at the mosquitoes that were devouring my legs – '. . . the latest craze. My niece has lost ten kilos since she started – just last year. Aerobics and dance together, you know, a solid workout.'

Downstage left, a brass image of Nataraja, god of the dance, was set in a crush of flowers. A semicircle of incense sticks fanned out before the image, like the spokes of a broken wheel, tips turning into wavering smoke. Standing just behind the image now, positioned so that her eyes could sweep over the front row, Padmasini tinkled a bell briskly. Her devotion was strictly mechanical. Her mind was elsewhere. Padmasini, dinner companion of Chief Ministers, winner of awards, frequent flyer, had raked the wingchairs with her eyes and had spotted Appa's elegant sherwani and silver hair.

The girl on the stage read something from her script about bharatanatyam's glorious unbroken three-thousand-year-old tradition. The dance captured the relationship between the Earthly Soul and the Divine Soul, she informed us.

'Padmasini's done something new to her blouse,' said the woman beside me. 'It disguises that big tire at the back. Who's her tailor?'

'Nonsense, it can't be the blouse. I keep telling you, it's liposuction.'

Now Padmasini's tailor bulked out her hips to compensate for newly acquired adipose around the chest; now he padded the bodice to offset the sudden burgeoning of the hips. These advances in costume design were closely watched each year by admirers and detractors alike. Between breast and hip, Padmasini's exposed abdominal flesh danced its own jelly-jig. Middle-aged patrons of the arts appeared to find this fascinating.

The dancer from New Jersey bounced energetically on to the stage, a plastic smile pinned to her face. Padmasini's fear of becoming passé in an age of innovations was reflected in her choreography. The music was speeded up. The mridangam player's face and shoulder muscles were pinched into obscene bulges with the strain. I winced as he assaulted his drum. The girl made frantic efforts to keep up with the music. She didn't complete any of her movements. She cantered all over the stage, two beats shy of synchronization.

I would have liked to write the review: 'Let us subtract from the overall impression the gold lace on her costume, of which she wore twice the normal allowance. What mark shall we assign what was left? Two on ten for incompetent footwork, with a penalty for screamingly coquettish eye-rolling and bad emoting, this reviewer regrets to say, even though the danseuse's daddy is the owner of the biggest software consultancy in Newark, New Jersey.'

What was truly, fantastically, grotesque was the – what can I call it? – the *sexiness*. It was a grovelling, bootlicking, desperate sexiness. The dancer clearly found it difficult to believe in it herself. There was absolutely no dignity in it. It was a special kind of stagey sexiness pioneered by Padmasini, a sexiness that had become the norm with bharatanatyam dancers. But what made me squirm with revulsion seemed to make the rest of Padmasini's audience perfectly happy. At any rate, no one complained. Press reviews of Padmasini's performances or her students' were, at worst, a kind of orphanage gruel – bland, indifferent, leaving one wanting more of something, anything, as long as it wasn't one more glib remark about the 'spirituality' of it all. Spirituality, that bogus trick. I *hate* the word spirituality, hate it, it makes me want to throw up, it fills my guts with acid. I *hate* the blindness and smugness and laziness and snobbery and self-conceit of the people who trot it out.

At best, Padmasini's reviewers were abjectly admiring. The Emperor may be mother-naked, his foul prick covered with warts. But the exigencies of advertising didn't allow the Press to actually call his sartorial bluff. Everybody knows, nobody cares. As Appa once put it, the dancer's father may turn out to be Croesus, and then where would the Press be?

During the interval, Appa made the chief guest's speech. He didn't even tweak it as he once used to do. Once, even I, who had heard the speech over and over again, did not realize how much it was a matter of variations on the same all-purpose theme. Appa's philosophy had bled colour and intelligence over the years. He had played the cultural bureaucrat for so long that it had drained the ardour behind his words. The words still spilled from his mouth almost without his volition, but the traits that produced them were worn to a nub. I read books from his library – Marcus Aurelius, Marx, Ivan Ilyich, Tolstoy, Ibsen – and wondered: how did the man who wrote in these margins, the man who marked these passages when he was my age, how did he become so empty and complacent? And I fervently hoped that it wouldn't happen to me.

Tired aphorisms, cracker-barrel wisdom. 'Out of sound all creation was born,' he said sententiously. 'Out of the Lord Siva's ankle bells. Out of the syllable "Om".'

After the speech, the dancer came out wrapped in a shawl and garlanded everyone. Appa came off the stage and looked at his watch. There were probably at least fifteen minutes of interval left, since the dancer had to have her costume changed by inexperienced helpers backstage. The hall was emptying rapidly.

Appa beckoned to Janaki. They stood together against a background of Plastic Woven Baskets and Pure Pappadums. Amma tensed in her chair. Her face suddenly looked distorted, as if it would crack with the strain. She was winding the tassels of her sari around her fingers, and then unwinding them, faster and faster.

Padmasini came down to join Appa and Janaki. Amma stood up swiftly and manoeuevred herself into the group. I tagged along for a laugh.

Appa cleared his throat. 'Padma,' he began, with the self-conscious shoulders of a bringer of bad tidings. Janaki smiled a sultry smile that curved like a scimitar, glinting with the spit her anticipating tongue washed over it. 'Padma, I have to–'

'Have you heard the news about my father, Balan?' Padmasini cut in.

Appa looked at her blankly.

'Kalyani may have told you – my father is terminally ill in Kalyanikkarai. My mothers heard from the doctors that they can't do much for him. They are here for the day. They're travelling to Kalyanikkarai early tomorrow morning. The doctors have given him only a few weeks to live. A month, maybe.'

'I'm very sorry to hear – what is it – the illness, what–'

'An aneurism. It has apparently opened up beyond

repair, and he is bleeding into his stomach cavity. They're pumping in blood to keep him alive, but they don't think there's much hope.'

'Surgery?'

'It's too late for that.'

'What a shame!' Appa said. He was flustered.

'How *sad* for you!' Janaki cooed.

'Since I obviously cannot go to the US in June, Balan, I hope you'll find someone else to go.'

Janaki's face changed abruptly, like those new trick billboards whose images seem to spin around as one goes past. For a second, her eyes shot venom at Appa. So you gave me the tour because *she* couldn't go, her snapping eyes said, then she was in control again, checking her fingernails. I'm as disappointed as you are, Janaki, I wanted to say to her. I was hoping for some drama.

Amma looked pale and nervous.

Padmasini broke the sudden silence in a brisk, let's-get-to-business voice. 'So, Balan, I'm going to be in Kalyanikkarai for almost two months, I hope you can set up something for me to do there.'

'I know just the thing,' Appa said, his face relaxing now. 'NATAC has set aside a budget for a lifetime award–'

Padmasini looked pleased, Janaki horrified.

'–for a dancer or a dance teacher from a traditional hereditary community. We could set aside, say, sixty per cent of that budget for a documentary on this person, instead of giving all the money to the person himself. You find a traditional dance master in Kalyanikkarai or somewhere within driving distance of it and the funds are yours. The budget will cover your directorial fee, the film equipment, the cameraman, an assistant, if you want to use one, your travel, your stay in Kalyanikkarai. Of course, we must cover the honorarium for the man himself. You just need to type up a budget statement, I'll handle the rest.'

'A traditional teacher,' Padmasini said. 'A documentary. I need to think–'

'That nattuvanar, bit of a lush, who came to see me a few years ago? The one whose book of lyrics you published – wasn't he from Kalyanikkarai? Or am I mixing him up with someone else?'

'Velu? I've lost touch with him. He's probably dead from liver disease by now. He was already looking pretty yellow by the time I sent him packing. A documentary – wait, I was thinking of – a friend's son – you know Shah, don't you? He's a budding director and cameraman. If NATAC is funding the film, I can use him.'

'Hmm.' Appa slipped a finger behind his glasses and rubbed his eye. He did that when he was exhausted. In the background we heard the dancer's bells jingling in preparation for her to come on again.

'And I know a woman in Kalyanikkarai,' Padmasini said. 'She's not a nattuvanar, but a dasi – a devadasi. That would certainly count as traditional, wouldn't it?'

'A devadasi? Of course! A perfect solution.'

'Goodness,' Janaki suppressed a yawn with the tips of two manicured fingers. 'I thought those devadasi-type creatures had all vanished off the face of the earth long ago.'

'It would be a pioneering effort,' Padmasini said, looking at Janaki, rubbing it in. 'Breaking new ground. I could choreograph myself into the film too. The footage of this woman could be intercut with footage of me talking about rediscovering the forgotten foremothers. A nice touch of rebellion and novelty. Yes, it would work for me. Why don't I take Hema along to Kalyanikkarai, to help me? Let's talk later, okay? I have to go backstage now, and hold the silly girl's hand, or she'll have stagefright again.'

'Padma,' Appa said. 'We'd better get some details on paper before you leave – tonight, if it is not too inconvenient. If you want to go to Kalyanikkarai soon, we don't have much time.'

'Will you come home with me, then – all three of you, of course – after the show? My mothers are here for the day. They've come to collect their things. They didn't realize they'd have to stay in Kalyanikkarai for a long stretch. You could cheer them up a little.'

'I don't think–' Appa began, but Amma cut in, 'Of course we will see them.'

'I hope you'll find the documentary makes up for slumming in that terrible backwater, Padmasini,' Janaki said.

Padmasini ignored her and bustled up the steps. The rest of us wandered back towards the chairs.

Janaki pouted. 'So, Balan, Padmasini gets the lollipop. Not bad, considering it's supposed to be the consolation prize. If you'd let me do it – there's a terrific market abroad for every kind of strong woman or woman rescue story. It would be ideal for someone who could see this devadasi from a feminist point of view – you know, poetic visuals, but a storyline: the modern dancer connects with the liberated women of the past, sisterhood, that kind of thing. Padmasini won't be able to do it.'

'Well,' Appa said mildly. 'A NATAC documentary's really a very simple thing, Janaki. She won't need to do anything fancy. If she gets a few snippets of footage and edits them into some kind of order, she's set to go.'

'Anyway, I'm off.' Janaki collected the Biscuit King from his seat. He had begun to nod off. 'This is the last show I'm going to for this year. I came mainly to see you. It will be good to get away somewhere where there are bathtubs that actually have water in them, and where the lifts work.'

In the whole conversation, no one mentioned the name of the woman they were going to give the award to. She was 'the devadasi'. What a shallow lot culture vultures are. How the officers of NATAC, wearing their government-issue blinders, trot nowhere, drawing behind them this unwieldy equipage of Festivals of India, publicity and diplomacy, awards and honours, documentaries and conferences.

In the van, going to Padmasini's place, Amma sank back with a great shuddering sigh. I looked down: her hands were trembling slightly. Appa, sitting beside Joseph in front, let his head roll back on to his seat. She had been worried sick – heaven knows why – about Padmasini's tantrums all evening; and he'd heaved up another speech from the place where he stored tired words that suited all occasions.

Luz Church Road, Alwarpet. Amma reached out and

ruffled the thinning hair on the crown of Appa's head. Under the flickering streetlights I saw the muscles around his jaw change, lift into a smile.

He turned around. 'If you knew she didn't want to go to the US, why did you nag me about finding her some sort of compensatory thing to do?'

'I didn't know she wanted to go to Kalyanikkarai,' Amma said. Her eyes were closed. 'She told me her father was ill, that's all. It didn't seem so serious when she mentioned it to me, and I forgot to tell you.'

The fumes from the slow-crawling buses were horrible. We rolled up the van's windows. When I turned my head sideways, my reflection stared back at me from the window on my side, darkened, transparent, superimposed on the grime of the city. We crept through Eldams Road, where the traffic was squeezed into a narrow tube of roadway between hills of piled-up dirt from the municipality's excavations. Was it the telephones this time, or the drainage, or the electricity? Someone was always digging up a piece of Madras. As soon as they filled up the holes and reapplied the tar, someone else came along and dug it up again.

Teynampet, Pondy Bazaar, Nagesh Theatre. My face undulated over a gigantic cutout of an actress dressed entirely in winking sequins. A cow ambled across the road to an unattended vegetable cart and helped itself to spinach. Mangy pye-dogs scurried along the pavement, yelping in habitual fear, keeping inches ahead of the stones slung lazily at them. They fetched up near a beggar who shared a bun with them.

'*What* on earth is *he* doing?' Amma said suddenly.

A paunchy, unprotected traffic policeman in the middle of Usman Road was hanging on to life by the skin of his teeth while his arms swirled out in comical arabesques.

'The government recently charged Padmasini with the task of improving the aesthetic quality of traffic direction,' Appa said solemnly, as if he was reading it from a newspaper.

'Oh, of course!' Amma said. They looked at each other, grinning, shaking their heads in disbelief. The drivers around the policeman stared, started, retreated, cursed and honked in confusion. And, I thought, here we are, going to the house of the genius who had left her aesthetic mark on everything, even the traffic.

9

Padmasini
Madras, 14 April 1990

'Take these boxes out and air the car thoroughly,' I said to the driver. 'I don't like it smelling of food. And next time, remember that I don't like chutney with the vadais.' The cabbage-juice diet makes me hungry all the time. I end up eating more than I would have eaten if I hadn't been on it. The fat sticks to me. Neurobion injections, Electral, steroids. I haven't lost a kilo in months, for all that.

I try to get the recitals over with earlier in the evening; not being able to have a proper meal at nine o'clock made me ravenous. Everything went wrong today. The New Jersey girl's parents had assured me that they had rented a good dance theatre, and by the time I realized it was this wretched wedding hall, it was too late to change things. No doubt Balan will make snide remarks about the poor production values – that is hiscatch phrase these days.

Still, the New Jersey dollars will make up for the lousy

show. The necklace was in poor taste, but it is going to be turned into cash anyway. It will go into the Padmasini Mahadevan Theatre Fund. I must remember that the lawyer will be here tomorrow with the details of the land purchase.

'A brilliant investment, Padmasini,' the lawyer said, when I outlined the project to him. My uncle trained him; he is one of the very few people I can trust. 'My niece from Arizona is a dancer, and her mother is always telling me how much theatre managers in Madras charge for their shabby facilities. You build a good dance space, with state-of-the-art equipment, and it will make you a millionaire all by itself.'

Damn. The servants have left the lights on everywhere. That Mamoi.

I learned over the years that the parents of my students were taken aback when I asked for a round lakh in arangetram fees; it was easier to ask for seventy-five thousand in cash and the rest in various kinds of 'traditional' gifts. Necklaces, bangles, gold coins, saris: anything that came to my mind, but I made sure it would add up to about twenty-five thousand. The parents protest, sometimes; they try to bargain. This girl's father was upset by the expenses. But once the girls are hooked, once five to seven years have been invested in their dance training, the parents cough up.

'Send Mamoi,' I said to the driver. He just looked at me. 'I don't care if you have to wake him. He's supposed to be my housekeeper. The lazy sod has left all the lights on, and I want to know why.'

The most terrifying thing is the idea of not being on

stage myself. The upstairs lights on as well – wait till I catch that Mamoi. A career that is fizzling out. Having bitches like Janaki becoming the new divas, while the culture vultures sideline me. The theatre will at least be a new project, and I can dance there as long as I like, since it will be my own space. Not that dancing is easy these days. Even sitting on the stage for two hours makes my knees hurt. The orthopaedic surgeon said, 'This dance form you do, it is cruel to the knees.' Yes, I knew that.

And in Maine, four months ago, my shoulder got so bad I had to see a specialist.

'Do you play a game in which you throw overarm a lot?' the specialist said.

'No,' I said. 'I do bharatanatyam. You know? Indian dance?'

'Ah,' he said. 'Feathers and drums. Pow-wows.'

It took four months of physiotherapy for me to be able to hook my bra again.

Mamoi stumbled in, rubbing his eyes to make me feel sorry I woke him. 'You think I make money for you donkeys to burn it up in wasted electricity?'

'Your mothers didn't want the lights shut off, Madam. They said the house was too dark.'

'Are you working for them or for me?'

'For both of you?'

'Who pays you?'

'Should I turn the lights off now?'

'Never mind.' Balan's van was coming up the drive. He'd replaced the Ambassador with a new Maruti van.

Balan had his office car. One personal car was enough. They'd buy a second car when Hema grew old enough to drive. Always check that about my students–

So, my dear, did you come to this class in your mother's car or your father's car?

We have only the one car, Padmasini-teacher.

I see. Well, you are a very pretty young woman, but my school is just so overcrowded these days. I'll see if one of my friends will teach you.

A second car was a useful indicator. Status, money, staying power.

'Mamoi, tell my mothers they have guests. Then go let the people in and make them some tea.'

'Yes, Madam.'

Balan's hand was in the small of Kalyani's back as she got out of the van. After all these years, the fact that they had lasted as a couple still hurts. He hadn't said anything to me, sixteen years ago, but I knew in my gut that he was thinking of asking me to marry him when Kalyani drifted into Madras. Sixteen years ago. I punish them both by holding Hema back in the dance school. But this strategy may have begun to backfire. The senior teachers at the school told me – reluctantly enough, since they knew I was Balan's friend – that Hema had begun to ask insolent questions. Wanted to know how my interpretation of Sita could possibly be called feminist, apparently.

I could teach that spoilt brat something about feminism. I could teach her something about being a single woman in this country of wives and mothers, about fighting to be recognized, about keeping that hard-won attention, long after my body wanted to stop moving.

If Balan pulled Hema out of the school, I would have no real hold over him. Balan still holds all the cards. Damn him for standing in my way.

What was I going to do with Hema during this Kalyanikkarai trip? I had no idea. People that age are simply uninteresting to me. Thank god I never wanted children. They are nothing but a distraction.

Doing business: now that was interesting. I could never understand the way of thinking that set the arts above business. Not many women have a head for turning a dance school into a thriving business, but I do. It is now a global business, I have schools and students everywhere.

The sight of couples makes me restless and irritable. Kalyani and Balan, even Janaki and her hideous husband. No. I have to drop this line of thought. It is better to think that I had a lucky escape from Balan: in those days he was full of zeal, he talked like a man who'd let his wife have her own career. But look at him now. Look at Kalyani, letting his hand on her back steer her towards the door.

Too late, anyhow, for me to start down another path. My mothers don't understand. What do you need money for, they keep asking. What are you going to do in your old age, with no children, no husband? They think I could choose at any point to give everything up and become a wife. A Kalyani. A second-class citizen with a second-hand life. Nothing of one's own. A pretty doll.

There weren't many men who'd marry a dancer with her own career. And now I am an *ageing* dancer with a career. I get proposals from old leering businessmen who'd as soon bed young mistresses as look at them.

Balan was looking at his watch as Mamoi showed him in.

'Padma, if I phone Delhi right away, we could firm up the plan to film this devadasi. Delhi has to approve the budget. Then we need to write to her – I hope you have a postal address for her. God knows how long she will take to respond. If it doesn't work out, I'll need to find an alternative, or NATAC will look silly.' He kneaded his neck muscles. 'This work is getting too much for me. I'm ready for retirement.'

I pointed him to the phone. Kalyani and Hema stood behind him, fidgeting. I didn't want him getting distracted. 'Kalyani, my mothers are waiting to see you. Why don't you go upstairs? Hema, you too. I'll join you in a bit.'

Balan punched in the Delhi long distance code, and the telephone number of the national coordinator of NATAC, his good friend, Akhilesh Pande. A typical Delhi sleazebag, reserving the best pickings for the Delhi diplomatic wives he slept with. At least Balan was too decent to do that. I should know, I tried to be his bit on the side after he married Kalyani.

'Akhil Bhaiyya!' Balan said. 'How are you? Good, wonderful. The family? That's marvellous, yes, I always knew he had it in him.'

I had picked up the phone the last time I was in the States. It had a speakerphone button. I gestured to Balan that I would like to hear the other end of the conversation.

Didn't want to be diddled in any way. He looked at me with raised eyebrows, but hit the button. I nodded my thanks.

'The reason I called, Akhil – since we're still looking for a Lifetime Achievement awardee from the south, I think I've got just the candidate for you. A bit of a departure from the usual, but it will have novelty value.'

'*Han*, Balan Bhaiyya, what's the good news?' Akhilesh's gravelly voice – he was tipsy or high. Ten-thirty on a Saturday night. We must have caught him mid-tryst. World's full of scum.

'You see – um – I have just rediscovered a dancer from a hereditary dasi – that is, devadasi – family who I believe is – uh – the greatest living exponent of the–' he looked at a question at me.

'–Kalyanikkarai style,' I said, and he repeated that into the mouthpiece.

'Arrey, a devadasi? Are there devadasis around these days? I thought they were all dead and gone.'

'Not gone yet, but may go any minute, Akhil. This one is seventy years old and uh – not too well. It would be a good idea to use modern video technology to capture this devadasi dancing on film; there are very few dancers from the old traditional dancing families left. You know, Hindu traditions are becoming quite the rage now.'

'You're telling me, Balan. Everyone in Delhi is talking of the golden age and the Vedas. Hindu tradition is better than a passport if you want to go to France or America. Hmm, a film on devadasis.'

'I'm giving the project to–' Balan glanced over his shoulder at me– 'Padmasini. She's right–'

'Padmasini? Balan, that woman is a major liability–'
Yes. That came out smooth and easy. They'd been
badmouthing me between them. Men groaning together
at unreasonable women. Bastards. They were definitely
going to bump me from the US Festival.

'Yes, Akhil. She's right here with me. As I was saying,
she is a wonderful choice for this project. I am calling
from her office, she is here, if you want to speak to her.'

'Give her my best wishes, Balan. I'll speak to her
another time. Can you send me the budget pronto?
Pronto–' He giggled suddenly. 'I like that word.'

'I'll have a detailed proposal made up in the next couple
of days. I'll mail it to you as soon as I can.'

'But the only thing – the budget was mainly supposed
to be for the awardee. The film will be quite an expensive
proposition, na? Devadasi fifty per cent, Padmasini fifty
per cent? '

'Oh, I think Padmasini, as a senior artist, will expect
a slightly larger share, Akhil. Plus, yes, filming will be
expensive. Think of the novelty value of it!'

'Novelty, yes, yes. Didn't someone shoot some footage
ten-twelve years ago of one old master from the south?'

'Janaki Narayanan, yes, she's now Janaki Kotiswaran.
A male guru's work. I went to the NATAC archives
last year to see that footage. It was never edited. It
lay in storage at NATAC Delhi until it was destroyed
by fungus. They said that it had not been preserved
properly.'

'These things happen, what to do.' I could see him.
Akhilesh Pande, in his plush chair, making little 'please
adjust' movements with his palm. Probably had his

other hand on his latest squeeze's rump. 'Well, send the proposal, Balan, but consider it a done deal, now itself. Nice words, na, done deal. I'll leave everything to you. I need to pass the filming budget, but you know me – you're the boss and I'm just the rubber stamp.'

Balan carefully placed the receiver on its cradle.

'All settled?'

'It's fine,' Balan said.

'Will you come upstairs?'

'I hope we aren't disturbing your mothers.'

'They said to bring you up no matter how late it was. They are going back to Kalyanikkarai by the early morning train, so this is their only chance to see you.'

'I could draw up a rough version of the budget right now,' Balan said. Typical male, didn't want to go see a couple of old women in distress.

'Of course, Balan. How much is the project worth?'

'About five lakhs, give or take a little. Part of it will go to the dasi woman, of course.'

'Don't give too much away to her, Balan. In fact, it would be best if you gave me control of the budget. I'll see that she gets a fair share. Pens and paper on the table there. Calculator in the left-hand drawer.'

'Thanks. It will take half an hour – your mothers can talk to Kalyani and Hema.' He looked at his watch again. Heavy lines curved downwards from his nostrils, like brackets around his mouth. He was getting old. 'We've got to get the details mailed off to Delhi quickly. When did you want to leave for Kalyanikkarai?'

'In a week, week-and-a-half.'

'That doesn't give us much time.'

'As I said, it doesn't look as if my father will last very long. All right, come upstairs when you're done.'

My mothers were sitting on the sofa. Their arms were locked together tighter than usual. They spoke in tandem, finishing each other's sentences.

'The Military Hospital is better for him now,' my own-mother was saying as I led Mamoi in with the tea tray.

'The nurses there are tougher,' my other-mother said. 'He was driving the nurses in the mission hospital crazy, throwing things at them.'

They'd been strangely excited ever since they'd arrived, bringing the news about my father. Shadow of death, I suppose. Their lives sad and stale, otherwise. Enough to put me off marriage for good, listening to their stories about being taken out of school when they were ten years old, to be married to boys who were fifteen and sixteen, boys who had hated the idea of marriage and had fought against it.

A pair of portraits hung on the sofa above them. This was their room, so I let those portraits be, or I'd have had the one of my father taken away. The Inspector, the bastard. The way he stared at the camera reminded me too much of the way he stared at me when I was a girl, before something angry and cruel came out of his mouth. The portrait had been touched up with photographic inks, to correct his squint, but there was no hiding the nastiness. In the other frame was my uncle, who had sheltered me in this house. His portrait was garlanded because he was dead. Soon the other one would be too. A fat sandalwood garland would cover up the stare nicely.

'He's been lashing out at the poor policemen,' my own-mother said. 'Men who worked under him before he retired. All they're trying to do is donate blood for him.'

'Strange, the fancies that come to the dying,' my other-mother said, turning to Kalyani. 'My husband, the Vakil – him in the picture here – he kept asking for his dasi mistress when he was dying.' They held each other, the Push-Me-Pull-You sisters, and cackled at the memory. 'He kept a dasi woman, you know. Rajayi, her name was.'

'You *knew* this?' Hema said, suddenly. She was the only one in the room who didn't know the story.

I sipped my tea to avoid looking at Kalyani.

'Everyone knew, child. He would visit her every evening before he came home.'

'Didn't you *mind*?' Nothing in Hema's upbringing could make her understand this placid acceptance. Or the claustrophobia of living in a small town in which everyone knew where a man spent his evenings.

My mother said, 'We'd been brought up not to mind, child.'

'They were opposites, the brothers. The Inspector hated dance, he wanted the tevadiyas stopped. But the Vakil loved their dancing. He even wrote songs for his paramour. He was the one who arranged a teacher for our Padma when she started begging to learn dance.'

'The Inspector swore he would break up the dancing in the temple, and he broke it up. We smuggled Padma to her classes in secret, but the Inspector found out. Oh,

171

he was *furious*. He was so angry he even arrested one of the dasis after he found out about Padma's class.'

'He arrested Rajayi. We thought there would be no end of fuss between the brothers.'

'He *arrested* her?' Kalyani's voice was too shrill. She tried again, softly, 'He arrested her?' So. She did not know her mother had been arrested. Interesting.

My eyes slid towards her after all. Her gaze locked with mine. She was working it out. You idiot, I wanted to say to her, how can you not have guessed that when I said I would be filming a devadasi in Kalyanikkarai, I meant your mother? Who else would I know of but Rajayi? My uncle's mistress for years, part of the family lore, even if I'd never met her?

'She went on dancing in the temple after they had passed a law against it,' my mother was saying. 'If a dasi was still dancing when they made that law, she got to keep the land the temple had given her for her service. If she had left the temple, then the land was taken away.'

'A thoroughly mercenary lot, the dasis,' my other-mother said. 'It's funny, though. We wanted to see this Rajayi, once, to see how she lived. We said we were going to the temple, and instead we went to her house. We sat on the veranda like passers-by taking a rest and looked through the window. I was saying to myself, here the Vakil must have sat; here the woman might have given him water to wash his feet before taking him inside. We thought we'd see all the things we family-women had heard of – dasi women lounging around, talking their loose talk, people writing poetry, men smoking and drinking, the guests matching and outdoing each others' witty sayings, the music–'

'But there was *nothing* in there. Not a four-legged chair to sit on, no musicians, no pretty girls and no cheroots. There was an old woman sitting on an old mat – it must have been Rajayi, but we thought, he can't have wanted her for her beauty.'

There was a knock at the door.

'Is that you, Balan?' I called. 'Come on in.'

Balan condoled with my mother about my father's illness. His eyes were wary. Thinking, did I get that right? Is she the wife or the sister-in-law? He didn't want to chat.

'Remember I'm taking Hema with me to Kalyanikkarai, Balan,' I said as I saw him to the door, to seal the contract.

He swept Kalyani away quickly, which was good, because I could see from her expression that she wanted to talk to me. And the last thing I wanted to do was back off from this project to film the mother in the name of some non-existent friendship with the daughter.

There's no money in friendship. Besides, I have this thing for Shah, the man I was thinking of using as the cinematographer. There's no money in an affair, either, but it will go down as a perk.

10

Rajayi

Kalyanikkarai, 4 May 1990

The letter came on a Wednesday morning – I remember, because Tuesday was Amalan's last day of school, and he had bought a bottle of red nailpaint for himself on his way back from his exam. I would not let him paint his nails during the school term any longer, not after all the times he got beaten up for it. His teacher tied his hair up with a rubber band once and made him sit with the girls, to shame him. I went to the school. 'Every now and then god makes some people different from others,' I told the teacher, 'and if Siva-Peruman in the big temple approves of Amalan, then I have no quarrel with the colour of his nails, and I don't see what you are punishing him for.'

The letter came the day Amalan's holidays began.

Mrs Rajalatchmi, it said, the government would like to give you an honour. I had no idea what that meant.

What kind of honour, and why me? I suppose I could have written to Lila, to ask if she knew anything about it, but the letter said I had to let them know at once if I would accept it.

At the temple, I said to Meenatchi, 'Just look at this. For years they don't even know I exist, these people, whoever they are, and I don't know they exist. Eh, princess,' I called to the pretty girl who works at the Canara Bank, 'will you be my first customer this evening and bring me good luck?'

'Just one arm-length of jasmine, paati,' she said. 'Don't wrap it, just tuck it in my hair.'

'Out of the blue they write to me,' I said to Meenatchi after I had threaded the jasmine into the girl's hair, 'and they want a reply *at once*.'

Meenatchi sat across from me under the archway of the south gopuram, minding the shoes that the worshippers took off before they entered the temple grounds. The girls in Meenatchi's family never learned music or dance, and went to school only up to the fifth standard. Meenatchi's mother had no man to take care of her; my mother had helped her mother when we had money to spare. Her sister went to Bombay, to Kamatipura, and disappeared. No one knows what happened to her.

'Eley, Rajayi,' Meenatchi said. 'Does this letter have a government stamp?'

'Why, yes – at least, I think so. But I cannot read the signature of the person who wrote it.'

Muthayya's daughter-in-law came by and bought five arm-lengths of mixed flowers, grumbling as usual that my measuring was wrong. 'I have the longest forearms of any flower seller in Kalyanikkarai,' I told her. 'Here, take your flowers, be happy.' I counted out her change, while six people from a family left their shoes in a muddled heap near Meenatchi.

'What does the letter say, exactly?' Meenatchi stacked the shoes in a neat row, with the delicate women's slippers on top, and put a token on them.

'It says, please let us know if you are willing to accept this honour. That's all. Do you have a clove to spare?'

'Toothache again? You should get them all pulled out.'

'Yes, and then what will I use for eating?'

She gave me a clove from her betel nut pouch and tucked it back into her waist. 'You know that harmonium player Latchumayya? He's getting a pension from the government. Maybe they have a pension for you.'

'I doubt it,' I said. 'I never had any luck with money. That bank girl asked me if I wanted a loan to start a chicken farm, and I said, the chickens will run it better than I can. A pension would be nice. I could pay a contractor to have my roof repaired. I have to patch it soon, the tenant says, or he leaves. He says there is mould in his clothes.'

'So, how much rent do you get for those two rooms?'

'The rent is not much, but it is half my income.'

'Then you'd better write and say you accept,' Meenatchi said, and turned away. She was huffy because I hadn't answered her question. I liked Meenatchi, but she pried too much about money, and when she learned something, she could never keep it to herself. Once, when she didn't realize I was standing behind her, I heard her say, 'You know who really hates the police? Rajayi. If you want to wind her up, all you have to do is mention the police.'

I took Meenatchi's advice, though. The next day I went to the post office to buy an inland letter. The girl behind the counter made a stylish fan out of ten inlands and said 'How many?' and sneered when I said 'Only one.' I had the government letter with me, so I could write a reply, address my letter right away, and send it off.

Every day I walked from my house to the flower bazaar to buy the flowers, from the flower bazaar back home to string the buds I had bought, to the temple morning and evening to sell the flowers, and back home again. Not bad for an old hag. My knee joints didn't like me breaking the pattern.

So the letter went off, and in two days I forgot all about it. Ask me what happened yesterday, and I won't remember. I remember all the things of my childhood. Wake me up in the middle of the night and ask me to do a varnam that Samu Vathyar taught me, and I can do it without a single step wrong. That is how old people's memory seems to work.

A week later, I was coming home from the flower bazaar with the basket on my hip, singing to myself.

This is the doorstep of the King
Of the city on the Kalyani's banks.

My basket was covered with a wet cloth. In the dog days of Chittirai, before the softening rains, the jasmine buds got bruised by the heat. I was going to string the jasmine at home.

This is the doorstep sheltered by walls
Made bright night and day by the Moon and the Sun.

Lila would remember that song; she played the princess leaning out of the window, listening to the fortune teller singing on the street. I always played the fortune teller.

I saw a big black car standing in the street, under the lamp post where I used to send Kalyani to study before we got the electric light. A man was standing outside a neighbour's door on the other side of the street, and he was pointing towards my door.

At first I thought: it is because of the elections. Last year, after the elections, the municipality changed all the street numbers. All the even on one side, all the odd on the other, so now people who came looking for a house with last year's address wandered about for half a day before they found it. Only the postman knew what was what and who was where.

Then I saw that the man was wearing a khaki pant–shirt.

The hairs on the back of my neck stood up. The basket fell out of my arms and lay half upended over the gutter. It was clumsy of me, two padis of fresh jasmine buds sprayed all over Musicians' Street. Eight rupees fifty paisa down the drain, with the drought driving the prices up.

The boy is in trouble now, I thought. Meenatchi said he was running with a pack of mischief-makers from the tourist bungalow. They have come for him, I thought in a panic. The police.

The khaki men and their ways are burned into my memory. Neither Lila nor I can forget how we would wait, shaking, for their raids to be done. My caste never had a good feeling about the police. In my grandmother Jagadambal's time, the police would come with the matron from the army hospital and hustle the women on our street to a male doctor who would force up their saris and poke at their privates. Our family had been exempt in those days, but we feared that humiliation all the same. In my mother's time there were half-a-dozen raids on our house.

In my dreams, all those policemen ran together. The one who came to the house the first time it was raided, taking Amma while Lila howled like a wolf cub, the one who slapped me when I fought with him, the one who said to my mother, holding my hands twisted behind my back, 'This hellcat won't do well in your profession, you better teach her to make your big tevadiya eyes instead of spitting and clawing.' And all of them wore the face of the one the town called 'the Inspector'.

Of course the Inspector would be an old man by now. He was older than me. The town said he had gone crazy. He had driven his servants away, even the field-workers, and his wife barely managed to get the rice harvest in last year, never mind the coconuts, fruit and betel.

My neighbour Muthayya, that great leaky-mouth, came out of his house to speak to the man in khaki. Muthayya's wife and son and brother-in-law and the daughter who had just given birth all spilled out of the door behind him, and all of them stared at my house as if there was a circus going on and they had paid good money for tickets.

Then the car's back door opened and a woman got out.

She looked at my house too.

So then I knew it was not the police. Ah, I am an old fool.

The woman was wearing dark glasses like an actor, and a fine white cotton sari. They did not make saris like that in Kalyanikkarai. From the city she must have come, from Madras. Now she would say something to Muthayya, and if he went to the vegetarian tiffin shop next to Baai's shop, everyone downtown would hear about it; if he went to the temple for the sandhya worship, everyone in the temple compound would hear about it. The temple's Ayyar would hear about it. If I kept my head down and crept about my business quietly, the street left me alone; if I drew attention to myself or my house in any way, the insults and trouble would begin again.

I could smell trouble coming because of this woman. So instead of going up to my door, I stood half hidden by the only tree left standing in Musicians' Street, and I watched and listened.

'*Adhuva!*' Muthayya spat. He pulled his nose. 'That *thing*. You should be ashamed, trying to find that *thing*'s house. A bad lot. The government wiped their community out, and a good thing too. They should have done it properly and *killed* the vermin, like rats. A thoroughly bad lot.'

The woman took a couple of steps towards my door. Muthayya hobbled across to her, the street scorching his bare feet.

'Can't you understand what I'm saying?' He clapped a hand to his head and tried again. This time in English. 'No Tamil speak? No go that house. Bad ladies!'

I could hate him, but I have never forgotten that when the police arrested me, and Lila had to hide, and our cow was lowing desperately for water and hay, this man watered and fed her. To avoid the sin of killing a cow.

The woman smiled, turned, and got into the car again. Muthayya seemed satisfied. His people went inside and all their faces appeared again at the two front windows of their house, peering, not minding the bars pressing into their flesh. The khaki man sat down under the old warning board that was hanging crooked over my door.

The Madras people were not going away, they were settling down to wait. Around my feet, the ruined buds were already opening to the touch of the hot red dust. I had to do something, so I stepped out from behind the tree.

'There's no one at home in that house,' I said.

The fire-god's star was in the ascendant. I sounded as if I'd sucked half the street into my voice, my throat was so clogged with dust. 'If you are thirsty or something,' I said, 'you go that way, up by the temple. The Samanar charity has a tent there with ice-buttermilk for free.'

'Ey, paatima, you know the lady who lives here?' the man said.

'And who are you?' I went a little closer so I could look at him up and down. Now I could see clearly that he was a car driver, not a policeman. 'And who are you to call me paatima, as if you are my blood-relation?'

'The lady in the car is a big dance teacher from Madras. She's looking for one Rajayi Amma's house.'

'Rajayi Amma, is it.' It sounded too respectful, not right, a joke. But I was tired and parched and sick of standing outside my own front door, so I said, 'All right, come in.'

He ran to the car and opened the back door and straightened up again with a plastic tray in his hands. It was covered with a white kerchief. It felt like the old days when I opened the door for a man who had come, bringing gifts, to see my mother or Lila or me. If you looked at me now you'd hardly think I could be any use to a man in that way.

The woman got out of the car, took off the dark glasses and put her hand over her eyes as if the sun was hurting them.

'Namaskaram,' she said. 'How are you?'

It was strange, unreal. I didn't know what to do, except go inside. It had been so long since anyone but my boy had come in by that door that I had forgotten how to be ceremonious.

'Come in,' I said again. 'Sit.' I waved her to the swing. It was still there, the chains tarnished and dusty, but serviceable. I told Lila she should use it as a litter for me when I was dead, and burn it with me.

'Oh, I cannot sit when you are still standing,' she said. 'You sit there on the swing and I'll sit–' She looked around as if to find a clean place on the floor, but everything was dusty, and her sari was white as milk. 'How can I sit on the swing at the same time as you?'

I was taken aback. It was the kind of old-fashioned respect we showed our masters. For fifteen years, when I was Samu Vathyar's student, and later, when I started taking Kalyani to him for lessons, I never once sat on a chair in his presence.

So why was my skin tingling, like walking into cobwebs?

I brought a grass mat and unrolled it for the woman. She took the tray from the driver and gave it to me. I lifted up the kerchief to cover up how confused I was, and saw betel leaves and betel nuts and fruit – bananas, pomegranates, oranges. There were two ten-rupee notes. I thought of the jasmine buds I had dropped and my fingers wanted to snatch up the money. I put the tray down without touching anything on it.

'You have come looking for me?'

'Rajayi Amma, I have come from Madras,' she said. 'My name is Padmasini. In a humble way, I am a dancer. Not like you, not a great old-time artist, but a fellow-worshipper of that god of dance.'

'How did you find me?' I said. 'I mean, no one – outside my family, and my neighbours – no one knows I have anything to do with dance, you see.'

'A friend gave me your address. I felt I could propose something that would let you earn some money. I understand your troubles. I may look well-off to you, Rajayi Amma,' she said, 'but I come from a poor family too.'

'My family wasn't always as poor as this,' I said. I didn't want her to think that we had always lived like this, with not a stick of furniture except that old swing, in a house that shook and shed plaster from the walls when the lorries roared past outside.

'The lorries make a terrible noise,' she said, looking out.

'It is because of the new bypass the government is building, up by the hill – they have already knocked down six houses where the hill sticks out, to make space for the new road. They are going to blast away the whole side of

183

the hill, so they won't have to tear down the Corporation School and rebuild it.'

'Blasting? That must be noisy too.'

'Very. What can we do? I only pray that the blasting doesn't undermine my walls.'

As soon as I said that I regretted it, because she looked up all around as if the roof was coming down then and there.

'This house goes back over a hundred years,' I said. 'It was gifted by the Kalyanikkarai Raja to my great-grandmother Kalyaniammal, for her services as a dasi in the temple and at the court. The street used to be full of musicians. Now it is dying. The government is waiting to shovel away our houses to make way for the new shops. But I will lie on the road and wait for the machines to run me over before I move.'

'Won't they pay compensation for the houses?'

'When have they ever paid enough to buy another house? And how can I afford to rent from someone else? As it is, the house gives me half my income. More than thirty years ago, when Ka – when my daughter started dance class, I had no money for lessons, so I threw up that wall, and rented out the rooms beyond it. I had the contractor knock two new doors in front.'

'So that is why the house looks – sliced in half. Why there is only one set of pillars in here.'

'The matching set of pillars is in my tenant's part of the house. We had already sold the fields and jewellery, bit by bit, till it was all gone. What did land fetch in those days? Not much.' Why was I telling her all this? I thought, and stopped.

'I would love to hear you tell stories about your past,' she said quickly. 'About your ancestors. I would love to capture such stories on film. You know? Like in the cinema?'

'I have no time to tell stories,' I said. 'Will you drink some water? It is such a hot day and I'm thirsty myself.'

'Don't trouble yourself,' she said, getting up at once, and going into the kitchen before I could stop her. She put a tumbler under the tap and opened it, and it spluttered and made empty noises. I filled a tumbler out of the big clay water pot and gave it to her. She put it down without drinking it. I filled up a cup for myself and drank.

'If I film you, the payment will be satisfactory,' she said.

I didn't understand what payment she meant. Should I pay her? Or would she pay me?

'What is the payment for?' I said.

'For your time, of course.'

'For my *time*? I don't understand. Must I teach someone dance, or singing, or what?'

'I see that I have explained it badly. It's like this, Rajayi Amma. The dance school I represent is working with NATAC, which is a government body, to make a film about a – er – traditional teacher and dancer.'

'Oh. Are you from the same organization that wants to give me an honour this December? Then maybe you can explain. I got a letter–'

'Yes, actually, I told them to send you a letter,' she said. 'It was through me that your name became known to them. I am responsible for the honour, in a very humble way.'

'You could have knocked me over, I was so surprised

when the letter came. Who could have heard about me in Madras?'

'As I said, a friend gave me your address.'

'Yes, but who – what is the friend's name? Was it Lilavati?'

'No,' she said.

'Was it Velu? Is Velu still alive?'

'No,' she said. 'It wasn't Velu.' But she did not say who it was. 'So I told Balasankar of NATAC – why, do you know him?' She was smiling.

When she spoke the name of my Kalyani's husband I jumped a little, but I recovered quickly.

'No, no, not at all, that is, I know him slightly. Is everything all right with – Balasankar and his family?' Lila and Kalyani wrote to me a few times a year, and Kalyani sent money when she could, but I never got as much news as I would have liked. I would have liked to sit this woman down and ask her to tell me everything she knew about Kalyani's life, what she did each day, how she passed her time, if she was happy.

'Yes, everything is fine with Balasankar. It is his organization that wishes to honour you this December. Will you come to Madras to accept the honour?'

'I've written to say yes.' Lila would help me work everything out so it would not harm Kalyani. She was clever at that kind of thing.

'That is good. Now, here's the plan. Now that you have agreed, I will film you in the next week or two. In December you can sing at a concert, we will show the film, I will get someone big to preside.'

'The ticket to Madras will cost a lot,' I said. 'I have to take my boy with me.'

'Don't worry about all that. You will be paid.'

As the woman talked, she seemed to be swelling up, somehow. Her manner was still respectful, but her eyes were hard and shrewd. What did she really want from me? I am an old woman, I thought; I need money; I may not be as good as I once was at judging the difference between good and bad, true and false.

I looked up and found she had asked me a question and was waiting.

'What did you ask?' I said.

'I said, do you ever teach the old dance plays to your students? Can you teach me the "Kalyanikkarai Kuravanji"?'

'I set up a class, to teach, but who wanted to come to a dasi's house? Not the local children. Once in a while, the dancers in Madras would come to learn the old dances. People like you. But they went to Samu Vathyar or to his son Velu, to the men – they didn't come looking for me. So, this money you are going to give me,' I said. 'You will pay it in December?'

'No, no, the money I will pay you is different from that amount. I will pay two thousand five hundred rupees, but only when the whole work I need you for is finished. This is for the filming. In December, NATAC will pay you for your ticket to Madras, for your stay, and for the concert itself.'

Two thousand five hundred rupees! It sounded like a lot of money. I said, 'Can I have some of it now? I have an obligation—'

'How much?'

'Five hundred.' I blurted out, without thinking, the exact amount the contractor had wanted for the repairs. If I'd had any sense I'd have asked for more and the difference would have seen the boy and me through the month.

'All right, five hundred. You'll have to sign a receipt saying I have given you an advance.'

The hairs on my arms and on my neck stood up again. People who brought papers and receipts were, in my experience, liars and thieves. But she was offering a good deal of money. Was it a good deal of money? Perhaps it was what she spent in a month on – on a new pair of bangles. Should I have bargained, asked for more? Would she think me naive?

It would be pleasant to have the pots and pans for cooking, instead of having them under all the leaks in the roof. The tenant wouldn't be so eager to leave. If he left, it was unlikely that I'd get a new one, with the whole street changing.

The paper she was holding out to me was in English. I could read some words, but most of it made no sense to me.

I suddenly remembered something Velu had said the last time I saw him.

'Tell me about your students in Madras,' I had said.

'The stupid dried-up cows.'

'What are their names?'

'I don't remember any names.' His memory had been washed clean by drink. 'But don't let any of that lot talk you into any kind of deal. Those Madras dancers are all snakes. Remember this. They will rob you blind.'

'Why?' I said. 'What happened?'

'They stole the manuscripts,' he said. 'They stole the olais that had been in my family for so many generations.' But he couldn't, or wouldn't, explain how this had happened.

'You need to sign here – and here,' the woman was saying. She was beginning to sound annoyed.

My hand seized up and I could not sign.

'I will think about all this and let you know,' I said, giving the pen and the receipt back to her.

'What? I thought we had–' She took a deep breath and spoke in a softer voice, 'I thought we had settled everything, Rajayi Amma. I even thought we could begin next Friday morning.'

'Oh, not in the morning,' I said. 'I still have to go to the flower bazaar, and string the jasmine and sell it in the temple.'

'But I'd be *paying* you, so you can spend the day working with me! I don't understand – you are being difficult!'

'No, I am not, Vilasini–'

'*Padma*sini,' she snapped. 'If you knew anything about the dance world in Madras, you'd know who I was.' So she was famous in Madras. All right. But I didn't know who she was. I heard Lila's voice in my head, and Velu's voice, saying, be careful, these Madras dancers are vipers.

'How can I stop working?' I said. 'You may learn a

dance from me or make a photo, a film, for a week, and then you'll go away. But after that, I still have to live, and my boy has to live.'

'Can't you not sell your flowers for just a week? That's all it'll take,' she said. 'After all, the payment should more than cover the earnings you will lose.'

She didn't understand at all. 'If I stop selling flowers, I'll lose my place at the temple gate. There is always someone waiting to grab my place, because it is a good one. Once you lose a place, you can't get it back.'

'Yes, I suppose I wasn't thinking of that. Where do you sit, in the temple, when you are selling flowers?'

'Under the south gopuram. Why?'

'To film you while you are selling flowers. That way both of us could have what we want.'

'Selling flowers has nothing to do with dance.' I didn't want her coming to the temple, making trouble for me there. 'Besides, the temple priests won't like that. There's an Ayyar there who'll make no end of fuss about it.'

'It will reveal women's power.'

'Women's *what*?'

'Nothing. I was joking. I'll come to buy flowers from you. All right, can we meet here on Friday afternoon then?'

'In the afternoon. If my heart agrees to the teaching, I will sign these papers then.'

The woman gathered the papers into angry hands and got up to leave. All honey one second and all mustard-and-sesame the next. Still, I felt inhospitable, turning her away without any food or anything.

'Here, take this fruit,' I said, picking up something

from the basket she herself had brought me. There was nothing else worth offering in the house, there was no milk, and no coffee.

'It is for you,' she said.

'My teeth are bad,' I said, 'and my boy won't eat all this.'

After I had given it to her I regretted it, because I could have stored it, and it would have been a treat for the boy. I felt old and stupid and out of my depth.

I went to get the kungumam pot, but when I came back she was already gone. I stepped outside. The driver was opening the car door for her.

'Go-and-come-back,' I called out. 'Go-and-come-back safely.'

Then I looked up where she was looking, and saw Amalan.

The boy was standing on the hill, watching us. I knew it was him, because no one else climbed up there these days. He started down the slope towards us. There were steps cut into the rock of that slope. The steps were narrow, and barely had enough room for a foot. You had to turn the foot out at an angle to climb them. They were steep, too – each step was more than two feet high. When I was young, I climbed up those steps once a year with Lila to dance in the small temple on the hilltop. I hadn't been there in years. The temple had collapsed into pillars and rubble, the boy said.

Padmasini was pointing at him. 'Look at that boy – he's going to fall.'

'I am afraid that he will, but he never has. He comes down that as if he is walking on level ground, like a Nilagiri mountain goat. That is my boy, Amalan.'

'Your son?'

'Yes.'

Amalan was gaining speed as he picked his way downhill, the heaped broken rock and tar barrels of the new road coming up to meet him. Then he was on level ground and running down the road towards us.

11

Hema

Kalyanikkarai, 9 May 1990

'Find an STD booth in Kalyanikkarai, and call me when you can,' Amma said. She had been nervous and wistful ever since I had agreed to go with Padmasini on her filming trip. 'Not too late in the evening, mind – it isn't safe for a girl to go out alone after dark in places like that.'

'Why don't you come with us, Amma?' I said to her. 'I'm sure Padmasini won't mind. Maybe it'll turn out you have some connection with the place, seeing as you share its name.'

'Would you like to go, Kalyani?' Appa put in. 'I can arrange–'

'No, Balan. Just call me, Hema-love, tell me what you did each day, the people you saw.'

Padmasini had gone to Kalyanikkarai a week ahead of us, and was staying at her ancestral home among the rice fields at the western edge of the town, with her dying father and her mothers. I travelled with Shah, the cinematographer, and Bazullah, his assistant, in a hired van; we reached Kalyanikkarai at about three in the afternoon on a Thursday. The van also transported Shah's cameras and equipment. We had all been booked into rooms at Tamil Nadu Tourism's guest bungalow near the old palace grounds. The van's driver was going to sleep in his vehicle, to look after the larger pieces of equipment, so they needn't be carried in and out of the tourist bungalow.

Padmasini met us at the bungalow. 'I don't need you this evening, Hema,' she said.

I had tried to find out what my duties were, as a member of this team, but it became apparent that Padmasini had given no thought to this question. Perhaps she had asked me to come along on an impulse, and was regretting it. 'Why don't you visit the big temple?' she said, as if she was eager to get rid of me now.

I was relieved to be alone after several hours cooped up in the van with three men. I went to my room to shower and change. I unpacked a few things and laid them out, among them a crumbling book called *A Walking Tour of Callianicarah* by Rachel Carstairs. Amma had borrowed it for me from the Madras Literary Society library. Since there would be plenty of daylight to read by, during the next couple of hours, I took the book with me and set out for the temple.

There was a steep footpath that dropped straight down

into the town, but the more tempting path followed the curve of the hill. Sheets of granite had flowed here under the pressure of some ancient volcano, making these hills and valleys. Granite boulders, breaking off from the mother-rock, were piled one above the other all around the path. Goats grazed on the tussocks of grass that grew around the outcrops of rocks. At a couple of points on the footpath, I caught glimpses of the river beyond the rows of houses. The water seemed an unusual colour, between salmon and rust, but that may have been an optical illusion. Beyond the river, the town thinned out into scattered dwellings among paddy fields and betel nut, sugarcane and coconut plantations, the patches of light and dark green stretching all the way to the horizon.

Ten minutes later, my walk, skirting the ruined palace buildings, brought me to the sacred tank around which the town's four main streets were organized. The temple's fortress-like walls were to the north of the tank. I walked alongside the tank, on the crowded East Main Street; on both sides were street vendors with betel leaves, flowers, brown hills of coconuts, and shops with palm cola and rose soda in green bottles. Beside the south-facing gopuram, there were bananas at outrageous prices because the children wanted to feed the elephant. The elephant belonged to another temple, the mahout said, but he brought it here for two hours every afternoon to make money.

'Feed my poor Gayatri, sister,' he said. 'Neither temple can afford to pay for her food. She must earn for herself.'

Being a complete sucker for animal hard-luck stories, I bought two bunches of bananas for the elephant. I placed them in her trunk, and she popped them into her jolly, smiling sack of a mouth. The mahout made her tap me on the head with her trunk, to bless me, he said, and she dripped elephant snot on me. I wiped it off with my dupatta and went on towards the temple's nearest gopuram. This gopuram, I realized later, was taller and more elaborately decorated with sculptures than the gateways that faced the other three cardinal directions. The finials on top were gilded, and flashed in the evening light. Workmen were constructing scaffolding out of wooden poles all around this gopuram: some kind of repair or renovation was under way.

I walked with the tide of worshippers around the temple's courtyard, first, and then into it, climbing the steps towards the massive pillared halls and the sanctum. Later, in the stone cloister that enclosed the temple's processional pathway, I found a quiet spot, and opened my book.

In the eastern quarter of Callianicarah (Rachel Carstairs had written), a short distance from the banks of the Calliani (the name of the city itself means 'banks of the Calliani'), the Siva temple nestles against granite hills that rise with disconcerting abruptness in the midst of the flat, rolling rice fields.

Like most South Indian temples, an antiquarian well-versed in these matters assures me, the Siva temple at Callianicarah is a palimpsest. The inscription on the inner walls of the temple's southern entrance suggests that the earliest rock-cut part of the temple, partly hollowed out of a granite outcrop, was the work of the Pallava kings, who reigned in these parts during the eighth and ninth centuries AD. Over the next three centuries, the Cholas built the massive sculptured gateway (the south-facing one) and part of the central tower in front of the rock-cut sanctum. The graceful pillared cloister that marks the perimeter of the temple's grounds was probably constructed at the same time.

The Naik kings added the Thousand-Pillared Hall in a more delicate, flamboyantly ornate style. Most of the paintings on the walls of the various buildings and outbuildings were commissioned either by the Naiks or by the early Rajahs of Callianicarah, once vassals of the Naiks, who broke with their masters and became independent princes. These Rajahs also raised the height of the central tower, crowning it with a gigantic cupola, and built the new fort and palace adjacent to the temple. The local people say that an underground passage was built from the palace to the temple, so that the royal family could escape to the sanctuary if the palace was attacked.

A considerable part of the palace has fallen into disuse and decay, for lack of upkeep, but the first Rajah's descendants still occupy those sections of it that stand intact.

I went back to look at the paintings in the failing light. On the thousand-pillared hall's ceiling, wasp-waisted, attractive women drawn in grainy earth colours twirled their fashionable costumes in a press of tavil drummers and nagaswaram pipers, animals and people. On the walls of the smaller shrines scattered about the main temple, and of the cloister where I had sat, the sculptors of a later, less particular age had caught the gestalt of ceremonial processions. The dancers in the friezes were compressed into squat dwarfish curves, all hips and breasts and jewellery.

Trudging uphill past the palace, in the dusk, on my way back to the tourist bungalow, I tried to identify the buildings that still housed the descendants of the most recent rulers of Kalyanikkarai, but no structure in that mass of crumbling stone and brick seemed in the least bit habitable.

'I hope the woman isn't going to be difficult,' Padmasini said, the next day. 'Dasis have always been notorious for their mercenary ways.' She had packed her travelling circus into two vehicles. I was in her car, while Shah and Bazullah rode in the van with the equipment. Padmasini's driver was honking and cursing under his breath: the vehicles were inching down East Main Street, surrounded by a crowd of laughing children who were daring each other to thump the car's windows. 'Tomorrow,' Padmasini said, leaning towards her driver, 'we take the long route – I had no idea the shortcut was going to delay us so much.'

'Difficult in what way?' I said.

'She wouldn't sign the contract the last time I met her. She's laying down conditions about when she wants to be filmed – she wants us to work around the hours when she buys her flowers and sells them at the temple.'

We drove past a sign that said 'Musicians' Street'.

'Is that how Rajayi makes her living?' I said. I had learned her name only the previous day, from Shah, in fact. All through the preparations for this trip, Padmasini and my father had continued to refer to her as 'the dasi', and 'the woman'. 'Doesn't she teach dance?'

'Dasi women never had any business sense,' Padmasini said. 'They wouldn't know the first thing about setting up a viable school.'

The house we stopped at was the last one on the street. There had been houses beyond it, but they had been demolished, and lorries were carting the rubble away.

Rajayi's door opened. The way Padmasini had described Rajayi, I suppose I had expected her to look rather unattractive, but the woman who stepped through the doorway made my breath stop in my throat. The flesh of her face slanted away from striking cheekbones. She was making no particular attempt to please anyone. She stood in the doorway for a moment, absently drawing the end of her sari pallu over her right shoulder. Her hair was almost white, and her eyes were hooded; she had a quiet poise, an air of reserve even, that was contradicted by the sensuality of her mahogany skin, shimmering faintly with sweat, the huge vermilion kungumam on her forehead, and her betel-stained mouth. My first thought was that she had no business, at around seventy, to be as beautiful as that.

Shah fired up the generator in the van, adding to the racket made by the lorries. The neighbours came out of their houses to stare.

'What is in that van?' Rajayi said.

'The generator.'

'But the neighbours—'

Padmasini pursed her lips. 'It is necessary. We can't rely on the power in this house.'

Bazullah unrolled lengths of cable from the van and brought them into the house. I would have liked to do his job – tripods, umbrellas, light-metres, and some heavy lifting – at least I would have learned something about making a film. But Shah thought it would please my father to learn that his daughter had been protected from menial work.

'If your father notices this film,' Shah had said, in the van coming up from Madras, 'I'll be a made man.'

As he stepped into the house, Bazullah knocked his head against a board that hung over the door. It came loose. He tried to put it back, but the wall had given way around the nail, and it fell to the ground and cracked slightly. He apologized.

'You must be the tallest lad that came in here since that board was put up,' Rajayi said, her face relaxing into a sudden smile. 'That board has been up there for nearly forty years. Maybe its time has come. My mother hated it, and even fought the government about it.'

Shah had his camera out and was filming everything. 'My name is Shah,' he said to Rajayi. He was from Gujarat, originally, but spoke Tamil tolerably well. He filmed the cracked board. And he must have filmed me standing on that veranda, watching Rajayi with my mouth open. All the years I had raged silently against the brand of sexiness Padmasini seemed to have patented, I had also been my own interlocutor, and had accused myself of being intolerant, of fighting all female sexuality because I didn't like sexuality in myself. But here was Rajayi: here was unselfconscious and effortless sensual power in an old woman, in every way the antithesis of the frantic, eyelid-batting, not-sure-if-I'm-sexy-or-spiritual-but-look-at-me-look-at-me *faux* seductiveness that pretty much stood in for all emoting among brahmin dancers. Perhaps that was it, then: dasi versus brahmin mores.

Padmasini made Rajayi sit on the swing with the basket she had brought from the market, full of white fragrant jasmine, red kanakambaram dry as paper, bittersweet green kolundhu. She made her sign the contract while Shah positioned the cameras on their tripods and checked the light.

'Don't you have any proper jewellery?' Padmasini asked, putting the contract in her bag. 'Any gold?'

'No,' Rajayi said. 'Why?'

'We want to show you as a part of ancient Hindu culture – it would be nice to have some colour, some jewellery.' Padmasini did not quite say, 'I wish you were more glamorous,' but she looked as if she had said it.

Rajayi laughed. 'Well, putting shiny things on an old woman's throat and wrists won't make her look like a cinema actress.'

Padmasini sent Bazullah to the car, to bring her own jewellery case. She took out a necklace and a pair of bangles and made Rajayi wear them. Shah went over and pinned a microphone to Rajayi's sari.

She touched it with the tip of her finger. 'What is this?'

'Never mind.' Padmasini's smile was tight. 'Let's get on with the filming.'

'It's a mic – so we can record your voice,' Shah said. Then he said, 'Sing something for me, Rajayi Amma.'

'*En mel Chittirai banuvai pol metthavum kaigirai, Manmadha,*' Rajayi sang. You are like the midsummer sun, burning me up, Manmadha, god of love.

Shah put on his earphones and listened. He frowned.

'Her breathing – it's moving the sari border. I'm getting a disturbance.'

Padmasini went to Rajayi and pulled her sari this way and that. Shah listened again.

'Now – do you want to see how you look?' Shah said. He was about thirty years old. He had a nondescript face and a slightly receding chin, but his expression was kind. 'Here, you can look into the camera here – look, this is when Baz here knocked the board off, and here you are. If anything bothers you, let me know.'

'Shah,' Padmasini said, smacking her hand down on the swing where she had settled herself beside Rajayi, 'can't we just–'

'I'd like her to get comfortable with the camera,' he said. 'It will make a difference.'

Rajayi bent forward and looked where he was pointing.

'It looks like the face of a stranger,' she declared. She patted her hair down. 'Is my hair all right? I want to look nice in your photo.'

'Yes, yes it's fine,' Padmasini said.

'What do you want me to do?' Rajayi said.

'Just string the flowers like you always do,' Shah said, 'and talk at the same time.'

'That will be difficult,' Rajayi said, 'because I will have to take the flowers straight from the basket. I usually spread them out on the swing beside me. You need to be able to see each stem if you want to pick the flowers up one at a time.'

Padmasini's substantial behind had occupied the spot where the flowers were usually spread. She produced a powder compact from her handbag, powdered her nose, checked her face from different angles, and put it away. 'Let's get started,' she said briskly. 'Shah, am I in the frame?'

'No. Did you want to be? I thought you wanted to focus on Rajayi – all right, we're set.'

Two flowers above, two below, the banana fibre whipped around them, and then Rajayi's fingers were dancing by themselves, and as she talked, the garland she was making grew longer and longer and flowed over the edge of the swing.

'Tell us about your life, Rajayi Amma,' Padmasini said, looking at the camera. She sounded like a schoolteacher speaking to a small child. 'Tell us about your life.'

'Hmm. My life. What's to talk about?'

'Anything. Just *please* hurry up.' Padmasini had picked up a jasmine bud without noticing it; she was rolling it between her fingers, crushing it. The perfume floated up.

'After the rains, in a jasmine garden,' Rajayi said, looking at the basket full of wet buds, 'the moisture starts the scent and ravishes the senses. The garden at the back of this house was full of flowers. The coral jasmine, the cannonball creeper, so sweet that the snakes came to smell its fragrance, and the jasmine my mother trained on the trellis. The town boys kept ripping the jasmine plants off the trellis, years ago, but I kept planting new slips.'

Padmasini made an impatient noise. 'I didn't want you to talk about gardens. Tell us something about your music, your dance. Start again, Shah. Rajayi Amma, tell us about your ancestors.'

'Um – my grandmother Jagadambal could do the Simhanandanam – draw a lion with her feet – have you heard of that? They spread muslin-cloth on wet sand, and the lion's body would take shape wherever she stepped on the cloth. The sand would show through, you see. Of course, the important thing was to do it from memory, without looking down to see if the lion's shape was coming out right. The rhythm was a hundred and eight beats. She would leap from the tail to the eye, and when she opened the lion's eye, it would be the hundred and eighth beat exactly. The Raja–'

'Can you sing the notes for this?'

'–the Raja gave her a pair of gold bangles, my mother said, for this feat.'

'Sing us the notes.'

'I have the notes in a book in my grandmother's writing, but I can't sing it offhand.'

'What songs *can* you remember?'

Rajayi seemed to be searching for a thread in her thoughts. 'When I was a child, my mother took me to Samu Vathyar – he was a great teacher here, the son of her master – for my dance classes. She said he might teach me the Simhanandanam, but he said: the time for this is past. He said, I will teach you dances that these ignoramuses will understand. He was always cursing the ignorance of the audiences, because he had known better.'

Padmasini asked questions faster than Rajayi could answer them.

'What did Samu Vathyar teach you? Sing that.'

'Wait a minute, Padmasini. It's hard to get the pitch right. There is no tambura, see, nothing to accompany my old voice.'

'We're wasting film. Don't worry about the pitch. Just sing it, Rajayi Amma, you sound just fine.'

'If you had told me you wanted me to sing, I would have prepared my voice, set my pitch, chosen a few songs and rehearsed them. I didn't know singing was part of it. Now I've gone and forgotten the lyrics halfway through.'

'What were the gestures for that? Sing it, show us the gestures. Shah, did you get that? Good, excellent. Now sing another song.'

Each time Rajayi stopped, Padmasini became more annoyed. Her fingers tapped the swing irritably. Every now and then a lorry went past towards the construction site, and made everything shake, and the sound kept going off, Shah said, so Rajayi had to start again. Then when she was almost at the end of one particular padham, a blast from the hill shook the whole house, and they had to start over.

Padmasini looked around the bare room with the eyes of a scavenger bird.

'Bring down those pictures,' she said to Bazullah. The

205

boy took down three pictures. She held one picture on her lap so that Shah could film her with it.

Samu Vathyar, Rajayi said.

I flinched when Padmasini nearly dropped the second picture, but Rajayi caught it.

'That picture is of my mother, Kanaka,' Rajayi said. 'Let me dust it first.'

'There isn't time,' Padmasini said. 'Rajayi Amma, tell me about the woman in the photo.'

'My mother was the one who taught me to sing the love padhams, the long and difficult ones.'

'Sing one.' And when Rajayi finished, 'Teach me the abhinayam for that song, and Shah will film it.'

Rajayi started to teach her, but Padmasini's arms stretched out in front of Rajayi's chest and face. Rajayi shrank back to give her space. Padmasini did her own gestures; she did them before Rajayi could do hers. Padmasini's left arm caught the wire and unhooked the mike from Rajayi's sari.

'It's a muddle,' Rajayi said, stopping. 'Are you teaching me or am I teaching you? My movements won't look right if I cannot stretch my arms – thank goodness Samu Vathyar is not here to see me making a fool of myself like this.'

'Now tell me about the man in this picture.' Padmasini was holding the third picture on her lap. The man in it looked familiar – I was sure I had seen him, or maybe the picture, somewhere.

'I am tired now,' Rajayi said. 'I am an old woman. And I have to finish the flowers.'

'Of course, Rajayi Amma. But I am paying you, and paying for the generator and for these people helping me. I have to get more done today.'

'Very well. That man in the picture was Sundaram Iyer. He was the most famous advocate in these parts. He was famous even in Madras. Everyone just called him the Vakil.' Of course – Padmasini's uncle; I had seen a similar picture in Madras, in her house. Did Rajayi know of his relationship to Padmasini? It appeared not.

'Who was he to you?' Padmasini said.

Rajayi hesitated. 'When he was young,' she said, 'he was as handsome as the god of love. They said when he stood up in court, his opponents trembled. He had a great knowledge of music. It was the music that drew him to this house. After my dedication at the temple–'

'Were you dedicated?' Padmasini cut in. 'Wasn't the dedication ceremony banned?'

'Not yet. We had to ask the Magistrate for permission, if we wanted to be dancers and have the rite to marry the god.'

'Really? Amazing – did the Magistrate give his permission?'

'Oh yes, he did. I signed a document in front of him.'

'Do you have any of those documents?'

'I don't know – it has been – twenty-five, thirty years since I even thought about any of these things.' Rajayi's eyes swivelled around to a trunk in the corner of the room. Padmasini's gaze followed hers, and alighted on the trunk like talons.

Padmasini made Bazullah drag the trunk out in front of the camera. She made him force the lid open.

'You must have some old manuscripts in here,' she said. She put her hands into the trunk and rummaged about. 'Surely you have some – old compositions, lyrics, written down by your mother or grandmother? Those song books you mentioned?'

'No,' Rajayi half closed the trunk again. 'No, I have no song books that would be of interest to you.'

Padmasini sighed. 'I have heard people in Madras say: who needs the old repertoire, who needs these dasis and nattuvanars? Because they – people like Velu, for instance – don't really teach their students anything. So selfish, wanting everything to die with them. But I – I say, they still have so much to give the world.' Her hands were still fishing inside the half-closed trunk. She drew out a paper. 'Is this the document?' she said. 'The one about your dedication?'

'What are you doing?' Rajayi said, reaching for the paper. Padmasini was holding it up in front of Shah's camera.

'This is a very important part of history – it must be filmed, Rajayi Amma.'

'*No!*' Rajayi's voice was suddenly sharp. 'No, it has that – that word in it, that word *prostitute*. I don't want you to film it–'

But Padmasini signalled to Shah that he must continue. He smiled apologetically and went on doing what he was doing.

'It will help people understand more about your past.'

'*No*, it won't. If they haven't understood all these years, why should this make them understand? Muthulakshmi Amma used the word 'prostitute' – she was an MLA, a famous woman with ties to our community, and she made the law which stopped our dance in the temples. Do you know how my mother fought against the word?' Rajayi said.

'Tell me more,' Padmasini said. Shah made close-up shots of the document, then panned to Rajayi's distraught face.

'My mother said that word was our downfall.' Rajayi's voice was shaking. 'As long as we refused to use that word about ourselves, we were safe. The Vakil and I even wrote a petition to the government about it – yes, that man in the picture – and we took it around and got two hundred and ninety signatures of other dasis on it. That word took everything from us, and you want to film that document. Can a mere name take away a *man*'s livelihood, eat his wealth up from month to month, make an outcaste of him?'

'We will not film it, then, if you feel so strongly about it.' Padmasini signalled to Shah and the camera swivelled away, but it was already done. She pointed to herself. The camera turned towards her. She clicked her tongue. 'It's so sad. A word, a name, can destroy a woman. It happened to Sita-Devi herself. Rama's own wife she was, and all it took was the gossip of washermen to make them try her by fire.'

Padmasini forced the trunk's lid higher, covering her nose against the dust. She pulled out four strings of ankle bells. One pair was strung on fine twisted rope, once white, perhaps, but now discoloured. Who knew how many years of sweat and dust and dancing the discoloration represented? This pair was wound tightly into a pair strung on red rope.

'Why have you kept these bells all these years?' Padmasini said, holding them up so that the Shah could film her doing 'research'. 'Is it for sentimental reasons?'

'Samu Vathyar chose both sets of bells, matching them for perfect pitch. I keep them to honour him, and to honour the dances he taught me. Anyway, who'll pay good money for bells? They buy brass by weight. There's not much weight there.'

'Can I take them then? I could use them for an exhibit.'

Rajayi looked flustered and distressed. 'I – I don't know.' She got up suddenly, took a cup, filled it from the pot and had a long drink of water. Shah filmed this too.

'Can you give back the bells?' Rajayi asked at the end of the session. 'I would like to keep them. And I must return these to you.' She unhooked the clasp of the necklace that Padmasini had lent her, and slipped the bangles off her wrists. 'Oh – by the way, my boy, Amalan, he says you promised to get him a necklace or a pendant or some such.'

'He wanted one like this–' Padmasini fingered the pendant that hung from the pearl necklace around her own neck. 'This one is gold and garnets, of course, but I'll get him a cheaper imitation version. I probably have one lying around somewhere in my luggage, or I'll buy one on East Main Street.'

'I have told him to stop pestering you about it, but

he has set his heart on it. If he takes something into his head, he won't let go of it. '

'Don't worry,' Padmasini said. 'I'll get him something. Here are the bells – perhaps you will sell them to me if you won't give them to me.'

'Let me think about it.'

'All right. I will come by again this evening, and learn some more padhams from you.'

'Not this evening,' Rajayi said. 'I'll be late leaving for the temple – I haven't eaten yet – and I'm going to have to run all the way there. I will have no strength to sing when I get back.'

All around us was the debris of our visit – banana fibre and flowers that had fallen from the basket while Rajayi was making garlands; cable-ties, packaging from some equipment Shah had unwrapped, a bulb that had gone out on one of the lights and been replaced, the pictures that had been taken down from the walls, cups of water, a plate of biscuits that Rajayi had brought out for us when we came in, the ankle bells, documents from the trunk.

Bazullah was looping cables around his forearm. It was clear that he wasn't going to be asked to clear up.

Padmasini said, 'I'll be here at noon tomorrow, then.' The driver opened the car door for her and she got in.

Suddenly, seemingly out of nowhere, a boy appeared on the other side of the car. He was about fourteen or fifteen and skinny. His ribs, heaving slightly from exertion, showed through his bare chest. His body gleamed with moisture; water was running from the shirt he held clutched to his belly, making streaks down his shorts. His eyes were lined with kohl, and his fingernails were painted scarlet. He stuck his head in at Padmasini's window.

'Can I have the pendant today?' he said.

The driver ran around the car, took him by the arm and yanked him away from the window.

'Don't,' Padmasini said softly. 'I haven't finished my business with his mother. Better not upset her.'

'Okay, madam,' the driver said. 'Okay, but you watch out, you pansy bastard, I'll get you one of these days.'

'The pendant?' the boy insisted softly.

'If you keep asking me, boy,' Padmasini snapped suddenly, 'I'll get annoyed, and you'll get nothing. If you shut up, maybe I'll get it for you.'

'All right. Don't tell my Amma I asked you,' he said.

'Go away now,' Padmasini said, 'and quit bothering me. Hema, get in the car, will you?'

'I'll join Shah and you at the tourist bungalow in a bit,' I said. 'I want to take a little walk.'

The boy hummed a film song as he went into the house, throwing the front door open with such exuberant energy that it swung around and smacked into the wall. I followed him back in.

'Eley, Amalan,' Rajayi called out, 'you're showering us with plaster again. Can't you open the door like a human being?'

'Look what I got.' He grinned, unrepentant, and unwrapped the shirt. A long black fish flopped out. 'The Ayyar saw me, but the fat old sod couldn't keep up with me. Can we have a piece for lunch? Have you made the rice?'

'I'm the one who answers for your thieving ways, Amalan – *I* can't run from the Ayyar, do you understand?' Rajayi took the fish from him. 'Oh–' She looked at me blankly. 'I thought you had gone. Amalan, this lady is from Madras. Wash your hands and speak to her.'

'The fish are killing each other in the temple tank,' Amalan said to me. 'If you put puffed rice on the top step, they will climb eight steps to reach it, they're so hungry. They'll just walk up the steps like creatures with legs.'

'There are too many fish in that tank,' Rajayi said. She had taken out a sickle. She placed her foot on the wooden handle and, crouching down, began to scale the sides of the fish against the sickle's edge.

'Will you share our food?' She paused. 'But perhaps you are a brahmin? Do you eat fish?'

'I love fish,' I said.

She smiled. 'Then stay.'

She sliced just below the bright red gills, reached into the cut and pulled the guts out. Amalan collected the guts and scales on a piece of paper, placed them on the back doorstep and whistled. A pair of cats appeared and ate everything, paper and all.

Rajayi cut the fish into steaks and rubbed them with salt, turmeric and chilli powder. She put a tiny dribble of oil into a pan on the kerosene stove and dropped the fish into it. I carefully hung the pictures in their old spots and put the little sandalwood garlands back on them. I made a neat pile of the packaging and put the documents and bells back into the trunk.

The house filled up with the smell of frying.

I looked around the big open room where we sat, and around the kitchen. There was no place where cooked rice might be stored – there was no fridge, and no covered pot on any of the shelves. We had not given her time to cook rice.

'I need to buy something, Rajayi Amma,' I said. 'I'll be back in a couple of minutes.'

The tiny Annapoorna 'Meals Ready' Hotel at the corner of Musicians' Street and East Main Street took less than five minutes to pack three helpings of lemon rice into leaf packages.

'I've brought some rice,' I said, coming back into Rajayi's house.

Rajayi wiped her hands on her sari and took the package from me. 'You bought food? For me – for us? Child – it is good of you. I just got started washing the rice – I haven't even put it on the stove.'

Rajayi brought out three plates and began to spoon out the contents of the leaf bowls. I found the broom behind the kitchen door and began to sweep up the flowers.

'No, no, you are our guest!' Rajayi exclaimed, taking the broom from me. 'Come and eat with Amalan and me. Are you Padmasini's daughter? Did she ask you to bring the food?'

'I'm her student, Rajayi Amma. My name is Hema. And no, she didn't.'

'Do you like the fish?' Amalan said.

'It's delicious.'

'That Madras lady promised that if I made Amma teach her padhams and all, she would buy me a pendant like the one she was wearing. Has she gone to the jewellery shop yet, do you know?'

'I don't think so.'

After we had eaten, Amalan reached into a cardboard box in a corner of the room and came back with a blouse of some kind.

'Look at my waistcoat,' he said. He pronounced it 'vas-coot'. 'The actors in the cinema wear these.'

Rajayi was putting away the leftovers. She looked up, frowning. 'Where did you get that?'

'My friend at the tourist bungalow gave it to me,' Amalan said. 'He *gave* it to me. Some actors from the koothu troupe left it behind in the bungalow, but my friend couldn't sell it.' His words came out in a rush. 'Cinema dancers have the beads and stones sewn on so they won't shake when they dance. I'm going to be a cinema dancer. My aunt Lila in Madras is one. I'm visiting her this year. Have you seen that cinema *Salangai Oli*? The best bit is where it is raining and Kamal Haasan drinks from a bottle and dances on the edge of the well.' His eyes danced; he sang the song from the film. 'Thakita thadimi thakita thadimi thandaana–'

'I don't know what is so fascinating about that song. About that saniyan cinema dance,' Rajayi snorted. 'This boy can dance,' she said to me, 'but he is in love with the cinema.'

'Look at this cloth – like moss, look.' Amalan stroked the waistcoat's velvet against the nap, his scarlet nails startling against the emerald-green fabric. 'I want that pendant for this spot, in the middle of the chest. It has red and green peacocks in it. Their tails are fanned out, and their beaks are touching. Amma will sew it on for me.'

'That will be beautiful,' I said.

'Amalan,' Rajayi said, 'have a bath before you go out again. Your clothes are a disgrace.'

'I can't help it,' he said. 'The powder from the rocks falls on everything. And I used my shirt to catch the fish.'

'Have you been watching them blasting the hill again? One of these days a piece of rock is going to knock you out.' Rajayi hoisted her basket on to her hip. 'If you take water from the sump, fill it up again. And mind your manners and talk to Hema, because I have to go.'

'Thank you for the lunch, Rajayi Amma,' I said.

'Oh, child,' she said. She bent down, touched my cheek for a second. 'I should thank you. I will go-and-come-back. I will see you tomorrow.'

'Rajayi was a revelation,' I said to Amma on the phone that evening. 'When she did the gestures for the padhams, she didn't look in the least bit *spiritual* to me.' For some reason this discovery filled me with delight.

Amma laughed. 'No, I'm sure she didn't.'

'She was too – *real* – for that brand of bullshit. Too *street*. So real, the Madras phonies will never be able to tell how good she is. And her son, Amalan – he's a *beautiful* boy, huge flashing eyes, a bit of a cross-dresser, I think, and crazy about Kamal Haasan. That's odd – he's too young to be her son – he's probably fourteen–'

'Sixteen,' Amma said.

'Really? How do you know?'

'I – oh, Padmasini said something, I think.'

'He's small for his age, then. You know what he did, after Rajayi left? He sprang up on the rim of the well in the backyard and did this absolutely brilliant riff on Kamal dancing on the rim of the well in *Salangai Oli*. He actually *danced*, didn't just goof around the way Kamal did.'

'Oh, that sounds dangerous,' Amma said. 'Hema, don't let him do that again.'

'Of course I won't. As soon as I figured out how to stop him without startling him into falling in, I did. How are things with you?'

'All right. There was a locksmith here today when I came back from the library. Your Vijaya Paati is changing the storeroom locks, or some such thing. Call me again tomorrow, will you, kanna? I miss you.'

12

Rajayi
Kalyanikkarai, 9 May 1990

I had to run all the way to the temple, since I was late, and I was breathless when I got there. I sold most of the flowers, to my great relief, and bought milk for Amalan and lamp oil for myself on the way home.

'Look at her strutting along,' Muthayya's wife said loudly through the window when I passed her house. 'Stupid city people, coming here to make a noise and keep company with women like that.'

My tenant was sitting on his part of the veranda. 'Why do they want to make a film about you?' he said. 'I don't know if I like it.'

'Be patient,' I said. 'They will give me some money, and I will have the roof repaired.'

Amalan had picked the stones from the rice and cooked it while I was gone, and we both ate it with the leftover fish. We sat outside on the veranda and watched the moon come up over the rooftops, the bats skittering about under the tiles, the owl that sat on the electric wire. The owl, in its turn, watched the bandicoot in the gutter.

When the owl gave up on the bandicoot, I filled up the clay lamp with oil, put in a wick, and lit it. I sat on the swing and let my shadow rock on the wall, keeping me company. I kept the tube-light off to save money. I switched it on only when Amalan was around and awake. He was asleep now, curled up on the mat like a small child. I covered him with an old sari. He was looking thinner than usual, smelling like a mouse – sixteen-year-old boys seem to smell like mice no matter how often they have baths.

Because there had been people in it all day, the house felt empty after they had gone. Voices floated in from the street. Muthayya's new granddaughter was crying, and the bells on the ends of the cradle tinkled softly as her mother rocked her asleep. The trunk was at my feet, where the helper boy had pulled it out. Padmasini had held out the things in it, and the man had made photos of them. The girl, Hema, had put everything back in the trunk.

If you could sell memories for cash, the things inside it would have gone too. I suppose that was what I was doing. Selling my memories to a woman from the city.

I had not sold the trunk, though its paint was almost gone. I had not sold the swing where he used to sit, while I sang and accompanied myself on the veenai, my Vakil, his silver betel leaf box beside him, gleaming intermittently as the swing moved and it caught the fitful light of the lamps. There was plenty of money for oil those days, and we lit six of the big brass lamps, each one with five or seven wicks. I trimmed the wicks carefully to please my mother. Each flame had to be round as a gold bead, she said.

When I finished singing, the Vakil would follow me to my room. I wonder sometimes if the tenant stands by the window, as the Vakil and I did, looking out at the moon. There the Vakil would take things out of his bag that were only for me, not for my family: books for me to read, flowers for my hair, bangles. Once he bought me three saris of exactly the same design and colour, because they were on sale. He was pleased with his bargain. Funny how men can be wonderfully clever in their professions and have so little common sense. He would leave his gold glasses on the bust of Gandhi-Thatha on the dressing table. That bust was smashed by the police, I think; it wasn't here any more when I came back from the sharanaalayam. I should ask Lila if she remembers what happened to it.

This morning I was conscious of nothing more than that Padmasini was crowding me, confusing me. Yet, when I think about it, I realize that I enjoyed myself. Other than Lila, whom I had seen exactly six times since she left for Madras so many decades ago, there was no one left in my life who spoke the same language as me. I was so angry with Velu when he betrayed my trust that I swore I would never say another word to him; and yet, when he came back to Kalyanikkarai, we wore the night out talking.

The things in the trunk pulled at me. So I brought the little clay lamp over, set it down near me, and opened the lid again. Before I knew it, I was seeing faces in front of me that I had long forgotten, as if it was yesterday that I had seen them, not forty or fifty years ago.

The document they had made a photo of in the morning was drawn up by a lawyer who could write English. He came to our house the day after Samu Vathyar said I was ready to dance in front of an audience. He was the same one who had helped my aunt Komala's brothers seize all her land.

'This is ridiculous,' my mother said to the lawyer, 'getting the white man's permission to do what our ancestors have done for generations. What is the Raja thinking, I wonder. Does he know about these things?'

The lawyer shrugged. He drafted the document for us, with my mother watching.

Petition of Miss Rajalatchmi (Rajayi), age 16, of Kalyanikkarai

With the permission of my mother, Kanakambujam, I wish to be dedicated to the Kalyanikkarai Siva temple, as I am not willing to be married. I wish to continue our house name. My mother also is of this profession. I now request permission to be a prostitute according to our religion. I request that I may be sent before the Medical Officer.

Dated: 15.9.1937

'What's this about the medical officer?' my mother asked, when the lawyer translated the finished petition for her. He had slurred over the word 'prostitute'; I had heard it, but she had not.

'Uh – ah – Kanakamma, all women of the – profession – have to be examined – for ah – diseases,' the lawyer said, fiddling with his pen and his inkstand.

'Are you saying we are prostitutes?'

'No – yes, well, you have to say that. It's here on the petition. It's the wording they want because of the new law, it can't be helped. Our Raja held off as long as he could, but apparently the Dorais in the military have another epidemic of the clap on their hands.'

'*Prostitutes!*' my mother cried. 'That is not what we are. My sister Komala used that word too, and I refused to listen to her. She learned the word from our worst enemies. That Kokku Missy, the Christian woman. We are dasis, under the protection of king and temple–'

'All that is changing, Kanaka,' the lawyer cut in, packing his bag with documents. 'There's soon going to be no difference between the way they treat the bazaar women and people like you.'

'That will never happen–'

'Haven't you noticed?' he said, huffing with exasperation, putting his bag down and spreading out his hands. 'You've been raided by the police more than once – doesn't that mean anything to you? All around you, for the last few years, the singers, the drummers, the nagaswaram players, and the dasi folk have been selling their houses to go to the city, to look for work, to look for husbands or patrons, to act in the cinema, to join political movements. All your people, one by one. Even your sister. Why don't you go with them?'

'This is my land, this is my calling, this is my house.'

'Listen, Kanaka–'

'Besides,' my mother said, nodding towards the temple, 'I have promised *him*.'

Soon after Komala left for Nallur to live with her Eurasian patron, two of my mother's and Komala's young cousins had fallen ill with the smallpox. My mother had tucked a sprig of neem on the doorframe to warn her neighbours away from the contagion, and nursed the children. Boiling the rice gruel, consoling her aunt, fanning the girls in their beds, she wondered if the goddess was showing her anger at Komala's defiance. In a panic, she promised the goddess that if the disease spared Lila and me, she would dedicate me in the temple.

The goddess of the pox took the younger niece at the end of the week; the elder one finished up so scarred that it was decided that she would be married off to a man of our own community, since she was no longer fit to dance. The dasi girl's face was her fortune; there was no point in teaching dance to a girl who could not attract a generous patron. Lila and I were untouched. My mother felt that she owed Siva-Peruman something.

The lawyer got our signatures on the petition, shook his head in despair, and left.

My mother was preparing the offerings for the dedication rite when her sister Komala turned up unannounced. This turning up was a habit with her.

'You are condemning Rajayi to lifelong slavery,' she said. 'To prostitution.'

'What a word to use,' Kanaka gasped. 'And you a woman of our community!'

'What are you? A woman without a husband! Does that not say "prostitute"? If someone wants to insult a man, what does he call him? A tevadiya's child, a bastard.'

'Some of us have sold our bodies, perhaps. Women who could not get a patron. But was I not like my patron's second wife?'

'You were nothing. A woman without self-respect.'

'But the upper-caste women, the pappathi wives, are they any better off? Their profession is cooking and cleaning and bearing children; they are mistreated by husbands, by mothers-in-law; if their husbands die, they wear widows' beige, and have their heads shaved, and spend the rest of their lives treated like beasts.'

'Yes, I know,' Komala said. 'They are oppressed too, like us, denied their rights. We are all slaves to men, and men are slaves to religion. It's religion that we need to do away with.'

'Is this what Kokku Missy is saying these days?' My mother was bewildered by the new rhetoric.

'I haven't seen Rachel in two years,' Komala said. 'I've been working with the Self-Respecters. You must have heard of Periyar.'

'Ramasami Naicker, that godless rebel? Of all the people in the world – the one who says god doesn't exist?'

My mother said Komala had fallen into the egotistical cycle of having faith and losing it. To lapse, to be disillusioned, is to have entertained the illusion in the first place that god took a personal interest in one's affairs.

'Did Siva-Peruman break the hand of death when it fell on our niece?' Komala cried. 'Did he poke our brothers' eyes out, then, when they took all my land and money? Get it into your head, god has gone away and left us to fend for ourselves.'

My mother's faith was much humbler and more practical than her sister's, and therefore it was also steadfast.

'Who looks after every living thing?' she said. 'Not a blade of grass can grow on this earth without god. If there is no god, then who keeps that and that in place?' The moon, the stars.

Komala loved a battle. How, when my mother tried to justify her choices, she would shake her head – no, no, no, you've got it all wrong – until my mother would come to me and say, 'If everyone – even my own sister – sees this one way and only a few of us see it another way, we must be wrong.' She would search my eyes. 'Do you think I was wrong all along?'

When I was young, I could never think of a good answer. When I grew older, I said, in a tone as fierce as my aunt Komala's: 'You are right – there is nothing wrong with our profession. They should not seize our land and our livelihood from us – they are not seizing the men's land, and they are not stealing the livelihood of the brahmins in the temple. Brahmin singers are praised for their music, and are called artists. Why should we not be recognized for the same things? You are right, Amma, you were right all along!'

On the occasion of my dedication, Komala suddenly

225

conceded victory. Perhaps she felt something tugging at her – something of her childhood with my mother, all the love and regret on both sides. 'You believe what you need to believe,' she sighed. 'I shouldn't be trying to change your mind. Take care of my Lila, and of yourself. This time, I will leave you an address: write to me.'

When our anxious relatives asked her to go to Madras with them, my mother refused. 'I promised to dedicate Rajayi at the temple. My promise saved the life of my child,' she said. 'One can't break a promise just because it's hard to keep.'

What was to say? Belief was not a matter of choice. For my mother, our Siva-Peruman of the big temple was just there, like this swing, and could hardly be wished away by loss of faith. He had saved us once, from the smallpox; this time, he might not help. There was no guarantee – whoever said there would be? But our lives were tied up with him. One did not stop feeding one's husband, my mother said, because he had become feeble and could not work any more. One did not turn out the dog that had protected one's home for years simply because one night the robbers came and took everything one had. One did not reject the god in the big temple because he had been impotent against this robber without a face who had taken our livelihood and our art from us. This movement against our customs, these people who wrote in the newspapers, these lawyers who seized our lands, these temples who terminated our services, these high-caste women on the street who sneered at us now, though once we sang and danced at their weddings – how, my mother said, was Siva-Peruman to deal with all of them?

Was my mother really keeping her side of a bargain made when it seemed as if god was setting a price on our survival? Was it a sacrifice? Or was it fear and shock and inability to move? A stone from a slingshot scatters the flock of wildfowl, though it strikes only one bird. Sometimes it seemed to me that my mother was that one bird, stunned by the sudden changes, unable to soar up and away with the rest of the flock. She felt that if our art was forfeit, there would be nothing left.

'What will I do if I'm taken away from all this?' she said. 'No other life makes any sense to me. I will live here and die here. I will dance until my death. It is our obligation and our pride.'

Or was it hope? My mother kept thinking that something would change, that people would not just give up on our dance.

'Rajayi,' she said, 'your singing grows more melodious every day, your dancing is a feast for the eyes.'

She thought the appetites of ordinary people were on our side; the man driving his buffaloes home who heard the drums and the nagaswaram in the distance; the woman who set her basket of coconuts on one side and sat down awhile to watch us. She did not notice the thatched cinema theatres and the bright posters on the town's walls. She did not notice the dwindling audiences at the dance plays on the temple platform.

'Has not our family's dance gone back so many generations?' she said. 'Our tradition has passed through time like gold wire through pearls. Our ancestors were legends, Rajayi, they were revered. The town talked all year about this one's kurathi, that one's singan. People came from miles around – you can't imagine how it was – drawn by their reputations.'

Neither my mother nor I could bear the emptiness of admitting that we had truly been abandoned, like a temple tank with no water in it, like the dry bed of a river, like wood wormy with holes. We could not bear to think that there was nothing we and our daughters were fit for in the world.

My mother paid for my debut in the temple. In the old days it would have been a patron. Then she waited for a suitor to ask for me, but times had changed. There was no patron.

'The trouble is, Rajayi, your beauty is of the statuesque kind,' my mother said.

I don't know if I was much of a beauty. My arms were strong and muscular from years of training under Samu Vathyar.

'You carry your head like a flower on a thick shoot,' she said. 'A stately flower that won't bend with the wind. And that trick you have of turning slowly to face a man and look him in the eye – you must stop doing that.'

I did not change my ways. Men were nothing to me, except Samu Vathyar.

'Eley, keep your eyes down,' my mother coached me desperately. 'Good god, what shall I do, the girl is frightening her suitors away.'

It was easier with Lila, who was plump and lovely and

had her mother's dimples. She had not been dedicated, but we now danced together at weddings and at the temple festivals. Wealthy men asked for her, and she and my mother chose a patron for her from among them. The man who became her patron didn't actually build her a new house, but he did patch the cracks in this old one.

When the young policeman came to ask for me, my mother was relieved. He was not in uniform – he had failed his exams, they said, and he was not yet called 'the Inspector'. He was trying on the character of the landlords who came to dasi houses. The silk veshti and shirt sat awkwardly on him; the turban was comical; the shoulder-cloth with the yards of gold lace drew attention to his pigeon-chest. He wore a bracelet of jasmine flowers around his wrist and a thick gold watch in his shirt-pocket, and was clutching a cane, even though he was a young man. His servant carried a carved silver spittoon shaped like an hourglass and a brass platter heaped with gifts.

Standing with me at the window, Lila made an inventory. "There's a bottle of perfume, foreign perfume,' she said, 'and Afghan Snow, and a silk sari, and fruit and flowers.'

But all I saw was that the man's eyes were hard. I saw ugly, cruel lines around his mouth. The town feared him, and my skin prickled when he looked up at the window.

'Oh, no,' I whispered. 'No.'

A gecko clicked his tongue.

'Listen,' Lila said, 'the lizard has spoken. He's the one for you.'

She shuddered theatrically. We squawked with

sudden laughter, unable to control ourselves. My mother had taken the platter from him, happy that I was to be matched at last.

Glancing out of the window, we knew he had heard us laughing. His expression darkened, as if the wind had blown a cloud over his head. I wanted him to go away, quickly.

'*No*,' I said urgently, when my mother came into our room to ask me for my consent. 'Not him – oh, not him!' My mother looked mortifed. Too late, I realized he had followed her into the house.

He set his turban on his head, picked up his cane in his left hand, and with his right, whipped his starched shoulder-cloth so angrily through the air that we took it for what it was, a slap in our faces. We watched him leave, stricken, embarrassed by our bad behaviour, and angry with him for disturbing our peace.

'He heard you laughing, you silly girls,' my mother said, coming back inside after she had seen him to the door.

'Did you refuse him?' Lila said to her, still laughing immoderately.

'Yes, I did,' my mother said. 'I didn't like to say yes, and I didn't like to say no. He's already a policeman, you know. I hope it will not bring trouble. He's the son of the big pappaan landlord. He's the younger brother of that Vakil everyone is talking about.'

My mother's music notebooks were in the trunk. A man came from Madras, years ago, and asked for them. He said he would write out the songs and bring the books back. Lila sent him packing. 'The city people will steal everything from us,' she said. 'They'll shave us bald and disappear, and if you want to remember the words of your own mother's padhams ten years from now, you'll have to go begging them.'

Beneath the notebooks was a bundle of silk. A densely wrought gold bangle rolled out. It was my mother's; I had kept it to honour her memory when my need was less dire, and then, when I might have sold it for food, I had hidden it here from myself. Lila had a matching bangle. There were brown stains on the silk, from something unidentifiable. When the flowers fell out of the silk, they gave me a shock, the way one is shocked when a flock of partridges erupts from a bush at one's feet. Brown flowers, decades old. I had placed in this silk a jasmine-string for a keepsake, because the Vakil had given it to me, and he was leaving for Madras. I had known then that I would never see him again.

I opened the silk out on the floor. In it were the letters the Vakil had written to me. On top of each letter he sent, the date was scrawled in a sprawling, confident hand. The letters began in 1939.

In Pudukottai, our relatives told us, the dancing in the temple had stopped. In Mysore, the Raja had bowed to public opinion. Our Raja was impervious to this opinion, which called us prostitutes, but what of his son? When he became the Raja, what would he do? When the old Raja had a dance in his durbar, the young one stayed away. It spelt doom for us. But people would understand, my mother said; she said they would understand how rich and beautiful the dance itself was, and it would be saved, and we would teach it to girls from brahmin families. So many brahmin girls were already learning it – look at that Rukmini in Madras, whose fame had spread everywhere.

I said, 'Why don't we write a petition and take it to the Raja and to the government in Madras where that politician Muthulakshmi has been making speeches against us?'

My mother and I got all the dasi women of Kalyanikkarai and Nallur together. Singers, dancers, women who worked in the temple. The clever young Vakil, Sundaram Iyer, who had passed his exams in England, would help us draft the petition in English. Three bullock carts, that day, set out for his house. But when we got there, his servants told us he was not at home. A fine day we had chosen to meet him, they said. He was at the freedom-fighters' rally – hadn't we heard? He was making a speech. The freedom-fighters had put up a platform near the river.

They agreed to convey our request to the Vakil when he returned from the rally. Quickly, as if they were shutting out an infection, they slammed the door in our faces.

The bullock cart drivers turned around and started across the fields. Then, at the edge of the town, at the far end of South Main Street, the carts could go no further because of the crowds. The women who lived nearby, my mother and Lila and I among them, got off the carts and began to walk home.

The freedom-fighters' procession came around the lake, which was not a lake any more. This arm of the Kalyani – its connection to the river flowing from the mountain silted up as the river changed its path – this arm had grown more stagnant, a backwater for a decade or two, then a cesspool, a nothing. Weeds had grown along the banks, and after a few summers the water had dried up entirely, leaving harsh cracks. A temporary platform had been built near the lakebed. A man stood on the platform. He was saying: if small kingdoms like our Raja's did not give up their independence and merge into the country they called India, Bhaaratanadu, they would suffer the fate of the lake.

The freedom-fighters flowed on where the river had widened, slinging itself against the right bank, wearing itself a new shortcut. On the sand they burnt the cloth and books that had been imported from England, and we were mesmerized by the flames bursting up and dancing on the faces of the people of Kalyanikkarai.

Their sacrifices made, they turned from the ash-piles towards the town again. The men wore Gandhi-caps, the women wore khaddar saris. They sang: *Vande Mataram!* They held banners that flapped in the wind. When they saw us, the women turned and spat on the ground.

'Since when have we become women that people could spit at?' the dasis shouted. 'Your husbands,' they laughed, 'we slept with them all.'

'Hush!' my mother cried.

The wives of many of the men we knew were in that procession. The wife of Sengalvaraya Shastri, who had been my mother's and my aunt Komala's music teacher for ten years, went past with averted eyes. The son of Sabesa Iyer, who taught Lila and me Sanskrit and Telugu, would have stopped and smiled, but was swept away.

They sang: *Vidudhalai, Vidudhalai, Vidudhalai!*
Freedom! Freedom! Freedom!

When we stopped watching and started to make our way home, a strange contest began, about who would occupy the middle of the road. The freedom-fighters had large banners slung between two poles; Gandhi Thatha smiled down from one banner; on the other, Mother India, dressed like Lakshmi, but with Durga's fierce lion behind her, blocked our path. The women who held the poles would not let us pass.

'Go back!' the women cried. 'Move aside! We stand for the nation!'

My mother lost her temper then. 'What do I know about your nation?' she said, planting her feet in the road and refusing to move while the crowd pushed us this way and that. We will die, I thought, they will stamp us out here, on the road in the middle of the town. 'What do I care?' my mother shouted. 'I serve the old Raja. I serve the temple, I serve art.'

The policemen cried, 'Can't you see there is no place for you!' They struck her arm with a lathi; startled, she turned, and the wave of people broke around her and past her. I threw my arms around her and held her upright. If she had fallen, she would have been trampled to death.

They were enthusiastic and alive, the high-caste women at the head of the procession. Every week they wore their khaddar saris and seized their banners and marched in the streets; they gathered in the marketplaces and burned the white man's books and the white man's cloth; they worked their gold bangles off their wrists, grimacing as the metal scraped their flesh, and threw them into a collection bag for the cause of freedom. For the first time in their lives they stood, the boldest among them, side-by-side with their husbands, instead of walking with bowed heads six paces behind. They sang, full-throated because the wind took their voices away: '*Bhaarata samudaayam, Bhaarata samudaayam, Bhaarata samudaayam vazhgavey!*'

And we – we did not belong in the world they knew they were making. And we all knew it. We leaned against the walls of houses, yielding. Even my mother. Angrily and grudgingly yielding, since they treated the road as their own.

Three days later, the Vakil sent us a letter. My mother tore it open carefully.

'It's too early for any kind of news, surely?' Lila said.

'I don't think it's news – he says he will come and discuss the petition. He will help us. It is a good sign.'

Inside the letter, there was a sealed envelope with my name on it. Now the paper was yellow by the light of my little clay lamp, and brittle as old leaves. It came apart at the creases, and I had to put the four pieces together to read it.

My dear Rajayi,

I hope this letter finds you well, as it leaves me.

You see how everyone is doing something or the other for the nation's sake – marrying widows, starting aircraft factories, dining stiffly and stoically with people of other castes and faiths. I found myself walking through the street, committed, with the rest of the khaddar-clad rabble, to building a bonfire out of British manufactures, emblems of our subservience (textbooks! foreign-made knowledge!). I was invited to make my contribution to the flames.

I, alas, was not patriot enough to give up the exquisitely leather-bound sets of classics – literature, philosophy – that I had ordered in England.

There was a certain mustard yellow coat, I remembered, that my honoured father had given me to wear at Cambridge. I hated that coat; people stared at me when I put it on and walked through the cold of England, thinking elevated thoughts. I did not like the coat better when I came back to this land. I left home three days ago, carrying that coat, set it on fire, and watched happily as it blackened and burned.

But when I turned around, I saw you standing at the corner of the street, and saw the women in our procession shouting abuse at you. I was afire, like the wretched coat. The freedom struggle went out of my mind altogether. I asked the man beside me, my uncle Sengalvaraya Shastri, who you were, and he told me your name and your mother's name.

Let me know if you will see this confused patriot in your home one of these evenings. My uncle says you are an extraordinarily gifted singer.

Give your mother and your elders my respectful greetings.

Your slave for ever,
Sundaram

It was a whimsical letter, and I was intrigued. I agreed to see him.

When he came to see me, I struck my veenai strings with a passion and skill I did not know I had; I was at my best. My mother kept the etiquette of dancers and singers. There was a language we learned as girls, of love, of sensual pleasing. The language was already dying in those days. How did we forget a language so rich?

All was ceremonial; the music, the man listening with respect and appreciation, his eyes and his heart full.

The Vakil became my lover, and he became a convert to our cause. He read us what he had written in the *Grihalakshmi* paper.

> *Consider the consequences if suddenly, without warning, the 35,000 temples of Tamil Nadu barred all women performers, devadasis or not.*

'Are there really thirty-five thousand temples?' my mother asked.

He grinned. 'It's a good number.'

He read us his outraged replies to people like Kokku Missy, who argued, in the *Callianicarah Herald*, the English paper, that there should be no more dancing.

> *What a myth, that nautch dance has become vulgar. I haven't seen any dasis with my eyes who are vulgar, but who am I to contradict the egregious, interfering authorities who tailor the facts to suit their narrow morality?*

My mother and I cut the pieces out of the newspapers carefully.

The Vakil drafted a petition for the dasi women, as he had promised, listening carefully to my words and my mother's, and turning them into English.

We already enjoy the freedoms which women's associations all over the country are campaigning for. If to this were added a modern education for our children and a recognition of our traditional skill in the arts, we would take our rightful places as guardians of the arts of music and dance, and be honoured in this great country.

The handwritten draft he had made, in the flowing hand of those days, remained with us. The petition had been typed by a clerk in the Vakil's office, and the women had gathered in our house to sign it. I remember the pages filling up with the names and signatures of women. How strong and hopeful the signatures had seemed, how numerous! The Tamil curlicues elegant; the signatures made bold and ornate so that they would cover more pages and give an impression of numbers; some names signed in English even. Gnanasundari, Karpooram, Mangalam, Kanakambujam, Thamarai, Alamelu, Lilavati, Malarkodi, Suryakanti, Mekhala, Sarojini, Valli, Swarnam, Dhanashri, Andal, Ambigai, Nandita Banu, Sudarkodi, Hamsa, Subbalatchmi, Meenatchi, Vasantalakshmi . . . and my signature was there too, Rajalatchmi.

So many women. I have not seen them or heard from them in years, except for Meenatchi and Lila and one or two others.

We marched to the Raja's palace to place the petition before him. We thought we knew everything there was to know about the power of bodies massed in the streets. Had we not fed the splendour and noise of every temple procession for centuries, our ankle bells matching the thunder of the drums, matching the hoofbeats of stately horses, the heartbeats of the crowd? But marching as mothers and sisters going out to claim justice, that was different. I understood the grim fire that had burned in the faces of the women who had marched for Mother India.

At the palace they told us the old Raja was ill. The young one received us, smiling, and took the petition from my mother's hands. He smiled too much, and committed himself to nothing.

So the petition was presented, and so it was ignored. It changed nothing. Among the yellowed papers, not in the Vakil's writing, but a scribe's, was a copy, for our benefit, of the main points of the Devadasi Bill that was our death-blow.

A woman who takes part in any dancing or music performance is regarded as having adopted the life of prostitution and becomes incapable of entering into a valid marriage, and the performance of any marriage ceremony, whether before or after this Bill, is hereby declared unlawful and void.

A hundred times I saw that document in my mother's hands. She read it again and again, as if she hoped that between readings the letters would form themselves into a different set of words and sentences, the ones that she had hoped for. The ones that would take care of the pride and livelihood of her daughters and her daughters' daughters. But there it was in writing, the death of all her hopes.

The Devadasi Bill was passed in the Legislative Assembly, but still the Vakil came to the house two or three times a week. He had become my patron; he said I was the love of his heart. When I danced in the temple or at a ceremony in the town, I sang and danced the varnams and padhams for him.

My breasts are swollen with love, my nipples are hard,
watching the koels calling to each other in the mango-tree,
waiting for him. A minute
stretches into an hour, into an age.
The evening has slipped away,
the flowers in my hair have faded.
He will not come tonight.
Dear friend of my heart, what would I do
if you were not here with me?

For eleven years the Vakil came and went, and he left his gold-rimmed glasses on the bust of Gandhi Thatha when he came to my bed. He said his life would be worth nothing if he could not live with me, always, he said. Always.

'You are a thief,' he said. 'You steal my time.'

'You could come less often,' I retorted.

'Not the Raja himself,' he said, 'nor the Raja's father, nor the Raja's priapic grandfather, who enjoyed many women in their time among satin sheets, cooled by

240

peacock-feather fans, celebrating the rites of spring, could possibly have known such exquisite' – he pushed the sari away from my body, as he spoke, he buried his face between my breasts – 'such exquisite, such unbounded pleasure. I am your slave forever.'

The next time my aunt Komala came back to Kalyanikkarai, in 1948, my mother was dying of pneumonia. It had been a long dreary monsoon, and the rain had poured down without let. But ten minutes before Komala arrived, the sun had burst out briefly.

'I've been waiting for you,' my mother said to her.

In a corner of the room, my mother's patron sat in an armchair. Komala looked at Lila and me for an explanation.

'His wife turned him out,' I whispered.

'She has nothing for herself, and she is supporting a man?' Komala said. She started to say something to her sister, swallowed it back.

'Where is Rajayi?' my mother said. Her eyes searched the room.

'I'm here,' I said.

'Put me where I can see the gopuram.'

Komala Chithi put an easy chair just outside the door, just short of the street, and we carried my mother out to it. She was light, mere bones. She groped for my hand. 'I want you to promise that you will not stop dancing,' she said. 'Once a year, on a festival day of your choosing.'

'I promise.'

It began to drizzle. The door opened and the man, her

patron, came out to hold an umbrella over my mother. In the rain, facing the temple, like a queen under a ceremonial umbrella, Kanaka sat until her heart stopped.

We cut out what the Vakil wrote about her:

Kanaka represented the power of an art that brought things into alignment: the benevolence of the gods with the fertility of the king and the fertility of the earth. The well-being of gods, kings, ordinary people. There was great beauty in her art, both because it was functional and because it was performed with grace and dignity and skill.

When I grieved for my mother, the Vakil was there to console me. But I had had no children by him, and this pained and worried me. There was no other tie than our love to bind us. I felt the fragility of the bond. I began to prepare myself for the end of it, especially since the white people had by then been finally driven out of the country, and the Vakil began to speak of admiring this or that political leader. He was becoming restless. His success as an advocate no longer satisfied him, and he wanted to do something grand with his life. The nation was here at last, he said. He wished to play his part in it.

He said, 'My brother-in-law is asking if I will join the Congress Party. He has influence; he has already spoken to the party's officials.'

'They will welcome you into the party.'

'What do *you* think?' he said to me, lying sideways on my bed, his cheek pillowed on one hand, the other hand playing with my hair. That day he sounded playful, not serious.

'Does it matter to you?' I said. 'Do you want to be a powerful man?'

'Not while I lie in your arms. I could dream my days away in your bed. My thief.'

The world was seeing dasi women in a way that menaced our idyll. People could not be public figures and continue to keep dasi mistresses. I felt his struggle. The *Grihalakshmi* and the *Swatantra Advocate* published vicious letters. He tried to warn me away from them, but other people actually took pleasure in bringing them to me, pretending concern.

Will a certain would-be engineer of the nation's destiny and member of the Congress Party explain what his car was doing outside the home of a woman whose family has had a traditional connection with Vice?

A few nights after his brother-in-law's visit he sat on his side of the bed, his back dejected, and said, 'I wish–'

'You wish what?' I had scratched his back with my fingernails. I knew what was coming and had been angry, and had left something for him to remember me by. Gently, I touched the weals I had made a few moments earlier.

'Nothing. Nothing – I'll tell you tomorrow.'

That day, I took the flowers he had brought me and coiled them in a piece of silk. I was sure there would be no tomorrow.

The Vakil joined the Party after all. In the same expansive hand in which he wrote me love letters, he wrote a farewell letter (how well I remember the pain of opening it, knowing that if he had not come to tell me, if he could not bring himself to face me, then it would be the worst news).

I know you will be unhappy to hear this from me. My brother-in-law suggested that I might be the right person to stand for a Legislative Assembly seat. Whatever my private views are on the importance of your art to this country, and whatever my feelings are for you, as a public man I cannot have what is seen as an illicit relationship. I can no longer write to you – how I regret this development.

I will have a trusted friend put money in a bank account for you. It will be there – a small sum, but like a salary, every month.

Forgive me, forget me. Destroy this letter, if you care for me.

But I did not destroy it. Not because of what the Vakil was afraid of, that I would use it against him, but because it was the last thing to me in his hand. I held it to my heart.

So who is the thief? I wrote.

You have taken my heart with you, but I will not reproach you. You must do what your brother-in-law and your wife want you to do. I hope you are happy in Madras. I dreamt of you last night, becoming a great man, a politician. May god grant you success and happiness.

Your gift of the red silk sari has reached me. What shall I give you in return?

What shall I do, now that you no longer sit on my swing

244

and watch patiently while I tune the veenai? I would take
up my veenai and play it, but who will understand the
words? The veenai stands in the corner by itself these days.
I cannot bring myself to play it.

I did not post this letter. The Vakil won his seat, and he remained faithful to me in his way. The money was paid into the bank account for some fifteen years. Then he too died, far away from me, and it stopped.

By the window, where the rain now comes through the gaps in the roof, there was a carved mahogany seat where a humpbacked brahmin clerk called Sarangapani had sat all night once, just to be able to boast to his friends that he had spent a night with a dasi. Long after we had all gone to bed he had sat there scribbling in a notebook, and at five in the morning he had handed my mother three verses of a javali.

'Why,' she exclaimed, 'these are very good,' genuinely surprised that this timid sheepish man who crept back to his wife by dewfall could write of love and betrayal in verses that scanned and could be set to a seven-beat talam. 'What ragam shall I set it to?'

'Paras,' he said, shyly. 'It is a plaintive ragam.'

So my mother had set it, and I had sung it to the Vakil.

The woman with the girdle sang to her friend:
I did not think he would discard me,
The fickle one.
My bangles are dropping from my wasted arms,

245

My heart is failing.

My love is going so far away.

When brahmin composers created songs that moved people in the gut rather than in the head, my mother said, we could be sure they had created them leaning up against the wall of a dasi's house.

Where had all those people gone, I thought, after the Vakil left. By 1950, my mother was dead. My uncles were still fighting with us over the little land left to us. Komala Chithi, too old and tired to travel around the country making speeches, and having run out of causes to take up, was the warden of a working women's hostel in Nallur. My cousins were dead, or married, or scattered, or divided from us by feud. There should have been children and grandchildren here in this house. But by 1950, the year the Vakil won the seat in Madras, only Lila and I were left in the echoing house that had once had so many people living in it and passing through it.

Three weeks later, the Inspector was waiting for me in the temple.

The lamp guttered; the wick was burning lazily. In a minute the flame sank into ashes and my shadow, rocking back and forth on the swing, sank into darkness. I wiped my eyes, put the letters back in the trunk and brought the lid down. I rolled out my mat beside Amalan's and readied myself for sleep.

13

Rajayi

Kalyanikkarai, 25 May 1990

A windless morning. On mornings when the leaves did not stir, the town of Kalyanikkarai was most like me: an old slattern in a faded sari with outmoded fancywork, drowsing in a raddled heap.

My feet scuffed the street. The red dust got in my hair, and on the cloth over the jasmine in my basket. When the old Raja was alive they would have watered the streets. Sometimes the peacocks used to fly over the walls of the palace and strut along the streets near the temple. No one harmed them.

The coconut thatch over the shops had grown greyer and more brittle than when I was young, but the town's oldest streets, the ones around the temple, had not changed much. They were narrow, crowded with hazards: tradespeople, bicycles, rickshaws, cows, heat-struck pye-dogs, baskets and carts and children. The painted clay gods stood on the same steps they stood on when I was a girl. The man in the prayer bead shop was the son of the man who used to hang his beads in bunches from the roof and make heaps of crimson and scarlet kungumam, yellow turmeric, and herbal powders for every ailment, on the counter. The shop smelt of cinnamon and liquorice root. We came here for two-sided white combs good for removing lice. Kalyani worked here for a while, after she came back from Kokku Missy's house.

The new shops were coming up big and bright on either side of the new bypass-road. They looked different, smelt different. Cold and frightening and costly.

Three days ago Amalan gave me a terrible shock. He had gone to Baai's shop to pay off the dues for the month, and to buy rice and soap.

'What took you so long?' I said, when he came back. 'I was starting to think something had happened to you.'

'I saw a dead body, Amma,' he said. 'Inside a black van with rose garlands so high I could not see the face. I followed it for a while.'

'Oh, Amalan, that is bad luck,' I said.

'Baai said the dead man was a famous police inspector,' he said. 'Everyone just called him "the Inspector", Baai said. The Chief Minister gave him a medal for something he did. Baai wouldn't believe his daughter had been coming to our house, because he was always vowing to wipe out people like us. Her car, in which she came here, was going along slowly behind the black van. They were going to the cremation ground.'

'Who are you talking about?' I said.

'She's the Inspector's daughter,' Amalan said. 'The

fat dancer from Madras who said she would buy me a pendant. Baai said she is staying in the farmhouse in West Kalyanikkarai, with the betel nut trees and the rice and coconuts.'

'Padmasini? Padmasini is the *Inspector*'s daughter?' I said.

'Yes,' Amalan said. 'What's the matter?'

'Nothing, Amalan,' I said. 'Nothing.'

Perhaps the boy had heard some rumour, mixed it all up in his head. Padmasini had made her film for four days. On the fourth day she had said there would be three more days of work, but she had not come. I waited for hours, and was late, again, getting to my place in the temple. She did not send word. Since she had disappeared without paying me, I assumed she had been displaying the behaviour of the Madras viper. I realized I had no address to write to her.

But if she was indeed related to the Inspector, as the boy seemed to think, she may have been kept away by his death. Perhaps she would come back, after all.

I had been feeling restless and stifled in the house; the sound of the blasting had grown intolerable. So this morning, I went straight to the temple from the market, thinking I would string my jasmine in the cool part deep inside the colonnade. The sculptors the Nayaka rulers brought from Tanjavur cut stone the way we might cut soap. On the stone walls, the inscriptions recorded which territories had been annexed and which treasuries had been sacked; which kings had married which queens and which priests had been assigned lands; which women had been engaged to be dasis, and how many measures of rice or cubits of land they were owed. They were carved in a kind of Tamil I could not read, but the old priest, the Ayyar's father, once brought me here and read each one out to me.

On the ceiling above me and above the Nandi-bull, in the thousand-pillared hall, there was a mural of dancing women in a procession, with drummers and nagaswaram players. Their skin was cracked like mine. The stucco on the ceiling had flaked away, and a thigh or an elbow had dropped into dust, an arm was cut off at the shoulder and began again at the wrist. When my ancestor Jagadambal died, the Raja made the artist paint her likeness into the ceiling there. No one in the family remembered which of these women she was.

This corner of the colonnade had been my mother's favourite place. I fancied that I could still detect, faintly, the hot silver smell coming off the border of my mother's sari and off her jewellery, and the smell of my mother's sweat after she had danced along the processional path.

It is natural; when one grows old, so many people one knew are dead. The Inspector, though! Dead and cremated, bringing so many years of hatred and fear to an unsatisfactory end. It had to be him. Why did Padmasini lie to me about being from a poor family? Why didn't she tell me she was the Inspector's daughter? Surely – surely she had recognized the Vakil in the picture she had held on her lap!

In this temple I was dedicated, and here I continued to dance and to help with other tasks after my mother died. My foremothers had been given no menial tasks, but I was put in charge of cleaning the ritual vessels. On the far side of the temple elephant's post was the well where Lila and I had, before the procession on that festival day, polished the brass pots and lamps from the main sanctuary and from all the other shrines around the temple. I was going to dance in the procession, as I had every year since I had been dedicated.

I tried to add up the years in my head: was it forty years ago? The bitter smell of tamarind mixed with rock-salt, heated by the sun, that afternoon, stung my memory.

'I know what you are thinking of,' Lila had said. She sang, '*She waits for a warrior, a warrior worthy of her, a warrior like you.*'

'Oh, be quiet!' I said. I was moping for the Vakil, who had been gone some three weeks.

That was when the man's shadow fell across my body, though from the way his shadow moved, I realized he had been standing there for a while. I had been rubbing the tamarind and salt into the verdigris that had built up in the filigreed crevices of the brassware. My sari had fallen away from my breasts when I leaned forward. I had looked up to see the Inspector's face. His eyes had been on me. I covered my breasts, and went on scrubbing. We finished, and loaded all the vessels, flashing in the sun, into the basket. Lila hoisted the basket on to my head.

As we passed the Inspector, our eyes down, he said, 'Perhaps I can be your warrior.' He put up his right forefinger and smoothed his moustache, eyeing me with a mixture of pleading and arrogance that repelled me again as it had repelled me the first time. I could sense violence held in tightly by his skin; it seemed to smoulder just behind his eyeballs and pulse in the veins on his forehead.

Ten years earlier, he had been rejected. He was asking again; his brother, the Vakil, had gone to Madras; my mother was dead. What was I to do?

'My brother has left for Madras – he is joining the Assembly. I'm sure you know this. You have no protector now. I could take his place.'

Lila's dimples deepened. The man's eyes swung sharply to her, and the anger in them sobered her.

Not meeting his eyes, I said, 'We must talk through an elder.'

'I already asked for you once,' he said, 'after your dedication, and your mother refused me. Who would you like me to talk to?'

'I – I don't remember seeing you before,' I said. My skin prickled. I shuddered in revulsion, and then moved about to conceal it, but he had seen. 'I will let you know.'

When we were climbing the sanctuary steps to take in the lamps and vessels, Lila said, 'Rajayi, you're not going to accept, are you?'

'No.' I looked over my shoulder. He was still standing at the post, staring after me.

'Here, I'll carry the basket for a bit. Your mother refused him, so why should you worry?'

'A bad feeling, that's all. Ever since he heard us laughing like a pair of idiots.'

'So we laughed. If we had to worry about annoying someone every time we sneezed or smiled–'

We passed the Inspector again on our way down the sanctuary steps. 'If you know what's good for you you'll stay at home tonight,' he said casually. 'I'll be on duty during the procession.'

I had promised my mother I would dance once a year, at the festival in April. I was determined to do this even though the Devadasi Bill had become, they told me, a law. I was planning to defy the law.

'Maybe we should let it go, just this year,' Lila said doubtfully. 'Maybe we should–'

'I am going ahead. But you stay out of it.'

'I didn't like the way he was looking at you, I didn't like it at all. You can't prevent me from joining you, anyhow.'

That night, Lila and I joined the procession in our usual way.

I finished tying the flowers and ate my lunch quickly behind a pillar. I must have dozed off then, sitting up. When I looked up, the shadows of the pillars were falling all the way across the stone path, and it was time for me to take the jasmine strings to the south gopuram and claim my space. I always trod carefully in the temple at this time of the day – in the late afternoon – because I knew that the Ayyar would be lurking, waiting to bilk the evening worshippers.

The old priest was frail, now, but he still performed the rituals in the sanctuary. His son, the one they called the Temple Ayyar, hated me. I always had to look over my shoulder to see if the Ayyar was going to come and start trouble for me. He took pleasure in destroying me with words.

I went down the colonnade steps and came around the corner of the Amman shrine. A group of people was standing in front of the shrine. Until I came up to them, I did not see that one of them was the Ayyar, scratching his back like a buffalo against a pillar.

'Is she asking for money?' he was saying. In front of him were Shah and Padmasini. The helper boy was carrying the usual umbrellas and all the machines; Shah had the camera in his hands.

'Don't give her any money,' the Ayyar said. 'She has not been employed by the temple. She's swindling you. You shouldn't be talking to her. You have no idea what kind of woman she is!'

In a panic, I tried to draw back behind the pillar, but as soon as I moved, he saw me.

'You!' he said. 'Come here! I heard the talk in the town about you,' he said. Curses on that Muthayya. 'So who are these people coming here to talk to you? What are you telling them?'

The stone of the courtyard was hot. A group of white sightseers went past, squealing because they had taken their slippers off at the temple gate, and the stone slabs were cooking their tender feet. The Ayyar stood there with his droopy nose, and his pink complacent lips pillowed in flesh, like a buzzard waiting to swoop. Passers-by began to stop, eyes glittering with curiosity.

I said, 'This lady from Madras is asking about my ancestors, and about dance. It is nothing.' I looked for Hema. I felt she would have taken my side. But she was not with them.

'Why do you want to know about dance from this

old hag?' he said to Padmasini. 'She and her ancestors, common whores. Now the research people come asking us if we know any devadasis – in my time they were just tevadiyas. They led a shameful life.' He clenched his fingers and opened them suddenly, spraying my foremothers into oblivion. 'Scotch,' he continued, holding up an arm and touching its elbow with the fingers of the other hand, measuring a full bottle. 'Drinking with men. They spoiled this temple's name. They spoiled dancing.' His mouth turned mean at the corners. 'They don't even remember any dances or songs.'

'Yes, well,' Padmasini replied, 'they were considered wives of the god–'

'Wives of the god! Do you know where-all she has been? Selling her body cheap to truck drivers, clerks, drunks, gangsters!'

My ancestor Annakili Naachiyar stepped on a scorpion when she was dancing in the god's procession, and it did her no harm; she was bitten by a snake, and it did her no harm. But if I, Rajayi, lost my temper and insulted this man back, the man would make sure I lost my place in the temple. I couldn't afford to lose my livelihood twice over.

The knot of people was tightening around us. There would always be people willing to be entertained by the humiliation of others. Suddenly the Ayyar turned to Padmasini, as if a thought had struck him.

'Who gave you permission to film here?' His eye wandered over Shah, the camera, the machines.

'We are not filming the temple itself,' she said. 'We want to use it as a background, and it will not be in focus.'

'You still have to show me the paper. You should come to the office first, before filming.'

'What paper?'

'The paper from the Religious Endowments Board. Otherwise you should not bring a film camera into the temple grounds.'

'Our filming has been arranged by NATAC – you know? The government? The man in charge of it has probably applied for permission from the Chief Minister himself. The Chief Minister is my friend.'

'But you don't have the paper yet?' he said. 'You can't show it to me now?'

I wanted to say, he has no authority to ask you – who was he, after all? – but I had to go on living and working there, and the man could make my life intolerable if he chose.

I wished that the crowd hadn't gathered, that they hadn't begun to whisper to each other, 'What is the problem?' The umbrella boy put down his burdens and rubbed his shoulders where the straps had bitten into them; then he picked them up again, as if he had been told never to let go of those machines. I wanted to tell Padmasini: give the Ayyar the bribe he is waiting for, quickly, so that we can get away from him. But she was acting as if she did not understand where his questions were leading.

'Giving money to a parasite like that,' the Ayyar was saying. 'Do you know what they say about the dasis? They used to eat the temple's rice, but now they have to make do with beggars' rations. It is their karmam coming back to haunt them.'

The crowd muttered. Someone laughed.

The air I breathed burned in my chest, poisonous with insult, and with my anger which I could not speak. I stood still, not shifting from foot to foot. It turned my attention to the burning flagstones under my feet. I turned into myself, to the place inside me that could not be touched, that was impervious as the rock from which these pillars were carved. My mother's face came to my mind, and she was saying: my grandmother covered those finials with gold. And her mother before her, and that one's mother, the women had stood fierce guard over their art and their dignity, like those stone demons with maces on their shoulders who flanked the door of the Amman shrine.

'How much are you paying her?' the Ayyar said. His tongue came out and wet his hanging lip. 'If you want to continue to film, the temple must be compensated too.' Now perhaps the scene would draw to a close, now that he had brought the talk around to a bribe.

Shah seemed to understand. He walked aside with the Ayyar. The crowd drifted away.

'You were not in your house this afternoon,' Padmasini said to me in a reproachful voice.

'I had to sell my flowers. Now it is late—'

'Just today,' she said. 'We will film near the sanctuary, and then you could sell flowers while we get some film of the temple.'

I sighed. 'Put away your machines and come and see the god. The old Ayyar – this man's father – he still cares for the lingam in the sanctuary with his own hands. And he will tell you stories of a different sort from his son.'

The Ayyar came back. Shah gestured to the boy. We moved in a small procession towards the sanctuary.

The old priest had a kind face and a slow, thoughtful way of speaking, as if he weighed every word before he uttered it. He had decorated the lingam with sandal-paste and flowers. He seldom left the temple during the day, even though the trustees didn't pay him much. He liked to tell stories.

'Once, when a king had wronged his people, and taxed them when the harvest was poor, the Kalyani river flooded the land. This lingam, about to be washed away, was taken to her breast by the goddess Uma; it was saved; the story goes thus; and see,' he showed us, 'the pearls in Uma's necklace, pressing down upon the stone of the lingam, left this double row of indentations. '

'May the goddess who kept the flood from this land–' the old man held out a pinch of sacred ash from his tray, Padmasini cupped her palm and took the ash '–may the goddess give you a long happy life with your husband.' I wondered if there was a husband. I had not asked Padmasini about her own life. I had been too busy answering all the questions she had put to me about mine.

We stepped out into the corridor near the sanctuary. The old priest ushered us out courteously. His son hovered, overcome by curiosity and greed. Shah set up the machines.

'Were you dedicated here, in this sanctuary?' Padmasini asked, facing the camera.

'I was married to the stone outside the Pillayar shrine out there,' I said. 'In our temple, the tevadiyas were always married there.'

'Don't use that word!' the Ayyar said. 'Can't you see they are making the film?'

'That was the word they used in those days,' I said. 'There was no disgrace in it.'

'Everything has a name,' the old priest said. 'Every god has a favourite tree, flower, time of day, dance, instrument, ragam. There were sixteen ways of worshipping god. In the old days, in the temples, we pleased the gods.'

I noticed that Shah had moved the camera around to face the old priest.

'There is a story about Rajayi's ancestor,' the old priest said. 'In the land of the red Kalyani, in the days when this temple was just a simple shrine carved out of a rock, a bad-tempered king became angry with the dasi Annakili Naachiyar and dismissed her from his service. Then the king wished to proclaim his glory by building the tall tower, the vimanam, over the sanctuary. It was all ready: the walls rising up in tiers, the niches, the carvings. Only one thing remained–'

'–the great dome over the tower,' I said, taking up the story because the old one broke off to cough. 'That great ball of stone' – I nodded at the tower – 'had to be lifted into place. The king had a ramp built, its sides high. He had strong pulleys built by the carpenter; he had miles of thick rope woven.'

'The great stone was cradled in ropes,' the priest continued. 'The ropes were passed over pulleys above the tower, and down on the other side. The king's own battle elephants were harnessed to their ends. One of my ancestors, the royal priest, chose the day; the whole city came out to watch, the legends say, it was such a grand sight. Then the mahouts began to walk the elephants forward.'

'And do you know what happened?' I said. '*Nothing.* The stone wouldn't budge. No matter what they did. They broke coconuts, they prayed, they made vows and offerings.'

'That night, the priest saw the god Siva himself in a dream. "If you want to finish the temple," Siva-Peruman said, "my favourite Annakili must place her hand over the rope." In the morning, the priest ran to the palace and told the Raja about his dream. The king found Annakili, begged her to forgive him, and brought her to the ramp. She touched the rope, the elephants moved, the stone rolled up the ramp and into place.'

'They say a child could have pulled it up, it was so light.'

'It's a true story,' the old priest said. 'There is a pit half a mile from the temple, where the king's fields used to be – they say that was where the ramp began.'

'A marvel of early engineering, the archaeologists have called the temple's cupola,' the Ayyar said, thrusting himself in front of his father. 'I can take you inside the well of the tower. The walls are full of paintings. It is a rare privilege to see them – it is difficult to arrange, the government is worried that the light from torches will fade the paintings, but I have influence.'

Shah turned his camera away from the Ayyar. 'Let's go and film by the temple tank. Did you say there were fish in the tank?'

'There would be more, if the town boys didn't steal them,' the Ayyar said. 'Eh Rajayi, if I catch your boy stealing fish from the sacred tank again,' he said, turning to me, his face suddenly twisted, 'I'll break his kneecaps, you hear?'

'Yes, Ayyare,' I said.

And with that final sally, he let us go.

14

Balan

Madras, 28 May 1990

It was still dark when I woke. I reached for my watch: 6 a.m.

There would be a few moments of respite before the hard light of summer leached colour from grass and sky. Madras was facing a water shortage again. I'd have to remember to tell Joseph not to wash the van. Kalyani's side of the bed was empty. She had probably gone downstairs to write.

'I wish my ideas would come to me at a more convenient time,' she said, the year she published the second book. 'But they always float into my head like this, between sleeping and waking. By the time I get to pen and paper they're gone. Would it bother you if I wrote in bed?'

'I sleep like a log,' I said, 'as you know.' It was one of our jokes, my sluggishness in the mornings. Since then

I had often woken to the hiss of her pencil racing across the pages of the notebook she kept on the bedside table. I found this surprisingly soothing and companionable. Mildly amusing, too, that the author of the slight Madhan – or was it Mohan? – and Mala books should take her labours so seriously. If she had forgotten to bring the notebook up with her the night before, Kalyani would force herself out of bed and stagger downstairs to write before she lost the idea.

I lay in bed, listening to the muffled distant roar of early morning traffic. The US tour was coming up in less than a month. A short stopover in London, a few meetings with old friends in the cultural relations circuit, and on to Chicago for the first leg of the tour. Another mental note: I needed to check the hotel bookings in Connecticut. We had planned to stay in an empty apartment, but the family that had offered it to us had had some crisis, and needed the apartment.

Ten years ago, I would not have thought it possible to get tired of travel, but more and more, these days, I found myself resenting it as a burdensome chore. There was too much to do and too many details to remember. Most of the performers I travelled with were festival circuit veterans, familiar with the routines, but the occasional group of folk dancers or tribal drummers could make a tour a nightmare. Their clothes were unsuitable for cold weather, their manners embarrassing; they drank too much on the flight, they leered at white women and tried to pick them up, they lost their passports, they complained about the food. The entire village would show up at the airport to say goodbye. I was taking some new Kathakali dancers from a small Kerala town on this trip – I'd have to keep an eye on them.

When, a considerable while later, Kalyani had not come up with my coffee, I felt a flicker of annoyance. Perhaps I had woken earlier than usual; perhaps my watch was wrong. The slight anxiety I felt before a long trip disrupted my sleep sometimes. I leaned over to Kalyani's side of the bed for her alarm clock. The movement of my arm sent her books flying off her bedside table. I walked around to her side of the bed and picked them up. They were from the Madras Literary Society, and like many of the dusty old tomes from that fascinating and poorly funded library, their pages crumbled when touched. Their debris – book crumbs, for all the care Kalyani took to turn the pages without destroying them – lay like confetti on the floor by the bed. I glanced at the titles: *Callianicarah Revisited*, by Rachel Carstairs; *The Callianicarah Gazetteer* by Sundry Hands. That awkward British spelling. Research for the setting of Mala and Madhu's latest adventure, or perhaps something Hema was reading before she left.

I was returning the books to the nightstand when I saw the note that was lying on Kalyani's pillow.

I smoothed the note out on the bed and saw that it had my name on it. I put on my reading glasses.

It was scrawled in an urgent hand on a sheet torn from her notebook. I read it twice without any sense of what it meant.

Balan,

There is something I never told you – I was never able to tell you. Before we met, I was briefly in love with a man – my dance master. We slept together (god, how coy that sounds) and I had a child by him. The boy is being brought up by my mother. He is sixteen now. This morning, my aunt Lila phoned to say she has had a telegram from my mother – the boy, his name is Amalan, is in trouble. (I never told you about my mother because of the boy, I didn't want you to find out.) He stole something, realized he's been found out, and has disappeared, has run away. I have to go to them – to Kalyanikkarai. I know I can't come back to you after. I'm sorry. Don't think badly of me. Please take care of Hema – don't let her miss me. I love her so very much. And I love you so much, though you will probably find it maddening that I should say this. Forgive me – I was never able to tell you because I feared losing you, and now it seems so stupid that I hid it. I have gone to Lila's house (cowardly – I admit it, I could not tell you this face to face, I have tried before). The train to Kalyanikkarai leaves at 3 o'clock. I'll come back at noon to pack a bag.

K

The 'forgive me' was heavily underscored.

The doorbell tinkled once, hesitantly, to herald the maid reporting for work. And then again twice, impatiently, announcing that the milkman had left four packets of milk in the basket on the doorstep. 7 a.m.

I heard everything and heard nothing, sitting on our bed, Kalyani's bed and mine. She always liked good notepaper, I thought irrelevantly. I had given her the notebook from which this sheet came, with its gold edges. I crushed the note tight in my hand and smoothed it out again.

I examined the sixteen-year-old pattern of our marriage and saw no flaw in the design, nothing that warranted a message like this. There had been no serious quarrel, no disappointment. Things had been going well for us. I had been a good husband, a steady provider.

I willed myself to consider meanings and consequences. I cast about for rationalizations. She could not be abandoning me now, when I had preparations to make for one of the three most important NATAC tours of the year. The Festival – did she want to go to the US with me, was she manufacturing drama so that I would take her with me? No; I knew this explanation did not fit. We had sworn that we would not use government funds to take family trips, and we had stuck to it. Of course she could take a trip, we would take a trip together, on our own time. (But what time did I have that I had not committed to NATAC?)

Something must have come up between us; some dissatisfaction she could not tell me about, some injury I had inflicted on her. She was punishing me. She would laugh, perhaps, and say: 'It was a cruel joke, but I needed to know you love me. It's all right now, Balan, everything's fine.' Was it her birthday? An anniversary? But that did not fit either. She was not like that. If I missed her birthday, I bought her a gift on some other day, and she was content.

Was it the quarrel we'd had the night after Padmasini's show? I was very brusque with her, true, but that was because I was tired. I was too tired to cope with her sudden outburst about the way NATAC managed its funds. What had she said? 'Balan, if NATAC lets Padmasini take such a huge chunk of this lifetime award budget, what will the dasi dancer get?' She was attacking me, of course, not NATAC. I told her it was none of her business. Later I remembered that Kalyani came from a dasi family, and I regretted what I had said. And we made up.

Perhaps she was ill. 'Can't come back after' – oh, I thought, what nonsense. She lived on her nerves. She had been on the brink of breakdown once or twice. She would be back. She couldn't, wouldn't, survive on her own. She needed me.

Downstairs, my mother began to tinkle her prayer bell. 7.30. Had I been sitting on the bed blankly for thirty minutes?

I read the words again, and yet again, and some sort of understanding came to me. Rage brought the blood rushing to my head – how could she do this to me, how could she be so selfish – and panic drained it again – I would have to tell Hema, I would have to tell my – please let it be a nightmare, let me wake now – tell my *mother*.

I went to the bathroom and splashed cold water on my face. My arms and hands shaking the way they might shake if I had carried an object too heavy for me; my knees buckling. Nausea. The towel rack and the haggard face in the mirror spinning, mocking me.

Amma sat at the dining table, pinching garlands out of cotton. How many of those damn garlands did her gods need?

'Your coffee – it is sitting here, cold, with that layer of cream on top that you hate. She's late again. I had it ready. It isn't my fault.'

'Amma, no one is blaming you.'

'I have something for you.'

'What is it?'

She pulled her bunch of keys out of her sari at her hip, sorted through them and pulled one off the keyring. 'This key – it is to her cupboard. I had it made so you can see what she is up to. She has been up to something – I keep telling you, and you – you'll find something. Don't tell her I had the key made.'

I sat very still. The key was in my hand.

'What do you mean, she is up to something?'

'There are other men, Balan. Yes. When she goes out, look in her cupboard.'

'Kalyani isn't – she isn't here today.' I noted with disbelief that I was stammering.

'What? Where is she?'

'Something came up during the night. With – with her family.'

'In the *night*? Just like *that*? What are you telling me? What *family*?'

'She had to – do something. In a hurry. She left me a note, that's all.'

Amma finished the garland automatically. Her hands never stopped, no matter what was happening in the world; in a nuclear war she would be the same, her religiosity driving her, always a hand hovering over a lamp, a flower for the gods, a tintinnabulation of prayer bells. She draped the length of cotton over a model of Rama's feet, in mythological rather than functional sandals.

'Rama, lord,' she said, placing her head on the plaster feet, 'are you testing me again?'

Gaudy oleographs of her gods, their halos carefully drawn by hand around their heads, their shapes obscured by the cotton garlands, hung on every wall in the house. I looked away.

'Am I hearing you right, Balan? Are you saying that a wife simply vanished into the night, left a note – no, I won't say anything. It isn't my place to speak in this house, after all.' She began fluffing out more cotton.

I braced myself for the innuendo, the accusation.

'No *normal* woman would leave her husband and go away in this kind of *hurry*. Why didn't she explain, why didn't she get your permission? Where can she need to go that she must creep out like a thief?'

I said, 'Someone in her family – someone must be ill.' Kalyani herself had vanished, she had escaped the interrogation.

'*Must* be, is it? You don't know? You don't know who, or how ill?'

I wished I hadn't started the lie about the illness. I hadn't thought it through.

She stared back at me impassively. A muscle worked at the side of her jaw, a faint suggestion of triumph, and I wondered briefly if she had made Kalyani leave me, somehow, if she had harmed Kalyani.

'I *warned* you – a thousand times. Her kind will never settle down – it's not in their blood.' Her voice trembled. 'I should know, seeing what your father's dealings with them were.'

'Amma. It isn't helping, this talk of *her kind*.'

'She's run away with someone. There, I've said it. You can tell me off now.'

I gathered my breath for an angry retort, checked myself, and expelled it in a rush. I remembered a time when my mother had been different. Tiresome, straitlaced, tyrannical, but more loving, and more kindly. Happier, perhaps. Then Appa got involved with the Pro-Art Progressives, arranging concerts for dasis. So many dasi women in those days, washed up, along with all the other wrack of modernity, on Madras's shoreline. But his professional interest in the dancers was mixed up with his libidinal one. He began to come home after midnight, or not at all. It was perfectly obvious to me, in my teens then, that he had a mistress – it must have been Lilavati. It was painfully obvious to Amma. How she wept and raged. Those pilgrimages, those prayers and sulks, all driving Appa further from her.

I looked at Amma with the lines etched in acid on her face, and thought, so this is how she felt with Appa. This being pierced by a fierce, hot claw, I thought, is sexual jealousy, and there is no immediate antidote to it.

'What sins did I commit in my past lives,' she was saying, 'that I have to put up with this? It seems we cannot ask even for *chastity* these days, we have become so modern. Who knows where she is gadding about?'

'*Amma*.' My voice was hard. I wanted to retreat to a place of privacy, but there was no place in the house, no place in the *world* private enough for this welter of emotions: all this fear, fury, confusion.

Amma said again. 'It's in her blood, she can't help herself.'

'What do you mean? Why do you say these pointless things?' I was shouting, losing control. The whole thing seemed absurd and melodramatic. Such things happened to families in which couples had been forced by their elders into uncomfortable partnerships, in families where the men were fist-happy, scabrous brutes and the women miserable overworked slatterns. Not to me, not to a man of some education and culture; not in this house, where the mirrors were Belgian and the bronzes genuine fourteenth-century Chola, where we knew how to love and respect each other.

'You say she's gone to see family,' Amma said. 'And I say, what family? Who does she have in this world apart from that – that – *slut* Lilavati?'

But that was where she had gone, I remembered. It was where I could reach her. I will go to Lila's house, I thought, and she will come back with me, and it will be all right again.

When I got dressed and went to the garage, I found Joseph washing the van.

'Why didn't you ask me?' I found myself shouting. 'With the water shortage and everything, why – oh, never mind, give me the keys.'

'Let me drive you, saar,' Joseph said.

'No,' I said.

It would be all right, I told myself over and over, as

I wove through the congested streets of George Town. But my mind would not work. I was an intelligent man, an educated man. This one thought – that Kalyani had slept with another man – this one thought had driven out every other coherent thought. It was humiliating. I was a beast, snarling and lashing its tail, tasting in my mouth fear and revulsion and self-pity, smelling of feral rage. The irony of it was that I could not take this humiliation to anyone else. I had to be secret.

Yet I wanted to talk about it.

There was no one to talk to but Kalyani.

For some time now, she had not shown her love in the ways she used to. On the balcony, suddenly, while we were sitting together, snatching up my hand and pressing it to her chest, 'Do you love me? Promise me you will never leave me. Promise me.' Crying when I left on a trip that would last three days, in the beginning. These days she waved to me cheerfully from the balcony.

There was, inevitably, I suppose, the cooling of passion. A year or two after our wedding, she had begun to shut herself away from me. Not physically, but mentally. How could she do that suddenly – be private and engaged, as if this world were well lost – me, Hema, this home, this life I had offered her – her mind wholly elsewhere, absorbed; in what? Tell me what, I said sometimes, tell me what you are thinking.

Nothing, she said, not hiding the twinge of annoyance because I had dragged her back from her singing or from a daydream. It seemed to threaten everything, the whole basis of our life together, if she could slide a window shut against me like that, sitting two inches away from me, my arm actually draped along the back of the sofa, her head actually resting on it. My arm has gone to sleep, I had to say, or: my shoulder hurts, I need to shift. When we were newly married, I could not bear it when she seemed indifferent to me, not for a minute. My body hurt me. I could not work. But as soon as she wrenched herself out of the reverie or stopped humming her song, I was happy. I could work again, I could stop paying attention to her.

Yes, she was a little disappointed in me. She fell in love with the fire-breathing idealist, and had to live with the successful bureaucrat. Idealism, that dim memory, the luxury of the young. The forties and fifties are the years of three-ring binders, ergonomic chairs to keep the vertebrae from buckling, unread library books, dreams of escape. Paris, New York, London, Athens: they were once distant, full of allure. Now I travelled through their airports several times a year, trying to placate the prima donnas from Delhi and Madras who felt they had not been given the best seats in Business Class, or the most expensive hotel rooms. I searched frantically for some way of repairing mridangams after American Customs had torn them open looking for drugs. I went into the toilet stalls at Frankfurt after some folk dancer from Bihar had used them, to check if he had pulled the flush. I suffered unspeakable boredom on the long flights.

I accepted the limitation of Kalyani's love. I never betrayed her trust, not with the young women, dancers and singers, in whose proximity I stayed in hotels far from home. I had never been unfaithful in deed, though I had wrestled with temptation. Somewhere in all this I kept a spark burning for her.

In Lila's house, I found Kalyani alone. She opened the door, saw me, and flinched.

'We'll talk later,' I said. 'Come back home.' Meekly, she gathered her things and locked Lila's door behind her. 'Isn't Lila here?' I held the van door open for her.

'She left by the early morning train. Your mother–'

'What did you expect?'

'I'm sorry.'

Back in our house, we found my mother pacing up and down, on the balcony, up and down; though she did not pass our bedroom window, or look in, she came far enough towards it for us to see her shadow bobbing on the curtains. I pulled the window shut.

'Oh don't, it's so suffocating!' Kalyani cried. She sat on the bed, twisting her sari end in her hands. Her packing was half done. She seemed unable to concentrate. She was behaving as if she had already left me, as if she had made that decision. Should I not have been the one to accept or reject her? But she was restless, waiting to go – to her son.

I could not fathom this mother-love that pulled her back to that child, conceived in blind lust.

'Kalyani,' I said. 'The man – your child's father.' That was said equably. Underneath, I was seething. *His* child by *her*, another man impregnating her where I did not and could not. 'Is he in Kalyanikkarai?'

'What do you mean?'

'Are you going to him?'

'No. I don't know. I don't even know if he is still alive.'

I did not believe her. I saw him, his head resting on her belly big with his child.

'When you gave birth, did he . . . did you play with

the baby together? Did you feed the baby, did he watch you–' I never had that, the pride of a man watching his wife's breasts satisfying his child's hunger. My first wife did not live long enough to feed Hema. Would he have turned the baby's head with a forefinger, brushing the breast, if it did not latch on properly? I saw him running his tongue over the wet nipple after the baby had drunk, a little jealous, wanting to taste.

'No. He never saw our child. Not when Amalan was a baby.' She said that wonderingly, as if she would have liked him to have seen. He had abandoned her; I had given her a home. I had given her love.

'You should not have lied to me.'

'No, I should not have.'

'You should have told me.' I had rescued her from poverty, from heaven knows what else. I let her forget that she had been rescued. I never put the burden of gratitude on her.

She wanted to leave me to go to that child whom she gave up sixteen years ago. Did our love of sixteen years mean nothing to her, did Hema, who accepted her so completely as her own mother – not a moment of resentment – did she mean nothing?

I suddenly remembered how Hema would crawl into the bed between Kalyani and me when she had nightmares, her body sweaty and wriggling, irritating me.

'You're seven years old, Hema,' I would say. 'Too big to crawl into our bed every time you have bad dreams.'

'Oh, let her come to us,' Kalyani always said.

'At her age, I was–'

'–in a room with your sister,' Kalyani would say

immediately. Now would my sister have to know? Had Amma already told her? 'You don't know what it's like not to have siblings. If Hema had a sister or a brother, I daresay she'd find comfort there, but she has to make do with us.'

'All right. Only – how the child does jerk and wriggle about.'

Was Hema not enough? Hema, who had said to me, on more than one recent occasion, 'Appa, it simply isn't right, the way Vijaya Paati treats Amma, and how you accept it. If you won't do something about it, I will.'

There had been days, some years ago, when I felt I could not understand Kalyani at all. My patience was tried by her unstable moods, her refusal to talk to me, her air of secrecy. She cut herself with razor blades. I felt the crisscross scars on her thighs. Strange creature: even at her most neurotic, she was careful to mutilate parts of her body that were not on public view.

'Isn't this a little – *crazy*, Kalyani?' I suppressed in myself the traces of revulsion. I saw her through those crises. I helped bring into being therapeutic Mala and Madhan. Were her fictional children not enough?

After all these years to have my bitter, truth-seeing mother proved right. It was all tainted, it was dirty and meaningless.

I too can throw it all away, I wanted to say. I can drive you out of my home, you slut, you liar, and no man will condemn me for it. I said to myself, I will rip her imprint from my body, even if I must flay myself. I will dispel her scent. I will be alone again, and whole, get back the integrity of my self without dependence, and never love another woman in my life.

But I would throw away sixteen years of our life together.

'Tell me what it was like,' I said.

'What?'

'To be with him, to – to sleep with him. That man.' Had he been a better lover than me?

'But you made love to your first wife, Balan. I neither expected nor wanted you to be a virgin. And I never asked you what it was like with her, though I was curious.'

'That was different.'

'How? How was it any different from my love for Velu which never came in the way of my love for you?'

She was trying to trap me into admitting that I had a double standard. I could not think why it was different. But it *was*.

'It is different because it is generally better for a woman if a man has more experience. The important thing is, I did not hide anything from you.'

'You gave your first wife a child. You made a child together.'

'Yes, and I told you–'

'And you told me that we would not have a child because you were sterilized when she died.'

'Well?'

'You were not. We could have had a child, if you had wished. You had the vasectomy a month before our wedding.'

'How–'

'Last year, when you asked me to send you a blood report from your medical files. When you blacked out at the airport in Frankfurt. I didn't mean to see the report of your surgery, but I couldn't help it – the dates were right there in front of me.'

'All right. You lied and I lied. You may not believe this, but I had myself sterilized to protect the child we might have had. Amma would have made things impossible, and I did not have it in me to turn her out or leave her in this house on her own. She had been a mother to Hema when there was no other woman to look after her – she had been kindness itself. I did not want to have to choose between our child and Amma. And I lied to save you hurt.'

'All right.'

'My lie changed me, Kalyani. It changed my life. I had never lied about important things before. And this was a big lie, wasn't it? Denying a woman the possibility of a child. Of a child by her husband, I suppose I should say now. Having denied you that, everything else I did followed directly from it – adapting myself to a job I would have lost very quickly if I had hung on to my ideals, making sure you could stay in this house that you loved so much–'

'I wish you had not done any of that. I'd have been happy in a hovel with you.'

'Kalyani, stay here with me.'

'I cannot.'

'Then at least tell me who he was, the man you had this affair with.'

'Why do you want to know? What difference will it make?'

'You said his name, you called him Velu. Tell me.'

'He was an adept, Balan,' she said. 'He could keep two different rhythms with his two hands and recite in a third.'

'What was he like?'

'He was harsh with me,' she said, 'but he taught me everything he knew; he held nothing back, though I could not afford to pay him for my lessons. The kind of teacher who teaches his pupil everything he knows – out of love, and I don't mean physical love – is a rarer thing than a lover. That kind of love, Balan, it isn't quite the same as the love I feel for you. It happens all the time. It is hard for a pupil not to be a little in love with her master.'

'What did he *look* like?' I said. She was being evasive.

'He was much older than me. Balan, you met him. Don't you remember? Ten years ago, the man whom you helped set up as Padmasini's choreographer? Vadivel Vathyar – Velu – from Kalyanikkarai?'

It was bewildering, the thought of Kalyani in love with the wizened, unwashed alcoholic whose face swam up into my memory. The shock of it – that I had met this man and spoken to him – hit me physically. The rival, manifested as flesh and blood, I discovered, was not a whit more tolerable than the rival conjured up by the imagination. How he must have laughed at me as I helped him. Had Kalyani and he seen each other secretly then? Had my mother been right about her *blood*?

I felt rage tightening me up until I struggled for breath. I forgave her. Then I took it back. Then I forgave again. I went out and tramped round and round the house to ease my heart, smashing my shoes down into the grass and gravel, frightening the women. Two pairs of anxious female eyes following my farcical perambulations.

I went back upstairs again. I didn't want to know the details. I wanted to know the details.

'How many times?'

'What?' She was folding a sari on the bed; flapping it out and folding it again, as if she would set the world to rights in this way.

'How many times were you – did you – sleep with him?'

'Balan, what does it matter? It's over. Can't you treat it as finished?'

'How many times?'

'Once,' she said, finding the insight to lie. 'Just once.' But I knew she was lying. She had measured the magnitude of her error in telling me about this affair. Should she have stolen away, leaving no explanation? Would that have left me whole and sane?

Her folding and packing done, she sat like a child with her hands folded in her lap. 'Just once.'

The images that passed before my eyes grew more lurid, more lacerating. I imagined the man's hands on her breasts, on her sex. I imagined her doing to his penis what she did to mine. I felt pinned and helpless.

She should have told me.

Would it have made a difference?

No.

I suddenly remembered, with a rush of sentiment, how I had pointed to the star Arundathi during our wedding. Arundathi the constant. I had forgotten. How I had infuriated everyone, laughing at the solemn wording of the wedding mantrams, how I had challenged the priest. Only the Arundathi had made sense to me. The man shows it to his bride. The little ritual had provided a lovely excuse to be away from the wedding crowd, alone on the balcony with her, under the stars.

Didn't they describe the cuckold as the man with the horns? But no (this agony was actually physical, it was making acid rush into my stomach), it was the other fellow who had the horns, and the cuckold was the one who was spitted on them, *skewered*–

'What are you doing,' she cried. 'If you slam your fist into the wall, you'll break your bones!'

Impaled on the hellish poison-tipped points like – I had no analogy, I had no name for the feeling, I could kill her.

But was I in a technical sense a cuckold? Could I be a cuckold if I had been betrayed before I was married, not after? I went back to her, tried to put my arms around her. I was furious that she was just sitting there passively, her packed suitcase at her feet, though she need not leave for the station for another hour. She pushed me away

'Balan, where has all this feeling been stored?' she cried at last, more in exhaustion than in anger. 'How could you, how *dare* you, after treating me with such indifference and courtesy all these years, so that I was coming to think that nothing I did would matter to you, suddenly unleash this – this – *cyclone* on me? All this jealousy and rage?'

She turned from tidying the top of her dresser to ask me this, and I found myself studying her beauty despite her swollen-eyed dishevelment. I found myself watching her as she blew her nose, as she absently ran a comb through hair that still fell to her hips, as she moved suddenly to stroke the strings of her tambura, as she reached up to the print over our bed and wiped the glass.

What to tell her? It was not true, the indifference part. How was I to explain the way I felt about her? The overpowering hunger, complicated, half of it because of her beauty and her intelligence, half arising from an illicit dream of power over her that I could never confess to? How to explain to her the repressed yet burning eroticism of the brahmin man?

But she had ceased to defend herself. She turned away from my questions. Her whole self was elsewhere. And at two o'clock, she pushed a small heap of jewellery towards me – 'I don't want your mother to think I am robbing you of your property.' Things I had given her. 'I am keeping one or two things–' she held something out, I could not see what, 'you can have them back if you want to.'

No, I said, no, I don't want the things–

At five past two, refusing to let me drive her to the station, refusing to let me go with her, refusing, even, to let me carry her suitcase to the waiting autorickshaw, saying goodbye to Kuppu but ignoring my mother, she was gone.

It was unreal. The bed was empty on her side. The library books had been left. This was a new country, a nightmare landscape, obscured by sudden deafness and blindness and disorientation. I floundered stupidly, my palms and my face suddenly wet.

'I can't sleep,' my mind said over and over. 'I can't sleep.' Just before midnight, I picked up the telephone and dialled the number of Hema's room in the tourist bungalow. When she answered the phone, I couldn't bring myself to say anything about Kalyani.

'The film's almost done, Appa,' she said, making conversation. 'We were supposed to finish it yesterday, but there's been a ruckus over some jewellery Padmasini left sitting in a purse next to a window in the bungalow – ask me why she was in the bungalow in the first place?'

'Why?'

'Trying to get into Shah's pants. The horrible thing is that one of the boys who stole the jewellery is Rajayi's son–'

'Kalyani's son.'

'No, Rajayi's.'

'He's Kalyani's son.'

'Appa, what is it? Are you trying to tell me something? Something's wrong–'

I explained, haltingly and with some misgivings, what I had learned about Kalyani.

'I didn't make the connection earlier, Hema. She must be related to Rajayi, she said something about her mother, in the note she wrote. I only just remembered.'

'Oh. Oh, god.' Her voice soothed me, slow, unexpectedly thoughtful for a girl – woman – of nineteen summers. 'I don't think I fully understand what Amma's relationship to Amalan is, but this makes sense of several things I've noticed. I don't know what you are thinking, or what you want to do, but I am on Amma's side. You know I've always been on her side.'

'Then will you go to her, if you can do it safely? I am sorry about calling you this late at night–'

'Of course. I was already planning to help search for Amalan, for Rajayi's sake. I'll go to Amma, if she is at Rajayi's. Will you come here tomorrow?'

'Thank you,' I said, 'and good luck with the searching. Yes, I'll come to Kalyanikkarai. I'll leave at about five-thirty in the morning, so expect me late in the afternoon.'

The key my mother had given me was in the pocket of the shirt I had worn in the morning. I took it out, opened Kalyani's cupboard. I touched the cotton blouses and petticoats and silk saris that smelt of her, and held the clothes to my face, inhaling. She had not taken very much, I realized. Was she coming back? Or was she rejecting everything I had given her? I found an album wrapped in silk and studied our wedding pictures.

I found author copies of her books – Mohan, not Madhan, and Mala – and read each one. Suddenly I understood Hema's annoyance with Mala, and I saw Kalyani pouring her paralysis, her helplessness, into this character. I understood something about Kalyani's life with me, under my mother's shadow, in this house.

In a drawer, wrapped in woollen shawls I had bought her, that she never had occasion to use in Madras, at around one in the morning, I found the notebook I had given her this year. She was writing the history of her family. There were chapters on her childhood, chapters about our courtship. There were gaps in the narrative. I skimmed rapidly until I reached the chapters about her Vathyar.

I began to read.

15

Kalyani

Kalyanikkarai, 1971–1973

When I came back from the mission house, after more than a decade of being away from Kalyanikkarai, I avoided my old acquaintances. A chasm had opened between the girl I was when I belonged to them and the woman I had become after years of belonging to Aunt Rachel. All my life since then I have built frail notional bridges from past to present, from one self to the other, and have not expected them to bear me safely across the gap.

I had built up hopes of being a school teacher, with my English education, and at first, the Kalyanikkarai Government Elementary School showed interest when I applied for a job. Then the headmaster heard that I was a dasi's daughter, and the school closed its doors to me. There was a shop on East Main Street near the temple's south gopuram that sold things used for worship: kungumam powder, turmeric, clay dolls of gods, brassware for rituals. The owner needed someone to sit in the shop in the mornings when there was not much business. My wages reflected this, but I was glad to have a job.

One evening, two months after I had come back, I met Velu Vathyar on Musicians' Street.

'So you've done all right for yourself,' Velu Vathyar said. 'Never came to see us. Not once.'

'Aunt Rachel – Kokku Missy – would not let me.'

'She was not watching you when you came here. You should have come to see us at least, even if you didn't want to come back to dance. My father missed you. He is a sick man now.'

I hung my head. It was indeed shameful that I had not visited Samu Vathyar when he was ill, and he on the same street as us. It was impossible to explain the strain and disturbance of moving between those worlds, my mother's and Aunt Rachel's; to explain the inertia that made me long to remain in one element and one world for a stretch of time.

'So,' Velu Vathyar said, 'why are you back now?'

'I'm back home for good. Aunt Rachel's nephew came and took her away to Australia.'

'Are you coming back to dance?'

'I never thought about it.'

'Come back and learn,' he said. 'It will please my father.'

I went to see Samu Vathyar after work that evening. He lay on a string cot, a gaunt old man. His ribcage expanded and contracted with each breath he laboured to take. He peered at me, not looking in the least bit pleased.

'Why did you not train to be a school teacher?' he growled. He was as terrifying as ever, even with his vision almost completely gone now. The ripe opaque cores of his cataracts were visible in his irises. 'Eh? Why come back to this?'

'I don't know,' I said.

'Hmm. Tuck your sari up and get in position,' he said. 'Let's see if you have any talent left.'

I began to dance again.

Over the next few weeks, Samu Vathyar taught me a new varnam. The absence of people (his wife had died, his girls had married and gone away) in the booming hall made his tapping-stick sound hollow. Velu brought him food, changed his clothes, plumped his pillows, fetched the doctor. He taught the younger students their steps. There were brahmin girls in the class now, smug and thin-lipped. There was need for their money and their goodwill. They brought their own water, to stave off the pollution of quenching their thirst in the home of a nattuvanar, so many rungs lower than them on the caste ladder.

The control of the traditional masters was worn away by this difference in caste. The new pupils danced indifferently. Since Velu Vathyar knew quite well that neither they nor their parents would tolerate the old pedagogy – the sticks flung at the stumbling legs, the dancing for hours without a break, the curses and insults – he developed a sort of ferocious patience. He withheld the best dances from the brahmin girls. He filled his mouth with betel leaf and betel nut. When he could not bear to teach, he went out and spat noisily into the drain. His betel-chewing was an insult.

I had to wait for my lesson until the brahmin girls had finished and left. If I lost my balance or moved clumsily, Velu was foul-mouthed. My shani, my curse, he cried, mocking me because he could not mock the brahmin girls. Gnanasoonyam, ignoramus. I tried on the movements he taught me, tried on the mind that went with such movements, the ethos that had produced them. Growing up as Callie, I had not learned what Kalyani would have learned by instinct, by osmosis: how to love, how to respect, how to seduce, how to insult, how to walk, how to spit, how to make a bed, how to pick flowers, how to count money, how to hate. I felt as square and angular as furniture; as wooden. My arms felt unfamiliar. I felt discomfort in every one of my tight muscles.

I learned the gestures for the varnam: a woman preparing a bed with flowers; a woman pointing to her own breasts that were heavy with desire; a woman sending her parrot to her lover, with a message. Of course I had danced a varnam at my arangetram, but that was before I knew the meanings of the lyrics. *I want to make love to you, lord of the fifty-four kingdoms on the banks of the Kalyani.*

If I hesitated before the sexual explicitness of the gestures, Velu's mouth became wry. 'So you've learned this from your white Christian Mamma,' he would say. 'So you can't make the bed to receive your lover or describe the beauty of a woman's breasts any more.'

288

How did my mother dance so differently from me? Her dance was part enactment (so remote, so ritualized, the neck flicking lightly from side to side, keeping the beat, no vulgar grasping at the real), and part conversation (so easy, so natural, like talking to one's cook or one's husband). I had to *act*. All the dancers in the class now were *acting* their emotions; they had been watching the way actors emoted in the movies; they didn't know how to *enact* anything. How? I thought, envious, thrashing about in my body, how did my mother do that?

But the world that had called for enactment was obliterated. It was dead already, though I tried to revive it in my body.

After many months of dancing with Samu Vathyar and Velu, I began again to feel the fluency of my body. When I had been a child, I had danced what I was told to dance; now I understood more about the composition of each piece, about music and rhythms, and about teaching dance so that it was subtly adapted to the body or the personality of the student. I began to teach the younger children in Velu's class, and I took a small share of their fees home. I still worked at the shop. The money helped my mother and me survive from month to month. The only other income was rent from a portion of the house which had been sectioned off, if I remember right, the year I began to dance.

Samu Vathyar died in his sleep one summer night. Velu Vathyar continued to teach me. His hand had begun to shake when he wrote down the notation for a song. Wasn't he, I wondered, too young for that? The tremor would roll down his fingers into the curlicues of his *thadinginathom* in Tamil, making the letters hard to read. I had not read Tamil for years. Now I could read it well enough when it was printed, but I slowed down when it was hand-written. He lost his temper when I could not decipher his notation for the songs I was learning. He blamed my Christian Mamma.

When he taught me, I was compelled to give the dance everything I had. The hollows of my neck became cups of sweat; my muscles, even though they were supple again, ached. With me, he still enforced discipline of the old-fashioned kind. Not the kind that the modern individual would tolerate, but the kind that broke down the self to reveal the dancer, some grander, stronger force than the self, all hamstrings and energy, all seduction and poetic intuition, underneath. He was the medium of my surrender to something transcendent, apart from myself. I needed him, for I had been taught too much individuality by Aunt Rachel, and I did not know how to exercise my craft simply and directly, without the veils of analysis, timidity, moral doubt.

It was almost logical for a woman whose art did not flow unimpeded by self towards god or king or world, the way my mother's had done, but needed a human medium; it was almost logical, I realize now, to take her master for her god, and then by degrees for her lover. Years of searching his face for infinitesimal signs of approval, years of waiting patiently as he tapped out combinations of steps with one hand, kept time with the other.

The universe had to be pared down to this: a leg

stretched just so, a movement of the hands so precise it was a stillness in the movement of the world. My feet described clean squares and perfect circles. The expressiveness, the emotion, they had to come from passion that was deeper than geometry, and Velu was there, the water that wore down the rock of my self.

Until I married Balan, everything I really knew, deeply, everything that accorded with my impulses and felt agreeable to my body, came from Samu Vathyar and Velu Vathyar. When I came back from the mission house, and for years afterwards, when I thought of Velu, I could have wept with gratitude. I actually did weep when I was feeling volatile. Watching Hema struggle with her loathing of Padmasini, I was often on the verge of telling her what a teacher might be to a student.

And what was I to Velu? The complex combination of rhythms he thought up needed a body to bring them to fruition.

In that empathy – in that moment of being the female body which would interpret and complete the man's creation – love was easy, inevitable.

I watched Velu, fascinated by the way he did things. Eating, for instance: he heaped the rice on his plate. He washed the white glutinous grains with buttermilk, placed them precisely in his mouth and swallowed them sensuously as if they had a strange glory, as if he had never seen rice before and would never again get a handful of it to eat. I could see it going down the tunnel of his throat. I had become used to white people's table manners at Aunt Rachel's board. Now I gave them up again. I watched the way he spoke the solkattus for the dance, the syllables coruscating in his mouth, the tongue imitating the slackness and tautness of the mridangam's skin, the slow beats resonant and weighty, the fast beats like a pebbly rush of brook.

And acknowledging to myself that I was in love with him (a little, I said to myself), I noticed how differently he treated me from the way he treated his brahmin students. He took no fees from me. He taught me everything he knew, not just the compositions he considered valueless, not worth shielding from the marketplace.

In Velu I saw an adamantine, even self-destructive stubbornness. He had set his face against the new regimes of dance, of government, of everyday life; but he made no avowals of faith in the old, unlike Rajayi. He seemed as remote and as unwavering as the pole star; in his cynicism, he seemed to have grasped the truth of things better than my mother, a dancer who had wavered and succumbed (it is better to give up dancing, she said; if only I could get a proper job in a shop! Be a teacher in the school!); better than Aunt Rachel, a Christian who had wavered and succumbed (the dasis, she said, were vestal virgins; she had learned this when she went to Madras, it was so fascinating yet reasonable, she said; Jesus was the Lord of the Dance too). Velu was nothing; not Hindu, not Christian, not atheist like my great-aunt Komala; he was a maker of dances obstinately labouring over his creations though they were no longer in demand. He was the most powerful man I knew, because he saw the truth (this is a dying art, he said, accepting what his father had told him, and we will have to let it go), and he would make no concession at all to the world.

He kept, instead, a covenant with the bottle. He had the erratic memory of the frequently drunk. There had been a cook at the mission house whose sweat and breath had smelt like this. So, I concluded, that was why his hand trembled.

I had never associated Velu with sensuality. Indeed, I had wondered if he noticed me at all, looking as he did during lessons at a point three inches to the left of my legs (but he always noticed when I made a mistake). I was startled, one day, by my sudden awareness that he desired me physically. I was tidying his betel leaf box, throwing away the broken tips of betel leaf, pushing all the fragments of nut into one compartment, smoothing out the long curling tongue of tobacco leaf. I heard his rough breathing, looked up, and saw him watching me. He did not touch me. I loved him the more for it. For months, then, nothing more than that quickened breathing, audible when there was dangerous proximity, that heightened awareness of each others' presence, after the students had gone home, after the street had grown quiet.

One evening after class, I heard the clinking of bottles on the terrace above Velu's house. I had never been up there, though looking up from the dance class below, I could see it through the strip of glass skylight. I went up stairs that were dirty from years of neglect. Velu was packing a worn carpet bag with empties from a great pile of bottles. A bottle was open beside him, and he was pulling from it. I had never actually seen him drinking before, and the loss of dignity – the comical bunching of the muscles of the face, the fuzzy expression – upset me. He would go now, I thought distractedly, he would walk down Musicians' Street with these bottles in his carpet bag, he would go to the wine shop on West Main Street and he would spend the fees his students had given him on drink, not food.

I had wanted for months to do something for him that would express my love. I had had childish dreams of rescuing him from a fire, perhaps, or from a boat that was sinking. I would at least stop him from going to the liquor shop, I thought, and, bold because I was being impulsive, half-laughing, I caught his hand and wrestled the bottle from his fingers.

Velu froze. It was not my action, I realized; it was his own response that was startling to him. His breathing unsteady, his hand moving almost involuntarily, he brushed the tips of my breasts, through layers of protection: sari, blouse, brassiere.

His touch was pleasurable. I had felt pleasure when I had discovered my own body's circuitry. Aunt Rachel had caught me mid-exploration once, and had read me a lecture on chastity, looking anywhere but at the hump of offending fingers over the offending nipple, under the cover of innocent half-sari. Under the sly groping of the mission house cook, my body had stiffened into martyrdom, and I had waited for the hands to be removed. But I liked the feel of Velu's hands on my breasts.

Velu struggled with the pin that held my sari to my blouse. He clumsily unhooked the buttons. He pushed helplessly at the straps of my bra. This reciprocal urgency I had never known before, this strong wish that the bra should fall away (I unhooked it at the back), that he should see my breasts.

I knelt in a heap of discarded clothing.

He was troubled and tender, as if he did not understand how we had moved from the fantasy of master and pupil to this friction of bodies. If I was aware of his sour alcoholic's breath or the roughness of his hands, with the five calluses where his teaching stick chafed his palm day after day, it only made all this seem more real, human, somehow.

I lay still on my back while he grazed my skin with his fingers, as if he were writing on my jumping skin, in curling Tamil script, the lines of a song.

In my imagination, I had even been through some version of this act with him a few times, not crudely, not with details like the feel of the rough floor hurting the small of my back, but delicately. In my fantasies, my sex had been available to him at once, without the intervening moment of undignified tugging (he was not used to underwear; his women, taken quickly in the market brothels, had worn nothing under their saris). In my fantasy, he had enveloped me, and I had been as contented as a child in her father's arms, specially chosen, wrapped, encircled, loved. And I had dreamed incongruous things into the act of our love; an English twilight from Aunt Rachel's recollections, Orientalia from her walls, an odour of lilies from the church.

That was how, in the inky downslope of an evening, under the flamingo clouds, between the end of dance class and the time of my mother's return from the temple, in the blink of an eyelid, in a mood of reckless abandon, I defied Aunt Rachel and my mother, and joined the ranks of the Fallen. And moreover, not having been struck by lightning, and having tasted the drug, and wanting more, and no longer caring to be a vestal virgin in order to dance, and finding that the heat of Velu's loins was still outpacing Velu's conscience by a yard or two, I fell perhaps a couple of dozen times more. A sort of pleasant sleaziness crept into the classes, which continued as before. Towards the end of the class, knowing what was coming, we felt an expectancy that was almost a relaxation.

On Monday mornings, when the shop was closed, Velu and I slipped away to walk among the hills that rose up so near Musicians' Street. In the palace orchards, the trees were untended. We walked under the ragged arches of banana leaves. Velu pulled down a livid cup of banana flowers hanging from one tree.

'You can drink honey out of them.'

I opened the pink-and-purple fleshy envelopes of the inflorescence, found the flowers, picked one and sucked from it, the nectar sweet as it touched my tongue. We walked on, touching the walls; the buildings, the royal stables, once full of horses and elephants, crumbled like soft biscuit. Other lovers had been here over the years, had scratched their names with shale on the patches of plaster, had vanished into time.

What would I do, the question was unavoidable, what was I going to do with myself? This work in the shop, the dance class, surely it was not going to be my destiny?

'You are at a good age to be married,' my mother said.

'I want to dance,' I said.

A young Christian teacher who knew me from the mission house was asking to marry me, she said. He had grown up in Kalyanikkarai too. Marriage, she said, think about it: marriage and security and children.

No, I said. I would wait.

The mission house man married someone else.

Walking south down a little footpath off Musicians' Street, to the east of the old palace outbuildings where my great-grandmother Jagadambal had once stabled her mare, one came to an odd hollow surrounded by rocky hills. In the middle of this hollow, where the rock had been shaved to the quick by ancient quarrying – the quarry had provided much of the granite from which the temple was built – a flat, smooth sheet of water lay cupped. It was clean, but dark and oily looking from being almost always deep in the shadow of the rocks. It gleamed like an eye. The pool was a mystery, opaque bronze and black water. In the harsh light of noon, sunlight lay trapped in it like a lode of fool's gold; washed out, easy on the naked eye, as if seen through smoked glass.

One Monday morning, about seven months after Velu and I had begun our affair – because that is what I must now call it – I had shaken Velu off when he suggested that we walk together, and I had walked to the quarry by myself.

To think. To try to think, at any rate.

What would I do, I thought, what would I do now?

Around the pool in the quarry, the rocks swooped

upwards into the sky, streaked with centuries of rain, haunted by a feral smell of bat, hung with fat hives over which the bees stirred, shimmering black.

I sat on a pillar that had tumbled from the shrine high up on the hill, and had fallen across the path that ran towards the palace grounds. I listened to the clinking echo of the hammers in the quarry, where the stone workers came to cut rock for kitchen counter tops as they had once come to cut rocks for the carving of pillars and cornices.

I looked up where the path led, shading my eyes from the sun, and imagined I saw Aunt Rachel striding across the chasms in a solar topi and sensible shoes, startling the bats, a paragon of health and attentiveness to detail. I imagined I saw my mother climbing the steep stone steps to the shrine on the hill, where she used to dance once a year.

I had once tried to climb those steps. The steps were little rock-cut depressions; there was barely room for a child's foot on their surface. My mother was going up, and she had assumed I would walk up as she did. Three-quarters of the way up, I had been overcome by terror.

'I can't go any further,' I had called out. I clung to the rock and moaned.

'All right, we'll go down then,' Rajayi said.

'I can't turn around and walk down!'

Rajayi tried to make me go down sitting on the rock – ignominious descent enough. I began well, but my foot dislodged a small stone, and its terrifying fall was my body pitching down the rocks, bouncing.

'I can't go down either,' I cried. 'I *can't*.'

I had climbed down, finally, backwards, feeling for

the steps with my feet, looking up at the great beehives hanging like pendants above me.

Velu had promised not to get me with child – he had said he knew how to prevent pregnancy, he was being careful. Only when I knew beyond doubt that I had missed my period twice did I feel a wrenching, gut-hollowing panic. Jesus, what would Jesus say? What would Aunt Rachel say? My mother – what would my mother say?

The pool's eye looked at me, watching and waiting: what will you do now, it said, and what will you do? Will you go forward, or will you go back?

Without knowing what she was saying, without thinking, swollen with rage at the withering of hope, at the waste of everything, Rajayi had cried, 'Oh, curses on you and the child in your womb!'

'Take it back!' I moaned, terrified. 'Take it back!'

Rajayi slumped on the swing. 'Of course. I didn't mean that. You have done a foolish thing. If you lie on the sugarcane, the ants will get you.'

After this outburst she made no reproaches. But she came with me to Velu's house the next day.

'How were you planning to take care of her, Velu-Thambi?'

Velu wiped his face. He had been thinking that he would throw the bottle away and start over. I would dance in the big city, in Madras perhaps, and we would be married, even though I was young and he–

'–old enough to know something of the world,' Rajayi said harshly.

'Old men take young women as wives all the time,' he said. His voice was weak, uncertain. 'There is no taboo against it.' But you are not old, I wanted to say.

'You have been a drunk for years,' Rajayi said. 'What they say in the town – a lush, a reprobate. And my child, and the child you have made with her, they must depend on *you*?'

'For the first time in a decade,' he said, stiffly, 'I am completely sober. I have thought about how I will deal with my – our – future.'

'You will need money.'

'I will go to Madras and teach there.'

'Velu Thambi, you'll need money if you want to go to Madras. Where will you raise enough to get started?'

Rajayi's bluntness spurred Velu to borrow money, to wash his clothes and pack them in a suitcase. He took the notebooks in which he had transcribed the compositions of his grandfather and father; he even took the family's treasures, the palm leaf manuscripts carefully preserved, full of the compositions that were part of his heritage. He wrapped them in silk, enfolded them in clothing. He left for Madras, promising to write as soon as he had found work and rented rooms for us. We would be married in the temple, my mother said, and she would come to Madras to help when the baby was due.

We waited, my mother and I. There was no word from Velu. Was it, I wondered, that the adamantine strength could resist the siege of modernity and money, but could not resist the bottle? Perhaps Rajayi had hidden his letters to me, not wanting me to throw my life away. Was he searching for me on a station platform in Madras, while I waited for him, growing heavier and heavier, no longer able to work, here in Kalyanikkarai? Had he found another student, another woman to have an affair with? Was he walking with her on the edge of the sea as we had walked in the desolate grounds of the palace?

'We have to go to Madras,' Rajayi said at last. 'He is not going to come back for you. We must have help when you give birth. We will go to Lila. She will take us in.'

'We can't just go to Madras like this.'

'Why not? I have written to Lila, and she has written back. There are hospitals there for you to have the baby.'

So, towards the end of 1973, we took the train to Madras. The baskets of saltfish at the station made me sick. We stayed with Lila. At the Hospital for Women and Children, where I was merely one pregnant woman among a hundred; where the labour rooms opened into each other and six of us women, giving birth at the same time, heard each other cursing or screaming, felt each other pushing; where a gentle and expert doctor ran from one pair of legs in stirrups to another, and the nurse thumped me on the thighs and pushed me back on the table when I raised my back to bear down; at the Hospital for Women and Children, Amalan was born. He was born six weeks before he was due, his skin blue and his lungs weak. The nurses took him from me and placed him in the nursery, but Rajayi insisted that they bring him out to be fed. His life hung by a thread for a few days, and then, when we were giving up hope, he suddenly grew stronger and was allowed to go home with us.

301

'Stay a little longer,' Lila said, rocking the baby on her veranda. 'We need to make plans.'

They sat in a huddle, my mother and Lila, they passed Amalan back and forth between them, they pulled his toes, they sang rhymes to him. They discussed my future while they patted him asleep.

Lila said to me, 'You must stop nursing the baby.'

'Why?' I said. 'He's not even three months old.'

'Because we must think of the future. Your body has to return to normal. We have to start going out so that you can be seen – look at you, if you don't feed him for two hours, your milk comes spurting right through your sari.'

Amalan would not take to the bottle. He spat out the rubber nipple, frantic and frustrated. His head twisting this way and that, he searched for my breast.

Lila set down the flat stone on which she crushed bark and herb and liquorice root for the baby's tonic. She ground neem leaves on it and applied the bitter juice to my nipples. Amalan tried to suckle, tasted the neem, and puckered up his face. I watched, bemused but still hopeful. I had given myself over to their plans – the break from Amalan would be temporary, Lila said, I would bring him back into my life when things settled down, when I had a man.

There had been no sign of Velu. I had looked for him at the concerts I had begun to attend with Lila.

In the mission house, soon after I was brought to it, Aunt Rachel took away the bright skirts my mother had sewn for me, and gave me a drab blue tunic to wear. The dress had belonged to a mission house girl who had outgrown it. I put my hands in the pockets: there were red seeds in the pockets. She must have picked them up for their brightness, and saved them.

Here are seeds, I had thought, suddenly happier, feeling the loss of my mother less; my lap had seeds in them. I had pockets; a new dress, anyhow; I had bright red seeds of happiness in the drab dress.

I had let Amalan go with my mother to Kalyanikkarai, and, as I wept for him, there had been Balan.

16

Kalyani
Madras, 1973–1977; 1980–1982

The Ambassador was almost at the gate when the man lurched across the road into its path. Joseph wrenched the steering wheel around.

'Oi, chief!' he shouted, all the more loudly because my presence ruled out swearing. 'Have you said goodbye to your family?'

The man got up on shaky legs.

'Falling in front of good people's cars and bilking them,' Joseph went on. 'Making cash for booze.'

'Wait,' I said. 'Help the man into the house.'

It was the first time I was seeing Velu since he had left Kalyanikkarai for Madras. The house was quiet; Balan was at work and I had just dropped Hema, nine years old that very morning, off at school.

'I did not know–' Velu looked around the living room at the genuine Tanjore paintings, the silk curtains, the brocaded cushions, confused. He had not expected to see me. 'Someone – someone gave me this address for Ba-Balasankar.' He looked at a paper he was palming.

'I am married now,' I said softly. 'Balasankar is my husband.' I turned, and behind me, Vijaya was coming down the stairs.

'Who is it?' Vijaya said.

'Someone come to see Balan. I'm trying to find out who he is.'

He understood, and took his cues from me. Vijaya went into her prayer-room, and left its door open. I went to the kitchen and asked Kuppu for some coffee.

It was an imperfect conversation.

'This Madras is incomprehensible,' he said. 'It's a strange place.'

He coughed suddenly, convulsively, before he had time to cover his mouth. I watched him wipe the specks of phlegm from the table in front of him, moving a pile of books to do this. In his hand was the familiar grimy shoulder towel. He had not refashioned himself for the city after all.

'You don't sound too good,' I said.

'I'm all right. What about you, though?' He coughed again. The cough became a fluid roar, like a waterfall, continuous. It shook his body and left a rasp in his voice. I waited until he stopped before giving him the coffee.

'Drink it while it's hot,' I said.

'I came to ask – Balasankar, your husband. Can he – is there any way–'

I saw his difficulty. 'Are you looking for work, Vathyar?'

The 'Vathyar' eased his heart a little. His face softened.

'I taught Padmasini Mahadevan for about two years when I first came to Madras. You know her? Then I stopped teaching her – there were words between us. Now–'

'Yes?'

'Kaliswaran, from Kalyanikkarai, do you remember him? He said she's looking again for a teacher to train her students.'

'Would you be willing to teach in her school again? To go back to work for her?'

'I have–' he coughed again. 'I have no choice. I need the work.'

'I will speak to my husband.'

As he got up to leave, he pointed to a book in the pile on the glass table. 'May I look at it?'

'Of course,' I said. 'It is a copy returned today by someone who had borrowed it. I have other copies – my husband wrote the preface for it. You can have it, if you like.'

At the door, he stopped and turned to me. 'You haven't changed,' he said. 'Your husband is a lucky man.' His eyes were rheumy, wistful.

So in 1980, Balan helped Velu mend fences with Padmasini. When Hema began classes with Padmasini a couple of years later, I saw him occasionally at the dance school. Padmasini had made him her factotum; he helped out in a general way in the school and choreographed dances and wrote solkattus on demand. He only taught the older students, because he frightened the little ones. His small acts of defiance had now become his habits. He seldom bathed, washed or shaved; silver stubble covered his jaw; the towel that he slung over his shoulder in lieu of a proper shoulder cloth was brown and covered with stains. He stopped sometimes and rocked back and forth furiously on his feet, like a man who was trying to remember something. He wouldn't last long in the school. Why do you have to do this, I thought; why can't you yield a little? But he could not yield, he would die rather than tidy himself up and teach made-to-order dances.

Velu sat on a grass mat in Padmasini's school. One of his few remaining students, an American-born dancer, came out of the bathroom after having exchanged her sari-and-pyjamas for a pair of jeans. She collected her notebook, her tape recorder, and handbag; her shoes swung from one hand. 'So long, master,' she said, her voice sprightly. She was relieved to be going home. Velu nodded indifferently.

'You never wrote to me,' I said. 'Why?'

'I was ashamed. I could not make a living. After I returned the money I had borrowed, there was nothing. I hated the teaching – there were no students like you.'

'Is Padmasini paying you enough?' I said. The girl had put on her shoes outside the door and was clattering down the stairs. 'She is a notorious miser.'

'The salary buys booze and betel leaves,' Velu said. He drew his dented betel leaf box closer to his knee. He propped its lid open. 'So, what do you think of this one's dancing?'

In the other room a shrill voice recited the steps: *Tha-thai-thai-tha! Dith-thai-thai-tha!* Young feet stamped their way rhythmically across the floor, Hema's among them.

'What can I say?' I said.

'You don't have to mind me. I'm beyond taking any pride in any of my students.' He had his own names for the girls. One was the Duck – she waddled. There was the Buffalo, who lumbered, and the Turkey, who had a dewlap. This one was the Crane; she had long skinny legs.

'You should see them. Each year it gets worse, the girls from America who come to Padmasini. Teach me exactly this or that, they say to me. Like choosing vegetables in the market. This one is bone-lazy. Her mouth works much harder than her limbs. Talk, talk. Beauty, Art. Wants a break every fifteen minutes to write everything in her notebook. If I sneeze, she writes it down to take to America. She tapes everything. She asks questions. She doesn't want to *work*. Dancers used to dance with their bodies in my day, not with their pens.'

It was a long speech for him.

'Vathyar.'

'Yes?'

'I haven't forgotten a single dance you taught me.'

'Do you practise?' He looked around the room as if he would ask me to stand up and get into position, start a varnam.

'I don't dance any more,' I said. 'I sing when he . . . when my husband has gone out.'

'When he has gone out.'

'Yes. But tell me what happened when you first came here.'

308

When he first came to Madras, and began to teach Padmasini, Velu Vathyar conducted her concerts, as a nattuvanar and teacher was supposed to do. The first five or six concerts went well. The second was at the Kapaali Temple. By December 1973, the prohibition of performances in temples, enshrined in the 1947 Act that had taken their livelihoods from the dasi women, had more or less fallen into desuetude.

The police winked at the festivities.

'What-to-do,' they said, 'the late Kalyanikkarai MLA's own niece is dancing. A brahmin woman.'

Just before the sixth concert, Padmasini discovered a man with a much more up-to-date style of singing than Velu's.

'I would like him to sing in the background, with you, Vathyar,' she said. 'It will be a help to you.'

'But I don't need help,' Velu said. He did not care for the young man's style; the young man was singing playback for the films and had no idea how to maintain a tempo that made sense for dance.

'We'll see how it goes,' Padmasini said, shrugging. 'And, Vathyar, make it a little faster this time. Let's not get stuck in the slow tempo.'

The performance went well. The reviews were good. The English papers talked of the Soul's Awakening as seen in the dance.

'Spirituality was in every lineament of the dancer's body,' said *The Hindu*.

The *Indian Express* expressed satisfaction that the Mayor was present. '"We commend the dancer," the Mayor said, "for dancing to such rare lyrics, lyrics that would be forgotten but for the sense of responsibility to the past demonstrated by people like Padmasini."'

The *Madras Evening Star* said: 'The Governor of Tamil Nadu graced the occasion, and noted: "It is heartening that the baby of bharatanatyam, the glorious divine dance of our ancestors, was not thrown out with the bathwater of the devadasi system."'

'Rukmini Devi presided,' the *Coromandel Post* noted, 'and said that bharatanatyam was a jewel that had fallen in the mud of a certain caste and become dirty, and people like Padmasini were showing that the dirt could be washed off.'

At the seventh concert, the new singer tuned the tambura, and the drummer set the mridangam's skins to his pitch. Padmasini whispered into the sound technician's ear. They began. The new singer sat beside Velu this time, rather than behind him. Velu understood. Padmasini had turned off his microphone, so that he sat there like a dummy except for his cymbals. The new singer knew the twists and turns of each song. He had rehearsed every move. When Padmasini wanted to signal something, it was the new singer she looked at.

This, for a master, a musician, a proud man, was the ultimate humiliation.

'You do not need my singing any more,' Velu said to Padmasini, returning her payment for the concert. She wouldn't take it from him. He flung the money into a corner and walked away. There would be other work for him.

But there wasn't.

The mothers of prospective students collected in the

homes of their friends and gossiped. 'Isn't Velu the one they say is a drunkard? We heard from Padmasini – better avoid him, she says.'

'His style is *so* old fashioned.'

The mothers exchanged views on the old love poetry. 'This Velu – he teaches the old dasi repertoire. Our daughter is from a respectable family, we can't let him teach her all those dirty erotic songs.'

'Yes, we want devotional pieces.'

'We want a style like Kamala Laxman's, in that movie, *Nam Iruvar.* You know, where she dances on the giant drum. Velu can't teach that sort of thing.'

It was the brahmin girls in Kalyanikkarai all over again, with the edge of cut-throat competition. The teachers and singers in the smaller towns had supported each other. Here, in the city, they were all competing for the same students and the same honours. And the brahmins were ubiquitous in the arts. They had occupied the radio stations, they ran the dance theatres, they had colonized the government's funding bodies. They were happy with what they were doing. They were taking ownership of other people's heritage.

'Try the Tamil Isai Sangam,' the clarinet player Kaliswaran said. 'They are the only ones who make a space for non-brahmins.'

But by this time – it was three years since he had left Kalyanikkarai, and he had no cause to be sober – Velu was back drinking. Where he could get legal liquor he drank it; where he couldn't, he found moonshine. He cultivated drinkers and wheedled liquor out of them. His skin was yellow. He owed three months worth of rent for the hole in the wall in which he lived. He went to see Lila. She turned him away: 'Where were you when Kalyani was waiting for you?' she said. 'Where were you when your child was born? Don't you come back to me, now, don't you show me your face again, you miserable soak.'

In 1977, Velu ran into Padmasini at a concert.

'I hear you have some manuscripts from your family,' Padmasini said. 'I know someone who'll publish them for you. There will be money in it.'

'I can give you my own notebooks,' Velu said. 'My family's manuscripts are precious. I don't want them going out of my hands.'

'I want the manuscripts,' she said. 'The notebooks won't be any use to me.'

He was given a paper that said he would no longer use those compositions himself until the book was published. He stared at the paper, disbelieving. Padmasini wanted him to stop using these songs that had belonged to his family's tradition for generations?

'This can't be right.'

'Yes, Vathyar. That is how these things are done.'

He went to his suitcase and took out the manuscripts. The palm leaves were heavy inside the silk cloth. He placed them gently on the bed and unwrapped them. The manuscripts had been inscribed on the leaves with an iron writing tool, and bound together, by an ancestor who had been worried about his failing memory. There were six of them in the bundle, the fruit of years of labour. Velu had said, in Kalyanikkarai, that he would never sell them. His father had given them to him, and he would give them to his son. Now he thought: what was the point?

Velu took the manuscripts to Padmasini. She inspected them, fingering the clasps that held the leaves together.

'But these are in Telugu!' she exclaimed.

'The old dance-teaching families always wrote in Telugu,' he said. 'My notebooks are in Tamil, though. You could take them instead.'

'No,' she said. 'I'll take these. Come and collect your advance tomorrow. The rest of the payment when the book is published.'

What happened about those manuscripts? he wrote to Padmasini three months, six months later. The tiny advance had dribbled away. The lodging house's landlord was banging on the door again, threatening to cut off water and light. Had the book come out? Could he have his palm leaves back?

There was no reply. Padmasini is on tour, the servants said when he telephoned. When he visited: she wasn't back from America, from France, from England.

At last he gave up the manuscripts as lost. He wrote a furious letter to Padmasini, packed his bag once more and went back to Kalyanikkarai. He met my mother there. She wrote to Lila and me about their meeting. It was hopeless, she wrote; he was cynical and full of self-loathing, and the drink was going to kill him. He had barely spoken to Amalan. He and his surviving brother had sold the ancestral house on Musicians' Street, and he was renting a room in the market.

Six months later Velu ran out of money again. He took on new students, giving them classes in their homes.

'You'd better start at the beginning,' he said to the students. It was not the drink speaking, he meant it.

'I've been dancing for fifteen years!' The dancers were indignant, their mothers outraged.

'You have been dancing for fifteen years, but you haven't been dancing well or correctly.' He would not compromise, he would not yield. He had no idea of the new diplomacy or the new fashions. They took two classes, three; they threw him out without paying him. This was when he came back to Madras, and came to see Balan about renewing his relationship with Padmasini.

The manuscripts that Velu wouldn't part with in Madras suddenly appeared in Delhi. Padmasini had found a penniless scholar who transcribed the lyrics from Telugu into Tamil. He did not wish to see his name immortalized on the cover; all he wanted was to be paid. A starving singer Padmasini had picked up during her travels in interior Tamil Nadu set the compositions to music; not in their original form, but with innovative twists. She did not need to acknowledge him either. NATAC published the final version of Padmasini's discovery, with an English commentary by Balan that explained the uniqueness of the compositions. The book brought Padmasini recognition as a scholar, a linguist, a researcher of rare archives, a reviver of traditions, as well as a composer and performer. It was not until Velu came to see Balan, and toppled a pile of books on a glass table, that he realized what had happened to those palm leaf manuscripts that he had brought with him from Kalyanikkarai.

By then he did not care.

Velu teetered on the brink of being a comic lush, but never quite lost the dignity that arose from a dry awareness of repressed talent. It is what we all had in common: Rajayi, this man, me. We had within us the volcanic pressure of a craft that had been honed and polished, laboured over lovingly, cherished, fed with hope and discipline and ambition, and then lodged within us useless. Except that, being a man, he had more licence to act in the world. He could exercise his craft once in a while, when rich women asked for it. After all, he was Samu Vathyar's son, even though he was no more than gaunt stripped bones rattling in a yellowing sack of skin. A dedicated alcoholic, a cadaver, the bilirubin creeping into his blood.

Velu scraped by for another year or two, living in a tiny room in one of Padmasini's outhouses and teaching in her school. His tenure was spiralling to a close. He had been arrested for trying to 'rob' a bank. It amounted to him lurching up to the teller and saying, 'I am a musician and I need money now.' He threatened the teller with a kitchen knife. No one took his attempt in the least bit seriously, but Padmasini still had to stand bail.

'I thought he would be useful, I thought he'd teach me something new. But he never taught me anything,' Padmasini said, sipping her tea one Saturday morning.

I sat with her while Hema was getting her dance lesson. 'He's disappeared now – hasn't come home since the police let him go. The driver found him lying in the ditch last week. He's forgotten everything, the bastard. How does he expect me to support him when he keeps annoying the students like this?'

('Ah, that Velu!' they had said in Kalyanikkarai, when he was young. 'What a remarkable talent, what an imagination, what a sense of rhythm, what a genius!')

'I shouldn't have let Balan talk me into having him back,' Padmasini said. 'Now I'll have to think of a way to get rid of him. He's disgusting. His room is so cluttered with rubbish – the remains of meals, dirty clothes, discarded newspapers – the servants won't clean it. The only thing he actually clears out of there is the bottles. He trades them in for more liquor. Handouts, handouts. I'm so *sick* of him. I don't need him. I've put up with him for years, out of pity. You know, Rukmini Devi herself said long ago that the best thing for this dance would be for the traditional teachers to be replaced by brahmins.'

The doorbell rang. Someone shouted; a moment later, there was a harsh sound of retching outside the dining room.

'Mamoi!' Padmasini called to her housekeeper. 'If that is Velu, get rid of him!'

'Madam, what do you want me to do with him?'

'Kick him out of the house!'

'He says this is his house. He says–' there was muffled laughter, a cry of dismay, a smell of vomit. I got up from my chair. 'He says he has come all the way back here to throw up on your carpet.'

316

'Put him out in the street.'

Velu stood in the living room, a bottle in his old man's hands, his eyes screwed up, grinning with delight. He wiped his mouth with his towel and stood swaying over his own vomit.

'Oh, he's *disgusting!*' Padmasini cried. 'Someone is going to have to clean him up! I'm not going to touch *that.*'

I took Velu into the outhouse's bathroom, bathed him, feeling myself shrinking from his old cirrhotic flesh, his stink.

'She says you must leave,' I said. He tottered to his room, leaning on my arm. 'I'll find some money for a hotel room.'

He was searching among his things, throwing clothes about.

'What are you looking for?'

'The olais – the manuscripts.'

'They're gone,' I said. I packed his things into a bag. 'Shall I go with you to find a room?'

He looked at me as if he was not sure who I was. 'No. No, I'm all right.'

He swung his carpet bag up and went staggering out into the day. It was the last time I saw him.

17

Rajayi
Kalyanikkarai, 28 May 1990

I was out of my mind with worry for the boy, but I could not help the feeling of gladness when Lila said that Kalyani was coming by the afternoon train. I thought, foolishly, of how I would take her face in my hands and kiss her as I used to. It was more likely that she would be distant with me. What was the price of Kalyani coming to me? I did not dare to name it yet. I was grateful. Let the consequences wait.

I had failed her, I had failed the boy.

It was different with Lila. She has been with me always, my sister. When I needed help she came, and I went to Madras to look after her when she brought her children into the world. Now Lila has gone to talk to the police, while I sit in this wet darkness, waiting and praying that Amalan would come home to us before the police found him.

I remembered when time had stretched taut like this, empty, elastic, each minute separate from the next. It's funny, how children fill up time, even when they are out at school or playing all day. Why did that come to me like a new thought? It is what women have always known. I knew what I would lose when Rachel Missy came to take Kalyani away, even though I had asked my aunt Komala to write to her: the meaning she gave my life, the purpose, the fullness. Buying milk in the mornings, packing her lunch, standing at the door to watch her walk to school. In the evenings, oiling her hair, and combing it – so thick always – and plaiting it, and then, after she had eaten, sitting on the veranda or the swing with a lapful of fidgeting child, glad of the musky smells of the rain, of the jasmine buds in her hair opening against the warmth of her neck, of her sweet hair oil. The garden growing hazy and unreal outside with the rain, and our corner of the house, where I might be telling a story or singing to her, seeming like the only solid place.

We deprived Kalyani of those pleasures, Lila and I. We never gave her a chance to cherish her son. But perhaps she sat like that with her stepchild in her lap, perhaps she told that child the stories I had told her of kings and demons and their doings on the banks of the red river Kalyani.

Waiting is always the hardest thing, harder than doing something. I should have gone to the police station with Lila, but I had a dread of the place.

I waited like this for Kalyani's half-yearly visits.

After my mother died, after the Vakil went away, after Lila left for Madras, I began to understand the rhythms of my own grief and reconciliation to grief. I no longer expected either extreme grief or great joy to last. I knew to the hour at which point joy would be snatched away; and I knew at which point sorrow would leave me and consolation come. So when I realized Kalyani was not safe in this house, and decided to send her to Kokku Missy, I knew how I would ride the grief out.

Still, for three days before Kokku Missy came for her, I sat like one paralysed. I had cleaned every bit of the house to receive the white woman, but after the work was done, there were Kalyani's things to pack, and I could not bring myself to do it. I dawdled for three days, looking at the debris of our life together, reminding myself of the things she would need in her new home, but not able to put them into a bag or a basket. Not wanting the end of the happiness we had, the two of us together.

When Kokku Missy came, Kalyani wrapped her arms around my legs and would not let go. How will I finish this? I thought.

'She will learn to read and write,' Kokku Missy said in her earnest way. Her jutka waited outside. Kokku Missy would travel anywhere, by any means of transport.

'To read and write?' I said. Reading and writing were the birthright of dasi children, long before the brahmins even thought of educating their daughters.

'I mean in English, of course,' Kokku Missy said. That made sense to me. English seemed to be the language of the future. There would perhaps be opportunities, even in the big city.

'She still has her hair combed,' I said, showing Kokku Missy the plaits I had made that morning. Something hard was in my throat. I could not swallow. 'She can't really do the back yet. It's so thick.' I had always been gentle when I tugged and teased the tangles out of those bushy waves. 'You will take care of the child?'

I did not want to say 'my' child. But I also wanted to shout it, to cry it, as the cart creaked, turning towards the Nallur road, and the horse clopped away through the drizzle. My child.

I fell ill, then; I must have been pining for Kalyani. There was no one to help, and I thought I might die, and leave Kalyani unprovided for. When I was somewhat recovered, I wrote to Kokku Missy, asking to be allowed to see Kalyani once in a while. I never heard back. I wondered if I should go to Nallur – it wasn't far – to see her but was afraid of Kokku Missy.

Finally, after months of this, I wrote a letter to the Vakil.

I have sent my child Kalyani, who is now ten years old, to study with the Christian lady they call Rachel Missy. Will you find out for me, if any of your colleagues goes to Nallur, how she is doing? I want to know if they treat her well. I should like Kalyani to come and see me once in a while, or I would travel to see her. I have written to Rachel Missy about this many times, but have had no reply. I know I have promised not to write to you, but there is no one else I can ask.

321

Months passed, once again, before I heard from Kokku Missy.

I try to instil a sense of Christian virtue in my little heathen charges. I agree that it is unnatural to tear the child away from the woman who has given her suck. I could certainly allow her to see you once every three months. But I do not want her to drift back to the sort of dancing class in which the women of your caste congregate. I said this to the gentleman – the pleasant and able lawyer – who came to see me on your behalf, and he assured me that you would keep your end of the bargain. I must say I am thankful to have met him. He was able to introduce me to a comrade in the legal profession who helped me with some legal questions I had.

What a self-righteous woman that Kokku Missy was. A few weeks after this letter came, my heart hammering, I looked out of the window and saw Kokku Missy's jutka draw up at the door. Kalyani tumbled out, and I felt that strange loss one feels when one realizes that children will not keep the shape one remembers or stay the same size.

Kalyani slept under a net in Kokku Missy's house. She slept restlessly here, when she was allowed to come to me, no longer used to the mosquitoes. I sat up at night, fanning the mosquitoes away from her face, wondering at this love I felt. The girl looked like the goddess in the stone mandapam on top of the hill, slender, fine-limbed. I wished I could put off the moment when the jutka would come to take her back.

At first Kalyani liked coming back, and then I saw the change in her. She did not like what she read on the board, which she could read now. One day, when she heard the ice cream bell, she ran out as she used to; then she turned and came back in.

'Here's the money,' I said, eager to please her.

'No, I don't want it,' she said. 'Aunt Rachel says these ice lollies are unhygienic.'

I knew she was floating free of me. She was pulled too hard two different ways. Again there would be loss, I realized, again I prepared myself. I remembered how we had drafted the petition to the Raja and the government. 'Give our girl-children English education, help them to become doctors and teachers and serve the nation,' we had said, and that was what Kalyani would do, I said to myself. All would be well in the end. My child's destiny would be different from mine. The thought was both exhilarating and frightening. What would we say to each other? How would we know each other when she grew older? But she would be happy. I dissolved my earlier dream that she would be a dancer into new dreams: she would be a doctor, a government officer, a teacher.

My child, lovely as the full moon.

My mother said god would forsake us if we neglected our duty to him. If god was not punishing us now, why was Amalan in trouble? I only wanted to see his face again, to feed him again. I looked back at the things I had said to him in the last few weeks, I searched for the kindnesses I had shown him, something outside the ordinary business of living. But I only remembered that I had nagged him for forgetting his chores, and berated him for pestering Padmasini about the pendant.

He must have felt that it was owed to him. She should not have promised it to him. Only let him come back to me, god, I prayed.

Perhaps he had come back and hidden himself in the house somewhere. He did sit quietly sometimes, without kicking at the wall or drumming his fingers on something. I switched on the light. There was no one – his mat was still in the corner, rolled up. The rainflies began to come in. I switched off the lamp again and groped my way back to the swing. I sat down and rocked myself, waiting for the morning.

One could not protect children from the world. One could not throw one's body between them and harm.

'Of what account is she?' I heard the Inspector's voice from – how many years ago? – from behind a pillar in the temple on the other side of the river, when Samu Vathyar was blessing Kalyani after her arangetram. We had chosen that temple, rather than the big temple of Kalyanikkarai, to keep the law off our backs. But he had found us out, followed us. And I, in my forgetfulness and complacency, had exposed the child to that. I had allowed her to make her debut.

'A tevadiya's daughter,' the Inspector said, leaning against a pillar with a thumb hooked in his belt. 'I can take her to the police station, and nothing – nobody – will protect her there. But you know that. No one in this town will say a word against me.'

Samu Vathyar had taken my shaking hands in his.

'Don't worry,' he said. 'Velu will see you home.' He left in the cart; I had to stay behind, to tidy everything up, pay the musicians and the temple workers. It was past midnight.

Velu saw Kalyani waiting for me on the temple steps, rubbing her eyes. 'Her feet are sore,' he said. He put his upper cloth on his bare shoulder and swung her up easily. She was half asleep. He carried her down the steep steps. Only the drunks lingered by the temple walls and Velu took a swig from a bottle one of them held out. 'To give me strength,' he said, laughing. He never drank in front of his father, but already, when his father was not around, he was beginning his lifelong affair with the bottle.

Holding her on his shoulder, her bangled arms lolling against his back, all the jewellery she had worn for her dance against his shoulder blades and his chest, slapping against him or cutting into his skin with every step, he trudged across the bridge with her. Drunk though he was, he took the shortcut easily, balancing on the bunds between the squares of paddy now harvested and ready for the next crop. He brought her into the house and laid her down gently on the rolled-out mat. Removing his upper cloth to wipe his face, he found it wet with her dribble, and smiled like a father, an older brother.

But when I trusted him to be her teacher, he betrayed us all. How could he not have had regard for Kalyani's future? I did not ever think, or want to think, that Amalan should not have been born. What happened, happened; there was no help for it. But was that where things could have gone differently for us? Or was the trouble always in our stars? Or did trouble only come because I agreed to do what this woman Padmasini asked?

It seems like fate, that Padmasini should be the daughter of the Inspector. When the policeman came yesterday to ask if Amalan had come back – a young policeman, not at all like the Inspector, a young man with a kindly face – the memory of her father came up and out at me, hood spread out, ready to strike.

'If you know what is good for you,' the Inspector had said, in the temple's grounds, 'you will not dance in the temple procession tonight,' He said that in the month of Chittirai, in 1950, on the night of the big festival. He was no longer a callow, ugly youth with a cast in his eye, or a clownish lad who had tried to imitate the ways of the Chettiar landlords and had been mocked by silly young women. He was a man, heavily built, an Inspector of police, used to giving orders, feared by the town. A Sandow who exercised on ropes hung from the roof-beams in his house, the gossips said.

That evening, Lila and I set up the brass lamps we had washed, poured oil in them, and made the wicks ready. We draped the festival idols in new gold cloths and flower garlands.

For me, it was an unlucky day. I had been nervous, and had pulled the string holding my ankle bells too tight. The string had broken and the bells lay all over the flagstones at the back of the temple. Lila, always quick with her hands, restrung them as well as she could.

When the idols were brought out on the palanquins – the old wooden chariot was destroyed, no one knew how to repair it – the worshippers came from every house; even baai left his shop in his nephew's care and came to watch, putting on his skullcap for respect. As usual, somewhere at the back, the drunks were fighting, their noise half drowned by the pipes and the thundering tavil drums. The people of Kalyanikkarai could still celebrate a festival like the beating of one heart. Without thinking about it, they fell into step with the drumming, the backbone of the procession: *kuntha-kunthakum, kuntha-kunthakum, kuntha-kunthakum*, the five-beat rhythm for the setting out from the temple.

I remembered every detail. The street dogs chasing something, a cow trying to stretch its tether to allow it to reach a marigold garland that had fallen from the idol of Uma, the beaded palanquins on the men's shoulders, the gay tassels dancing with every step, the venom-green petromax lanterns that swung from poles.

Carts rolled behind the procession with the old and infirm. The children in bright clothes and checked ribbons ran behind the carts. Samu Vathyar was at the head of the musicians, reciting, his voice clear as a bell. Velu was only a boy, but he had a pair of cymbals too.

Kuntha-kunthakum, kuntha-kunthakum.

'It's a smaller crowd than usual,' Lila shouted, over the tremendous power of the nagaswaram pipes. She was short of breath. Growing heavier had done that to her.

In four different places around the temple's circumference we danced. The old palace elephant was missing, and the Raja's great bobbing umbrella. We missed the dancers who used to dance with us, but Lila and I were full of energy. The policemen were there in large numbers. They marched rigid and slightly aloof, to show that they were there to keep pickpockets from practising their trade. Lila caught sight of the Inspector and nudged me between dances, as we walked to the next halting place.

After the festival, when I came back home, I was tired. I had begun to take off my jewellery when I heard the noise. The Inspector was kicking the door deliberately, to show the power of the police-issue boot. The door was never painted since his assault on it, though the hinges were repaired and the lock was replaced. The burn of his boot against the wood, the dinge of that night's terror, is still there.

'What do you want?' I cried.

'Come out!' he said.

'Why must I come out? I have done nothing!'

'Where is the other one?'

'She has left for Madras,' I lied, thankful that I had made Lila listen to her patron and go to his house for the night. She had been worried about me.

'Get into the jeep quietly,' he said. The police jeep stood outside, a uniformed driver at the wheel.

'It is unjust. I have done nothing!' I said again.

'Call your neighbours then. Rouse up the town and see if they will help you.'

I said nothing. A dasi woman had no neighbours.

'I warned you this afternoon,' he said. 'I took pity on you and warned you.'

I wrapped my hands around my stomach to steady the flutter there. I braced myself against the wall. He caught my wrists and began to drag me out. My glass bangles broke, and the pieces were bright on the floor. The stick swung in his hand.

I had taken off my ankle bells and they were on the swing. Dragging me with him, he bent down, picked them up and threw them through the broken door. They flew all the way across the street.

'You're not going to need those any more,' he said.

They fell into the gutter. Muthayya's daughter – the one whose seventh child was born only three months ago – Muthayya's toddler saw them fall, and ran out of the door to look at them. As the Inspector pushed me into the jeep, I heard her mother's hand falling across the child's face. The child screamed. When I came back, weeks later, she would not smile at me. The bells still lay where the Inspector had thrown them. I brought them in and put them in the trunk.

There was a constable in the back of the jeep. 'All right,' the Inspector said. 'Take her with you.'

'You are lucky,' the constable said to me. 'It is the sharanaalayam, not the jail for you.'

The sharanaalayam had once been the hospital for the white people's army. Dasi women hated it.

In the sharanaalayam, they made me take off all my jewellery. They gave me a receipt. It mentioned a ring the Vakil had given me, the gold bangle that I wore on my right hand, and the bottu, sign of my marriage to the god, which I wore on a gold chain around my neck. Nothing else. The gold bracelets, the hair pieces and the earrings disappeared silently, and there was no one who could even say who took them.

The warden led me to a dormitory. It had rows of grey iron beds with threadbare mattresses.

'Put your things here, but don't go to bed,' the warden said. 'You are wanted in the outhouse.' She was an old widow, a woman of no means, less than nothing. She averted her eyes from me when she led me to the building. I heard the latch falling into place on the outside of the door.

The outhouse had once been part of the stables where the visiting doctors' horses had been rubbed and fed. Now it was where the night-watchman slept by day. It smelt of river-mud and seaweed; its windows gave on the Kalyani. As soon as I looked out of the window and saw how quiet it was around me, my heart began to beat painfully.

Through the windows the rainflies came. They died by the score all around the lamp. The sickening odour of their fat mingled with the smell of damp earth. The thunderstorm was sudden, unexpected.

The Inspector came in through the outhouse door. He turned around and shut it; he shot the bolts above and below. He stood over me, his stick swinging in his hands. His breath and his sweat smelt of brandy.

Ever since, when I saw the midges around the street lamps, the Inspector's face came back to me.

'How many men have you fucked?' he said. 'Twenty? Fifty? A hundred?'

I watched his hands coming closer to my breasts. The room wheeled around me. The bulb hanging from the ceiling swung in the wind from the open window, his shadow and mine grew large and small on the dripping walls.

He pushed me down on the watchman's bed. I waited for his rage and his need for revenge to be sated. The first time he raped me, I knew he was disappointed; I must have accepted my violation too stoically, I did not protest, I did not show enough fear. It was not my looks he wanted any more, or even my body. It was my dignity he wanted to take from me. He wanted me to fear his step, his smell.

'Whore,' he gasped as he ejaculated against the wall of my throat. 'That will stop you singing,' he said. 'That will stop your voice.'

I did not think it was either the first time he had done such a thing or the last time. He was the kind of man to whom hurting is like a love potion.

'Whore, whore, whore,' he said, turning me on my stomach, hurting any part of my body that could be pierced. 'You laughed at me, you and the other whores.'

It was an age before he finally rolled off my body and wiped himself. Holding his reddened handkerchief in one hand, he said, 'If you speak to anyone about this I will make sure the same thing happens to your girl children.'

He opened the door and went out. All my life since, it was not what he did that stayed in my head, but this thing he said so casually, with perfect seriousness, before he left. 'I'll make sure the same thing happens to your children.'

My sari was bunched around my feet and stained with blood. I was too tired to move. I lay on my side where the Inspector had dropped me until the warden came in, a cup of tea rattling in her frightened hand.

'Will you have a bath?' She cleaned me up apologetically. 'My nephew is a constable, he works under that man. He got me this job. Try not to hobble like that. The other women – they mustn't – they mustn't talk.'

When I went back to the dormitory, trying not to hobble, the other women stared at me, heavy with knowing. They were either old women, too poor to take care of themselves, or women who had been arrested – petty thieves, prostitutes – and brought here to be reformed. One toothless destitute threw her thin regulation khaddar sari over her face and howled for no reason. With her hands, she beat her breasts, reliving who knew what grief.

'Don't mind her,' the warden said. 'She's crazy.'

The old woman began to sing a song. It was a song of the villagers, and it had a bleak simple tune.

He is a frog in the well, mother,
I am a jasmine garland.

The other women joined in.

He is a mangy dog, mother,
I am a bright gazelle.

A tide of wailing and screeching laughter washed over everything – the harsh linen, the rough damp walls, the bodies bare of jewellery.

He is a dried-grass broom, my mother,
I am a tassel of silk.

The women sang and wept and laughed. They rocked themselves on the creaking iron cots, until the warden burst through the door.

'I'll have the police on you,' the warden cried, and fled from the shaming laughter of the women. She locked herself into her own room to shut out the sound.

A spatter of rainflies lay around the bed they gave me, thrashing their wings away from their bodies. The whole dormitory smelt of their death, their fat.

The warden put me in a tailoring class. I started by stitching buttons. I was grateful that I was not given a garden job; walking was terribly painful. Lila came to see me early one morning. She had been hiding in her Chettiar patron's grain attic.

'What about the cow?' I said. 'What about our Gowri?'

'That Muthayya is taking care of her.'

'That is something. Muthayya, of all people.'

'Rajayi.'

'Yes?'

'Rajayi, you know we can't do this dancing any more.'

'You are thinking of leaving,' I said, dismayed.

'I will go to Madras,' she said. 'They are making films there. There is a director who is looking for women to act.'

'Lila, the things they say about the cinema – it isn't a good profession for women. They say the directors cheat you, they exploit you.'

But Lila would not hear any arguments against the cinema or against the director she was going to write to.

I looked at her in despair. 'Why would you believe what this director is saying? Who is he, anyway?'

'My Chettiar knows his brother. He has money, Rajayi, and money is what we need. The land is gone; we don't know how to keep ourselves. Your Vakil is gone too. Are you still hoping he will come back to help you? What good are we women without patrons? Helpless as babies. God, look at that old hag. You and I could end up like her.' Lila spat a long crimson trail of betel juice against the wall to show the warden how much she disliked her.

They sent me home after keeping me in the sharanaalayam for about a month. The cow had not been taken. I stroked her head; Lila would sell her to get money to go to Madras. When we realized I was pregnant (the irony of it; I had been barren with the man I loved), she decided not to leave for a while. She brewed me a medicine to take the child from my womb. But the child clung to her life, and in the end I was glad.

Lila took care of me. She fed me rich food, and cooked in a corner of the garden so that the smell of the seasoning would not make me throw up. I could not imagine the house without Lila in it. I said to myself, I will have the child. I will take such good care of her that she will thrive, and we will have each other.

Still, when Lila's patron gave her money to go to Madras, and she packed her bags, I wanted to cry out, 'Don't leave me now! I have no one else!' But there was no help for it. I walked with her along the station platform.

The train pulled out. 'Eat well,' she shouted. 'Don't tire yourself out.'

Lila's plump waving hand was finally withdrawn. Too pretty, I thought, too pretty and too innocent of city ways to be a success in Madras.

Lila was in Madras by my seventh month. For the sake of our old love, she said, I should have the baby there, so that she could look after me. In the end it was I who sold the cow for the train fare to Madras, and for the stay there. Kalyani was born at the end of the year in which the Vakil left for Madras. Strange it felt, when Amalan was born; it all seemed so familiar, the nurses in their uniforms, the hospital rooms, the muggy Madras weather, Lila carrying tiffin boxes full of fried fish to make the milk come down.

I came back to Kalyanikkarai when Kalyani was three months old. I wondered, often, what Lila was doing, if she was safe. I wrote to her. When she was doing well and had money, she would write back. When she was doing badly, when she had been abandoned by yet another man, there would be silence.

The rain flies started yesterday. They knew the thunderstorm was coming; all evening they swarmed in clouds around the street lamps. In the morning I found their wings everywhere, and their waxy bodies lying in heaps on the front step. Every year they came and died around the house; every year, before the monsoon, the lizards on the walls gorged themselves. I took a broom and swept the rain flies away, trying not to think about so much death.

A long time ago, that Inspector. He is dead too. The policeman who knocked on the door and asked if Amalan was home was a different man, with a kinder face.

I will go to the temple and make an offering for the safe return of Amalan. For my Kalyani's happiness, and for Lila's too.

18

Kalyani

Kalyanikkarai, 28 May 1990

My nerves were rubbed raw by Balan's rage, by Vijaya's triumph.

'You've shut me out already – how can you do that?' Balan kept saying.

'Because I know I cannot come back to you.'

'Why not? Why assume that?'

'Would you have me back, now, knowing I lied to you? Knowing I had an affair?'

'I – I don't know. Talk to me, tell me everything.'

His confusion was pathetic; fleetingly, it made me want to cry, to comfort him. But after years of indecision, I had made a choice; I did not want to be diverted from it. The emotion passed.

'I cannot, Balan. There is no time.' I said it quietly, without inflection.

After so many years of fearing the loss of everything that anchored me, after the terror of loneliness, I had reached a state of placid acceptance, even eagerness to be finished with this life.

'There will be time if you'll let me drive you to the station.'

'No, Balan,' I said. 'I will take an auto.'

I could not bear to be inside the house, in the disturbance that Balan was making around himself. My packing done, I went out to stand on the balcony. The windows of the house were shadowy, the curtains blowing lightly. I memorized each detail, taking it into the darkness in myself, folding it carefully like old clothes in a chest. Perhaps I liked endings more than I knew; perhaps I had grown used to them. Now I was hopeful of seeing a son for whom I had suppressed my visceral love long enough. I was trying to imagine how my mother would look, so much older than when I last saw her.

A breeze curled through the jasmine, through the arali, bearing scents almost too poignant to bear.

The Kalyanikkarai Express picked up speed. The rhythmic clatter of the train was soothing. The ticket collector checked my brown stub of ticket at Tambaram; after that, I was left alone.

The train's wheels moved to a rhythm: *didithai, didithai, didithai*. Samu Vathyar made me dance the didithai step all around the perimeter of the temple, when I complained of aching thighs. He sent Velu Vathyar to supervise my agony. I finished the last step, panting, and collapsed on the temple steps. Velu stood over me, chuckling sardonically.

At Villupuram, a man went through the coach with a basket of fruit. A woman bought a guava, sliced it with a paring knife, salted it, and shared it with her daughter while I watched. The train went torpidly first west and then south.

I realized suddenly that I was tired. I had not slept since I had heard the news about Amalan. The train clattered over bridges, rocked me asleep, jolted me awake again. When it stopped at the stations, the fans slowed down, and it grew stiflingly hot. I bought a women's magazine and fanned myself with it. 'Ten Secrets to Make a Man Love You', the cover said.

Outside, the darkening landscape was growing familiar. So familiar, so dear to me: the open country, the dusk-softened chequerboard of fields and streams, the lights that flickered on in the houses in distant villages and in ghostly pumphouses on the sides of hills. At the stations, the tea vendors passed under the lamps like ghosts, their cries unexpectedly earthy and strident.

As the train lurched into the last long curve of track before Kalyanikkarai, throwing my body against the window, I smelt rain. I smelt home. A thunderstorm was coming; grey clouds hid the moon. The Kalyanikkarai temple's south gopuram loomed in the distance, a towering darkness. Pale yellow lights glowed at intervals from the niches set in its walls – not the old lamps, surely; they would have gone out in this wind; electric lights, probably. If I had been less anxious, the sight would have made me glad.

Outside the station, a group of teenaged boys leaned against their motorcycles.

'Ey, baby!' one of them called, rocking his hips. Would Amalan, now sixteen, look like this, would he behave like this? In the autorickshaw that brought me from the station to Musicians' Street, I couldn't focus. The shops spun by in a blur of light and dark that hurt my eyes. The electricity had gone in some parts of the town. Hurricane lanterns hung from hooks in the shop roofs, swinging wildly in the wind, making everything rock and tip as if it was going to fall over. The auto twisted through the familiar streets. We passed the south gopuram.

There had been changes in Kalyanikkarai, but no more than I had expected. Until we reached Musicians' Street.

'You've got the house wrong,' I said when the driver stopped.

'57, Musicians' Street. This is it,' he said, yawning. 'They knocked down the other houses.'

The street beyond our house had been swallowed up. Peevish Muthayya's house still stood across from it, but a broad smooth clearing swooped through the space where the other houses had stood. It had swallowed Velu's home – Samu Vathyar's ancestral home. I paid the driver under the light of the single street lamp. There still was electricity on this street. Around the lamp the rainflies had gathered, hundreds of them.

The darkness was all around the lamp, thick and spongy and venomous. There were faces at every window near my mother's 's house, even at this hour, but not one face was friendly, and not one body stepped out of any of the doors. In the house I found Lila alone. She had come

340

by the morning train to be with my mother. She heaved herself up from the floor, helped me take my bags inside. Dust rose up and made me cough.

'She tries to sweep it up, your Amma, but it's falling much faster than before,' Lila said. 'She's gone to the temple. Two bags?'

'Yes. I may have to stay. Have you heard anything?'

'Nothing. The police are looking for him. He's hidden himself well enough. There is no doubt that he stole the jewellery.'

'Do they have any idea, any guesses, about where he is hiding?'

'They think it is somewhere in the palace grounds, or among the hills near the quarry. They've looked twice, but there are so many places you can hide.'

'It's the third day he's been gone?'

'The third day. They are bringing dogs to look for him tomorrow.'

'Hunting.' I shuddered. 'There must be something we can do.'

'How much money do you have?'

'Not much. About a thousand. But I have jewellery. I thought of leaving it all behind, but I did not want to take off my thali, and I thought the bangles could be sold.'

'Good. We may be able to do something in the morning. Look for him, maybe, pay off that bitch who filed the police complaint.'

'Who?'

'Padmasini.'

'Oh.' The world spun, nothing made sense. 'He stole from *her*? What did he take?'

'A pearl necklace with a gold pendant, some gold bangles. Expensive stuff. I spoke to the police. I said he was just a boy. They laughed at me, Kalyani. He is friendly with a couple of older boys, brothers, from the tourist bungalow. They had this trick of putting a pole into the rooms through the window bars – people have been leaving their windows wide open because of the heat – and they hooked whatever could be pulled out. Clothes, loose jewellery, handbags with handles.'

'How do the police know all this?'

'The manager at the tourist bungalow was suspicious. One of the brothers worked as a cleaner there, the other one worked in the kitchen. And they had found a fence. The middleman got caught with some jewellery, and the police picked up the older boy last night. They beat him up at the station. He told them Amalan had been their lookout. Most of the time they only gave him what they couldn't sell. This is the first time he took something valuable. The police are more interested in this boy's brother than in Amalan, but they won't let Amalan off without a bribe. Balan could–'

'No. I can't ask Balan. But I could talk to Padmasini. I could ask her to withdraw the complaint. Let's not wait until the morning. Let's go tonight, first to the police station, then to Padmasini's.'

'All right. Her father died, did you know? The bastard.'

'Yes, I spoke to her after the funeral. Balan telephoned to give her his condolences.'

'Would you like to see your Amma? She has been waiting for you. We must make sure she comes back home before the rain comes down.'

342

I felt dread at the awkwardness of it. I wanted and did not want to see my mother. I wanted desperately to see my son, and I did not want to see him. Guilt and regret complicated love.

As we reached the south gopuram, the prayer bells began to boom. In the sanctuary, even this late in the night, there was bargaining; importunate requests and hopes were wafted towards the great lingam in wisps of camphor smoke. Cynic though I was, I found myself irresistibly stirred by the mysteries of the sanctum: concealment, revelation, sounds and smells. The worshippers shimmered before me, pierced through by their faith. The power of human need was focused here to the point of burning; beating at the doors of the gods, petitioning – save me, help me – in a din of drums and brass bells. Siva, lord, give me a boy child, give me money, let my daughter have a safe birth; Pillayar, elephant-headed one, let my son get the government job, give me good health until the harvest is brought in, let me survive this disease of my bowels.

Even I, sweating, rejecting the blindness and superstition of it all, saying no, no, there is no such god, even I, immune to the seductions of faith, shuddered with the intensity of it, and involuntarily added my plea under my breath: help him, save him. Into the ear of the Nandi, where the worshippers whispered their hopes, I found myself saying, let me not lose him. Let me hold him in my arms.

In the shelter of the cloister that went around the temple, my mother sat, the end of her sari pulled tight over her shoulder. Not for her then, as for the married women, the luxury of comfortable middle age, the loosening of the petals of the self. She was as tightly furled as a bud, hugging her dignity to herself. Only her beautiful shoulders were still flung back with a dancer's nonchalance. They were the shoulders of a woman walking erect in a bitter wind.

So many years had passed that we had no way of greeting each other.

'Lila brought you,' she said.

'Yes.' My throat was tight and painful.

'Are you well?' We took refuge in inanities, in ceremony.

'Yes. Are you well?'

'Is your husband well? Your daughter?'

'Yes, they are all well.'

'Lila said you could not come, not unless you came for good.'

'Yes.' I longed to reach out and touch her, but I could not. My arms were tied at my sides. 'It will be all right.'

'I hope so. How will we manage for money?' Years of privation had made her practical. That was one of her strengths. I had grown soft with self-indulgence. 'Padmasini would not pay me anything else – not a paisa more until the whole film is finished, she said.'

'We'll manage,' Lila said cheerfully. 'Haven't we always? Now you should go home, Rajayi, in case Amalan comes back, and then Kalyani and I will go and talk to Padmasini about withdrawing the case.'

'Did you find out what the boy has taken?'

'A purse – it had a necklace with a garnet pendant, some gold bangles, money.'

'If I had known the boy was your – son? If I'd known he was *your* son, I wouldn't have reported it,' Padmasini said. 'I'll phone the police, withdraw my complaint.' She studied my face and yielded to curiosity. 'Is he really your son? You aren't making this up?'

'He is really my son.'

'The father–'

'He is gone.'

'Typical man. God, this is so strange. He is, could be, my uncle's grandson, then. How can I help?'

'Padmasini, we need money,' I said. 'I don't have enough to bribe the police. He may have stolen other things. If they find him, they will not just let him go.'

Her face grew hard. 'I have given Rajayi money,' she said. 'I paid her a thousand and she's supposed to get two thousand more, plus train fares. Can't Balan–'

'Padmasini,' I broke in, 'I know how much you were given for this project. Five lakhs. A couple of thousand is nothing. It isn't even the miserable share Balan and you agreed upon for the person you were going to film.'

'I set a price with Rajayi, and she agreed to it.'

'Three thousand,' Lila said, 'is not much to pay to make a film of someone's art, someone's whole life.'

'Then she should have sent me away. She shouldn't have taken my money first!'

'The police want more money, Padmasini,' I said

quickly. I should not have gone to the police station. They looked at my clothes and jewellery, and they decided to hold out for more. They could smell money. 'Lila and I spoke to them. I will sell my jewellery and return it to you tomorrow. I don't have enough cash now.'

When we went back to the police station, the men with authority had all gone home. Lila placed the envelope of money on the table and spoke to the night constables. They eyed the money, but they dared not take it. Come back early in the morning; come back early, and we will be able to help you, they said. You could make good some of the losses. We'll look at the FIR and tell you.

A young man in a torn bloodstained shirt lay slumped against the wall of a barred cell at the end of the room. He looked at us with dull eyes. I began to ask the police if he was the boy they had beaten up, and if we could help him too, but Lila shushed me.

Back on Musicians' Street, I waited on the veranda, too anxious to settle down to wait inside the house. If I count to fifty really slowly, Amalan will be back by the end of it, and all this would have been a dream, I said to myself. When I was a child, wishing desperately for something, I would play this game with myself.

I counted to fifty, slowing down as I reached forty. I turned back to the house, thinking, now something would have changed, now there will be some news. Someone came to the house. A young constable. I ran to the door; my mother jumped up to greet the newcomer, her face distorted with worry, dropping the blanket Lila

346

had wrapped around her. But he had only come to find out if Amalan had returned on his own. He was going to bed now, he said. He would start searching the quarry in the morning.

Two houses away a street light flickered and would not catch. The fireflies made pinholes of flickering light among the leaves. My stomach was an empty pit. The rain began again at midnight.

Rajayi came to the door. 'Come in out of the rain, my love.'

The light of a torch came bobbing down the street, towards us.

'Amma? It's me, Hema.' She covered me with her umbrella, put her arm gently around my shoulders. 'Appa phoned. You don't have to explain anything. Tell me what I can do.'

Rajayi raised her hand to the O of her mouth, her face suddenly animated by astonishment.

'This is my daughter, Hema. Balan's daughter and mine.'

'You are blessed,' Rajayi said. 'The child has a generous heart.'

I crushed Hema to my side. 'If you and Lila will wait for Amalan here, Hema and I will walk a little way towards the quarry, to see if we can find him. Look, Hema has brought a torch and an umbrella.'

'Be careful,' Rajayi said. 'The rocks will be slippery.'

Hema and I began walking, huddled under the umbrella, the soft rain like a veil around us.

'Amalan!' I called into the darkness. *'A-ma-lan!'*

In the night, the moon was reflected in the quarry's pool like metal shavings. *'Amalan!'* Hema called. 'Where are you?'

There were signs of human presence near the water. On a rock some quarry worker's clothes were spread out to dry; beside it were signs of late-night merriment. Shattered glass of liquor bottles, the charred remains of a fire. There was a faint smell of excrement.

The rocky passes became wind tunnels; our hair flew across our eyes, blinding us, and the wind carried our voices away. The inhuman grandeur of the rocks frightened me, their indifference mocked me. And yet I could not help regretting that they were breaking the granite down, humbling it, bringing it down to human scale.

The rain stopped, leaving behind a mist full of stars. Here, in the quarry, they seemed to float into our faces, the fireflies that haunted the damp hollows of the hill. The boy must be cold, I thought. The rain pooled here and there in shallow cups and depressions among the rocks. An occasional shaft of lightning speared the rocks; there was still rain to come.

'Am-a-lan! Am-a-lan!' we called, until our throats seized up. 'It's all right, you can come home! Your Amma is waiting for you!'

We sat on a wet rock to rest for a few minutes. Hema threw a stone into the water. The ripples opened like a mouth screaming.

We walked on, around the hill, finding the shortcut to the palace woods. They were full of pitch-black wet

348

silence broken only by thunder. The grass bent away from the wind; it curled with blowing.

'Amalan! *Amalan,* call if you can hear me!'

The rocks took up my voice, bouncing it in different directions. There was no answer.

'Amalan! We are not the police. Answer us!'

In the moonlight, the waterlilies in the pond near the palace had turned a smoky blue. They were bruised from the rain. The palace's eaves dripped. We looked in the broken-down stables, in the abandoned outbuildings. Far away to my left, a single lamp glimmered in the niche of the south gopuram, like a sign of hope.

Rajayi told me a story when I was a child.

Once, centuries ago, the Kalyani washed the stone steps of the temple. When a new king took his place in the Kalyanikkarai durbar, he was first bathed in the waters of the Kalyani. Then there was a king who did not honour the river and, beating desperately against its inner bank, the river changed its path and abandoned Kalyanikkarai.

This king's wife found her child eating the naaval fruit she had set aside for an offering to Murugan. She smacked the child and sent him out into the courtyard. The child wandered into the forest, crying. When the king's servants looked for him in the evening, the child was gone.

The queen was heartbroken and went searching for the boy on the banks of the deep-flowing Kalyani, now so far away from the palace.

'*Kalyani-aaray, en kanmani enge?*
En kanmaniyai poga kandaayo?'

'River Kalyani,' (my mother sang to me), 'where is my dear one?

'Have you seen the apple of my eye?'

And as she wandered, she came upon a tree whose branches hung low over the river, and there was her child sitting on the branches with another child, the young god Murugan of the six faces, and they were both eating the naaval fruit that hung in great bunches from the branches of the tree.

At dawn, Hema said, 'Should we check the house again?'

The rain had turned to mist and damp. We turned around and headed home, chilled through now, stumbling and uncoordinated, glad of each other's warmth under the umbrella. The sun rose, dispersing the mist, as we came up to Rajayi's house.

I stopped suddenly. 'But where are the steps?'

In the dark, in the night, I had not been able to see beyond the end of the street. Now I saw that where the steps used to lead up to the small hill-shrine, a great slab of rock had been blasted away, and the new bypass cut into the hill's flank. The hill's recent wound shimmered blue-white where the light touched it; all around it the granite was darker, with grey-brown streaks.

Rajayi ran out into the street at the sound of my voice. Her eyes travelled up the hill's scar. 'That face of the hill was blasted away in the last few days,' she cried. 'He always comes down that way. If he wants to come home, that is where he will – we must go the long way around, must go up–'

In the distance we heard the baying of dogs.

'Kalyani, you go – no, you are afraid of high places. Lila – come with me, we have to get up the hill before he tries to get home–'

The dogs were above us, on the hill somewhere, getting closer.

'I'll go,' I said. 'Hema will help me.' I gathered my sari up and began to run up the winding footpath towards the top of the hill, and Hema ran with me.

Silhouetted figures appeared at the edge of the sheer rock wall above. There was sudden confused noise: men shouting, the baying of dogs, a woman screaming somewhere, a lorry braking. The granite hills sent back the woman's scream and the squeal of the lorry's brakes. The echo went on, bouncing from hill to hill.

19

Kalyani

Kalyanikkarai, 30 May 1990

Lila and I went twice to the police station, but the police were evasive. Patience, the sub-inspector said. If we were patient, we would see Amalan's body. It was in the District Hospital, there was paperwork to do. The doctor had to certify his death, and then they would need someone to identify him. When we went home, a van was waiting under the lone tree near Rajayi's house on Musicians' Street. I looked at it without recognition.

A tall man stepped out from under the veranda. I could tell he wanted to speak to me. Balan? He was a stranger down the length of a long corridor. He seemed too far away to matter, not real.

Balan made the police release Amalan's body. With Joseph's help, he brought Amalan home and placed him on a litter in the backyard. At the hospital, they had tied his feet together to hold them in place. They had stuffed cotton wool in his nostrils. Why did they do that? I wondered. Were they afraid he would start breathing again, suddenly and embarrassingly?

Rajayi bathed Amalan's stiffened limbs, slowly and with infinite gentleness. There was surprisingly little visible damage on his body. But his internal organs had ruptured.

Balan and I brought Amalan into the house, and we lifted him off the litter because a body must lie on the bare floor. He was going back to the earth; he would become ashes. I went to find Amalan's clothes. There was nothing in the small cardboard suitcase Rajayi pointed out to me that was not patched and worn. Hema left the house quietly; twenty minutes later she came back with packages. A new shirt, new trousers – the right length – a new veshti.

'Thirteen generations of dancers,' Rajayi crooned to Amalan, choosing the veshti over the trousers, wrapping it around his waist. 'You were the last of us.'

The redemption I had dreamt of – one day, I would tell Balan about Amalan, and we would welcome Amalan into our family, we would all live together – it seemed such an absurd idea.

When the wind blew, I hid from the rain. Now the garden is withered, now I am full of regret. The flat landscape of thwarted hopes.

Rajayi had gone into shock when it became clear that Amalan had not survived the fall. When she was slightly recovered from that, she had wept, freely and without restraint. Now she seemed resigned. I wondered what she was seeing. Amalan's face at three years, absorbed, sticking coral jasmine into a heap of mud, at five, tearful as she waved to him from the school's gate, at nine, faded and famished after a long summer day's games? His eating and his sleeping under her care; his colds, his scraped knees; his report cards, his dancing, his hero-worship of a movie star. The fights about – what? Baths, perhaps, or homework, the trouble he got into, the dirt he tracked in. About money. About noise. About things meant for supper that had been eaten by lunchtime. Some day, when she was able to dwell on these things, she would tell me what Amalan had been like.

'Did I sell your life for money, my boy?' Rajayi keened over him, spoke to him as she struggled to get the shirt on. 'The money they gave me, this honour they are going to give me – what will I do with them now? It was for your sake, boy!' She began to sing a lullaby; she made up the words as she went along. The story of Amalan's life, his agility, his innocence. She brought a green embroidered waistcoat from his suitcase and draped it over his chest.

None of the things in my life that had certitude, not Balan, not books, not the contours of Hema's face, not rice and sugar and coffee, none of these things made sense. Nothing could be cordoned off. Everything was infected. But in the end, if I waited long enough, perhaps it would all cohere again.

Balan was exquisitely tactful. He appeared when we needed him, effaced himself when we did not. Briefly he had held me in his arms and said, 'I have been a fool,

Kalyani. Forgive me.' I could not find it in myself to be attentive to him, or even to Hema. But my mother – how could I not admire this? – my mother surrounded them with soothing and sensible words; she observed the decencies. Balan had travelled a long way. Was he tired, was he hungry? She could not offer him anything in this house of death, but there was a hotel, just at the end of the road.

I turned away.

I brought a comb that had been left on the windowsill in front of an old cracked mirror. Amalan's hair grew straight up, springing with energy, and at the crown it was like a satellite picture of a coming storm. I smoothed his hair down as well as I could, trying not to touch the place that had struck rock. I wondered at his ragged boy-arms, that we had crossed over his chest. He was stick-thin, the skin pocked with wounds old and new, ringworm, and on his face the white marks of deficiency. His arms were scratched. His lips were charred almost to black; he must have been thirsty before he died. There was a long infected gash on the side of one leg; I drew the veshti over it, hid it from view.

So there were all these styles of dying, I thought. There was dying with a flower blossoming from the bone, a skull-cap of blood, on the hillside by the highway. There was dying slowly from the roots upward, all nourishment denied. There was the yellow-skinned dying from self-destructiveness and alcohol. There was inward dying, with no outward sign to show for it.

The morning went by in a thick haze; voices and faces came out at me, retreated. I tried to make sure Rajayi was all right, but Lila was always before me, solidly reassuring, the real pillar of Rajayi's strength.

A small respectful trickle of men and women passed through the house. Where had they come from? Rajayi was astonished, touched. One or two men came from among her relatives; she had last seen these cousins, she said, at her mother's funeral. A man introduced himself to me as a clarinetist, and placed a small garland over Amalan's feet. 'You don't remember me,' he said. 'I am Kaliswaran. I played for your arangetram. You must have been nine or ten years old.' He would be one of those carrying the bier.

The flowers and garlands piled up in a gentle wave around Amalan. Kaliswaran sat down by Rajayi, and they talked.

'I didn't know you were back in this town, brother,' Rajayi said.

He said, 'In Madras there is no work for clarinet-players, and I came back to this soil.'

There were quite a few tremulous hands; one man kept nodding at me, and I nodded back at him, twice, thrice, before I realized it was Parkinson's, not a greeting.

The clarinetist had the musician's disease – alcoholism. He got up to shoulder his end of the bier, to take it to the burning ground; he sat down again abruptly, and they realized he was drunk. They left him sagging against the wall, staring at his feet sticking straight out from under his veshti. It was unexpectedly farcical. Who would take the pole at that end? Balan stood up. He was taller than the small men of the small town.

The bier was borne away at last by the men, Balan

stooping to match the height of the others. Rajayi was held back, crying, by Lila and another woman; her arms reached out beyond the door to the black van in which they were taking Amalan to the burning ground. As the van moved away, I looked down. On the street was a carnage of rose petals, scattered to sweeten and purify the way so that other people might not feel the pollution of the death.

Suddenly, Padmasini was standing by the door, saying something to a man who stood beside her with a camera slung around his neck. I hadn't seen her get out of her car; she must have just come.

'Enough,' the man whispered. 'You said just some footage from the outside. Let's offer condolences and leave.'

'Just a little of the people,' she said. 'Get that image, an atmosphere of mourning. Unobtrusively. It makes sense. It's tragic.'

'No. I won't do it. Padmasini, it's not a good time. We can't intrude on their sorrow at this point.'

'That's a cliché, Shah, and you know it. "Intrude on their sorrow." I want to do this for Amalan, in fact, and for the sake of the women, to commemorate them all – Rajayi, Kalyani, their ancestors. Finishing the film is my salvation.' She did not meet his eyes. 'You're here to do a job.'

He shook his head. 'You're unbelievable. But I won't go in there to film.'

They came into the house. The man said: 'I'm Shah. I'm sorry.'

They spoke to my mother; then Padmasini came up to me and said, 'I am so grieved by all this. I feel responsible, somehow. I am sorry.' I nodded.

Her voice was unsteady and I thought, at last, here was some feeling, in a woman I had thought armour-plated. But perhaps it was just drama, perhaps it was just regret that the film she was making would not be completed. Or would it?

Later in the afternoon, after Balan came back from the burning ground, I wanted to sink into the comfort of his arms, but I could not do this in front of my mother. I could not take comfort in something she could not share. I sat beside her instead.

That evening, the street was full of people. Hema went out and learned that the crowds had gathered for the inauguration of the new bypass. The road was unfinished where it touched the hill – there had been unforeseen delays – but the Minister had agreed to come today, and they had to go ahead with the celebration. We listened to the ruling party's propaganda songs, deafeningly amplified. The Minister made a speech. In the middle of the applause, there was a knock at the door and Balan opened it.

'Who is it?' Rajayi said.

'Workmen,' Balan said. 'They said they have been engaged to repair the roof tomorrow. Are they to go ahead and buy the materials?'

So the business of living began again. The next day the workmen came to the house. We heard the rhythm of their hammers on the other side of Rajayi's wall. As they patched the old timber and unloaded the tiles from the lorry, the thin treacherous rain began again.

After the funeral, we stayed on for a few days to help Rajayi. Balan seemed to understand what I wanted. Without being obtrusive – he stayed at the tourist bungalow – he made arrangements for the house on Musicians' Street to be sold. It was clear that Rajayi could not live in it by herself: she would move to Madras, and Lila and she would live under the same roof again.

It was time for me to leave; I too would go back to Madras, to Balan, to Hema.

Balan wanted to visit the temple before we left, and I went with Hema and him. On the innermost walls of the temple, in the hollow soaring space above the shrine, long-torsoed women glowed in the light of the guide's torch. The ochres and yellows of their skirts shimmered like living pollen, the blues were ground from azurite, the reds from tourmaline.

As we came back out, Hema noticed that the men on the scaffolding around the south gopuram were painting the sculpture with enamel paint. On a board propped against the wall, the Archaeological Society of India claimed credit for this move. Balan telephoned their Madras office in some distress to ask why the stone was being daubed with plastic.

'To preserve it, sir,' they said.

20

Madras, 15 December 1990

Vijaya

'I have put up with the woman for long enough,' I said to Balan, when they all came back from the woman's native town. 'I won't take her mother in. I just won't, Balan, and she can have lost *ten* children.'

'You don't have to take anyone in, Amma,' he said.

'There is no place for an old woman in this house,' I said. 'I will go to an aashramam in the hills.'

'Of course, Amma,' he said. 'If it is your wish to retire to an aashramam, choose one, and I will arrange for you to have the best rooms there.'

'There is one in Kodaikanal,' I said. 'I could die in peace there.'

'Do you have the address?'

'So eager to get rid of his own mother, so eager to welcome strangers into his home.'

'Amma, listen,' Balan said. His voice was very clear and sharp, unlike any voice he had used with me before. 'I am not going to say this again. Kalyani's mother will not live here. I will not subject her to the insult of your company. She will live with Lila, and I will arrange for her to get one of the government pensions. I don't say this in anger, but I want you to understand. As for where Kalyani and I will live, *you* have a choice: you will make it once, and once only, because if you don't keep your side of the bargain the choice will be ours.'

He was standing squarely in front of me, his arms crossed in front of him.

'Sit down,' I said. 'I'll ask Kuppu to make you some coffee.'

'Here is the choice,' he said. 'I've found a house, and Kalyani and I both like it. Either we leave and live on our own or, if you wish it, we continue to live here with you, on condition that you don't utter *one single word* more against Kalyani. You make her welcome again, as far as you are able, or you leave her alone.'

'Very well, then, take your wife's side against your mother,' I said. 'I am not to warn you when your wife and her newly discovered mother get together to scheme and plot and undermine your interests and–'

'You appear not to have heard me.' His voice smacked into me like a fist. '*Not one single word more*, I said. I have been quiet for far too long, out of pity and respect for you, but Amma, I am fifty-one years old, and I must have peace in my own home. I must be allowed to care for my wife and my child, and not have to expose them to your narrow views, which I don't share. Very well, if you want to be orthodox, live on your own. I will take care of you, I won't neglect you, but I will not live with you. I have thought about it carefully, and I must have this chance at happiness. We – my wife and I, and my daughter – we must have this chance. It occurred to me that you were making us all so unhappy that I stayed on tour to avoid being at home, but where was Kalyani to go?'

'You are all against me,' I said. Unaccustomed tears came to my eyes, and I held my sari to them. 'You have been seduced–'

'You have made the choice,' he said. 'I will need a couple of weeks to make arrangements for the house. After that, we will move out.' Then he turned around and left, shutting the door carefully behind him.

I cried as I had not cried since Balan's father died. Would I be able to endure the woman's sneering, her triumph?

She has won and I have lost. We all know it. Hema, especially, knows it. She has become more obstinate, less amenable in subtle ways. There are battles every day, there is a drawing of lines and boundaries all around me. Now, when I have a headache, I have to speak to Balan on the telephone. It is hard to keep his attention when we no longer live under the same roof.

Today Balan asked me if I would like to go to the screening of the film they made on the woman's mother.

'Why would I? I would get one of my headaches, Balan,' I said.

So they went without me. And I said to myself, 'Why would I want to watch your wife's bitch and cunt of a mother be glorified in the Music Academy, by all of Madras?' Cunt, I said to myself. Cunt, cunt, cunt.

Balan

Every poison has its antidote, they say. Counteracting the jealousy released in my body, Kalyani's fragility; the Kalyani I first saw reappeared, looking as if she would break in half. She was so lovely still, my heart so wound about with her. She agreed to come back with me to Madras. So then, facing more squarely than I have ever done the question of our marriage, I understood why I held my love back; she had never been sure if she would stay with me.

To stay in a place, you have to know how you arrived there, why the journey was made. Past and present must be made coherent. This has happened for Kalyani, and she will, at last, be content.

She would not let me touch her for a while. It made my need grow. Last month, she came back to our bed. She took comfort in physical love, I satisfied my need, and we will be at peace, I think we will be at peace. Though there still is debris everywhere, the sense of death is receding like a flood.

She has worn no flowers in her hair since her son died, but today, she let me buy her flowers again. She asked for eight arm-lengths. It was a sight to behold, on Lila's veranda: the four women in a circle, pinning lengths of the jasmine in each other's hair, around them a bubble of laughter and warmth. Hema, touched by the splendour of it, was radiant. I was outside, feeling extraordinary pleasure at being able to look in, because I had never seen any of the women in my family touch each other like that, or make the air hum, like that, with love. In the car, later, the jasmine threw off its perfume, and the sense lingered of female connection, of an ancient dance that engendered life.

I have even come around to thinking, knowing the thought will be never tested, that I would have accepted Kalyani's son into our home if he had not died. This and other illusions about myself I cling to. A sardonic, mocking version of myself stands apart from these illusions – the illusion that Kalyani needs me, for instance. But I don't have the strength to confront them. Hema has that kind of strength. I can see her in mid-life, telling herself nothing but the truth, reinventing herself, if that is the price to pay.

Hema adores her new grandmother and is fascinated by her new great-aunt. A good thing; she has decided not to stop dancing, just to change teachers. And it pleases Kalyani to have her daughter learn from her mother. They get together twice a week, all four women, at the new dance school where Rajayi has begun teaching master classes in padhams to already trained students. It was all Hema's and Kalyani's doing, but NATAC provided some funds.

'You have to do something to save this form,' Hema said to me.

Her clarity shamed me, and her vehemence. I felt shame and great pride at the same time. I learned something from the generosity of Hema's love for her mother, from the grief she felt for the brother she had never known. Her capacity for righteous anger jogged my memory. It was something I too once had, and forfeited in the course of becoming a government man.

Something came back to me in the middle of all this: the recollection that it was the kind of dance and music Rajayi represented that I had once believed in. I had planned to devote my life to it, with the idealism of a young man. I am not that young man any more. That job is too big for me. But at the preview of the film I thought: any record, however flimsy, is useful. My god, I thought, imagine never having seen this.

That Shah is a man to watch. Definitely a find. The film is his handiwork. I had expected the usual pedestrian document, but he has produced something close to art. Padmasini sat by me at the preview, fretting terribly. She kept saying Shah had left important things out, which probably means he managed to edit her out of the footage to a considerable extent. Where he has let her into it, the quality drops.

One bit in particular I relished, shot by the temple tank. I am looking forward to seeing that again this evening. You can see the moment when it occurred to him to turn the camera (he does it so slowly, brilliant man) from Rajayi's face on the bank to its image floating among the lily pads in the water. On the way the camera rests on Rajayi's heels, criss-crossed with cracks. The tank waters down the sunlight nicely, and there is a perfect image of Rajayi as she sings that padham Kalyani once sang for me. So – great art has to burst upon one like this; not clothed in beauty, as I had believed it would be, but with gnarled fingers and chipped nails, on cracked and bleeding feet. I felt humble suddenly, watching that scene. I felt ignorant.

I've already signed Shah up for other NATAC documentaries.

Oh, well. I am old enough now to know that the film will make not a jot of difference in the world. It is such a small thing; such a small problem of such a forgotten group of people, and the world has moved on to other things. Even their troubles are not as great as the troubles of others. We can't undo old violence. But I will announce NATAC's new scholarship today, for children of hereditary dance teaching families, so that they can learn from their own kin.

Kalyani

We have picked Balan up, and, driving towards the Music Academy for the screening of the documentary on Rajayi, we pass the man who sells bottled aphrodisiacs under a tree in Panagal Park. What is Balan thinking? When we were young, we opened our selves and bodies to each other with reckless candour. Middle age has more to hide; now we muffle the diminuendo of our selves – the low hum of our struggles with time and failure – with closed doors, shawls, secrecy. There are strange epiphanies. One day I found a bottle of hair dye, unused, in the wastepaper basket in his study. A copy of *Anna Karenina*, unread, lay on his pillow; I know he found my notes about my family, hidden in the cupboard drawer in which I kept my woollen things, never used.

Balan turns around to smile at me. Something has been saved, at any rate.

The children released from the Ramakrishna Mission School run out on the pavement, barefoot; the orderly girls file out of Holy Angels Convent in their brown and white checked uniforms; stunted trees die inside wiremesh cages; restaurants and cafes fill the air with a sudden fragrance of coffee. A hot metallic smell comes off the road, cut through by the biscuity fragrance of a bakery, the air-conditioned smell of a sari shop, the smell of shit among the shanties of the very poor, the impossibly contrapuntal perfume of roses and lilies at the Pondy Bazaar flower market.

Big city, city of hopes. Choreography of sex-starved boys posing, commuters caught in the deadly scramble for places on the footboards of leaning buses, master tailors cutting silk, mattress-makers beating cotton, girls bargaining for cheap Tiruppur cotton panties on the pavement. City to which all art is so hopelessly tangential, and the art of the old princedoms especially so. What would a dancer like Rajayi do with this reality?

Grief has released small dry patches of our lives, and we can step from one to the other like crossing a wet floor, so that we can go on living. It is still treacherous. At the preview, in the background of one scene shot in Rajayi's house, Amalan appeared, craning his neck with a boy's curiosity. I look at my own palms sometimes, feeling them connecting again with Amalan's body. I see him in my dreams.

I dreamt of fruit-bearing trees last night. Tall outcrops of rock enclosed a tiny orchard. I looked into the valley through a gap in the rocks. Grass in their hair, buried in leaves, two children peered back at me, with fingers curled around black branches.

'Do you know who Rajayi Paati reminds me of?' Hema said. She has been so kind; so much the mother, when I have been the child. She went to the cassette player. 'Listen,' she said. 'I taped this from the BBC because I liked it so much. It's called "Strange Fruit".'

I listened to the voice of an American woman called Billie. 'Isn't that a man's name?' I said, but there was Billie Jean King of course. I want to describe the effect of the song, but the vocabulary of music criticism is full of clichés. What is the thing in Rajayi's voice, in Billie's voice, that brushes my hair against the nap, warms me, goes through to my bones? Is it like a burr in a dialect, a melding together that is richer than the sharp cold lines of standard speech? Is it the faint tremolo, the ragged edge of grief? It is an aching sound. A caged songbird may make that sound calling to birds outside the window. Do Rajayi and Billie sound so different from the brass-throated brahmin singers who draw spirographs with the scale because they understand the acoustics of desire, restraint and suffering? The old connection between art and fertility and death?

Rajayi's music is like a peepal leaf that has lain for a season on the edge of a pond; veined, empty of gaudy chlorophyll, washed by obsidian waters, old.

The film is surprisingly good. Rajayi doesn't come across like a store-bought antique, deliberately distressed, or like a forgery, aged by chemicals, or like a piece of bad dialogue in a historical novel, quaintly archaic. It must have taken tremendous tact to pull that off. That cameraman – he neither romanticizes her nor empties her art of its poetry. There's clever cutting between scenes in which she has been filmed in the house against the ugly tube-light and the crumbling walls, with Amalan's trousers hanging on a nail behind her, and the parts in the temple. The sound of the trucks, the blasting occasionally audible. If the past must be seen, then it must be seen in its full fragility, in its incongruity with the present. There was a moment when Rajayi's arms were captured against the whirl of a ceiling fan in one of the temple's annexes. It is better to admit this incongruity at once than to diffuse it under golden light. The art must speak through interference, if it is to speak at all.

Without history, it is hard to move forward. Something has been saved, something has been recorded. Hema has begun to learn from Rajayi. That is a way of moving forward.

Hema

They are sitting side by side in the car, and Appa turns around in the front seat and looks at them. He smiles. I wonder if he is seeing what I am seeing. I had always thought Amma the most beautiful woman in the world. But against Rajayi's mind-stopping foursquare simplicity, her massive beautiful shoulders, her poise, Amma's beauty has become ghostly. Cotton wool against teak, cloud against the earth-brown shoulder of a hill.

Wouldn't you think those prissy, mealy mouthed brahmin ladies who are taking over the dance would just see something like Rajayi's dancing and realize they can never cut it? That's why these people need those stupid 'innovations', cardamom and chillies over rotting meat. People like Padmasini who never imagine that dance might be something more than the worldly, egregious rattle of one step after another.

Rajayi is on the stage, waiting to begin the singing part of the evening. I've been watching the rehearsals. I'm awestruck by her. Her singing is never self-indulgent. She privileges neither the music nor the lyric; she resolutely rejects the schmaltz of hidden sob, the sweet lubricity of simulated passion.

She has shown me something that I might have searched the whole earth for and never found; something that could shape my life. How can I be of use to her? What can I do for her? Because I want to do something.

In the film, there are moments that are miraculous. Rajayi's hands coming into the middle of the frame, moving slightly in front of her shadowed face. Her arms are both strong and withered. She is walking towards the camera, somewhere in the temple, not dancing, but saying something about her ancestors. Her interrupted shadow is picked up now by the pillar, now by the floor. The setting sun is in her eyes and she is blinking uncomfortably. The red cotton of her sari flares out softly against the stone floor.

I know what I will do when I am ready for a career. I will make films on art. I'd like to be a filmmaker, just to catch a moment like this.

Lila

All reason has gone out of the film, Rajayi said. But I said to her, finish this, do what that Padmasini-cow wants, remember what our mother said.

Before our mother Kanaka's funeral, Rajayi slipped two of her mother's gold bangles off her wrist, taking one for herself and giving one to me. The goldsmith who makes ten bracelets a day, our mother used to say, if he spent a month on one, it would be perfect, and so must your movements be. Remember this.

And watching the film, I know Rajayi remembers.

Rajayi

The music has been stopped so long inside me, has grown so sharp, that it is cutting its way out of my body. I expected to feel old and tired, but my padhams are coming out fierce. They hurt.

The songs will hurt, because I must sing the reputation the world gave me, a lover who could not acknowledge me, a god who made a bad husband. A child I had to send away and a child dead on the road.

I must sing the respectable wives turning to spit at the sight of me. The town baring its teeth, menacing me. Its teeth were glass, there was glass in the yard under the tree of the orchid.

My hands come up to dance to the song praising the Raja's doorstep, but I am singing my own door that was kicked in and the hands that dragged me out. An outhouse, a smell of marsh mud and rainflies, pitting my will against a man's will.

Of my people, so many have died; those who survived left for the cities, searching for anonymity. For years I've been hearing silence where there used to be voices singing and feet stamping. I must sing the corners of the house where the children hid themselves in their games, Lila and I and the others, the places where our lovers leaned their canes and umbrellas when they came to sit on the swing, I must sing the pages filled with notation in my mother's hand.

I must sing the place which had been my grandmother's land, the soft monotonous green of paddy fields, broken only by the betel nut trees, the place where factories have now been built.

Thirteen generations of my family I sing, my mother and grandmothers for thirteen generations, orienting their selves to the dance and the temple. Once my mother tried to train the jasmine plant sideways into its trellis; but no matter what she did to the tendrils, by the morning they grew straight up to the sun. That was how we turned to dance. By my time our family meant nothing in the temple, but it was a place to go. Years upon years of going nowhere but to the temple, coming nowhere but home, and my mother saying, Rajayi, never forget that I promised you would dance in the temple at least once a year.

The women affirmed life, death, god, the king. They knotted meanings out of things, the brass lamps, the clay vessels, the poet's words, and released these meanings back into the wide world.

The lights on the stage shine like the lanterns of processions.

I see a road stretching backwards, the women standing along it at regular intervals, like telephone poles, like milestones, like lights in a railway tunnel. A punctuation of women, my ancestor at the head of it, Annakili Naachiyar, who made stone rise up in the air like a feather. What I sing is a fragment. It is tiny, because my memory has failed, but it is also precious, priceless, because it is what remains of that glory, of those women who stood with their hands on their hips, balanced lightly and insolently on one leg, the other leg flowing slightly away from the body, carrying the curve of waist into the earth, and behind these proud women the road stretched until it disappeared into the sky.

Acknowledgements

I am deeply grateful to my teachers, my friends, and my family: to K.P. Kittappa Pillai, T. Brinda, and Shyamala Mohan, especially, but also to R. Muttukannammal, P.R. Tilagam, and others, for opening a world of dance and music to me; to Dr B.M. Sundaram for unique insights into South Indian dance history; to S. Anand, Jane Borecky, Edmond Daly, Teresa Hubel and Gyongyi Hegedus for sharp, affectionate and helpful critique of drafts of this novel; to Hari Krishnan, Rex, Davesh Soneji and Vidya Sankaranarayanan for friendship and solidarity in the weird world of bharatanatyam in Canada; to Lois Mansfield and Samantha Pearson for letting me have 'writing retreats' in their homes; to R. Sivapriya for guiding this novel into print; to Janani Ganesan and Arushi Singh for editing; to Sarada Ramaswamy, R. Padmanabhan, Subbulakshmy Natarajan, and Sarada Natarajan for providing ideals to live by, and for familial love; and to Nigel Joseph and Richard Joseph for perceptive critiques of my writing, and for the gift of enduring joy.

juggernaut

THE APP FOR INDIAN READERS

Fresh, original books tailored for mobile and for India. Starting at ₹10.

juggernaut.in

CRAFTED FOR MOBILE READING

Thought you would never read a book on mobile? Let us prove you wrong.

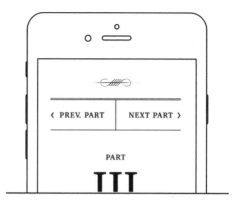

Beautiful Typography

The quality of print transferred
to your mobile. Forget ugly PDFs.

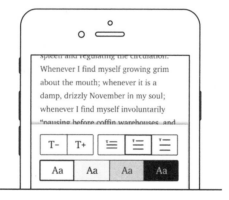

Customizable Reading

Read in the font size, spacing
and background of your liking.

juggernaut.in

AN EXTENSIVE LIBRARY

Including fresh, new, original Juggernaut books from the likes of Sunny Leone, Praveen Swami, Husain Haqqani, Umera Ahmed, Rujuta Diwekar and lots more. Plus, books from partner publishers and loads of free classics. Whichever genre you like, there's a book waiting for you.

DON'T
JUST READ;
INTERACT

We're changing the reading experience from passive to active.

Ask authors questions

Get all your answers from the horse's mouth.
Juggernaut authors actually reply to every
question they can.

Rate and review

Let everyone know of your favourite reads or
critique the finer points of a book – you will be
heard in a community of like-minded readers.

Gift books to friends

For a book-lover, there's no nicer gift than
a book personally picked. You can even
do it anonymously if you like.

Enjoy new book formats

Discover serials released in parts over
time, picture books including comics,
and story-bundles at discounted rates.
And coming soon, audiobooks.

juggernaut.in

4

LOWEST PRICES & ONE-TAP BUYING

Books start at ₹10 with regular discounts and free previews.

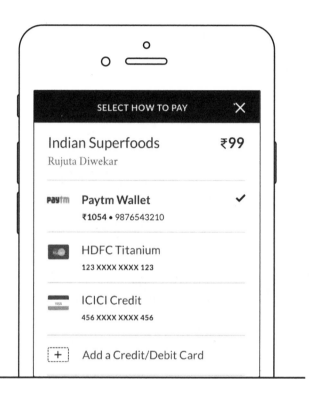

Paytm Wallet, Cards & Apple Payments

On Android, just add a Paytm Wallet once and buy any book with one tap. On iOS, pay with one tap with your iTunes-linked debit/credit card.

Click the QR Code with a QR scanner app
or type the link into the Internet browser
on your phone to download the app.

ANDROID APP
bit.ly/juggernautandroid

iOS APP
bit.ly/juggernautios

For our complete catalogue, visit www.juggernaut.in
To submit your book, send a synopsis and two
sample chapters to books@juggernaut.in
For all other queries, write to contact@juggernaut.in